P9-DGE-014

D0014920

THE CROW

THE THIRD BOOK OF PELLINOR

Alison Croggon

CANDLEWICK PRESS
CAMBRIDGE, MASSACHUSETTS

Copyright © 2006 by Alison Croggon
Maps drawn by Niroot Puttapipat

First Candlewick Press edition 2007

First published by Penguin Books, Australia

Library of Congress Cataloging-in-Publication Data is available.

Library of Congress Catalog Card Number pending

ISBN 978-0-7636-3409-4

2 4 6 8 10 9 7 5 3 1

Printed in the United States of America

This book was typeset in Palatino.

Candlewick Press
2067 Massachusetts Avenue
Cambridge, Massachusetts 02140

visit us at www.candlewick.com

FOR BEN

One is the singer, hidden from sunlight
Two is the seeker, fleeing from shadows
Three is the journey, taken in danger
Four are the riddles, answered in treesong:
Earth, fire, water, air
Spells you OUT!

Traditional Annaren nursery rhyme
Annaren Scrolls, Library of Busk

A NOTE ON THE TEXT

The *Crow* is the third part of my translation of the eight-volume Annaren classic text, the *Naraudh Lar-Chanë (The Riddle of the Treesong)*. The enthusiastic response of readers so far confirm my initial instinct that this story could move outside the cloisters of academic study and fulfill its initial function. This we know quite clearly, from a note attributed to Cadvan of Lirigon, which is inscribed on a forepage to one of the extant versions: the purpose of the *Naraudh Lar-Chanë* is, he says, to "delight all hearers" and to "introduce those unfamiliar with Bardic Lore to the ways and virtues of the Balance." Instruction, then, was important to those who wrote it down for their contemporaries; but its first intention was "delight."

As for "instruction": like the rest of the vast trove of parchment and reed-paper documents unearthed in Morocco in 1991 and known, misleadingly, as the Annaren Scrolls, this text repays study. It is one of the richest single sources for what we know of daily life in Edil-Amarandh, and gives us clear and vivid pictures of many of its peoples, from the complex Bardic cultures of the south to the various societies of the frozen plains of the north. It is quite likely that in its own time it served the same purpose as it does for us—that in part it was written to educate Annarens about the diversity of cultures amid which they lived. But unknown millennia later, this instruction has a special piquancy, bringing to life a civilization now long vanished from the face of the earth. The translation I present here cannot pretend to have captured in contemporary English all the subtleties and intricacies of the original text, and for this I am sorry; but I hope to have preserved at least some sense of its beauty and excitement. Those who wish to know more can find some sources of information in the appendices that I have included with each volume.

The first two volumes of Pellinor, *The Naming* and *The Riddle*, concern themselves with Maerad of Pellinor, a young Bard who discovers she is the Fated One prophesied to save her world from the rising darkness of the Nameless One. *The Naming* records her meeting with her mentor and friend, Cadvan of Lirigon, and their increasingly perilous journey to Norloch, the center of the Light in Annar, in order to reveal her destiny and bring her into the power of her Bardic Gift. In the course of her quest, by chance or fate, Maerad finds her brother, Cai of Pellinor, whom she had long thought dead, and also reveals the corruption that now lies at the heart of the Light in Annar. *The Riddle* traces her adventures with Cadvan as they flee the forces of both the Dark and the Light across the green lands of Annar and the frozen wastelands of the north, where she is captured by the Winterking, Arkan, a powerful Elemental being. The story finishes on Midwinter Day, after her escape from his northern stronghold, Arkan-da, and her discovery that the Treesong—or at least, half of it—is inscribed on the lyre that she inherited from her mother, and has owned since she was a child.

The Crow—originally books IV and VI of the *Naraudh Lar-Chanë*—shifts focus from Maerad's story to that of her brother Cai, known as Hem. We last saw Hem when he parted from Maerad at the end of *The Naming*, as they fled Norloch; and now we pick up the story on his arrival with the Bard Saliman in the populous and ancient city of Turbansk. Here we see a society very different from Annar in many ways—despite the commonalities of Bardic authority—through the naive eyes of a bewildered young boy and against the darkening background of gathering war. The battle against the depredations of the Nameless One intensifies as the immortal despot of Dén Raven (known more commonly in the south by his usename, Sharma) threatens to destroy all the cultures of the Light in Edil-Amarandh.

As in the previous volumes, for the purposes of this text I have treated Annaren as the equivalent of English and left untranslated some terms from other languages, in this case, most commonly, Suderain—the language spoken across both the Suderain and the Amdridh peninsula. A couple of Annaren experts have questioned this decision, arguing that in doing this I give a false sense of the centrality of Annaren and imply that it was an imperial language like global English, which, for all its wide usage, it was not. I can only note their objections here, and answer that it seemed to me to be the best solution at the time as the original text was, indeed, written in Annaren.

As I worked on the text, it was impossible to resist reflecting on how many parallels exist between our own time and that of this ancient story. Our world has darkened considerably in the early years of the twenty-first century, suggesting to this reader at least a contemporary relevance in some of the descriptions of war in the volumes that make up *The Crow*. The *Naraudh Lar-Chanë*'s subtextual concerns about the relationship between human beings and the natural environment seem equally timely. This is, in part, a function of the universality of all art. But I can't help reflecting sadly that it says little for the human race that we are no closer to resolving these questions than we were in the days when Bards and the Balance held sway.

I have now spent so long on this task of translation that it is almost impossible to imagine my life without it; and it is fair to say that I did not realize, when I began to translate *The Naming*, how much it would take over my life. The work is still a long way from completion: there are still the final, and most difficult, two volumes before me. This is not a complaint: the many hours spent debating intricacies of Annaren syntax or the finer points of Bardic ethics, the days in libraries poring over ancient scripts or microfiche, attempting to decipher some arcane detail of life in the vanished realm of Edil-Amarandh, have been among the most rewarding in my life. And this work has made me many friends, both readers and those who have helped me in my research, who have enriched my life immeasurably.

As always, a work of this kind is created with the help of many people, most of whom I do not have the space to acknowledge here. Firstly, as always, I want to thank my family for their good-humored tolerance of this obsessive work—my husband, Daniel Keene, for his support of this project and his proofing skills, and my children, Joshua, Zoë, and Ben. I am again grateful to Richard, Jan, Nicholas, and Veryan Croggon for their generous feedback on early drafts of the translation. Chris Kloet, my editor, has my endless gratitude for her unfailing support and sharp eye, which has saved me from many a grievous error. Among my many colleagues who have kindly helped me with suggestions and advice, I particularly wish to thank: Professor Patrick Insole of the Department of Ancient Languages at the University of Leeds for again permitting me to quote generously from his monograph on the Treesong in the Appendices; Dr. Randolph Healy of Bray College, Co. Wicklow, for his advice on the mathematics of the Suderain Bards; and Professor David Lloyd of the University of Southern California, for his acute and valuable analyses of the complexities of political power in Edil-Amarandh during many pleasurable conversations. Lastly, I would like also to acknowledge the courtesy and helpfulness of the staff of the Libridha Museum at the University of Querétaro during the months I spent there researching the *Naraudh Lar-Chanë*.

Alison Croggon
Melbourne, Australia

A NOTE ON PRONUNCIATION

MOST Annaren proper nouns derive from the Speech, and generally share its pronunciation. In words of three or more syllables, the stress is usually laid on the second syllable: in words of two syllables, (e.g., *lembel, invisible*) stress is always on the first. There are some exceptions in proper names; the names *Pellinor* and *Annar*, for example, are pronounced with the stress on the first syllable.

Spellings are mainly phonetic.

a—as in *flat*. *Ar* rhymes with *bar*.

ae—a long *i* sound, as in *ice*. *Maerad* is pronounced *MY–rad*.

aë—two syllables pronounced separately, to sound *eye–ee*. *Maninaë* is pronounced *man–IN–eye–ee*.

ai—rhymes with *hay*. *Innail* rhymes with *nail*.

au—*ow*. *Raur* rhymes with *sour*.

e—as in *get*. Always pronounced at the end of a word: for example, *remane, to walk*, has three syllables. Sometimes this is indicated with *ë*, which indicates also that the stress of the word lies on the *e* (for example, *ilë, we*, is sometimes pronounced almost to lose the *i* sound).

ea—the two vowel sounds are pronounced separately, to make the sound *ay–uh*. *Inasfrea, to walk,* thus sounds: *in–ASS–fray–uh*.

eu—*oi* sound, as in *boy*.

i—as in *hit*.

ia—two vowels pronounced separately, as in the name *Ian*.

y—*uh* sound, as in *much*.

c—always a hard *c*, as in *crust*, not *ice*.

ch—soft, as in the German *ach* or *loch*, not *church*.

dh—a consonantal sound halfway between a hard *d* and a hard *th*, as in *the*, not *thought*. There is no equivalent in English; it is best approximated by hard *th*. *Medhyl* can be said *METH'l*.

s—always soft, as in *soft*, not *noise*.

Note: *Dén Raven* does not derive from the Speech, but from the southern tongues. It is pronounced *Don RAH-ven*.

Contents

DÉN RAVEN

APPENDICES

TURBANSK

Summer crowds of apricots occlude the sky
Small perfumed suns that fall onto the grass

Birds bicker in the branches and the branches shake
And showers glaze the fruits, a dew of glass

And so they bruise and blacken to a cloying stench
A feast for flies, although this too will pass

All sweetness gleams but briefly from the shade
Such webs as weave our selvings do not last

And even our corruption is a tiny thing
A sour breath that fades into the past

From the *Inwa* of Lorica of Turbansk

I

THE WHITE CROW

A DROP of sweat trickled slowly down Hem's temple. He wiped it away and reached for another mango.

It was so hot. Even in the shady refuge of the mango tree, the air pressed around him like a damp blanket. There wasn't the faintest whisper of a breeze: the leaves hung utterly still. As if to make up for the wind's inaction, the cicadas were louder than Hem had ever heard them. He couldn't see any from where he was, perched halfway up the tree on a broad branch that divided to make a comfortable seat, but their shrilling was loud enough to hurt his ears.

He leaned back against the trunk and let the sweet flesh of the fruit dissolve on his tongue. These mangoes were certainly the high point of the day. Not, he thought sardonically, that it had been much of a day. He should have been in the Turbansk School, chanting some idiotic Bard song or drowsing through a boring lecture on the Balance. Instead, he had had a furious argument with his mentor about something he couldn't now remember and had run away.

He had wandered about the winding alleys behind the School, hot and bored and thirsty, until he spotted a seductive glint of orange fruit behind a high wall. A vine offered him a ladder, and he climbed warily into a walled garden, a lush oasis of greenery planted with fruit trees and flowering oleanders and climbing roses and jasmine. At the far end was a cloister leading into a grand house and Hem scanned it swiftly for any occupants, before making a dash for the fountain, which fell back into a mosaic-floored pond in the center of the garden. He plunged his head under the water, soaking himself in the delicious coolness, and drank his fill.

Then, shaking his head like a dog, he surveyed the fruit trees. There were a fig, a pomegranate, and two orange trees as well as the mango, the biggest of them all. He noted with regret that the oranges were still green, and then swung himself easily into the mango tree and started plundering its fruit, cutting the tough skin with a clasp knife and throwing the large stones onto the ground below him, until his fingers were sticky with juice.

After he had eaten his fill he stared idly through the leaves at the blue of the sky, which paled almost to white at the zenith. Finally he wiped his hands carefully on his trousers, dragged something from his pocket, and smoothed it out on his leg. It was a letter, written on parchment in a shaky script. Hem couldn't decipher it, but Saliman, his guardian, had read it out to him that morning and then, seeing the look on Hem's face, had given him the letter as a keepsake.

To Hem and Saliman, greetings!

Cadvan and I arrived in Thorold safely, as you may know if the bird reached you. We are both much better than when we last saw you.

I was very seasick on my way here, and Cadvan and I had to fight an ondril, which was very big, but we got here safely. Nerili has given us haven, and you will have heard the rest of the news from the emissary.

I hope you have arrived in Turbansk with no harm, and that Hem finds the fruits are as big as the birds said they were. I think of you all the time and miss you sorely.

With all the love in my heart,
Maerad

Already they were being chased by monsters. Hem knew that an ondril was a kind of giant snake that lived in the ocean.

Cadvan was possibly even braver than Saliman, and Maerad (to Hem's twelve-year-old eyes at least) was braver still; but they were only two, and the Dark so many, and everywhere. And where was Thorold, after all? Somewhere over the sea, Saliman had told him, and showed him a shape on a chart; but Hem had never even seen the sea and had only the vaguest idea of distance on a map. It meant nothing to him.

Hem stared at the letter as if the sheer intensity of his gaze could unriddle its meanings, but all it did was to make the page swim and blur. The only word he could make out was *Maerad*. And what had Maerad not written down? What other dangers was she facing? The letter was already days old: was she still alive?

Very suddenly, as if it burned him, Hem crumpled up the letter and shoved it back in his pocket. Unbidden into his mind came the memory of when he had first seen Maerad, when she had opened his tiny hiding place under the bed in the Pilanel caravan and he had looked up, terrified, expecting a knife flashing down to slash him to ribbons, and instead found himself staring into his own sister's astonished eyes. Only he hadn't known she was his sister, then. That had come later. . . . He remembered Maerad as he had last seen her in Norloch, standing in the doorway of Nelac's house as he and Saliman rode away, her face white with sorrow and exhaustion, her black hair tossing in the wind. Hem bit his lip, almost hard enough to draw blood. He was not a boy who wept easily, but his chest felt hot with grief. He missed Maerad more than he could admit, even to himself.

Maerad was the one person in the world he felt at home with. In the short period they had been together his nightmares had stopped for the first time in his life. Even before she knew he was her brother, she had taken him in her arms and stroked his face when the bad dreams came. Even now it seemed amazing; Hem would have hit with his closed fist anyone else who took such liberties. He had trusted Maerad from the start: he sensed her gentleness, and underneath that, her loneliness and sadness. But more than anything else, Maerad accepted him just as he was, and didn't want him to be anything else. Maerad, he thought painfully, *loved* him.

Now Maerad was so far away that she might as well not exist at all. It was almost two months since he had last seen her, and she could be anywhere in Edil-Amarandh. And here all anybody could talk about was the war. It lay inside every conversation, like a fat evil worm. It might kill Maerad; it might kill him. They might never see each other again.

Hem puffed his cheeks and blew out a big breath, as if trying to expel his morbid thoughts. There was Saliman, of course. Saliman was everything Hem would have liked to be himself: tall, handsome, strong, generous, brave, funny . . . Hem had adored him, with a passion akin to hero-worship, from the first time he had seen him. It had seemed like a miracle when Saliman had offered to be his guardian and to bring him to Turbansk, the great city of the south, to go to School there and learn how to be a Bard.

Since he had first gained the Speech and had been able to speak to birds, Hem had dreamed of coming to the south, where—the birds had told him—grew trees full of bright fruits as big as his own head. And now, here he was. He lived in a grand Bardhouse with Saliman, and had as much to eat as he wanted, and dressed in fine clothes, rather than the rags he had been used to. But although he now sat in a tree surrounded by the sweet fruit he had once dreamed of, happiness seemed as far beyond him as ever.

For one thing, coming to Turbansk had meant that he had to part from Maerad. The unfairness of this struck deep, although even at his most surly Hem knew it wasn't anyone's fault. And he had found that he didn't like the School much. He wasn't used to having to sit still and concentrate, and he took the criticisms of his mentors badly, however kindly they were given. They also insisted on calling him Cai, which was the name he had been given as a baby, before he had been kidnapped by Hulls and placed in the orphanage where he had spent most of his childhood. He constantly forgot that it was his name, so he kept getting into trouble for ignoring his teachers, when really he hadn't realized they were speaking to him.

Hem brooded on the injustice of the Bards for a while, unconsciously plucking and eating another mango. It wasn't *his* fault that he didn't know anything. Nobody seemed to understand how hard reading and writing were for him, and when he stumbled over a word the scornful looks of the seven-year-olds with whom he did scripting classes scorched his pride.

But the core of Hem's discontent was that he was lonely. Saliman, the only person in Turbansk he trusted, was often away, or occupied with Bard business. And these days Saliman was usually preoccupied, even when they did have time to speak together. Hem was the only northern child in the School, and his pale olive face stood out among the black-skinned Turbansk children, who thought him rough and strange. He was already a veteran of several fights, and now they avoided him because he fought dirtily: he had no qualms about gouging eyes or pulling hair or biting. He didn't speak the Suderain language, which limited his communications to the Speech, and (Hem considered with chagrin, throwing the huge mango stone so it rattled through the leaves) it was impossible to lie in the Speech; it twisted your words around. It was proving to be a real nuisance. Though, luckily perhaps, it also meant the other students did not understand his Annaren curses and insults.

He thought of a class the day before, when he had been so bored he felt dizzy. Forgetting to stop himself, he had yawned uninhibitedly. The mentor Urbika, who was chanting in the Speech the First Song of Making, paused midline and fixed Hem with a piercing eye. It was a look comprised of irony, irritation, and compassion in equal parts, but Hem was oblivious to its subtleties. He was too busy picking sulkily at his sandals.

"Minor Bard Cai, do the great mysteries of the Making bore you, perchance?" she inquired. The other children tittered, and turned to stare at Hem, who only slowly realized that Urbika was speaking to him. He looked up, and saw that the whole class was staring at him, bubbling with suppressed mirth.

"Er, yes—I mean, no, yes, it does," he said, suddenly flustered, and burning with humiliation. Urbika had given him a long look, silenced the class with another, and said nothing more about it; but Hem brooded over that trivial incident for the rest of the day. Nobody laughed at him, *nobody*. One day he'd make them pay for it . . .

A noise of which he had been half aware now forced itself into the forefront of Hem's reverie. Some kind of commotion was going on below his feet. He looked down through the leaves and saw a brawl of feathers on the ground, six or seven crows attacking something in their midst. Consumed by curiosity, he dropped from the branch to the ground, right next to the fight. The crows were so intent on their business that they didn't even notice him. He saw now that they were savagely pecking a white bird that had obviously given up on any idea of escape and was now vainly trying to hide its head under its wing. Blood spotted its feathers where the crows had torn its skin.

Filled with a swift anger, Hem lifted his hand and cried out in the Speech, "*Der ni, mulchar!* Begone, carrion!"

A blue bolt of lightning leaped from his fingers and hit the attacking crows, which screeched in surprise and dismay and flapped off in a stench of scorched feathers. Their victim lay on the grass surrounded by scattered white feathers with blood at their tips, its eyes closed, its breast heaving. Very gently Hem picked it up, feeling its body trembling in his hands. He involuntarily drew in his breath at the bird's lightness: underneath the feathers its body was so small, a mere scrap of life.

Are you hurt, little one? he asked, in the Speech.

At the sound of his voice the bird opened its eyes, and then almost immediately shut them again. Hem regretted he hadn't taken notice of the noise sooner; it was likely now the bird would die of shock. He cradled it against his chest, cupping his hands around its head to create a darkness, which at least might make the creature feel less afraid. Though no doubt it was past fear.

He was thinking that it was probably time he left the garden when an angry cry came from the cloisters behind him. He started, and looked around wildly for a means of escape. A very large man in long green robes was running swiftly toward him, shouting in Suderain. The only quick way out was to swarm up the mango tree and drop down the other side of the wall, but Hem was hampered by the bird, and he didn't want to jolt it by moving quickly. He assessed his chances, cursing, and decided he had no choice but to stand his ground.

When the man reached him, panting hard with both exertion and anger, he drew back his hand to cuff Hem across his head. The boy flinched and steeled himself for the blow, but the man stopped with his hand still high in the air and stared at him in astonishment and what seemed to be rising anger. Then came a flood of questions, of which Hem understood little, apart from the word *Djella*, which he knew meant Bard. Hem realized that the reason he hadn't been summarily punished was that the man had recognized the distinctive robes of a student at the Turbansk School. He smiled as ingratiatingly as he could, and said, every time the man paused for breath, *"Saliman Turbansk de."*

The man gave Hem a skeptical look, and then grabbed him painfully by his earlobe and pulled him into the house. Hem concentrated on not falling over and hurting the bird he had rescued. He was propelled swiftly through wide hallways and shaded rooms smelling of sandalwood in which he caught glimpses of rich colors, glints of gold and crimson and azure. Finally he went through a large atrium. At the far end the man opened a huge bronze door and stepped out into the blinding sunlight of the street. For a moment Hem thought with relief that was the end of it, but the man still had an unrelenting grip on his ear. He was marched humiliatingly through the streets until they reached Saliman's house, which was thankfully not very far away. There his captor tolled the brass bell and waited stolidly until the door was answered.

The bewildered minor Bard who opened the door was blasted with a flood of Suderain. She spread her hands to stop the flow, looking sharply at Hem, and appeared to invite the man in. The man shook his head, and she fled to find Saliman. Hem and his captor stood outside in the heat in complete silence for some time. Hem passed the wait staring at the front doorstep, his teeth set against the pain in his ear. The bird in his hands was still alive; he could feel its heart fluttering against his palm.

At last Saliman came to the door. When he saw Hem his eyebrows shot up to his hairline.

"Hem!" he said. "What have you been doing? Alimbar el Nad! Greetings!"

The man, his sense of grievance exacerbated by the wait, poured out his complaint. Saliman answered him in Suderain, and Hem stopped trying to follow the conversation. At least Alimbar had let go of him. He stood patiently, rubbing his ear with his free hand. It seemed Saliman was trying to invite Alimbar inside, while Alimbar insisted that he would not enter. After a few more exchanges the man seemed a little mollified, and finally he bowed to Saliman, who held open the door for him. Saliman turned to Hem and waved him in also. His eyes were hard.

"You," he said in Annaren, "I will deal with later. I want you to go to your chamber, and to stay there."

Hem, who had been totally unfussed by Alimbar's anger, quailed before Saliman's. He nodded meekly and scurried off.

Back in his chamber, Hem carefully put the bird down on his bed. It gave a small squawk and then lay with its eyes shut, its breast heaving. Hem, who was familiar with birds, was puzzled: it was of some kind he did not know. It looked like a crow, but its plumage was white. It was obviously a fledgling, only just losing its baby fluff to adult feathers; its tail and wing feathers were stubby and short, and it had a scrawny, half-made look about it.

Gently, Hem examined its injuries. He couldn't find any great damage, apart from a couple of savage tears in the flesh of its body and neck, but there could be internal hurts that he couldn't see. No bones seemed to be broken, and it wasn't bleeding freely anymore. What worried him most of all was the shock; birds could easily die of it. He looked around his room, and saw the chest in which he kept his spare clothes. He summarily threw his clothes onto the bed, spread a cloth he used for drying himself on the bottom of the chest, and gently placed the bird inside.

There, little one, he murmured in the Speech. *You are safe now.*

The bird made a soft peep, as if thanking him, and Hem closed the lid so it would feel safe in the dark. Then he worried that it might not have enough air, and stuffed a shirt under the chest's lid so it wouldn't close completely.

If it was alive in an hour, he thought to himself, it would have a chance. In two hours, more of a chance. If it was alive tomorrow, it would definitely live.

It would need water. He had a jug and a cup on his worktable, but no dish to put water in for the bird. He could get one easily enough from the kitchen, but he didn't dare leave his chamber; if Saliman arrived and Hem was not there, he would be even angrier with him. He would have to wait until Saliman turned up.

He sat and fidgeted on his bed, wondering how Saliman would punish him for his latest escapade. Would he be thrown out of the Bardhouse? Hem uneasily considered the possibility: in his mind, it seemed quite likely. When he thought about it, there weren't many reasons for Saliman to keep him there; none of the other minor Bards liked Hem much; he was always getting into trouble, and he wasn't exactly shining in his classes . . .

Within a short time, Hem's fear had turned into a certainty. Where could he go, if he didn't live with Saliman? He would have to live on the streets. Perhaps he could get work in the marketplace as a caller, carrying the goods for sale and telling of their virtues. He could be good at that . . . and then he remembered he couldn't speak Suderain. He would have to be a thief, then. He was good at stealing things. Though it would be more difficult than when he was a small boy: he was tall now, and in Turbansk his paler skin meant that he had lost the ability to go unnoticed in a crowd. He would head north then, and find Maerad—he could steal things along the way to feed himself. The only thing was, he would miss Saliman.

And the other thing was Cadvan, Maerad's mentor. Hem admired Cadvan as much as he did Saliman, but he found Cadvan more forbidding. He remembered very well how stern the Bard could be. If Hem did find Maerad, he would find

Cadvan as well, and Cadvan would likely be very cross with him . . . but, on the other hand, Maerad would speak up for him. Then all three of them could go on an adventure together.

Hem brooded on his new future for a while, concocting an enjoyable fantasy in which his own heroic acts featured prominently, and then remembered the bird. It had been very quiet, and he was sure it must have died by now. When he opened the chest it was standing up, and it scuffled into a corner, trying to hide. Hem made some soothing noises, but didn't attempt to speak to it or lift it up. He noted that its beak wasn't gaping with thirst, which relieved his mind, and he gently shut the lid again.

It seemed ages before he heard steps in the corridor and a knock on the door. There was a pause, while Hem braced himself for a telling off and wondered why the door remained shut, and then Saliman said, "Hem? May I come in?"

Hem still wasn't used to these courtesies. "Yes, yes, come in," he said breathlessly, as he scrambled for the door and opened it.

Saliman stood in the corridor dressed in the red robes of a Turbansk Bard. His long black hair was tied back from his face in an intricate pattern of braids, and a golden brooch in the shape of a sunburst was pinned on his shoulder. He looked, Hem thought—glancing nervously at his dark face—not quite so cross as he might; surely that was the ghost of a smile haunting his lips. But maybe not . . .

Saliman was in fact looking in astonishment at the mess of clothes piled on Hem's bed. "I hope, Hem, that you are not thinking of running away?" he said, picking up a blue tunic.

Hem gulped. "No," he said. "I—I had to put the bird somewhere."

Saliman turned to face him, his face expressionless. "Bird?" he said.

"It was hurt. And they need a dark place, so they're not frightened. So I . . ." He faltered and stopped. Perhaps putting injured birds in clothes chests was not allowed in Bardhouses.

"Yes?"

"So I put it in the chest . . ." He gestured vaguely toward the other side of the room. "But I took all my clothes out first. So they wouldn't be dirtied. I didn't think it would be wrong," he added hastily, putting on his most virtuous expression, although whether his clothes remained clean wasn't something that ever bothered Hem. "I just wanted to help the bird."

Saliman stood very still, looking searchingly at Hem. Then he sat down on Hem's bed and rested his brow in his hands in a gesture of despair that made Hem grin despite himself, although he took care to straighten his face when Saliman looked up.

"Hem," he said at last. "Do you have any idea whose garden you entered today?"

Hem shook his head.

"I have just had a very long and very boring conversation with Alimbar el Nad. He is a consul of the Ernan of Turbansk, and is fifth in authority to the Ernani herself. It seems that he found you in his private courtyard, which he keeps expressly for his own use. Not even his servants are allowed there. And yet you seem more worried about whether or not your clothes are soiled . . ." He shook his head. "What were you doing there?"

Hem studied his feet closely. He wasn't going to admit that he was stealing mangoes if no one had accused him; he would be thrown out for sure. Saliman sighed heavily and stood up.

"After a great many courtesies and sweetmeats, and after offering to place the spell of bounty on his house, a most exhausting and complicated charm, I may add, and also promising that I would whip you soundly, I managed to soothe him. Alimbar is a hasty and impatient man, quick to take offense—and to give it, truth be told. I had to swallow my pride at least three times, and that goes hard for Saliman of Turbansk. But you almost caused a most difficult friction between the School of Turbansk and the Court, and it could not be worse timed."

Hem stared at the floor until his eyes burned, only half comprehending what Saliman was saying.

"Hem," Saliman continued gravely. "I am very angry with you, and I ought to punish you. But, to be honest, I don't believe it would make anything better than it is. So I will not be whipping you. Although perhaps that is merely to save what little shred of my pride remains."

"So you're not going to send me away?" Despite himself, Hem's voice wavered.

Saliman looked surprised. "Send you away? Whether you stay here or not is your decision, Hem, not mine. No, I would not send you away."

Hem gave an involuntary sigh of relief. He was not afraid of being whipped, although no one had beaten him since he had met Maerad, and perhaps he had lost some of his old toughness. But now Saliman was standing with his back to him, looking out of the window. He was silent for a long time, and Hem began to feel ashamed of himself.

"I'm sorry," he mumbled, when the silence had stretched out too long.

"But are you, Hem?" asked Saliman, turning around. "Are you really sorry? It is not enough to say so, and then to do the same thing again."

Now Saliman's face was very serious, and a fluttering started in the boy's stomach. When Saliman was happy with him, Hem felt exultant, but his displeasure hurt more than any whipping. Saliman was one of the few human beings he wholeheartedly respected, and there was an unsettling power in

Saliman's dark gaze, which seemed to see without prejudice or fear through any dissembling.

"Well?" Saliman's voice was gentle, but within it was a strength like steel.

"I *am* sorry," said Hem, a little more clearly. "I don't mean to cause trouble."

Saliman sighed again, and sat back down on the bed, patting the cushions beside him. "Sit down, Hem. Tell me, are you very unhappy?"

Hem blinked at the unexpectedness of the question. He had not spoken to Saliman about his feelings. He opened his mouth to answer, and then shut it again.

"Urbika tells me you are not making friends," said Saliman. "And she says you are struggling with the Suderain language, which can't help."

Despite himself, Hem blushed. He didn't like the thought that people were observing him like that. He struggled with himself. He had longed for the chance to pour out his heart to Saliman, to tell him all his troubles. Saliman would understand his constant nightmares, his fears, the difficulties he had talking to people, how he hated the other minor Bards. He knew that Saliman would not judge him. But now that the chance had come, it was as if his jaws were sewn together with wire.

"I miss Maerad," he said at last.

"That, alas, is a wound I cannot heal," said Saliman gently. "Although I can perhaps help with other things."

There was another long silence.

"Well," said Saliman, when it was clear that Hem would not volunteer anything further. "Perhaps we should look at this bird of yours."

Hem brightened up at the change of subject, and opened the chest. The bird cowered in the corner, staring at them unblinkingly. Saliman picked it up carefully, whispering to it in the Speech, and it relaxed into his hand.

"Do you think it will be all right?" asked Hem, watching Saliman anxiously.

"I think it has sustained no great hurt," said Saliman. He examined the bird closely, murmuring in the Speech. As he did, he began to glow faintly with a strange inner light. Hem, who had now seen a few Bards using their Gift, knew he was making a healing charm, and relaxed. He felt a strange affinity with this tattered, abused bird, and he was relieved that it was getting the proper treatment. He could do healing, but he wasn't confident about his ability.

After a short time Saliman finished, and he coaxed the bird onto Hem's wrist, where it perched, perfectly tame, as if it were a falcon. Its feet felt cold against his skin, and its claws dug in with a surprising strength. Hem chirped at it, and then said, in the Speech, *Are you all right, little one?*

Better, said the bird. *Hungry!* And it made an interrogative noise very close to the wheezing gasp of a baby bird asking for food.

"It's scarce more than a nestling," Saliman said, smiling. "But what is it?"

"I thought you might know," said Hem eagerly. "It looks like a kind of crow . . ."

"Yes, but it's white." Saliman regarded it with his head cocked to one side. "How did you find it?"

"Well, I was sitting in the mango tree when . . ." Hem stopped.

Saliman glanced at him ironically. "I had assumed that you were raiding Alimbar's fruit trees," he said. "Very expensive fruit it is, too. And then?"

Hem blushed for his slip, and told the full story of how he

had found the bird. Saliman listened attentively, and then
stroked the bird's head. "An outcast, eh?" he said. "Perhaps it
will not want to go back to its kin, where it will be persecuted. I
think it is a crow that was so poorly used because it is unlike the
others. Crows will do that. You may have found a companion,
Hem." He stood up. "I'll leave you to decide whether you want
to look after a crow. I have many things to do, and I am now
grievously late."

He walked to the door, and turned around. "I haven't for-
gotten your trespass," he said. "We'll say no more for today. But
I will do some thinking, and I judge that you ought to, as well."
Then he left.

Hem nodded absentmindedly; his attention was all turned
to the bird. It now looked very perky, but it was, he thought,
rather scruffy. It would look better when all its adult feathers
had grown and it didn't have grayish fluff poking through
them, which gave it a kind of ragamuffin look.

So, he said. *Do you want to stay with me? I can look after you.*

Feed me? said the bird.

Yes, I'll feed you. And keep those others away. You'll be safer.

The bird ruffled its feathers, stuck out its tail, and soiled the
floor.

But you'll have to do that outside, Hem added, thinking with
dismay of Saliman's rather stern housemaster. *Because people
will get cross with me.*

The bird turned its head, fixing Hem with one of its eyes.

I stay, it said.

So what is your name? asked Hem.

Name?

What do they call you?

I was not given a name, said the crow. *The flock would not name
me, when my wing feathers came, because I am wrong-colored. I have
no name.*

You have to have a name, said Hem. He thought for a moment, and remembered the word for *bird* that had been used by the Pilanel people he had briefly known. *How about "Irc"?*

Irc? The bird bobbed up and down comically on his wrist. *Irc! I have a name! Irc!* It soiled the floor again.

I told you, said Hem. *You'll have to do that outside.*

Feed me? Hungry!

All right, Irc, Hem said, sighing, but only with pretended impatience. *I'll feed you.*

II

WOUNDS

IT wasn't very surprising that Hem had not learned much of the Suderain language. He had only recently arrived in Turbansk, after a two-week journey south with Saliman all the way from Norloch, the chief citadel of Annar. They had fled the city as it trembled on the brink of civil war, and Maerad and Cadvan had stayed behind, planning to escape that night and head north on a quest for the Treesong. Nobody really knew what the Treesong was, but Hem had perfect faith that Maerad would return triumphant, having not only discovered its identity, but having saved the world from the Dark as well. For wasn't that what the old prophecies had said she would do?

As he and Saliman had galloped through the moonlit meads of the Carmallachen in the Vale of Norloch on the night they left, Hem had looked back over his shoulder and seen the towers of the ancient citadel in flames, with a great smoke spiraling upward and obscuring the stars. When at last they had stopped, Hem had passed the night in despair, sure that Maerad and Cadvan must be dead. Saliman had consoled him, saying that they were sure to have escaped, that there were secret passages that even Enkir did not know. Hem just swallowed and hoped. Beneath his boundless faith in Maerad's abilities was a dreadful fear that he would never see her again.

He didn't fully understand what had happened in Norloch, but Saliman explained that Enkir, the First Bard, and therefore the most important Bard in Annar, had revealed himself as a traitor against the Light. Moreover, Enkir had destroyed Hem's family: it was Enkir who had overseen the sack of Pellinor ten years before, when Hem's father had been murdered and his mother and Maerad sold into slavery. Hem himself had been kidnapped by the Black Bards, the Hulls, under Enkir's orders, and put into an orphanage in Edinur: a miserable prison where he had lived most of his short life with the other unwanted children.

Many of Hem's nightmares were about the orphanage; he would dream that he was still there, in a dank, pitch-black room crammed with children of all ages lying three or four to each stinking pallet; freezing cold in winter and sweltering in summer. It was never quiet: children whimpered and muttered and screamed all night, even in their sleep. Babies were put in with the rest of the children, and very few of them survived, although the older children tried to care for them. Hem had many memories of small blue corpses being taken out in the mornings. Sometimes what the children did to each other was worse than the neglect and careless brutality of the adults who ran the place: there was a vicious hierarchy among the orphans, reinforced by beatings and taunts, and any weakness was quickly identified and exploited. There was never enough food, and the children often sickened and died from the illnesses that raged rapidly through the crowded buildings. Only the tough survived; and luckily Hem was tough.

He had been taken out of the orphanage by a Hull, who brought him to a fine house where, for the first time he could remember, Hem slept in clean sheets and had enough to eat. But he was still afraid: the people in the house were sinister and cold, and he found out later they were all Hulls. They had tried to make him become a Hull like them, tempting him with their immortality. They showed him that Hulls did not die: even if stabbed through the heart, a Hull would stand up again, smiling, the wound instantly closed over. But an instinct

in Hem rebelled against their persuasions, which although
softly spoken, with fair and reasonable words, caused icy chills
to run down his spine.

Finally, at the dark of the moon, the Hulls tried to make
Hem a Black Bard by force. Although he did his best to forget
it, he remembered that night with a horrible clarity and it, too,
figured in his nightmares. The Hulls had ordered him to kill a
boy called Mark, whom he knew from the orphanage. When he
had refused, despite their worst threats, they killed the child
themselves, forcing Hem to watch, and burned his body in an
ensorcelled fire. Hem was then locked in his room without food
and left alone, too frightened even to sob in the darkness.

The next day the Hulls had been out on some foul errand,
and by chance Hem was rescued by two Pilanel men who were
robbing the house. The Pilanel had been kind to him, taking
him as one of their own because of his olive skin and Pilanel
features; but the Hulls had tracked them down in the wilder-
ness and mercilessly slaughtered the family who had cared for
him. Hem, hidden in the Pilanel caravan, had heard everything.

That was something else he had nightmares about.

After he had lain for hours in his cramped hiding place, too
terrified to venture out, Maerad and Cadvan had found him.
He had then discovered that not all Bards were Hulls, as he had
thought. Finding that he had a sister—someone who belonged
to him, someone who without question wrapped her warm
arms around him when he cried out and trembled in his black
dreams—was the most important thing that had happened to
him in his whole life. When he had been forced to leave her
behind, he had felt as if his heart had been cut in two. It was a
loss he tried not to think about, because it hurt him too much.

Meeting Saliman was the second most important thing that
had happened to him. Despite his anxieties about Maerad, the
ride to Turbansk with Saliman had been his first taste of real

freedom. The weather had stayed fine for most of the way, and although they feared pursuit from Norloch, he and Saliman had encountered no dangers. After Hem's body had made the first painful adjustments to horseback—for riding made his legs so stiff that he thought he would walk with bowed legs for the rest of his life—the journey had been an unalloyed pleasure.

Hem often wished he could ride again with Saliman through the mountains of Osidh Am, his favorite part of the whole journey. They had camped at night by still pools in the fragrant forests of larch and fir, and Hem would lie by the fire looking up at the bright stars through the branches high above him. During the day they often surprised small herds of deer, which would leap up almost under the horses' feet to crash away through the bracken, and sometimes they brushed past bushes full of butterflies, which would start up in a cloud of bright colors about their heads.

There were no other people for leagues, and a great peace began to rise in Hem's heart. It was the happiest he had ever been. On the other hand, his first sight of Turbansk, which was, Saliman told him, the most ancient city in Edil-Amarandh, had been bewildering and overwhelming.

They had arrived at first light on a summer's day, just before the dawn bell. The Great Bell of Turbansk, three times the height of a man, hung in a high belfry under a gilt cupola above the West Gate—one tower in that city of many towers, which glowed like an opulent mirage on the shores of the Lamarsan Sea. It was struck every day at the exact moment that the sun's disc appeared over the horizon.

As it rang over the city, it had seemed to Hem as if the sound itself was made of light. Sunlight and bell note spilled simultaneously over market and tower, house and hall and hovel, picking out the glittering domes of the School and the palace and the Red Tower, flushing the stone walls pale pink or warm yellow. The sun flooded the city's broad squares and trickled into the narrow alleys of the poor quarters, where the walls were painted in fading greens or blues or reds, and fresh washing was strung over the street from house to house like colorful flags; and on the great inland sea of Lamarsan a path of dazzling gold flared across the water.

In the markets, which teemed with people hours before dawn, the flaming torches faded in the sudden increase of light and the world flooded with color. The dew sparkled on the roses and jasmine and saffron in the flower stalls, and rainbows quivered over the scales of trout and salmon, and on the iridescent feathers of freshly killed ducks and pheasants as they lay on the marble benches.

From the food and flower markets spread a labyrinth of alleys lined with stalls and tiny shops, which sold everything from plain brass lamps to curious enameled fortune-telling boxes that were used to predict the positions of the stars, from robes of diaphanous silk to thick linen tunics, from rings and brooches to knives and cooking pots. The narrow streets were packed with people: bakers walking with trays of fresh loaves balanced on their heads; donkeys and pack mules loaded down with huge panniers or sacks; farmers from the Fesse, the land surrounding the city, carrying baskets of dates or live ducks, their heads poking from the top; women in bright, embroidered robes, their fingers sparkling with rings; children squabbling and playing; and hawkers marching up and down, calling the virtues of their wares.

There was a whole street of spice sellers, who sat behind their counters with bowls of precious ground spices before them, saffron and cardamom and whole nutmegs and cinnamon sticks; then you would turn the corner and find a street of shops full of songbirds and finches, fluttering in cages of copper wire. The next street was full of stalls with copper braziers that sold little tin cups of black coffee and sweet honey-filled cakes and hot bean pastries. Jugglers and minstrels plied their trades for the gossiping customers.

Hem stared, amazed at the ordered chaos of Turbansk, his nostrils flaring. The streets were aromatic with spices from the hawkers' stalls and everyone, men and women, wore musky perfumes. As the heat of the day increased, the perfumes merged with other, earthier smells—rotting vegetables and sweat and waste—so that Hem felt faint, as if he were drugged in some sweet stupor, moving through a constantly changing hallucination.

The people of Turbansk took great pleasure in personal adornment; at first Hem thought everyone in Turbansk must be fabulously wealthy, for he saw no one who did not wear golden earrings or bracelets or some intricately fashioned brooch. Later he knew that those who were poor wore trinkets of brass, with glass jewels; but to Hem they seemed no less beautiful than emeralds and gold. Nothing had prepared him for the rich colors and ceaseless movement, the countless men and women and children who moved with unerring grace through the teeming streets. To his astonishment, he saw no beggars: they had been everywhere in Edinur. He turned and asked Saliman if they had been banished from the city, and Saliman laughed.

"Nay, Hem, here the Light does its work. No one goes hungry in Turbansk," he said.

Hem mulled this over in silence. "Then won't people get lazy?" he said at last.

Saliman gave him a sharp look. "What do you mean?"

"If they don't have to work for food, I mean."

Saliman stared ahead for a moment, as if revolving thoughts in his head. "If a person doesn't want to work, that is their loss," he said at last. "To make things, to care for what one loves, to earn one's place in the city, that is one of life's great pleasures. It is not a Bard's business to tell people what to do: if they are hungry and ask for food, we give them something good to eat. We have plenty, after all. Then they are able to think what they might do best. If their best is sitting in the gardens watching the carp in the pools, then so be it."

Hem blinked in surprise. It seemed wrong to him, simply to give food away for nothing.

The city of Hem's daydreams so far surpassed them that his expectations had wavered like smoke and collapsed utterly. He scarcely remembered his first week there. It passed in a blur of unfamiliar voices and words and colors and smells: the fresh touch of linen sheets against his skin; the silken caress of his new robes; the tastes of the food, which flamed along his tongue, making him choke and gasp; the hundreds of faces he saw in the streets every day, each one a stranger. Although Hem wasn't afraid, this sudden profusion of sensation induced something very like panic. In the midst of his confusion the only still point was Saliman, who—perceiving the chaos of Hem's mind—for that first week took him everywhere. Hem haunted Saliman's footsteps like a little dog, never less than three paces behind him, as if he were the one rock in a turbulent and threatening world.

But in seven days the world stopped whirling and settled down, and Hem began to find his bearings. He was instated into the School of Turbansk as a minor Bard and now wore on his breast a brooch in the shape of a golden sun, the token of a Bard of Turbansk. Saliman told him to keep the medallion of Pellinor—the precious token from his babyhood, which was the only thing he possessed of his family's heritage—in a cloth bag that he hung around his neck.

The Turbansk brooch, a gift from Saliman, pleased Hem much more than his lessons, which, apart from swordcraft and unarmed combat, he found much more difficult than he had expected. Study bored him, even his studies in magery, and he was at best a mediocre student.

This puzzled Saliman, who believed Hem had a facility with magery. He had taught Hem a few techniques on their journey to Turbansk and, when he had time, showed him mageries that caught the boy's fancy. Hem was particularly adept with the charms to do with concealment, shadowmazing, and glimveils, and he had even mastered a disguising spell that was a speciality of Cadvan's, and which was particularly difficult. Saliman suspected this ability might have to do with his life in the orphanage, when he had been forced to keep his Barding powers hidden, as anyone suspected of witchspeak—which was what the ignorant termed the Speech—might be stoned to death. Yet in classes he acted the dullard, refusing to concentrate or focus his powers.

To Hem's dismay, Saliman had left the city for a few days shortly after their arrival in Turbansk. This was when Hem began to feel truly isolated. Saliman would not tell him where he was going or when he would be back, and despite Hem's pleadings would not take him with him. Hem felt it as a betrayal; a small betrayal, perhaps, but a betrayal nevertheless. Saliman came back for a day and then vanished again, and Hem began to feel lonelier than ever.

During Saliman's absences the Turbansk Bards were kind to him, but Hem found this almost as bewildering as Turbansk itself. He simply wasn't used to being treated with courtesy. The first time a Bard gave him the bow of greeting he had flushed red with anger, believing that he was being mocked; but fortunately Saliman was present and took him aside, explaining that it was the custom, and that he was simply expected to bow back.

Most often his confusion erupted without warning into explosions of rage. Perhaps Hem's greatest difficulty was that he didn't speak Suderain, but that might have been overcome if he had not also suffered from a deep mistrust of almost everybody who attempted to speak to him. Within days his fellow students had dismissed him as surly and aggressive, and before long some were taunting him, provocations to which he always responded violently. By the time Hem rescued Irc, he had punched three minor Bards hard enough to warrant visits to the School healer for both parties, and once had even used magery against a student, a practice so strictly forbidden in the School that Urbika had told him sternly that he would be thrown out altogether if he ever did such a thing again.

All this was in Saliman's mind as he contemplated his charge over the evening meal, a couple of weeks after Hem's escapade in Alimbar's garden. Hem was proving a more testing responsibility than he had expected, although he did not regret his decision to bring him to Turbansk. Beneath his exasperation, Saliman had grown to love this difficult, troubled boy, and he had a Truthteller's intuitive understanding of the contradictory emotions that were tearing Hem apart. What he didn't know, Saliman thought, was what to do about them.

Hem was on his best behavior, and so was acting as if he were made of wood; in his nervousness he had already knocked over a full goblet of wine.

I am a healer, Saliman thought to himself, *and counted great in that art in this city; but these wounds are beyond me. Perhaps only Maerad could heal them. . . .* He thought of Hem's pale-skinned sister, in her own way almost as damaged and lonely as Hem was, and sighed.

Saliman had arranged to eat alone with Hem that night, and Hem, conscious of his sins, was unusually tense and silent in the Bard's company. Only that morning he had endured yet another difficult interview with Urbika, who had patiently asked him why he felt obliged to use his single talent—that for unarmed combat—against his fellow students.

Hem had stood before her, silent and scowling. He could not tell her that it was because Chyafa—the minor Bard whom he had, shortly before, left with a black eye—had called him a dirty white *hlaf*. Chyafa was Hem's principal enemy in Turbansk: a strongly built, handsome boy with an air of superiority who dropped his taunts with a carelessness that only intensified their sting. To report the insult was to compound Hem's humiliation: Hem understood enough Suderain to know what *hlaf* meant. It was the word for carrion crow, which as an insult meant an ignorant barbarian, and it particularly hurt because it referred to Irc as well. A number of other children had laughed at Chyafa's witticism and Hem knew then, with a sense of furious helplessness, that it had become their nickname for him.

So he had said nothing, dumbly awaiting his punishment, and Urbika had pressed her lips tight with suppressed frustration. She was having a trying morning. Hem had been assigned the dawn duties for a week as a punishment, which meant waking before the first bell, shivering out of his bed in the dark hours before daylight to sweep out the Singing Hall and lay out bowls and spoons for the other Bards, and then working in the kitchen, stirring great cauldrons of dohl, the dried beans that were boiled with fermented milk and sweetened with honey for breakfast.

It was a mild punishment: privately Hem didn't mind these duties, since he liked Soron, who oversaw the kitchens. He was a fair-haired, heavily built Bard from Til Amon, and he had a trick of wordless, unpatronizing kindness. He kept Hem supplied with meat for Irc, without Hem having to ask more than once, and gave him any sweetmeats left over from the previous evening, and never asked him questions about himself; which paradoxically meant that Hem was more chatty with Soron than with anyone except Saliman.

Hem knew that Saliman was very busy; he had only that morning returned from one of his mysterious trips. This probably meant that tonight's meal had been arranged because he wanted to say something in particular. Hem feared, again, that he was to be sent away, that this latest outrage had torn even Saliman's patience with him. He was so nervous that his appetite had disappeared, and he merely picked at the fresh fruits piled on the table, although among them were some of his favorites: mangoes (sent as a courtesy, Saliman told him ironically, from Alimbar's private garden), star fruit, pomegranates, figs, green melons, and grapes.

Irc, who had been granted special dispensation to come, was perched on the back of Hem's chair. The bird had no such inhibitions, and gulped down the pieces of meat and fruit Hem fed him, wiping his beak on the boy's hair. He then gave a contented babylike cheep and moved to Hem's shoulder, where he crouched close against his neck. Absently Hem reached up and scratched Irc's neck and the bird made little crooning noises, stretching out his head in bliss.

"Irc certainly looks well," said Saliman. "You have been taking good care of him, for certain."

"He likes me." Hem gave a small smile. "But only because I feed him."

"There is more to care than food," answered Saliman. "Though I agree that is an important part of it."

"I've trained him not to do his droppings inside. Though it's taken a bit of persuasion," said Hem proudly. "Eh, little one?" Irc gave a sleepy chirp.

"Well, I am very glad of that."

The conversation faltered again, and Saliman sat back,

straightened his shoulders, and let out a long breath. "Well, Hem," he said. "There are a few things we must speak about."

Hem looked up, unable to conceal his agitation. He had been waiting for Saliman to say something like this.

"What are we going to do?" asked Saliman.

Hem cleared his throat. "Do? About what?"

"About you, of course."

There was a short silence while Hem mentally surveyed his catalog of misdemeanors. "I don't know," he said forlornly.

"In normal circumstances, I would know what to do," said Saliman. "It would simply be a matter of time; you are not used to life as a Bard, and it is a difficult life to adjust to, even for those who come here without your troubles. But time, I fear, is what we do not possess."

Hem slouched down in his chair, staring at the table. Did this mean that he was going to be thrown out?

"You know, Hem, that Turbansk is preparing for war."

Everyone knew that. Hem sat up straight again. "Yes," he said.

"I'm not entirely sure that you know what that means," said Saliman. "Which is why I wanted to talk to you tonight, although I should really be elsewhere. We have had terrible news today: the Iron Tower has marched on Baladh."

Hem nodded. Baladh, he knew, was one hundred and fifty leagues east of Turbansk. Like everyone else in the School, he had heard the news, which had arrived by bird courier that morning and spread through Turbansk like wildfire. The students had been whispering about it in the corridors, shocked and subdued, and a girl whose family came from Baladh had started crying in one of the classes and had been taken away by Urbika.

"We know very little yet about what is happening there," said Saliman. "I am grieved; many friends live there, and I don't know how they are faring, or even if they are still alive. Baladh is a School almost as old as Turbansk, and as venerable in the Knowing and the Lore. If it falls, and I fear that it cannot stand, it will be a loss beyond calculation."

For a few moments the strain showed on Saliman's face and, for the first time that evening, Hem was jolted out of his self-absorption. He stared at the Bard with surprise; Saliman's eyes were bright with unshed tears. Hem couldn't find the words to say what stirred in his heart, and he merely stammered, before falling silent.

"Well," said Saliman at length, "we will find out soon enough. And if Baladh does fall, nothing but a few small towns and hamlets will stand between Turbansk and the massed armies of the Nameless One, which even now issue from the poisoned land of Dén Raven. It will not be long before we too shall be facing the same fate."

For a few moments Hem felt himself fill with a black dread: this was the stuff of his nightmares, but unimaginably multiplied.

"In two weeks or so, perhaps less, perhaps more, Turbansk will be assailed by the Black Army," Saliman continued. "I know we cannot expect any help from the north. We will be lucky if we do not have an army marching on us from there as well, although I think Enkir still plays his double game. Most Bards in Annar do not know of his dealing with the Dark, and will believe what he says and mistakenly follow him; and I doubt not that he moves against all the Seven Kingdoms, from Lirigon in the north to the Suderain in the south. But all the kingdoms will resist, if that is what Enkir plans; and I think if he does move, it will be first against the western kingdoms, against Culain and Ileadh and Lanorial. So, no threat from the north; but no help, either." Saliman's voice was quiet, as if he were speaking to himself, but Hem listened attentively.

"But will Turbansk really fall?" he asked, thinking of the power and pride of Turbansk, its thick walls and high towers, and its thousands of people. "It is stronger and bigger than Baladh, isn't it? Surely . . . ?"

"Hem, I do not know if we shall prevail." Saliman smiled at him sadly. "It may be that I was born to see the last days of this city I love so well. Yes, we are mighty, and we are strong; but the force the Nameless One brings against us is the greatest seen since the Great Silence, when all Annar was conquered and the high cities of the Dhyllin cast to the ground. I fear that against the Darkness that rises now there shall be no prevailing."

There was no arguing against the bleakness of Saliman's voice, and Hem, whose mouth was open to ask another question, said nothing. Saliman was silent for a time, lost in his thoughts, and then filled his goblet again with wine.

"How do you know about the army?" Hem asked at last, to break the silence.

Saliman looked up, startled. "I'm sorry, Hem, I was thinking. Where do you imagine I have been these past weeks? I and others with me have been finding out what we can about this army. The army that marches on Baladh is more than even Turbansk can resist."

Hem looked at Saliman with renewed respect, and felt guilty for his resentment of Saliman's absences. He had had no idea that Saliman was doing anything as dangerous as spying out the forces of the Nameless One.

"But, for all the hopelessness of our situation," Saliman continued, "we shall not despair. I do not think we will hold Turbansk, but that does not mean that we will give it up without a fight."

Although Saliman spoke quietly, a passion throbbed in his voice that sent a strange shiver down Hem's spine, and he almost jumped up and shouted. But Saliman, who was not given to emotional utterances, visibly mastered himself, and smiled at Hem.

"Which brings me to you, Hem. I ask again, what shall we do? In a few days, all those who cannot fight, the old, the infirm, the children—and they include the younger students of Turbansk School—will be leaving for Car Amdridh, where there is more hope of holding out against the Black Army than there is here. Shall you go with them?"

"No!" It burst out of Hem before he could stop himself. "Not if you're not going! Don't send me away from you!"

Saliman stared gravely at Hem, and the boy looked down at the table, feeling foolish. It was as clear a declaration of love as any he had made in his life. But Saliman did not smile; his dark face was sad and thoughtful, and the gaze he cast on Hem was full of a strange tenderness.

"I have thought, for a number of reasons, that perhaps it would be better if you stayed with me," he said. "But it seemed also to me like a mad thought. Life will be very dangerous here, and to stay is to risk your life. I will demand a lot of you, if you remain with me."

"I'll do anything you say," said Hem, his voice cracking with urgency. He most profoundly did not want to be sent away with the students: he did not want to be banished from Saliman's presence.

"I will need you to be older than you are," said Saliman. "I will need you to be larger than you think you are, to think beyond your own petty concerns. I know you are capable of it."

Hem thought again of his behavior over the past weeks, and regretted it sincerely for the first time.

"I promise," he said. "I really do."

Saliman studied Hem coolly, as if weighing his value, and the boy blushed and bowed his head under the scrutiny. "I don't want you to make a rash choice, Hem," the Bard said at last. "I would not contemplate your staying if I thought it was certain you would be killed, but the risk, all the same, is very great, and it will be harder than you now think. I do not walk safe paths."

Hem looked up, and now the passion blazing within him was naked in his eyes. "I'll follow you anywhere," he said.

There was a pause, and then Saliman smiled, but it was not a joyous smile.

"Hem, my heart tells me that, like Maerad, you have some task in this struggle," he said. "I do not know what it is, but I believe it lies here, and not in Amdridh. And I think it is right that you stay here, as you wish. But it is not a decision I take without much misgiving."

There was a long silence while Hem struggled with a strange exhilaration. He knew he ought to feel afraid, that he did feel afraid, but Saliman's promise to keep him in Turbansk filled him with a buoyant light. Saliman, he thought, with a surprise that was almost painful, *trusted* him.

Irc, now wide awake, was bored by all the talk, and flapped onto the table to steal some food.

"That means Irc too, doesn't it?" said Hem, his eyes shining. "I'm sure Irc can help. He could carry messages . . . and . . ."

Saliman grinned suddenly, and all the strain seemed to vanish from his face. "As long as he keeps his house manners," he said dryly. "He does not eat as much as you, for all his greed, so perhaps we can afford him."

Irc gulped down his pilfered food and, knowing they were speaking of him, cocked his head.

You be good, said Hem sternly in the Speech. *Yes?*

I good, said Irc, turning toward Hem and knocking over Saliman's goblet, for the second time that night, with his tail.

Saliman rolled his eyes upward, and started mopping the table with a cloth. Hem scrambled up to help him, radiant with an awkward joy he was unable to conceal. For the first time since his arrival in Turbansk, he didn't feel unwanted and in the way.

It was going to be all right, he thought. It really was going to be all right.

III

THE SHADOW OF WAR

SURVIVORS from the siege of Baladh and the conquest of the Nazar Plains began to straggle into Turbansk over the next two weeks. First came a fleet of craft fleeing across the Lamarsan Sea, a motley collection ranging from tiny coracles of hide to the long sailing dromonds, bearing as many as could be crammed inside them. A day or so later the remains of the mounted forces sent by Turbansk to reinforce the Baladh defense rode through the City Gate; they had been routed, and little more than half of their original strength returned home.

Next came those who had been able to escape overland in the chaos of the battle. The first wave came on horseback, wild-eyed and gaunt, carrying many wounded with them; then families perched on wains drawn by exhausted horses and oxen, with thin, wide-eyed children who did not speak, and yet more hurt and dying; and lastly those on foot, filthy with the dust of the road, carrying children and others who could not walk because of hurt or age in makeshift sedans, or even on their backs.

By the time the first survivors arrived, the evacuation of Turbansk was all but complete. Those students at the School younger than seventeen were among the first to leave for Amdridh, many with loud protests; among the loudest were Chyafa's, who resented it mightily when he heard that Hem alone, among all the children his age, was to stay behind for the defense of the city. Hem enjoyed a sweet feeling of revenge when he saw Chyafa's gaze turned upon him with rancorous envy, but he found he did not feel the need, this time, to rise to his sneers. Hem merely smiled at his enemy and said nothing, and saw with satisfaction that it made him even more annoyed.

For days there was a stream of wagons and carriages and horses on the western road, carrying supplies and precious goods—the rarest of the irreplaceable scripts from the Library, treasures from the Turbansk palaces, the chief riches of every household—and all those who were not needed to defend the city. There were many grievous farewells; families were divided, fearing they would never meet again—parents from children, husbands from wives, brothers from sisters; lovers and old friends were parted. Hem witnessed many such despairing partings in the streets of Turbansk, and counted himself the luckier for staying.

And so Turbansk changed: there were few children playing in the streets, and then none, and the adults who made their ways through the city were solemn and preoccupied. Saliman's Bardhouse seemed empty, as only a few people remained there; he had been mentor mostly to younger students. Hem's chamber no longer echoed with the faint sounds of conversation and music and laughter, which usually filtered through from the many rooms. He was unsettled by the quiet; it brought home what was happening in the city, and sparked a growing sense of foreboding.

And as the stream of people pouring out of Turbansk toward the west dwindled and then ceased, others came in from the east and filled the empty houses, pausing briefly before they too—those who were not too ill or exhausted to move, or who were not staying to defend Turbansk—took the long road west. Now there were also people from the villages and hamlets of the Balkir Plains between Turbansk and Baladh, fleeing from the advancing armies. The forces of the Nameless One were burning everything in their path—house and vine and orchard—and a faint black smudge was visible on the eastern horizon, turning the sunrise the color of blood.

The Healing Houses were not large enough to house all the wounded from Baladh, and so the empty School was used as well, and Bards in white robes moved between rows of beds in the cloisters where only days before students had run and shouted and laughed. Hem was asked to help the healers, and he threw himself into the work with goodwill. Even Irc was pressed into service, and when he was not on his usual perch on Hem's shoulder, flapped around the buildings bearing scribbled notes or messages.

Hem saw a lot of grim sights. There were many people, including a dozen Baladh children, with terrible burns that had not been attended to properly in their flight, and they suffered excruciating pain. The healers used a strong drug distilled from poppies and exerted all their Bardic arts to dull their agonies; but many of them died.

When Hem first saw the shocking burns, on a tiny girl who could not have been more than three years old, he thought his heart would burst with anger. She did not cry, but held hard to her mother, staring at her with black eyes full of a mute, unanswerable appeal. Even when she died, beyond the help of even the greatest healers of Turbansk, she still held on to her mother, and the woman's hand had to be gently untangled from the dead fingers, which grasped as tightly as a vice. It was then that Hem asked Oslar, the chief healer, what had happened to the burned children.

Oslar was an old man even by Bardic reckoning, his hair very white and his skin very black, and his strong face was lined with a deep and patient sadness. Hem reflected that he must have seen a lot of suffering in his long life. "She was caught by one of the worst weapons of the Dark," he said. "It was the dogsoldiers."

Hem had heard of dogsoldiers, but up until then they had been just a word.

"What are they?" he asked, although he knew that Oslar was needed elsewhere and did not have time to answer his questions.

"They are not human, and I do not know if they ever were," said the old Bard, speaking plainly and looking him in the eye, as one adult to another. "They are creatures of flesh and metal and fire, made by some foul sorcery in the forges of Dén Raven, and they do not know what mercy is. They have heads like dogs with muzzles of blue metal. Their very bodies are weapons, from which they shoot a liquid fire. It sticks to flesh and eats into it. It's the strange fire, how it sticks, that makes the burns so bad."

Oslar looked across at the other beds in that room, with their small victims, and Hem swallowed, his mouth suddenly dry. "Now, Hem, I have work to do. Excuse me." Oslar nodded courteously, and Hem followed him with his eyes as he moved slowly from bed to bed. Hem knew the old Bard had slept very little in the past two nights, and yet he showed no sign of weariness.

He was grateful that his question had been answered, although the answer did not comfort him. Oslar, he thought, was a very great man. Then he felt surprised at himself: he didn't usually think things like that.

As Hem ran around the School of Turbansk, bearing potions from the herbalists or new dressings from the weavers, bringing a beaker of water to a woman too weak from childbed to walk, or holding a broken arm for binding, his anger smoldered and grew bright. He hated what had been done so wantonly to these people with every fiber in his being. He was no stranger to rage, but for the first time his feeling was tempered by compassion, and he discovered a patience within himself that he had not known he possessed.

Perhaps it was the example of Oslar and the other healers, including his mentor Urbika, who had stayed with most of the other Bards and was herself a gifted healer. Even if he made a mistake, which was seldom, they never spoke a sharp word to him, no matter how little they had slept, or how overworked they were. And so Hem learned, in those few days, how to listen to the ill, how to anticipate their needs, how to run fast in soft shoes so he made no loud noises that might disturb those who slept. Before the scale of the suffering before him, his previous complaints seemed petty and insignificant. He was too busy, in any case, to worry much about himself; his day was filled from dawn to dusk with countless tasks and errands, and Oslar himself began to teach him some charms of healing for the less serious cases. He was so tired by nightfall that, for the first time since he had been in Turbansk, he was not troubled by nightmares.

When Saliman told him one evening that the Bards were praising his work, and that Oslar had said that few minor Bards in his experience had shown such innate talent as Hem in the arts of caring for the sick, Hem accepted the praise, which was hard earned, with a new humility.

"Don't be offended if I say that I am surprised; I thought you would be too impatient for this work," said Saliman, with a smile, which for Hem was ample reward for every hour he had spent in the Healing House. "Perhaps you will be a healer when you are grown. Every Bard has to find out how their Gift best expresses itself; for some, it is a hard road. But I think you might be lucky. Healing is one of the highest callings; and there is always need for healers, even in times of peace."

Hem pondered Saliman's words in silence. He could imagine

himself as a healer. Perhaps one day he could be as good as Oslar.

"You'd have to work on your scripting, though," said Saliman, interrupting his reverie. "Imagine, say, if the herbalist made a love potion instead of a laxative because he couldn't read your instructions. The trouble you could cause!"

Hem grinned; Saliman was constantly nagging him to work on his writing, which was nearly illegible. Perhaps now he could see the point.

They were eating a quick meal before Saliman went out again to continue the endless work of preparing Turbansk for an assault. The food was plain, but tasty: freshwater fish from the Lamarsan Sea baked with dates, and a mash of pulses. Outside Saliman's rooms, birds burbled in the trees as they settled to their evening roosts, and a cool breeze brushed Hem's cheek. It was very peaceful. Hem suddenly wished, with a furious longing, that he could have come to Turbansk in ordinary times.

Saliman had just told him of the first attacks on Turbansk, by raider ships sailing from the mouth of the Niken River across the Lamarsan Sea, and Hem had seen soldiers in the eating halls, on their way to harry the Black Fleets, or returning exhausted and grim-faced. No raider ships had yet reached Turbansk, and, Saliman told him, none would: the harbor defenses were stout. But the raiders drew off Turbansk's strength, wearying their forces even before the main assault; and after the fall of Baladh, Saliman feared that a fleet of stolen ships would set out from Baladh Harbor to launch a major attack.

Because of the war, Saliman had not even had time to take Hem, as he had promised, to see the Lamar Falls in the Lamarsan Caves, the sacred heart of the Light in Turbansk, which he had said were one of the wonders of the world. If times had been different, perhaps they could have ridden there with Maerad . . . but Hem quickly shut off his thoughts about his sister: they were too painful.

"Will there ever be peace again?" he asked, a little sadly.

"Of course there will be." Saliman leaned back and closed his eyes, and Hem could see how weary he actually was. The skin under his eyes was purple, as if it were bruised, and his face was drawn. Hem wondered how long it was since Saliman had slept; he was willing to warrant it was more than two days. "If not in my lifetime or yours, then in someone else's."

Hem, depressed by Saliman's reply, didn't answer, and Saliman opened one eye and stared at him. "Forgive me, Hem; I should not jest. I am so weary, and the storm has not even hit."

"You must rest," said Hem sternly, with his new authority as a healer.

Saliman smiled wanly. "We will be ready soon," he said. "Then I will rest. For a short time."

Over the next few days the black smudge of smoke in the east grew closer and the Healing Houses began to empty. All the sick were to leave Turbansk, even the worst injured, although Hem saw the anxiety on the healers' faces as the patients were placed on the special litters that were to transport them. He knew they should not be moved, but he also understood that it was impossible for them to stay in Turbansk. Many healers went with them, to care for them on their long journey to Car Amdridh, although Oslar and Urbika were among those who stayed behind, and, very suddenly, there was little for Hem to do. He spent a day in the Bardhouse, bored and lonely but too depressed to go out, feeling a sense of doom growing inside him. His patience seemed to have disappeared with his work at the Healing Houses, and he was even irritable with Irc. That evening he asked if he could go with Saliman the next day.

"Perhaps I could help?" he said. "Irc was really useful in the Healing Houses, too . . ."

Saliman studied Hem's face. "It might be as boring as anything you are doing here," he said. "But yes, I should have thought of it myself. It is a little gloomy waiting alone for war to break over your head. Of course you can come."

So the next day Hem became Saliman's shadow, as he had in his first week in Turbansk, except this time the slender boy had a white bird on his shoulder. The Bards and captains and city consuls did not object, if they seldom took notice of him, and the sick panic that had begun to stir in Hem's stomach eased back slightly. When he looked into the faces of the men and women who talked so earnestly, at their determination and strength, he did not see how they would be defeated.

As a member of the First Circle of Bards, one of the ruling bodies of Turbansk, Saliman was in charge of many aspects of the city's defense, and by the end of the day Hem began to understand why Saliman had been so tired. That day he went to several different meetings at the School and the Ernan—the great palace that stretched gracefully under the shadow of the Red Tower—listening to reports from scouts and the captains who had been attacking the raiders on the Lamarsan Sea with fire boats, and conferring with the other leaders of Turbansk to coordinate strategy. If any of them thought it odd that Hem was present, they didn't say so.

Hem hadn't been inside the Ernan before, and was awed. Most of its riches had been stripped and sent away to Car Amdridh, but it still possessed a breathtaking grandeur that surpassed even Norloch. Norloch was a high citadel built into the living rock above the Norloch Harbor, tower above tower of white stone topped by the Crystal Hall of Machelinor, and it spoke of majesty and authority. The Ernan was not a tower but an ancient palace, and it was built for pleasure. It had been added to and changed by successive rulers over countless centuries until it was the largest single building in the city, surrounded by wide gardens planted with perfumed trees and rare flowers.

The palace spiraled inside high walls of stone, room after graceful room connected by archways or doors wrought of brass or iron in intricate grilles. The floors were of polished marble or mosaics of glazed tiles, depicting abstract patterns of flowers or stars. The rooms opened onto countless courtyards, each different: one contained nothing but white sand, raked into patterns, with black stones placed carefully upon it to induce contemplation; another held a fountain and a lawn of a pungent herb that refreshed the mind when it was walked upon; yet another was full of roses of every color, spilling in artful disarray onto marble paving. Some chambers had large windows that opened onto wide terraces, from which the sun could be watched as it set across the Lamarsan Sea.

Hem walked through the endless maze of the palace, hearing his heels echo on the floors, his mouth open. He had thought the School of Turbansk grand, but this made the School seem austere. Saliman saw his expression and chuckled.

"We give our rulers the same name as their dwelling," he said. "For the people of Turbansk, both palace and ruler embody the greatness of our city; and, perhaps, its folly. Some Ernani have taken this role too literally; the Bards and the people had to relieve one of his rule, when he became too expensive to maintain. And so we have this great palace, one of the glorious treasures of Edil-Amarandh."

"How do you not get lost?" asked Hem breathlessly. Saliman was walking very fast, and he almost had to run to keep up with him, Irc clinging to his shoulder and flapping to keep his balance. Hem feared being left behind because he thought he would never find his way out.

"I've been walking this palace since I was little older than you," said Saliman. "And that is many years. I am sorry that I have no time to show you its marvels. There is no place like it in the world, and there never will be again. . . . There are chambers here where the walls are decorated only with precious stones. There is a summer house built entirely of jasper, which was made five hundred years ago solely for the recitation of a certain poem by a famous poet of Turbansk. In the Garden of Helian there is a beautiful house of red marble made by the Ernani Helian a thousand years ago, so he could study the stars; Bards still use it for sky-watching. On festival days the people of Turbansk can enter here, and they come in their thousands to marvel and to feast in the gardens. And I suppose I feel the same pride in the Ernan's extravagant beauty as they do, although at times I wonder . . ." He trailed off.

Hem, dazzled by the splendors he was walking through, looked up questioningly.

Saliman shrugged his shoulders, smiling. "You will have noticed there are no corridors in this palace. In Annar, they build corridors; the Annarens like that kind of logic. This palace is built as a series of spirals. Here it is more complicated and oblique to get anywhere."

Hem privately agreed; he was hopelessly lost. But Saliman was continuing, musing as if to himself.

"Though in all the Seven Kingdoms power is complex," he said. "It is so, even in Annar. Norloch is relatively simple, because only Bards rule there. . . . Elsewhere there are two authorities, the Bards and the governing councils. And the Bards and the other authorities do not always agree on what is best to do."

Saliman halted and looked around the colonnaded hall through which they were now walking. "But often I think that Turbansk is the most complicated," he said. "The people of

Turbansk are born with politics in their blood. Cadvan would not last two days here; he would lose his temper and offend all the consuls, and from then on his life would be misery." Saliman grinned, thinking of his old friend. "Sometimes this is a good thing; it is far better that people talk than fight. But when something must be done quickly—well, it can make it more difficult. Our friend Alimbar, for example, despite our desperation, has been making my life more complicated than it need be, for reasons of his own. But we are very fortunate in our present Ernani, Har-Ytan."

Saliman stopped outside tall doors more impressive than any Hem had yet seen: they were of cedar burnished to a deep, rich polish, with great bosses wrought of gold in the shape of the sun entwined in flames of different colors, from deep red to white gold. Saliman looked down at Hem.

"Hem, you must be on your best behavior here. And Irc, too," he added in the Speech, looking sternly at the bird, who gave a faint *cark* and hid his head in Hem's hair. "Just bow as I do, and say nothing."

Suddenly nervous, Hem gulped and nodded, and Saliman bowed his head to the two palace guards, who opened the doors and admitted them.

Hem paused involuntarily at the threshold, blinking with dazzlement. Saliman was striding forward, so he rapidly collected himself and followed. He cast covert glances around the room, doing his best not to look as overwhelmed as he felt. The rest of the palace was, he realized, merely a rehearsal for the throne room.

The Ernani sat on a wide, low dais at the far end, on a throne of black enameled wood carved in filigree patterns with a marvelous delicacy so that, despite its size—its back stretched high behind the Ernani—it gave an impression of weightlessness. Behind the throne, reaching up to the ceiling, was a

giant golden sun like those embossed on the doors, which cast
a golden glow about the whole room. The walls, which were
pierced by long, narrow windows that ran from floor to ceiling,
were faced with plain panels of dull gold punctuated by murals
painted with an exquisite delicacy, each framed in the same
black enameled filigree of which the throne was made. They
depicted, Saliman told Hem later, famous stories of the
Suderain: one was of the Battle of the Dagorlad Plains, in which
the Ernani of Turbansk had held back the forces of the
Nameless One in the days of the Great Silence; another was of
the meeting of Alibredh and Nalimbar, who were fabled lovers,
in the water gardens of Jerr-Niken.

Hem and Saliman walked toward the throne on a path of
black onyx tiles that bisected a wide and shallow pool stretching for the width of the throne room and half its length. The
pool, filled with flowering water lilies, was stepped in three
shallow terraces, and water spilled over the lips of the higher
levels into the lower pools so the room was filled with its constant music, and the lilies gave off a subtle perfume.

To Hem, it seemed to take a very long time to walk the
length of the pool, and then across the plain expanse of polished black stone that stretched before the dais. About the
throne were set several low stools, of the same marvelous filigree as the throne itself, on which sat five people. They turned
and watched as Saliman and Hem approached and Hem recognized, with a flutter in his stomach, Alimbar, whom he had last
seen outside the door of Saliman's house. He also recognized
Juriken, the First Bard of Turbansk, and Il Hanedr, whom he
knew was the captain of the city soldiers, the Guardians of the
Sun. A tough-looking, thin woman—the chief guard, Menika—
stood silently by Har-Ytan's right shoulder in Turbansk battle
gear, and another woman he did not recognize, dressed in
formal robes, sat nearby, her head bowed.

The Ernani sat very still on the throne, watching their progress. Hem dared a swift glance, although by this time he was so awed he scarcely knew where to direct his eyes. The Ernani was the most regal human being he had ever seen.

She must have been fully Saliman's height, and her body was at once voluptuous and strong; if she had been less tall, he might have thought her stout. She wore a close-fitting dress of silk dyed craftily in many shades of red and orange, which shimmered against her black skin as if she were sheathed in a living flame, and her long hair was braided in tiny plaits in the style of Turbansk, beaded with rubies and gold so it fell in a glittering fountain down her back. A huge ruby blazed on her brow, and on her breast she wore a torque of gold emblazoned with the sun. Her powerful arms were bare, apart from bands of plain gold about her wrists, and a naked sword lay across her lap, in token of war.

When they reached the dais, Saliman genuflected on one knee and bowed his head, and Hem hastily copied him, wishing he had half of Saliman's grace. He was glad that he had been told not to speak; his mouth had gone completely dry, and he was sure that if he had said anything it would have come out as a squeak.

To his amazement, the Ernani addressed them in the Speech; he found later that the Speech was used in the Suderain for all debates of high policy, and although she was not a Bard, Har-Ytan spoke it well. Her voice was deep and musical, and seemed to resonate through the entire throne room.

"You are tardy, Saliman," she said. "We have been waiting."

The hair prickled on Hem's neck. He hoped fervently that she did not blame him.

"Forgive me, Har-Ytan, Fountain of the Light," Saliman answered. "I was detained by other urgent tasks. And only the most urgent could keep me from your glorious presence."

The Ernani laughed, a melodious ripple of mirth that sent a strange shiver down Hem's back.

"Consider yourself merely rebuked, then. Welcome, Cai of Pellinor." Hem was startled that she knew his name, and then blushed at being addressed. "Sit down. There is much to discuss, and little time."

Hem scrambled to his feet and followed Saliman to a stool, hardly daring to look up from his feet. Irc was infected by his abashment and didn't even squawk when the movement almost tipped him off his perch on Hem's shoulder.

Hem was surprised, after the grandeur of their entrance, by the discussion that followed (it was a while before he remembered that the First Bard and the Ernani were, in fact, equal in authority over Turbansk). All formality was put aside, and a discussion of the current defense of Turbansk was conducted briskly, with reports from each present on the latest developments.

Il Hanedr, captain of the city guard, said that his scouts reported the Black Army was two days' march distant, preparing to assault the Il Dara Wall twenty leagues east of Turbansk, the last major barrier before the Black Army. The Wall was manned by some ten thousand archers and infantry, mainly from the regions around Baladh, and four ranks, six hundred in each rank, of the Sun Guard. It was a giant construction made in the days of the Great Silence to resist the forces of the Nameless One, and Har-Ytan had ordered this ancient wall rebuilt and extended five years previously, when it became clear to her that an assault from Dén Raven was all but inevitable. It was a strong deterrent: a high double wall of granite with deep foundations, fortified with many towers. It stretched for a league across a strip of dry land that divided the Neera Marshes, and an invading army could be delayed there indefinitely, or be forced to march for leagues around the marshes.

"Imank is slower than we judged, then," said Juriken, raising his eyebrows.

"If the Hull were not so concerned to burn everything in its path, they might be swifter," Il Hanedr answered. "But the destruction has bought us a little time, although we might count it dearly bought. We would not have had time to muster so many had Imank moved more quickly."

"Each small advantage we have is bought dearly," said Har-Ytan. "So we must use it well. Is there any point, think you, in harrying the army as it approaches the Wall?"

Both Il Hanedr and Juriken shook their heads. "Nay, it would cost us more than it gained," said Juriken. "It would be sending our fighters to almost certain death, and such are the forces arraigned against us, it would not slow them."

"There is nowhere that death is not almost certain," said the Ernani.

Juriken hesitated, then nodded. "There is always hope," he said. But his expression was grim.

Hem's heart froze, and he stole a secret look at Saliman. But now it was Saliman's turn to speak.

Hem now learned that Saliman was coordinating the shoreline defenses. He said that the fleet of Black Army ships from Baladh that he feared was imminent had not been sighted by his scouts.

"Perhaps the fireships we sent against the raiders have made their own argument against attack from the Lamarsan Sea," he said. "But I think that is too much to hope for. I cannot believe that Imank, the captain of the Black Army, does not plan an attack from the Lamarsan Sea; those fleeing Baladh were not able to destroy all the galleys they left behind, and it is not beyond the enemy's power to build more. I fear three score at least being sent against us. What seems most likely is that they plan to send the galleys at the same time as the Black Army, to block our harbor and draw off our forces. We will not be able to flee over the water, if we do not hold the passage. And the caves will serve only for few."

There was a glum silence, and then the talk moved on to a general discussion. The city fortifications, Alimbar reported, were almost completed. Within the city were Alhadeans from Nazar and Cissians and Bilakeans from the plains between Turbansk and Baladh, as well as the remnants of Baladh's defense, all experienced at fighting back the incursions from Dén Raven that had become common over the past three centuries. They had retreated stubbornly before the advancing armies, harrying the outriding forces with some success, and had swelled the ranks of the Turbanskians by nearly twenty thousand. Juriken estimated that with the forces now at the Wall, the city had some two score thousand fighters, and supplies enough for all of them for three months, even if the harbor were closed off.

Hem brightened at the numbers; it seemed so many, more than he could imagine in one place. But Juriken was gloomy; he estimated the Black Army was ten times that size, and of that number, many were dogsoldiers. He was also uncertain about what kinds of sorceries Imank might be planning to use. After that, Hem noted that no one talked about victory; and he shifted uncomfortably on his seat.

Lastly spoke Indira, the stranger who had listened silently and intently to the entire discussion. She was an emissary from Zimek, a large School to the south of Turbansk.

Zimek, Hem learned to his shock, was to be abandoned, and all its peoples were now on their way to Car Amdridh. "Not all like it, naturally," said Indira, her face somber. "Many are angry at the thought of leaving their homes, and say we flee like cowards. But we all know our fate otherwise would be Baladh's, to be disemboweled by the Black Army as crows tear a carcass; we are strong, but not strong enough. This way, we choose when we leave, and what we take with us, although it breaks our hearts. We take all we can carry, and are burning all crops and stripping all orchards. There will be nothing for the army to pillage."

Juriken and Har-Ytan nodded. "How long before Zimek is emptied, then?" asked Har-Ytan.

"Two days, no more," Indira answered. "And then it is done." While she had been speaking she had shown no emotion, but now her voice broke, and she covered her eyes. Har-Ytan reached out and pressed her hand gently.

"It is well done," she said quietly. "Alas, all our hearts will be riven, ere the end of this."

After the meeting in the Ernan, Hem felt deeply exhausted, so Saliman sent him home and continued to the harborside to speak to the ship captains who were now coming in from yet another attack against the raiders of the Black Army. He came back many hours later, and after greeting Hem went to bed without eating anything. Saliman did not stir from his chamber until late the next day.

The smoke rose in the east, closer again. But the defenses of Turbansk were now ready.

The next day Hem found himself with nothing to do, and hungry. Saliman was nowhere to be seen. Instead of making for the butteries, Hem wandered toward the marketplace of Turbansk, wondering if he might find Saliman there, near the harbor.

It was the first time Hem had been to the markets since

Turbansk had begun to evacuate its population. Only two weeks earlier, they had been the bustling heart of Turbansk. The markets were where Hem most often went when he was feeling unhappy at the School; here he could lose himself in the crowds of people, wandering fascinated from stall to stall.

Closest to the School were the flower markets, an ancient cloistered hall of stone that was always cool, even in the harshest midday heat, because the stone was kept wet so the flowers would stay fresh. Next to them were the food markets, with their marble counters where stallholders displayed freshwater trout and bream and crayfish caught by the fishers of the Lamarsan Sea, or carefully piled mounds of luscious fruits and piles of greenery.

But now the markets were desolate and melancholy. The flower markets were completely closed, the stone tables empty, the windows shuttered and barred, and the noon sun struck back harshly from the suddenly naked walls. A few stray dogs nosed down the gutters of the alleys looking for scraps, and those people who walked through them mostly wore armor and strode purposefully, instead of sauntering, as the Turbansk people generally preferred, prepared always to be waylaid by an invitation to gossip over a cup of strong, sweet coffee.

Hem realized properly for the first time that those who remained in Turbansk did not expect it to withstand the coming attack. A small hope he had been nurturing in his heart shriveled and died; despite Saliman's bleak words, despite what he had seen and heard from the survivors of Baladh in the Healing Houses, despite yesterday's conference at the Ernan, Hem had continued to believe that perhaps all those who stayed in Turbansk did so because they thought they could defeat the forces of the Nameless One now marching against them. But the empty markets told him more eloquently than any words that this was a fool's hope; the thousands of people who now prepared to defend Turbansk did not do so because they thought they would win.

Why did they stay, then? Hem continued his glum meandering, preoccupied with the question. Why had he stayed? That one was easy: he did not want to be parted from Saliman. But why did Saliman stay?

Hem paused in the Street of Coffee Sellers and absent-mindedly bought a coffee from the single stall that remained open. As he handed over the copper coin, the stallholder said, in good Annaren, "So you are the young Bard in the Healing Houses?"

Startled out of his musings, Hem studied the man with interest. He was thickset, with the black skin of a Turbanskian. Deep laughter lines creased his eyes, and his teeth were very white and strong. A shortsword hung from his waistband. Why was he staying? "Yes," Hem said. "How did you know?"

The stallholder laughed. "Word gets around," he said. "And everyone has heard of your bird. We do not like to use our children in war, and so I know of no others as young as you who will remain here. My daughter, Amira, was very angry when she heard about you. 'Father,' she said to me, 'you send me away, against my will—although I can fight, although I would give my life to save the city that I love—and yet there remains in Turbansk a foreign boy from Annar who is younger even than me.'"

Hem smiled, and the stallholder continued.

"I told her, it is the law, but it is also the law of my heart. And I told her that perhaps she will fight anyway in Amdridh, if things go ill here. It did not please her." He laughed, but Hem heard with surprise that there was no bitterness in his laughter.

"But you are staying," said Hem.

"Yes," he answered.

"And do you think we will save Turbansk?"

At first the stallholder didn't answer. Instead, he pressed a little honeyed sweetmeat into Hem's hand, waving off Hem's offer to pay. Hem put it in his pocket for later. Then the stallholder said, "All who remain here are afraid that we see the last days of our houses. The Bards and the Ernani do not feed us false hopes: they say, the Black Army is very great, and our forces cannot defeat them. Send all that is precious to you— your children, your valuables—to Car Amdridh, where they can be better defended. But they have called for all who can to stay and defend our city, to buy some time for those who flee, and to allow Amdridh to ready its defense and muster all its forces. We will not simply abandon Turbansk, the jewel of the Suderain, to the carrionfowl of the Dark. And perhaps we can deplete the army, so those behind us will have less work to do." He smiled grimly.

Hem studied the stallholder, wondering at his bravery. "What is your name?" he asked at last.

"Boran," said the stallholder. "And yours?"

"Hem."

"A thousand blessings on your cup, Hem," said Boran, giving him the traditional benediction before drinking.

"And on yours, Boran," said Hem. He said it in Suderain, as he had at least mastered that phrase, finished the coffee, and handed the cup back to Boran. Then, thanking him, he continued his moody wandering, kicking a stone before his foot so it rattled on the cobbles.

IV

ZELIKA

HEM wasn't taking much notice of his surroundings, so when someone shot out of one of the side alleys and crashed into him he was taken completely by surprise. Irc flapped into the air, cawing in protest, and Hem was sent sprawling onto the ground. His first feeling was rage, and he grabbed blindly for his assailant, catching part of a cloak and holding it fast, even when a hard little fist hit him in the eye. He grabbed one arm and then another, and, panting with effort, wrestled his attacker to the ground.

He was sitting astride his foe, about to take revenge for what he thought would probably be a black eye, when he realized he was fighting a girl. She was glaring at him murderously, still struggling and spitting out imprecations. Hem's command of the Suderain language had improved considerably in his time in the Healing Houses, although it was still uncertain. Nevertheless, he understood enough to know that he was being called some very unflattering names.

He flushed, and would have responded in kind if he had not simultaneously noticed the ragged state of the girl's clothes and that she had been hurt; quite recently her lip had been split, and there was a nasty infected cut underneath her right eye. He swallowed his retort.

"I'm very sorry," he said, in careful Suderain. "I did not see you . . ."

The girl paused in her struggle to free herself and stared at him balefully.

"You should be more careful," Hem said.

"Let me go," said the girl.

Hem studied her curiously. She had the light-brown skin of those who came from the eastern parts of the Suderain, and spoke with the accent of Baladh. She must have arrived late in Turbansk, and somehow missed the last wagons that had carried the children to Car Amdridh. He thought she must be about his own age. She had tangled black hair, which spilled in loose curls around her face, and delicate features, which were somewhat mitigated by the anger of her expression. She was filthy; her tattered cloak was so stained it was almost impossible to tell its original color, and she carried a battered leather bag that clearly held all her few possessions.

"Please promise not to run away," Hem said. "I'm sorry, it was—" He didn't know the Suderain word for *accident*. "I won't hurt you . . ."

The girl paused, and nodded. Hem, normally so distrustful of strangers, did not doubt for a moment that she would keep her word. He carefully got off her, and she sat up, brushing herself down. Irc returned to Hem's shoulder and leaned forward, his head cocked, examining the girl with unalloyed curiosity. She would not look at Hem, and sat next to him with an air of affronted dignity. Hem groped around in his mind for something to say, cursing his lack of Suderain.

He suddenly remembered the honey cake that Boran had given him, and he pulled it out of his pocket and offered it to her. It was a little crushed, but still mainly whole. The girl stared at him doubtfully, and then snatched the cake from his hand and devoured it in two bites. She was clearly starving.

"What are you doing here?" asked Hem, watching as she wiped her mouth. "You should be on your way to Car Amdridh."

"I hid," said the girl. She seemed a little mollified after his offering. "I want to fight the Black Ones." She drew a knife from a sheath at her belt and pointed it at Hem; he could see that it was a cooking knife, sharp enough to cut bone, but not a fighting weapon. "I'll kill anyone who tries to stop me."

Such was the expression in her eyes, Hem had no difficulty in believing her; he was glad that she had not been able to reach her knife in their struggle. He felt a strange mixture of astonishment, admiration, and pity.

"No one can stop you," he said. "It's too late. The Black Army—" He waved his hands around, hunting for the words. "The Black Army comes very soon." He pushed the point of the knife aside, and she slowly put it back in its sheath. "So—your name? I am Hem."

"Zelika," she said slowly. "Zelika of the House of Il Aran." She looked at Irc curiously. "What is that bird? It is not a falcon."

"He's my friend," said Hem. "His name is Irc." He looked at the girl again; now he could see the gauntness of her features, and he wondered when she had last had a good meal. "Are you hungry, Zelika?"

She paused, and then nodded.

"Come with me. I'll get you food."

Hem saw distrust and desire warring in Zelika's face, but hunger won. When she stood up, he saw that she was slight, but she carried herself with a pride that added a little illusory height.

He began to lead her through the streets toward the School buttery. Perhaps she could stay at Saliman's house: there were plenty of spare rooms, and he thought that Saliman would not mind. She could get some new clothes and have a wash, and Hem could see to the wound on her cheek, which was festering; he had some balm in his chamber.

"You are not from Turbansk," said the girl flatly, interrupting his thoughts.

"No, from Annar," answered Hem. "My Suderain not so good."

"My Annaren not so good, as well." Zelika spoke in Annaren, with an atrocious accent, and smiled. For a brief moment Hem saw two dimples in her cheeks, and a mischievous light danced in her eyes, vanishing as quickly as it appeared. He glanced at her curiously.

"So why do you stay here?" he asked. "Everyone says Turbansk is—we can't . . ." Stumped again by his lack of vocabulary, he trailed to a halt.

"I don't care if I die," said Zelika. "I want to kill as many of the Black Ones as I can before I do." Hem looked at her again, at the strange, utterly focused determination in her face; it was almost madness. He had never heard a human being say anything with more conviction, and something like fear constricted his heart.

"Why?" he asked, although he thought he knew the answer.

She gave him an unreadable glance, as if measuring his capacity to understand. "My mother, my father, my brothers, my sisters, my aunts, my cousins, my uncles, my grandmother—" She drew her finger brutally across her throat, and her eyes blazed with hatred and grief, although her voice was flat and unemotional. "I saw it. My home was burned to the ground. I will avenge the House of Il Aren."

Hem said nothing: there was nothing to say.

"Why should I live?" said Zelika. "I have nothing to live for. I will fight them, and kill as many as I can."

"You need a better knife," said Hem.

They walked the rest of the way in silence.

At the buttery, Soron gave Hem a plum and a small bowl of cold dohl without any questions, although he stared curiously at the girl. They sat at one end of the long table in the eating hall, and Hem watched as she ate.

"You should not eat so quickly," he said. "You will be sick." He mimed vomiting. Zelika said nothing, but slowed down; she had been wolfing her food ravenously. When she had finished the bowl of dohl, she looked at Hem inquiringly. She obviously wanted more, but did not ask.

"How long since you ate?" he asked.

"I think . . . two, three days," said Zelika.

"No more now," Hem said sternly. "More, in a little while."

To his surprise, she did not argue with him. "I tried to take some bread from the market, but the man saw me and chased me. I ran and ran; that's why I ran into you."

"There are no crowds, and it makes stealing hard," said Hem.

"I never stole before," she said, with a disarming simplicity. "I don't know how."

Hem looked at Zelika more closely. He had taken her for an urchin, like the orphans he had known in his childhood, but it now occurred to him that she might be more gently born. He remembered her announcement of her name. Perhaps she was from one of the important families of Baladh. She fought well for a noble, he thought, remembering their scrap; in his short time at the School, Hem had quickly worked out that students from wealthier families were much softer in a fight than those who came from poorer houses.

"I should heal your cut," he said, with a trace of self-importance. He had dealt with many minor injuries at the Healing Houses. "Come with me."

Zelika followed him with a gratifying meekness to Saliman's house, and he took her first to the bathing room. "You should get clean, first," he said. "I'll get clothes for you. Wait here." He ran to his chamber and emptied his chest, and returned with a tunic and trews.

Zelika was sitting on the bench in the bathing room, looking suddenly lost and exhausted.

"Do you want a wash?" Hem asked.

She nodded dumbly, but did not move. Hem wondered for a moment if she expected him to wash her; he did not feel up to that responsibility.

"I'll wait for you, there," he said firmly, pointing to the hallway, and went out of the room, closing the door behind him.

There was a short silence, and then he heard the splash of running water. Hem sat cross-legged on the floor and composed himself to wait.

It wasn't long before Zelika emerged. She was wearing the clothes Hem had given her; they were slightly too big. Her hair had been washed and combed and hung in glossy ringlets down her back. Hem blinked, taken aback; she was much prettier than he had first realized.

He led her back to his chamber and dealt with the cuts on her face. They were not very serious, apart from the infection. He cleaned out the pus scrupulously and applied the healing balm, muttering healing charms in the Speech. Despite how much it must have hurt, Zelika did not make a sound.

As he finished his work, Hem heard the street doors open and close with a bang. Telling Zelika to wait in his chamber, he ran to see if it was Saliman: it was almost time for the noon bell, and he counted on the Bard returning home for the midday meal. It was Saliman, and before he had a chance to open his mouth in greeting, Hem breathlessly told him about Zelika.

"Is it all right that I brought her back here?" he asked anxiously. "I didn't know where else to take her. She wasn't hurt so badly that she needed the healers, and I cleaned her cuts myself . . ." Saliman's eyebrows were drawn into a frown, and Hem trailed off into silence.

"Turbansk is no place for a child," said Saliman shortly. "She should not be here."

"I'm a child," said Hem, suddenly feeling angry. "And I'm here. And anyway, it's too late now. All the wagons have gone."

There was a silence, and Saliman sighed. "We'll eat in my rooms. Everyone else is out," he said. "You may as well go and get her."

Zelika had come reluctantly to meet Saliman, and had at first sat silently, refusing to answer any questions, and concentrating on eating. Saliman had covertly studied her as she ate, as if turning over the little Hem had told him about her. When they had finished their meal, Saliman had said that she should leave for Car Amdridh that day; although all the wagons had left, a messenger was preparing to ride that afternoon, and Zelika could ride with him.

Saliman's statement pulled Zelika out of her blank passivity. She refused flatly to go. When Saliman pressed her, she stood up, screaming curses, and threw her plate at him. Hem, greatly embarrassed, tried to calm her down, and finally she just sat mulishly, her lips pressed tightly together, and would not speak at all.

Saliman watched her tantrum in silence with his arms crossed. When she was finally quiet, he asked her if she really knew what it was she was facing, and how little hope there was of victory.

Zelika glared at him mutinously. "I know," she said.

"I doubt you understand fully," said Saliman, with a hard edge to his voice. "I shall explain."

All through the Great Silence, Saliman said, Turbansk had

been assailed by forces from Dén Raven, but it had never been taken. Neither, as loomed large in the thoughts of everyone in the city, had Baladh fallen, nor the ancient fortified city of Jerr-Niken. But now Baladh lay in ruins, and the Black Army marched on territories it had never before invaded. Jerr-Niken had been sacked seven years before by Imank, the sorcerer-captain of Dén Raven. It was then that fears arose in the Suderain that the return of Sharma, the Nameless One, long prophesied, was now a reality.

During the Great Silence, Imank had been the Nameless One's chief captain. A powerful Hull, a bard who had traded his True Name for the secret of deathlessness, Imank had fled far to the south after the collapse of the Dark. It had not been heard of for centuries. The people of Dén Raven, freed from tyranny and enslavement, made treaties with the Suderain and Annar, and for some hundreds of years even used the Bardic system of dual government. For centuries all had seemed well, and little disturbed the peace.

But three hundred years before, in a sudden coup of un-precedented savagery, the Bards of Dén Raven, accused of spying by the then King, had been slaughtered or banished. Those few Bards who managed to escape to the Schools of the Suderain brought evil news with them: Imank had returned to Dén Raven. Adopting the guise of a wise and trusted counsel-lor, the Hull had ingratiated itself with the King, poisoning his mind and encouraging his greed and lust for domination; and when its power over the King was total, the Hull had sprung a trap on the Bards. Thereafter, for two centuries, Dén Raven had been ruled by a series of petty kings and despots controlled by Imank and a cohort of Hulls, who returned out of exile from the unmapped areas south of the Agaban Desert.

Since Imank's return, very few outsiders had managed to

penetrate Dén Raven, and the few who had brought grim reports. The entire realm had been transformed into a fortress, and the people of Dén Raven into a massive army. From birth to death every action of every person was overseen by the Eyes, Hulls who controlled the different regions and dispensed work and punishment. No rebellion, in word or thought or deed, was too small to be crushed mercilessly: merely to mutter a complaint was enough to merit torture in the dungeons of the Hulls, and to speak openly against the rulers was a death sentence.

"I have been there myself," said Saliman, and both Zelika and Hem looked up at him with wonder. "Merely to attempt to enter Dén Raven is to risk death and worse." He was silent for a time, his face overcast by dark memories. "I hope never to return there. It is little more than a huge prison. The Eyes of Sharma are powerful sorcerers, and they are greatly feared; they have ways of watching, perversions of Barding, which are an evil even to think of. Much of the land is poisoned: there are places where nothing will grow, and strange forests that glow red at night. There are beasts running wild who do not understand the Speech but are grown dumb and strange; they have something wrong with their minds, and their forms are misshapen. The Nameless is ingenious in all his devices; I don't doubt these also serve his purposes."

As Saliman spoke, Hem could see in his mind the landscapes he was describing, and the boy shuddered.

"The armies are fed by great farms, all tilled by slaves," continued Saliman. "The Eyes control all supplies; they live well enough, but the people fare poorly, and are given only enough to ensure they live. Those who win favor with the Hulls, of course, can do much better; some, the Grin, live in an obscene luxury and are themselves petty tyrants. They are useful to the

Nameless One, and so he suffers them to flourish. But nothing there is grown or made for pleasure or beauty, and even the leisures of the Grin are stamped with foulness and cruelty."

Saliman paused, and Hem swallowed, the queasy fear of his nightmares rising within him. The two children had listened in silence as Saliman spoke, Zelika frowning as she tried to keep up with Saliman's Annaren. They watched as Saliman poured himself a goblet of water and drank before he continued.

"We always feared that Imank merely prepared for the return of the Nameless One," said Saliman. "For fifty years we have been certain that the Nameless was in Dén Raven, but no one in Annar would believe us. Wishful thinking clouded the judgment of most Bards, but I fear that was the least of it. A subtle corruption has wormed its way into the heart of many Annaren Schools, although I did not know what it was until I saw Enkir, the First Bard of Annar.

"Perhaps if we had marched on Dén Raven before it had become strong, when Imank was merely harrying small settlements south of Jerr-Niken, it might be a different story now. But when Jerr-Niken was sacked seven years ago it was already, I fear, too late. What is about to happen is the culmination of long planning by the Dark, and the Light is weaker than it has ever been. I fear all goes the Dark's way; the best we can do here is measure our retreat. The Nameless seeks to be sure this time: if the Dark conquers, then all Edil-Amarandh will be like Dén Raven, a place of tyranny and fear, and Song and Knowing and Light will vanish from this world, beyond our reckoning."

Hem thought of the bony hands and chill eyes of the Hulls who had taken him out of the orphanage, and wriggled uncomfortably. A vivid image of Maerad as he remembered her in Norloch, laughing at one of Saliman's absurd stories, crossed his inner eye. Maerad wasn't much taller than Zelika, and she was only a few years older than Hem himself. And she was supposed to cause the downfall of all this terror and might? For the first time Hem's absolute faith in Maerad faltered: if even the strength of Turbansk did not suffice to hold back the Black Army, what could his sister do? He almost asked how Maerad was going to save them, but bit his tongue; he feared Saliman's answer would be comfortless.

"So this is what you choose to face, both of you," said Saliman, this time in Suderain and looking straightly at Zelika. "The main part of Imank's army now marches on Turbansk. I do not believe, though we fight to the last soldier, that the city will stand. Do you see why I say this is no place for children?"

Zelika leaned forward, spitting out her words. "The worst they can do is kill me," she said. "I'm not afraid."

"Zelika, there are worse things than death," Saliman said. His voice was calm, but it had a curious intensity.

"I know there are," said Zelika. For the briefest of moments, her eyes filled with a terrible, almost uncomprehending grief, before it was overwhelmed by blazing hatred. She jerked her thumb at Hem. "You let him stay; why not me?"

Saliman looked at both his young charges impatiently. "I have not time for this wrangling," he said. "And precious little energy. Not an hour since, I had word that the Black Army has reached the Il Dara Wall, and already we are hard pressed." Hem suddenly understood, with a lurch in his stomach, Saliman's uncharacteristic curtness when he had returned home. "But you have won one point, Zelika: I will not burden any messenger with you."

"Good," said Zelika, her eyes snapping.

"Then tell me: what do you think you will do here?"

"I will fight. I will do anything," she answered. "I will kill the Black Ones. What will *he* do?" She pointed derisively at Hem, who was now deeply regretting he had brought her home.

Saliman stifled a sigh. "Hem is a certain case—" he began.

"And so am I. Anyway, what makes you think Car Amdridh will be any safer?"

Zelika crossed her arms and leaned back in her chair, seeming to think the argument was settled. Hem glanced at Saliman with alarm. To his surprise, Saliman gave him an amused look.

"I like this Zelika, for all her wildness," he said in the Speech. "She has been ill-used, and is in great pain, and for those and other reasons I mislike greatly her staying here; but within her there beats a brave heart. And she is right; it is likely she will be little safer in Car Amdridh, if Turbansk falls. The Dark reaches for its full power, and its arm is strong. I have not the will to gainsay her desire to stay here. Not now, anyway. How many more strays are you planning on bringing home?"

Zelika, suspecting that Saliman was talking about her, looked from one to the other mistrustfully. Hem answered in his bad Suderain.

"No more," he said fervently.

Saliman answered in the same language, so Zelika could understand. "Then while we await our doom, she can teach you how to speak Suderain. Yes, Zelika? That can be the price of your meals." He smiled at her, and Zelika, uncertain at first whether he was mocking her, looked back blankly.

"So you will not send me away?" she said.

"It seems I cannot. So you might as well be useful." He held out his hand.

She stood up and clasped his hand solemnly, as if they were closing a bargain. "I'll teach him well," she said, with what Hem thought was an ominous determination.

Hem cursed inwardly, and felt even sorrier he had taken pity on Zelika. He should, he thought, have left the girl in the street where he had found her.

＊　＊　＊

The following day Saliman took Hem and Zelika with him on his daily inspection of the city, telling them they should see for themselves how Turbansk would be defended. Hem was at once pleased to go and jealous that Zelika was also invited, for it diluted his delight in Saliman's company. Perhaps Zelika sensed this, for she remained almost completely silent, although her eyes glowed with savage pleasure when she examined the fortifications. The inspection took most of the morning, even though they went in haste on horseback from post to post, as Saliman wanted to report to Har-Ytan and the First Bard by noon.

Turbansk was protected by two high walls, the inner higher by six spans than the outer. They stood about thirty spans distant from each other, and were connected by wooden bridges, which could be drawn back if necessary. The walls were topped with zigzag crenellations and behind the zigzags ran walkways connecting the many towers built along the walls. These were now manned by a light guard, but once the alarm was raised the towers would be bristling with archers and artillery. The huge West and North Gates, the weakest parts of the wall, were the most heavily fortified, with high towers either side and above. Before the outer wall was a deep moat, now filled with fire-hardened stakes that rose up to a palisade the height of a man, which itself drew up to the blank stone barrier of the first wall.

When Hem had first ridden into Turbansk, the space between the walls had been filled with flowering gardens and lawns. These had been ruthlessly uprooted and the entire area planted instead with stakes. All the towers had been strengthened and faced with iron to protect them, Saliman said, from fire missiles. Hem blinked at the transformation; it was as if the city had been stripped to its bones.

At Turbansk Harbor the fortifications had also been strengthened, the harbor's encircling walls built higher and also faced with iron. The harbor entrance was protected by a huge spiked chain, each link the size of a man, which could be raised or lowered from a mechanism within the harbor towers. The harborside was the only place where the strange suspension of activity did not exist: although ranks of ships lay at the long quays, the shipwrights were still building more, and it hummed with industry.

"Haven't we enough ships?" asked Hem, looking with wonder at the activity: to his eye there seemed already enough ships to carry the whole population of Turbansk. Saliman paused and turned back; he had been about to stride off to speak to the harbor captain.

"We have a great fleet, yes," he said. "Yet I judge we need more ships, and we will build as many as we have wood and time for. Just as in the armories, Hem—if you go there—the smiths still work all day. If Turbansk falls, the only escape for most will be through the harbor: we have to protect those who flee and keep the passage open. So, you see, the task does not end, even after we are besieged. But all the major work is done."

It was indeed a mighty navy: there were scores of small fireships, to be sent under sails filled with mage winds against an invading fleet, and rows of fighting triremes with three layers of decks for rowers, large triangular sails, and wicked-looking rams at their front to hole and sink enemy ships. There were other, larger ships being built; Saliman said these were to carry people and goods, should the city fall. But Hem felt heartened: it seemed to him impossible that Turbansk could be taken, with such strength at its command.

Lastly Saliman took them to the watch at the top of the Red Tower, from which they could see over the walls to the Fesse of Turbansk. This sobered Hem considerably. When he had last seen the Fesse, it had been a tilled country of gentle and luxuriant beauty, filled with groves of dates and olives and green crops and gardens. Now he looked out upon what seemed to be wasteland: most of the trees had been cut down, and the crops harvested or burned. The empty villages and hamlets looked completely desolate. No one moved in this bleak landscape, apart from a lone messenger riding the Bard Road east to the Il Dara Wall.

Saliman noticed his expression, and smiled with grim compassion.

"You are shocked, Hem?" he said.

Hem nodded, unable for the moment to reply.

"Not the least of the grievous costs of war are what we are forced to do to ourselves, in order to survive," said Saliman. He looked thoughtfully at Zelika, who did not seem nearly as shocked as Hem. "I assure you, Zimek would look yet more grim than this, and remember that Baladh now lies in rubble. We sacrifice much, in the hope that by doing so we buy enough time for victory."

Hem looked at Saliman, a catch in his throat. "Do you mean, to give Maerad time to find the Treesong, and fulfill the prophecy?" he said.

Zelika looked up, baffled.

"Aye, among other things. Our hopes rest on something so slender we are yet to know what it is. It is the sheerest folly, yes? The Nameless would certainly believe so . . . But it is hope nevertheless, and a hope I cleave to. Because I say to you, Hem: if it were not for Maerad and Cadvan, we would now have no hope at all."

That afternoon, when they had returned to the Bardhouse and Saliman had gone on to the Ernan, Zelika asked Hem who Maerad and Cadvan were. "What did Saliman mean, back at the Tower?" she asked, with an unusual shyness. She was speaking Annaren, a special dispensation for Hem, since she often refused to, and Hem knew this meant that she really wanted to know. He didn't answer for a time, wondering if he wished to share his sister with this strange, passionate, irritating girl.

"Don't tell me, then, if you don't trust me," Zelika said at last, shrugging her shoulders. "I don't care."

Hem felt a stab of contrition; he could see that under her bravado she was hurt.

"It's not that," he said. "Maerad is my sister and Cadvan is her friend, her mentor, I suppose. He's a great Bard, famous in Annar; he and Saliman are old friends. I'm not sure if I'm supposed to tell anyone what they are doing . . ."

"Your sister?" Zelika's eyes softened, and she looked at Hem with a new interest. "I didn't know you had a sister."

"I didn't know, for a long time," said Hem. He suddenly realized that Zelika knew even less about him than he did about her. "You see, I . . ." He stopped, suddenly nonplussed. He didn't know how to tell Zelika the story of his life, of the slaughter of his family in the sack of Pellinor, of the long, bleak years in the orphanage, his time with the Hulls and his rescue by Maerad and Cadvan. She looked at him inquiringly, and Hem, feeling a strange reluctance, began his tale. He had told his story to very few people, and to no one in Turbansk, since no one here had asked. It stirred up painful feelings he would rather leave sleeping inside him; but Zelika listened intently, without interrupting.

"I see: you have lost your family, like I have," said Zelika, when his telling stumbled to a halt. "Maybe that's why . . ."

"Why what?"

"Why—when you jumped on me in the street, when I realized you weren't going to hurt me—I thought . . ."

Hem waited patiently; Zelika was staring at her hands, twisting her fingers together.

"It is hard, when you don't have the words!" she said, looking up. "I mean, the first thing I thought was that we had something in common. And that seemed a very strange thing to think, when you were sitting on my chest like a sack of yams." She smiled hesitantly, glancing shyly at Hem. Unexpectedly moved, he smiled back.

"And what did you mean by . . . the Treesong, was it?"

"That's the bit I'm not sure I should tell," said Hem. "Maerad and Cadvan went north, to look for the Treesong. Nobody knows what it is. But you see, Maerad is the Chosen One, and the prophecies say that she will cast down the Nameless One in his next and worst rising. Which is now."

Zelika's eyes widened in disbelief, and then she started laughing. "Your sister! Cast down the Nameless One!"

Stung, Hem scowled at the ground. He was sorry now that he had said anything. "That's what Saliman says," he said. "And he says it's our only hope. That's what he meant at the Tower."

Zelika stared at him, her face serious again. "I'm sorry," she said. "It seems a very strange thing, that one girl should be able to do what all Turbansk and Baladh cannot. I don't think I can believe it."

Hem shrugged his shoulders. "You don't have to. It's the truth, all the same. Why would Saliman believe it, if it were not?"

"Maybe he has to," said Zelika. "Maybe if he didn't, he would be in despair."

Anger flashed in Hem at Zelika's doubt and he glared at her, his fists clenched. "Saliman's no fool," he said. "You should show some respect."

"I do respect Saliman," she answered, her face shadowed. "It's not that. But Hem, you know, I don't have any hope." She looked up, straight at Hem, and for once her eyes were not veiled. With his Bard-born perception, Hem saw for the first time the true extent of her inner devastation, and he breathed in sharply; it was almost too painful to bear. "I don't have any hope at all. Hope is not why I'm here."

"What do you want, then?" asked Hem.

"Revenge," she said flatly. "Revenge and death. There isn't anything else."

After that conversation, Hem felt a new closeness to Zelika, although that didn't mean that he found her any less annoying. As a teacher, she lived up to all his expectations; she was by far the most merciless he had yet endured. Saliman had instructed him, with an unusual sternness, that he was to work hard at his Suderain, and it was only his respect for Saliman that stopped him from rebelling, although it went hard for him.

Zelika took her pact with Saliman very seriously. They had lessons every morning, and the rest of the time Zelika would not permit Hem to speak anything but Suderain. She was very pedantic; she would make him repeat a word again and again until he said it absolutely correctly, which could go on indefinitely, and drilled him in the endless declensions of nouns and conjugations of verbs until he thought his head would burst.

Then she would solemnly make him sit down and have a "conversation" with her. Hem found this part of the lesson more irritating than almost anything else, because it seemed ridiculous and false, and he could never think of anything to say. He began to amuse himself by talking the most absurd nonsense he could think of, and then by creatively abusing Zelika.

When she chose to exercise it, Zelika had admirable self-control; she limited herself for the most part to correcting his grammar and pronunciation. But she did slap him once, bursting into a storm of tears, when he called her a "skinny cat." Hem was puzzled: it was by no means the worst thing he had said to her. It was a long time before he found out that it was the insult her brothers had used, when they wished to tease her.

Irc was bored by the lessons, and provided some entertainment by flapping onto Zelika's head and trying to pull out her hair, or creeping underneath her chair and pecking her feet at inappropriate times. When he disgraced himself by soiling one of her sandals, which she subsequently put on, he was banished altogether. Hem was very regretful, especially after the sandal incident, which amused him vastly; but he did learn much more quickly if Irc was not there.

In fact, although he did not admit it to Zelika, Hem was grateful for the distraction; the lessons relieved his boredom and dissipated the fear that otherwise filled his thoughts. He never regretted that he hadn't left with the other students, but this didn't stop him from feeling a deepening trepidation. Sometimes, as much as he dreaded its arrival, Hem wished the Black Army would hurry up, just to break the mounting suspense that filled Turbansk with a strange, dreadful anticipation. It seemed as if the whole city trembled, holding its breath, on the edge of doom.

V

THE WALL OF IL DARA

HEM dreamed. He was at the top of the Red Tower and Maerad was standing next to him. They both looked over the Turbansk Fesse, but in his dream vision he could see much farther: he saw past the mountains of the Osidh Am to Norloch, and across the whole of Annar. Tiny figures marched in ranks along the Bard Roads, and columns of smoke rose over all the landscape, and he knew, with a chill in his heart, that Annar was at war. With dread he looked east, toward Dén Raven, and everywhere was devastation, grove and field and village and city burned and ruined. Then it seemed that the clouds of distance lifted away, like fog in the morning sun, and very clearly he saw the citadel of Dagra in miniature, standing by the shores of a lake of black still water. Gripped in the vision, Hem shuddered: he didn't want to look anymore, but he could not stop.

The city of Dagra was arranged in a half circle parody of the Annaren Schools, with straight roads connected by circular avenues radiating from a central tower. It sprawled from the feet of high, stony mountains the color of dried blood. The main streets were lined by tall, blank-faced towers of stone, and behind them, in a tangle of small streets and alleyways, was a chaos of dwellings and workhouses, grim buildings with small slit windows, flat-roofed and often many-storied, bulging oddly where extra rooms had been added on to the original structure.

Nothing green grew there, to soften the rock and dust, and no waters flowed save a meager, dark river running into the black lake. Figures swarmed in the streets. Unwillingly Hem's eyes traveled up the radiating streets to their hub: he knew that at the center was the Iron Tower, the fortress of the Nameless One. Its grim battlemented shadow stretched over the sad city beneath its feet, and even its shadow filled him with a loathing so strong that his gorge rose. But some will forced him to look, and at last he lifted his eyes and saw.

The Iron Tower was founded on the roots of the Osidh Dagra, the Dagra Mountains, and loomed over the surrounding plains. It seemed taller than any tower that Hem had seen, taller even than Norloch, and was wreathed in spirals of noxious vapors, staining the sun's rays so they fell lividly onto the city beneath. Buttressed by massive iron wings, it towered from a wide base of rugged basalt stained red by iron oxides, battlement rising within battlement, wall within wall, up to a single high watchtower. Whereas Norloch was crowned by the Machelinor, the Tower of the Living Flame whose crystal pinnacle could be seen from far out at sea, the Iron Tower was surmounted by a huge blade, which flashed a searing greenish white when it caught the diseased light.

It struck Hem that the Iron Tower and Norloch were somehow the same, and the thought bit his heart with a painful horror.

Maerad's voice shattered the vision, and suddenly he was alone with her again. They were no longer standing on the Red Tower, but in a garden he did not recognize. *It is so*, she said in the Speech. *Dark and Light are both reflections of the human heart.*

She looked on him sadly, and Hem, filled with a helpless love he had no words for, leaned forward to embrace her, not only for his comfort, but to allay the sorrow he saw in her face. But as he reached out, he saw hooded figures behind her shoulder, and cried out: three Hulls stretched forward, their white bony hands clutching for Maerad, a red light in their eyes. And where his hands should have touched Maerad, they closed on air: she had vanished, and with her the three Hulls and the garden, and Hem was alone in a dark place, sobbing on a stone floor.

He woke with a start, the tears still wet on his cheeks, and stared sightlessly ahead, sitting up in his bed. Starlight from the casement shimmered faintly in his chamber. The dream was still vivid within him, filling him with a strange despair that was almost like tenderness; it hadn't been like his usual nightmares of terror and suffocation, and he had never dreamed of his sister before. Although the dread it had inspired in him still lingered, it faded before his thoughts of Maerad. Now she stood clearly in his mind's eye—he saw her direct blue gaze, her black hair falling in stray wisps over her white face, how her expression had softened when she had looked at him—and for the first time Hem felt the full pain of his sister's absence. Missing her was an anguish he did not admit fully into his waking life; but now, in the deep of night, it broke open his heart, a raw wound beyond healing.

Irc, who was on his usual perch on Hem's chair, woke at the sound of Hem's weeping and cawed sleepily, and then flapped over to the bed. He stood on the pillow by Hem's cheek, his white feathers catching the faint starlight, and cocked his head to peer at him with one eye. Hem put out his hand and scratched Irc's neck, and gently the bird came close and crouched next to the boy's trembling body, snuggling into his chest like a cat. Hem kept stroking the bird's white feathers, feeling them crisp and cool under his fingers, and Irc's warm creaturely weight, so light but so intensely present, gradually comforted him. At last Hem drifted back to sleep, and Irc stayed with him on the bed, his head tucked under his wing.

✳   ✳   ✳

One morning a couple of weeks after Zelika's arrival, Saliman announced he would be going away.

"How long for?" asked Hem, with dismay. He had thought that Saliman would be in Turbansk until the attack.

"As long as need calls me," said Saliman. "I am summoned to the Wall of Il Dara, where many evil things happen as we speak."

"Will you be fighting?" asked Hem, clutched by a sudden fear. What if Saliman did not come back?

"I do not go to fight, although there is a fierce battle there," said Saliman. "Do not be afraid for me. All the same, it is worth taking thought of what to do if I do not return. If I am not back in three days, you and Zelika should take ship out of the harbor while you still can. I have spoken to the harbor captain, Nerab: he will know you, and there will be ships leaving."

Hem stared miserably at Saliman, whose words did nothing to comfort him. "Can't I come with you?"

"Nay, Hem," said Saliman. "Oslar asks again for your help in the Healing Houses. Many wounded came in last night from the battle at Il Dara, and he is hard pressed. For the moment, you are needed here."

"Why did you want me to stay here, then, if I'm not to go with you?" said Hem passionately. "I don't want to stay behind—"

"I'm not leaving Turbansk," said Zelika, her eyebrows drawn into a stubborn line.

Saliman sighed. "Hem, Zelika, that is my order and my desire, and it is only if I do not return. I will not argue." Hem returned Saliman's stern, dark gaze with a despairing anger, his heart burning. "You stayed here, Hem, because my Knowing told me that there is a part you must play in this story, although I do not perceive what it is. It does not do for a Bard to go against his Knowing, even if it seems grievously mistaken: that is one lesson I have learned in a long and sometimes dangerous life. But if I am not here, there will be no one to guide you. Fate has many forkings, and some are darker than you are able yet to understand. And I must tell you clearly, as clearly as I can, that if I do not return from Il Dara, my foresight tells me that your remaining in Turbansk would do great damage to the Light, and to Maerad: and therefore I order you to leave."

"How could I harm Maerad?" asked Hem, bewildered and hurt. He had thought Saliman let him stay because he loved him, but now it seemed he spoke of a colder decision.

"That has not been vouchsafed to me." Saliman's face softened, and he leaned forward, lifting up Hem's chin so he was forced to look into his eyes. *"Hem,"* he said softly in the Speech. *"Be sure I love you, more I expect than you know. It cost me dear to allow you to stay here, with all the forces of the Black Army marching on this city: I desire your death as little as my own."*

Hem was taken by surprise. He was still fragile after the previous night's dream, and only just stopped himself from bursting into tears. Saliman had never said anything so openly to him, and much as Hem longed for Saliman's love, it also bruised him. And it made him feel more afraid that Saliman might not return: perhaps it was a kind of farewell.

Zelika had been listening impatiently; she did not understand what Saliman had just said. "That doesn't count for me," she said fiercely. "I won't leave. You'd have to tie me up and put me in a barrel to get me on that ship."

"Nevertheless," said Saliman calmly, in a tone that brooked no argument, "if I do not return from Il Dara, you will leave Turbansk."

Zelika folded her lips into a tight line, and said nothing more. Hem glanced at her out of the corner of his eye, wondering what she would do. He doubted whether anyone could make Zelika do anything.

*   *   *

Hem and Zelika forewent their lesson. Saliman left for Il Dara shortly after the morning meal, and he farewelled the children in the garden. Hem waited for him, looking around with new eyes at this garden he had come to love. It seemed almost unbearably frail, as if it could be swept away in the next moment, and this vision made the colors more clear, the outlines sharper, its beauty more poignant. Although the day was already beginning to heat up, the garden was still cool, and would stay cool until evening; it was well shaded, with many glossy broad-leafed trees and flowering vines. Birds and some little golden monkeys chattered in the trees. In the center, surrounded by white marble paving, was a pool, wherein swam many golden fish, their fins turning lazily under the water crocus. There were several benches around the garden, which would normally have been full of young students, either talking or studying, but now, except for Hem and Zelika, the garden was empty and its beauty was touched with melancholy. Hem didn't feel like talking, and waited by the pool, staring gloomily into the clear water.

Before long Saliman entered the garden, in the full arms of the mounted Sun Guard of Turbansk. He wore a corslet of hardened ceramic scales enameled in blue, and his arms were protected by blue-stained leather vambraces. On his breast, and on the gold helm he carried under his arm, were emblazoned the golden-sun symbol of Turbansk, and his braided hair was drawn back from his face with leather thongs. A shortsword was bound to his hip, and a bow lay across his back, and he carried a round shield, lined with albarac to drive off sorcery, on which was etched a rising golden serpent, the symbol of his family. Over all he wore a crimson cloak of linen.

The armor made Saliman seem like a stranger. Hem stood up, wiping his suddenly sweaty hands on his tunic, feeling shy.

Saliman took Hem's hand wordlessly, and Hem looked down at the dark, graceful fingers clasped around his and felt a lump rising in his throat.

"I plan to be back the day after tomorrow," said Saliman. "If I do not return by the end of the third day, swear to me that you will do as I ask, and leave Turbansk."

"But you will be back," Hem said vehemently.

"I plan to be," said Saliman, and smiled. It was the smile Hem most loved, the smile that heralded a joke or an amusing story. For a moment Saliman looked as if he had not a care in the world. "So do not fear for me too much; I am tougher than I look! I say these things in case of mischance—for mischance may always happen in war—not because I believe it will happen. Remember that."

Hem nodded, fighting back tears.

"So swear you will do what I ask, if by chance things go ill."

"I swear," said Hem.

Saliman pressed Hem's hand, and then clasped the boy's shoulders and kissed his forehead. "Go well, Hem. I have great faith in you. I will see you soon." He looked at Irc, who was watching from a nearby branch. "And farewell to you too, young crow. They are complaining in the kitchens about some missing spoons; when I return I think I must inspect your hoard."

Irc cawed in mixed amusement and alarm. *It's all mine*, he said.

No doubt, said Saliman dryly.

Zelika had wandered up as they were speaking, and now stood tentatively nearby, too shy to come closer. She looked, suddenly, much younger. Saliman clasped her also by her shoulders and looked down on her with a glint of humor in his eyes.

"Zelika, I have made Hem swear that he will leave Turbansk if I do not return. Will you do so?"

"No," she answered. "I am no oath breaker."

Saliman laughed, and ruffled her hair. "I thought not," he said. "I ask, nevertheless, that you consider what I request. I think that you are too precious to be wasted in war." He kissed her forehead, and she jumped with surprise.

"May the Light shine on you both!" said Saliman, and turned to leave.

"And on you," said Hem fervently. Zelika remembered the proper response a little late; she stood very awkwardly, a startled look lingering in her eyes.

The children stared after Saliman as he went back into the Bardhouse and disappeared. The garden seemed even emptier than before.

"He'll be back," said Zelika confidently. "He is a great warrior. I can tell."

"He is a great Bard, as well," said Hem. His voice was hoarse. He turned away to hide his emotion, and Zelika was wise enough to say nothing more.

Soon afterward, Hem and Zelika reported to Oslar at the Healing Houses. Zelika insisted on coming, although Hem had looked at her doubtfully, asking a little arrogantly what she thought she could do to help; but Oslar gazed down at them over his beaky nose and set Zelika to work at once pounding medicinal bark and roots into powder with a stone mortar and pestle.

Hem took up his former duties of caring for the wounded, and this time was given more responsibility. He was shocked by their number; there were not enough beds to hold them all, and makeshift pallets had been laid on the floor to hold the less seriously injured. There were no children, but Hem found the suffering of adults almost worse: one expected children to cry, after all. Even a few days of Zelika's intensive drilling had improved his Suderain to the point where casual conversation was not nearly so difficult, and he found it made his work in the Houses much easier.

Irc was again asked to be a messenger, and became a familiar sight, flapping through the cloistered rooms from one Bard to another. He was a very different figure from the comically scrawny youngster Hem had rescued from the crows a month before. Then Irc had been on the awkward brink of maturity, his adult feathers thrusting through the remains of his baby down. Now all sign of fluff had vanished; his feathers were sleek, and he was developing the heavy body of a mature bird. He remained, in his adult plumage, pure white from his beak to the end of his tail, but unlike a proper albino did not have pink eyes: his irises were instead a deep flecked gold, and his beak was black. He had the innate intelligence of his kind, and also a magpie's fondness for bright or glittering objects; Hem had not been able to cure him from his habit of stealing from the dining halls small silver spoons, of which he had amassed a fairly impressive collection. But through his constant companionship with Hem, Irc had a much wider vocabulary than most birds, and the Bards in the Healing Houses found they could entrust him with more and more complex messages.

The patients in the Healing Houses coined a name for the strange boy, because of his fairer skin, and the crow that so often sat on his shoulders. They called him *Lios Hlaf*, the White Crow. Hem smiled when he heard this, remembering how the same name had once been used as a taunt; now, spoken by the wounded men and women for whom he cared, it seemed to him to be a mark of honor.

*   *   *

Saliman did not return as he had promised, on the second day after he left. Hem and Zelika did not speak about it, but each knew the other was waiting for him. When they came home, they looked first to see whether he had returned: but Saliman's chambers stood empty. The few Bards who still lived in the Bardhouse were most often out, and on the second night the children prepared and ate their evening meal alone. They ate in Saliman's rooms, rather than in the dining hall, because it felt less lonely. Conversation lagged, because neither would speak about the topic uppermost in their minds: whether they should leave on the ships that were to carry the wounded out of Turbansk the following evening.

Hem had, of course, sworn that he would heed Saliman, but he was finding his promise harder and harder to contemplate. If Saliman did not return the following day, and Hem left, he would never know what had happened to the Bard, whether he was dead, or captured, or simply delayed. Hem didn't think he could bear not knowing, and was privately turning over in his head whether to stay, even for a little space of time. One more day, surely, would not count as breaking his promise. Zelika kept her own counsel.

After the meal, both of them were so exhausted that they went straight to bed, although Hem lay awake for a long time, his body humming with tiredness, the terrible sights he had seen during the day running through his head again and again. What if Saliman had been burned by the liquid fire of the dog-soldiers? Or perhaps he had been blinded by one of the black arrows or worse—many of them bore a terrible poison that made wounds that did not heal. Hem slipped uneasily into evil dreams, which he could not remember but which left a dark aftershadow when he awoke.

The next day Hem felt so depressed he could hardly get out of bed. He knew instantly that Saliman wasn't back; all night a part of his mind had been listening for the door to open, for the familiar steps in the house. He and Zelika broke their fast avoiding each other's eyes; they knew that if Saliman was not back by noon they would have to decide what they were going to do. They walked to the Healing Houses without speaking, and worked all morning with a furious intensity; more wounded had arrived overnight from Il Dara, and the healers were preparing to evacuate the worst hurt to the harbor as soon as possible. Hem spent the morning running errands and assisting the less seriously wounded, until Oslar looked at his drawn face and sternly sent him back to the Bardhouse, insisting he eat a proper meal. Hem met Zelika at the herbalist's, and they slowly walked back to the Bardhouse.

He knew as soon as he opened the door that Saliman had returned: his cloak lay on the bench inside the door, and his sandals underneath it. Hem stared at these objects, hardly daring to believe they were there, but he would know Saliman's shoes anywhere. He felt himself trembling and breaking into a sweat; it was not until that moment that he realized how much he had feared that Saliman was dead. All the weight lifted from his chest: his heart was suddenly winged, soaring with happiness. Forgetting everything else, he ran through the house, shouting Saliman's name; but Saliman was not there.

"He's probably gone to the Ernan or something," said Zelika, when Hem returned, crestfallen. "I'm hungry, let's get some food. We'll see him tonight, I expect."

Oslar had ordered Hem to rest that afternoon, so Zelika returned alone to the herbalist's. But Hem was soon back in the Healing Houses because he couldn't bear the suspense of waiting in the empty Bardhouse. He could feel that something had happened: the atmosphere was charged, and the sense of suspended waiting had given way to an air of frenzied activity. Almost everyone he saw in the streets wore armor, and small groups of people talked in subdued voices in the alleyways, glancing sideways at Hem as he hurried past them. It was a hot, windy day; the dust kicked up in Hem's face, drying out his mouth, and the wind made a low moaning as it swept through the streets. Or was it the wind? He sharpened his hearing; there was a distant noise that made his heart thump in his chest. It did not sound like wind, but something else, although really it was too faint to be sure what it was.

He spent the afternoon helping to lift people onto the litters that were to take them to the harbor. Here in the Healing Houses, the Bards were calm and patient as they always were, no matter what emergency they might have to deal with, and the anxiety that had been mounting in Hem all day subsided in his work. But then Oslar spotted him and sent him home, brooking no disobedience; and so Hem found himself again idle in the Bardhouse, starting up at every noise he heard in the street. Zelika came home as the shadows began to lengthen, but still there was no sign of Saliman.

The children waited in his rooms. The hot wind had died down, so they flung the doors open to the garden and watched the light gently failing outside. This tense, uncertain wait reminded Hem of something; he rummaged through his memory, trying to place it. Ah yes, it was like the time when he and Maerad and Cadvan and Saliman had waited in Nelac's rooms in Norloch as the day darkened, knowing that something had happened, not knowing what it was. The memory obscurely comforted him. Irc was in the garden, a silver glimmer in the shadows under the trees; it sounded as if he were squabbling with the meenah birds, with whom he had a fractious relationship. Hem thought briefly of calling him in, but refrained; all day Irc had been as busy as Hem, and he deserved some play.

At last they heard the outer doors open and close, and then steps outside the room. Hem stopped himself from leaping up, waiting until he stepped into the room, in case it was another false alarm, but it was Saliman. The Bard walked slowly into the room and stopped when he saw the children waiting there. He greeted them in a soft voice, embracing both, and drank some water before he sat down. They watched him in silence, containing their questions. Hem was shocked by the exhaustion on Saliman's face: lines ran from his nose to the corners of his mouth, and he looked older.

"Are you all right?" asked Hem. He felt shy; he wanted to ask Saliman what had happened, but didn't know how.

"I am tired," Saliman answered. "So very tired. And sick at heart. But yes, I am all right."

"But what's happened?" The words seemed to burst out of Zelika. She leaned forward, her eyes sparkling with impatience. "Something has happened, hasn't it? Has Il Dara fallen?"

Before he answered, Saliman crossed the room and poured himself a goblet of ruby wine. He offered some to Hem and Zelika, but they refused, wrinkling their noses; neither of them had yet developed a taste for the strong Suderain wines. Saliman sat down, and drank deeply.

"Ah, that's better," he said. "All is not dark, when the tongue is still able to savor such richnesses. You two don't know what you're missing." He smiled, and the lines softened on his face; he seemed briefly more like the normal Saliman.

Hem and Zelika waited tensely, twisting their hands, longing to hear what had happened to him, and yet not wanting to press him. Saliman sipped his wine again, and glanced at the children. "Forgive me," he said. "I have been talking all afternoon, at the Ernan, and I have not slept these past two nights. But I will tell you what has happened—you have a right to know.

"You are right, Zelika: the Il Dara Wall has fallen. I have ridden hard to get here; my horse is swift and our forces at the

Wall are not completely routed. Even as they retreat, they fight
the Black Army every step of the way to Turbansk. Nevertheless,
I judge the city will be encircled in a day, or less."

Hem felt as if his heart had been plucked from his chest,
leaving in its place a strange hollow. It was the news he had
been expecting, but even so it hit hard. He licked his lips: his
mouth seemed suddenly as dry as parchment.

"We knew the Wall could not hold out against the forces that
were thrown against it, but we still hoped we could hold out
longer than we did," said Saliman. "I went there because we
had word that Al Ronin, captain of the Il Dara Ranks, had been
slain, which is grievous news, as he was a great warrior, and we
counted on him in the defense of Turbansk. More, the ranks
said they were desperate, that they were beating back a foe that
came on endlessly, like the waves of an ocean, their strength
undiminished by any of our costly victories. I led there a force
of three horsed ranks of the Sun Guards—not nearly enough,
yet all we could spare, for we also feared that the Black Army
may yet surprise us. Imank may have sent a battalion to march
north from Baladh, circling the Neera Marshes and returning
along the South Road, to strike Turbansk while we spent our
strength defending the Il Dara Wall. Well." Saliman smiled
tiredly. "That is what I would have done, if I were Imank. But
there is no word of movement along the South Road, and we
must be grateful for the small mercies that are granted us.

"In the battle for the Wall our forces faced the entire might of
the Black Army: thousands upon thousands, in ranks so deep
beating against the wall that you could not, even from the towers, see the end of them. We had to cover a league of wall,
stretching either end into the Neera Marshes, through which an
army cannot march, and we had to protect the road, which runs
through a gate pierced in the south end. On the east side, we
had dug a deep moat and we filled it with stakes, and on the

other side of that yet another trench, to prevent the armies reaching the Wall itself.

"For five days, before he was cut down, Al Ronin held back the Black Army. Hundreds died in those five days, but very few of ours. As well as the Sun Guard, Al Ronin commanded Alhadeans and Bilakeans, who are famed archers, and the Cissians, among the fiercest fighters in Edil-Amarandh—in peacetime they are goatherds and metalsmiths, but they delight in the arts of war. Too few against too many, but they had a chance as long as Il Dara stood."

Saliman paused and wiped his mouth. "Firstly we heard that Imank ordered ranks to build a great ramp, sloping up to the heights of the Il Dara. Al Ronin could not oppose that at first, until they came within bowshot. Imank set a ram manned by dogsoldiers to break the gate, but that was beaten back again and again. The gate is protected not only by rock and iron, but by spells made in the time of the Great Silence, and it is not easily cast down, even with sorceries. But at the end of those five days the moat and trenches were filled with dead, so the oncoming ranks could walk across them to the Wall itself . . . and from huge catapults they began to cast up ladders made of chains, hooked at one end, which would grapple the wall. That is how Al Ronin died, hewing down a mighty captain from Dén Raven as he mounted the Il Dara.

"Thus we began to lose fighters, though not as many as the Black Army, and we still beat them back. But though we lost one to their ten, Imank could afford losses much more than we could: our blood was ebbing with each fresh assault, and our enemies numberless. So it was when I came there, with three ranks of the Sun Guard. Still, we might have prevailed for longer. We foiled their attempts to tunnel beneath the Wall—its foundations go very deep and are enchanted against breach— and although hard pressed, we were holding them from swarming over the battlements, and they could not break the gate. Imank even abandoned the building of the ramp after we assaulted it with catapults of magefire, and we counted that a victory . . ."

Saliman stopped again, and refilled his goblet, glancing somberly at Hem and Zelika, who were both listening in absolute silence.

"Of course, all idea of victory was an illusion," he said, when he was again seated. "We knew that, but we did not know what would happen next. Imank summoned the ranks of child soldiers. And that brought such horror on us that our courage failed us for the first time."

"Child soldiers?" said Zelika sharply.

"Aye," Saliman said softly. "Simply that they were children is bad enough. But these were *our* children. And they came to assault the walls of their own homeland. There were fighters there who were hacked to death by their own sons and daughters, whom they had thought dead, for they could not bring themselves to raise their weapons against them."

Hem stared at Saliman, shocked. "You mean, they just joined the Dark?" he said. "How could they?"

"Nay, Hem, it is not so simple. I guess these children were captured in the assaults on Baladh and the towns and villages of Nazar and Savitir. They are drugged or bewitched: they no longer know their own names or their own kin. And they know neither fear nor mercy. They are cruel beyond imagining, even though some are years younger than you. They fight like maddened creatures . . . In a time of many evils, I deem this is the greatest. It broke the heart of our defense."

"How many?" asked Zelika in a whisper.

"There were many ranks of them," said Saliman.

"I thought they killed everyone they took." Zelika's face was drawn with horror, and suddenly Hem realized that she feared

that her own brothers or sisters might be among the child soldiers. Saliman looked at her with deep compassion, and there
was a silence before he continued his tale.

"After the child armies attacked us, things began to go ill.
That night a tunnel we had not sourced opened up behind us,
and out of it poured at least a rank of Hulls and dogsoldiers.
Although we stayed them with great losses on our part and
blocked the tunnel, we began to realize that we could not hold
the Wall, and it was better to retreat in good order than in a
rout. But we had barely ordered ourselves for a retreat when
they broke the Gate. I know not what spell forced its enchantment, but I do know no living Bard can match those who made
the spells that held it. Hence I fear the more what foul sorceries
will be brought against Turbansk, since I doubt not that Imank
has used a bare tithe of that armory against us . . . So I left the
battle and rode here, more swiftly than I had right to ask any
horse, to bring this evil news as early as I may; and I rode on the
very wings of the storm. And soon all of us will be in the teeth
of it."

A silence fell. Hem looked down at his hands and noticed
they were trembling.

"I-I don't know what a battle is like," he said. "I've seen
fighting and Hulls and all of that, but nothing that big . . . it all
sounds so very big . . ." He wanted to say that he was afraid,
but he thought that if he did, Saliman would send him away,
and frightened though he was, he feared being sent away more.

"I know what battle is like," said Zelika, her voice quiet, but
very hard. "It is screaming, and a terrible noise, like in a metal-
smith's or a quarry, but much louder than you can bear. And it
smells of burning and blood and worse things. And it is faces
made strange, because they are angry or frightened or dying,
and the most terrible fear you ever knew, which makes you feel
as if your blood runs bright silver. And everything is horribly

clear and crooked; and something strange happens to time, so everything seems very fast and very slow all at the same time. And it is seeing growing things burned and cut down, and beautiful things smashed to pieces, and seeing the ones you love—seeing loved—" Her voice caught, and she bowed her head and said nothing more.

Saliman was silent a moment. "Yes, Zelika," he said gently. "That is exactly what a battle is like."

LAMARSAN

To admire beauty without envy is love:
To lie in the darkened garden to hear the song
Of the unseen nightingale is love:
If you would hold a knife to your heart
To spare another, that is love:
To love is to give everything away for nothing,
To open your house to the dark stranger:
The world is a pit of fire and shadows,
Those who love throw themselves into it wholly:
Ah my heart, only you know best
How love is the mortal flesh burning in darkness.

Murat of Turbansk,
Library of Busk

VI

THE DEATHCROWS

NIGHT fell over Turbansk. It was a night of velvet air, gentle and warm, and crowds of stars blazed in the moonless sky. Jasmine foamed spectrally over the walls of the city, its sweet scent falling pungent in the streets and alleys, and the starlight lent the flesh-colored stone of the buildings an eerie pallor. Turbansk seemed a lovely mirage that trembled against the darkness, its towers and domes as insubstantial as a dream.

Saliman had retired early, and Zelika had disappeared. Hem knew he was exhausted, but he could not sleep. He tossed and turned restlessly in his bed, and at last rose and threw on a tunic and slipped out of the Bardhouse, leaving Irc behind him on his usual perch, his head tucked under his wing.

Hem walked barefoot through the streets of Turbansk, listening to the night sounds: the cicadas shrilling loudly in the treetops, the occasional sleepy crooning of doves, the calling of frogs. Bats made graceful parabolas in the air, their high, tiny squeaks sounding between the trees. And there was also the strange moaning noise he had heard the day before, and had thought was the wind. It was louder than it had been, and with a stab of fear Hem realized it must be the braying trumpets of the Black Army, still distant, but closer now, closer all the time.

Although it was near midnight, Turbansk was not sleeping. Armed soldiers moved through the wider streets, some purposeful and unspeaking, others joking, and he saw runners taking messages from the Ernan to the guard towers. But as

Hem walked on, he passed some houses bright with lamps, their gardens strung with paper lanterns of many colors; and from them Hem could hear conversation and laughter, and strains of music—the dulcimers and flutes and drums of Turbansk playing the long, wild songs of the ancient city. The music, so defiant in its loveliness, plucked his heart with a special poignancy, and he stopped outside one house and listened.

When Hem had first arrived in Turbansk, he had scornfully told Chyafa that Turbanskian music had no melody and made no sense, and was far inferior to the music of Annar. It was, he reflected now, perhaps the reason why Chyafa had so persecuted him; for music was Chyafa's great passion and he was the most talented dulcimer player in their class. Now, as he stood by the wall, listening to the throb and passion of the music on the other side, Hem regretted his words: Chyafa had been right to say he was ignorant.

Whoever was singing, Hem thought, was a great singer. His voice wound through the complex rhythms and melodies of the instruments, binding them together into coherent harmonies; and then it would soar into its own dance, like a bird that suddenly leaves the flock in a moment of exuberance and acrobatically twirls in the air, showing off its grace and skill, before returning to the flock again. So the music moved through its repetitions, eternally the same and eternally different. And as Hem listened, he began to make out some words:

> *Blessed are the roses of Turbansk, blessed the bounty*
> *of their beauty,*
> *For their hearts are softer than skin and yet they*
> *open endlessly*
> *And out of their hearts spill colors to delight the eye*
> *And perfumes enough to make rich the moment of*
> *each who passes.*

The roses do not choose to give to one and not to another:
The poor man and the prince alike are given their grace
*   equally.*
Blessed are the roses of Turbansk, although they wither
*   and die*
And pass into shadow as each of us must pass into shadow.
The prince and the poor man are given this darkness
*   equally*
But their moment of Light is not less beautiful for its
*   passing*
Nor is the gift of their grace any less for the shadow that
*   follows them:*
Neither the prince nor the poor man nor the rose are less
Though the sun must go down behind the hills and the
*   hills down into dust*
Though even the Ernan's glory must come at last to decay
Though the petals wither and drop from the stem to the
*   ground.*
All shall pass, all shall pass, to the night that has no
*   morning*
Yet another morning will rise and buds will open in
*   new colors . . .*

Hem pressed his forehead against the wall and shut his eyes, letting the song's mingled lament and celebration flow into the deepest parts of his soul. The song finished and it was like the end of a dream; he looked up, startled, and realized suddenly how tired he really was. Slowly he walked back to the Bardhouse and went to bed, and this time slept deeply and dreamlessly.

Zelika was standing by Hem's bed, shaking him, and he turned over groaning, blurred by sleep.

"Wake up!" said Zelika.

Hem sat up slowly, his hair sticking out, and Zelika regarded him with scorn.

"You'd sleep in if the world was about to end!" she said. "It's late."

Hem looked at the light coming through the casement. It *was* late. He was surprised.

"I thought you'd like to know that the Black Army is here," said Zelika.

"What great news."

"So let's go to the Red Tower and see. I don't think anyone would mind. You have to come, though; I don't think they'll let me in by myself, but everyone knows you . . ."

Hem was still blinking, fuddled by sleep, and impatiently Zelika shook him again. "Well, come on!"

"All right, all *right*! But I don't have any clothes on and I can't get dressed until you get out of my room."

Just to annoy Zelika, Hem took longer dressing than he normally would. When he came out of his bedchamber, she was fizzing with irritation.

"I want breakfast first," he said, when she tried to drag him out of the Bardhouse.

"You can have breakfast *afterward*."

"I'm hungry," he said stubbornly. "I'm not going anywhere until I've eaten something."

Zelika saw that he might refuse to go at all if she kept pressing him, so she gave in with the sudden surprising meekness she could display when she realized other means were useless, and followed him to the dining hall.

The Bardhouse was absolutely deserted. Hem stopped dawdling because he was as anxious as Zelika to see what was happening. He took an apple from the store and gulped down a cup of water and then they wended their way to the Red Tower.

The guard at its foot simply nodded when he saw Hem, and he and Zelika climbed the endless spiraling steps, stopping every now and then for a rest, up to the very top.

They heard the Black Army before they saw it. The faint bray of trumpets that had lain underneath the busy music of Turbansk had now ceased; instead there was a low throb of war drums, like another pulse in the blood. The hair on Hem's neck prickled.

Two Bards, Inhulca of Baladh, whom Hem knew by sight, and Soron of Til Amon, his friend at the buttery, were already there, as well as several soldiers who were keeping a lookout, peering through the curious eyeglasses that Bards used for starwatching. Soron greeted Hem somberly and nodded toward Zelika.

"They're here, then," said Zelika.

"Aye," said Soron. "What was left of the Il Dara forces came fleeing through the gates in the small hours of the night. And they were not long followed by the vanguards of the Black Army."

"'What was left?'" repeated Hem. "'Why, are there not many?'"

Soron hesitated before he answered. "They said there were some ten thousand fighters at the Il Dara," he said. "And of those ten thousands, I think maybe ten hundreds came through the gate. And of those who came, many are wounded. For those left behind, they say there is no hope."

"So few," whispered Hem, exchanging a glance with Zelika.

"Many friends fell and will not return," said Soron. "But look. You will see why. And yet more come."

Hem and Zelika stood on their tiptoes and peered over the parapets of the Red Tower, and their breath stopped.

The Fesse of Turbansk, which they had last seen empty and deserted, now pullulated with masses of figures that looked from this distance like a huge swarm of ants. At first it just seemed chaotic, but as Hem stared he began to see an order emerge. The army was not milling around randomly: every part of it was busy. To the west, stretching down to the gentle shores of the Lamarsan Sea, rows and rows of brown tents were being erected, making a city that seemed almost as big as Turbansk itself.

Closer to the walls, great numbers were digging trenches; and structures of wood and iron, the siege engines of Imank, were already being built by teams of soldiers. Before the West Gate some hundreds were involved in furious activity. Hem squinted, trying to see more clearly what they were doing: it seemed to him that they were probably building a ramp, like the one Saliman had spoken of at Il Dara. He looked along the East Road and saw that Soron was right: although the Fesse already seemed full, yet more marched along the road, as far as the eye could see, rows and rows of soldiers interspersed with great ox-wains dragging in supplies, and larger animals he could not identify. Where they had been, columns of black smoke rose into the sky.

The only area that was clear of the Black Army was immediately before the city walls, which was empty for the space of a bowshot. And from the Red Tower, Hem could see the city walls bristling with archers, standing behind the zigzag battlements, and the sun banner of Turbansk unfurled from the top of every tower, glittering in the clear light.

Hem turned and looked down to the harbor, and then over the Lamarsan Sea. A haze lay over it, but then, with a throb of fear, he thought he saw a blur on the water in the distance: was that the fleet from Baladh, which Saliman had spoken of? He leaned forward, squinting, but could not be sure.

Hem thought of the slaughter at Il Dara, and a lump formed

in his throat. Irc gave a subdued caw, and wiped his beak on Hem's hair.

"We are too few," said Soron, echoing Hem's thoughts. "We have two score thousand. I cannot count how many stand there before the walls, but I do not need to count to know that if each fighter here killed three enemies, they would still out-number us."

"Saliman doesn't think we will stand," said Hem.

"No one thinks we will stand," said Inhulca, a tall Bard with a weather-roughened face and a nose that looked as if it had been much broken. He had the light skin of a Baladhian, and he looked on Zelika with open curiosity, although he was too polite to comment on her presence. "But we stand here, all the same. It is the calm before the storm." He smiled; Hem thought it a savage smile, and it sent a strange thrill down his spine. "But I am due at the Ernan. I will see you, Soron."

"Until later, Inhulca," said Soron.

The Baladh Bard left, and Soron glanced again over the parapet and then looked at the children. "Well, no one can fight without eating," he said, stretching. "I had to see for myself, but for the moment my part in this war is in the kitchens. Are you staying here, then?"

Hem had seen enough, and looked inquiringly at Zelika.

"No, I've seen what I wanted to see," she said. Her face was hard and closed.

"We'll come down with you, then," said Hem to Soron. "If that's all right."

"It's all the same to me, young Bard," said Soron. "If you have time to come to the kitchens, I'll give you both some seed-cakes and a dish of tea."

Hem brightened: Soron's seedcakes were a rare delicacy, and were especially delicious with mint tea. But it was the kindness underneath the offer that counted more. It was one thing hearing about the Black Army, and quite another to see it swarming on your doorstep. He felt more shaken than he had expected.

The calm before the storm, Inhulca had said. The streets of Turbansk did have a strange calm—a tense, still expectancy. The three of them hurried. Although there was no reason to hurry, everyone they saw was walking quickly as well, and nobody was speaking. Hem thought it was eerie. The market-places were completely deserted; even Boran the coffee seller had closed his stall. Hem wondered where Saliman was.

They were close to the buttery when Irc let out a sharp caw, and jumped off Hem's shoulder into the air.

Fly! cried Irc. *They are coming!*

What do you mean? asked Hem, turning around wildly. He couldn't see anything. Zelika and Soron stared at him in puzzlement. But almost before he had finished speaking, a shadow fell over the far end of the street. They all looked up involuntarily.

Before they had time even to cry out, Soron had grabbed the children's arms and started running. Irc swooped around their heads, jabbering wildly in panic.

"Put your heads down!" Soron shouted, panting. He was a heavy man. "Don't look up. *Run!*"

The sky was dark with birds. They flew low in close formations over the streets of Turbansk, in flocks so large that they blotted out the sun like heavy clouds. Even in that brief glimpse, Hem had seen them plummeting in groups of five or ten or fifteen, down from the flocks, to attack people in the street. As they ran, Hem could hear the singing of bow strings, and soft thumps as bodies fell to the ground, and then in the distance someone screaming, and then someone else. The birds made no noise at all. Something went past his ear, as if a sword had just missed him, a vicious swipe of air, and then another;

and then something struck the back of his head as if he had been hit by a stone. He felt no pain, but panic possessed him. If Soron had not been holding his arm, he would have been running blindly with no idea of where he was going. Suddenly Irc was on his shoulder again, cawing in distress and trying to hide in his hair, clutching him so hard his claws went through Hem's tunic into his skin. Hem heard Soron cry out, and something rushed up from them with a noise like a *whoosh* of flame, and he smelled scorched feathers and before his feet was suddenly a litter of small smoking corpses. They were carrion crows, he realized in that instant; but they seemed strangely the wrong shape. He had no time to wonder.

It was not far to the buttery, although Hem's chest was burning before they reached it. Soron thrust them through the street door, slammed it shut behind them and then leaned against it, staring at the children without seeing them, his breast heaving. They waited until they got their breath back, and then they walked to the kitchens. None of them felt like speaking. Something was tickling Hem's neck, and he put his hand back to feel. He was surprised to see that his fingers were covered with blood.

The way to the kitchens led through a gallery lined with long narrow casements. Zelika paused at its entrance, and peering over her shoulder Hem saw why: some of the windows were smashed; others were cracking under the assault of the crows, which dived recklessly against them with no heed to their own hurt. Half a dozen crows were already swooping through the gallery away from them, like a hunting pack. Irc cawed again, this time with defiance and rage, and Soron cried out in the Speech. A great bolt of white light leaped from his hands and hit the birds. They burst into flame and tumbled silently to the floor in a stench of burned feathers. Then all three ran through the gallery to the kitchens, to find the heavy door locked. Soron hammered on the wood, shouting, and a frightened young Bard, his assistant Edan, unbolted it and let them in, and then bolted it fast behind them.

The kitchen was darkened because all the shutters were closed, and a lamp was lit on the table. Besides Edan there were a number of people, some of whom had clearly run in from the street to escape the birds: two were bleeding from head wounds.

Hem, Zelika, and Soron sat down and breathed out.

"They are no ordinary crows," said Hem. It was the first thing any of them had said.

"Nay," said Soron. His face was grim. "I have not seen nor heard of the like. They do not hear the Speech, as do all beasts of Edil-Amarandh. They are some foul and twisted breed of the Nameless One's, curse him."

They're no relations of mine, said Irc huffily. Now he felt safe, he had regained his usual assurance and was sorting out his ruffled feathers with his beak. He seemed to have escaped injury. *Even my cousins, who hate me, would not do that. Those birds are not creatures—they are mad.*

Zelika's eyes were dark and huge. "They're evil," she said. "Twisted."

"Was there anything like this at Baladh?" asked Hem.

"No," Zelika answered. She did not say anything more.

"Edan," said Soron. "We need some tea. I am a little out of breath: would you brew some for the kind people here? Peppermint, I think; our stomachs are all a little shaken. And there are seedcakes that I baked just this morning in the cool room. Could you get them out?"

Edan started to boil water, and Zelika and Hem jumped up to help. In the ordinary tasks of preparing and sharing food the last of their panic began to dissipate. Hem wondered what was happening outside in the streets, what was happening to the archers on the walls: surely only Bards with their mageries could drive back those murderous flocks. Despite his fear, or perhaps because of it, he thought the seedcakes tasted particularly good.

The assault by the crows seemed to last for a long time. Since neither Zelika nor Hem could venture into the streets, they helped Soron in the kitchens, one ear attuned always to the soft menacing buffeting against the kitchen shutters. Then, very suddenly, it stopped. Hem, who was chopping root vegetables for soup, paused and glanced at Zelika. Without saying anything, they both went to the kitchen door and pressed their ears against the wood, trying to hear what was happening outside, and then cautiously opened it.

The skies were clear, and the children blinked as the bright sun poured onto the warm stone walls. In the tiny alley outside the kitchen were scores of dead birds in little piles on the ground, and everywhere was a litter of black feathers. They were heaped against the walls of the neighboring buildings. Some of the grilled windows, which were wrought in intricate patterns of iron, had dead birds wedged into them.

"They must have just dived and broken their necks!" said Zelika in astonishment.

They're mad—I told you, said Irc, and gave a superior caw.

Hem surveyed the mess silently. The sheer recklessness of the assault made his innards curl with horror. If they do that, he thought, I'm glad none landed on my head.

"We should get home, while we can," he said. "They might come back."

"They *will* come back," said Zelika scornfully. "There's no *might* about it."

Hurriedly they thanked Soron, who looked anxious but did not question them, as Saliman's Bardhouse was not far from the

butteries. Then they took a deep breath and ran home, fearing
all the time that another flock would blot out the sun. The city
was deathly quiet: they were the only people out. Every street
was littered with the bodies of crows; it was hard not to step on
them, though their feet loathed the feeling of the soft bodies
beneath them. Once they saw the body of a soldier in the street.
Even from a distance, Hem could see it was no use going to
check if he was still alive. They averted their eyes, and ran
faster.

The Bardhouse was empty. They went hesitantly into
Saliman's rooms, where lay the broken bodies of five crows.
Seeing this beautiful chamber so violated filled Hem with a
sudden fury: this was the closest thing to home that he had ever
known. He bent down to pick up one of the corpses, but Zelika
grabbed his arm.

"Don't touch them," she said. "They might be poison or
something."

Hem saw the point of that, so they went to find some pans
and brushes, and then tidied up the chamber as best they could.
Hem looked closely at the dead birds: seen close up, they bore
very little resemblance to crows at all. They were about the
same size, and were black, but their heads were too big and
their wings somehow misshapen. There were few feathers on
their heads, their eyes and necks covered with naked gray skin
pocked with stubble. They had the vicious stabbing beak of a
crow, only again it was too big. As Hem gingerly scooped one
body up in a pan, he saw that it had two heads: a second mal-
formed and incomplete head grew out of its neck. He stared at
it, overwhelmed by a sense of deep wrongness: somehow this
horrified him more than anything else he had seen that day.
Then he went out into the garden and was quietly sick.

After they had restored some order to Saliman's rooms, closing fast the wrought metal shutters in case the birds came back,

they started on the rest of the house. Most of the rooms had been shuttered, as their occupants had long left for Car Amdridh. To their relief, there were no dead birds in Hem's and Zelika's rooms. It was better to keep busy; neither of them dared to venture out into the streets again, and Hem was beginning to wonder where Saliman was, and what was happening in the city. Behind everything he could hear the low, constant throb of the war drums outside the city, and the occasional bray of horns. The noise seemed to echo inside his skull.

Saliman arrived not long afterward. He was clearly in a hurry.

"Hem, Zelika—thank the Light you're all right. I'm sorry I couldn't be here sooner. As you might guess, I've been busy."

"We've been tidying up," said Hem. Irc, perched on Hem's shoulder, cawed in agreement. "There were some of those . . . crows on the floor, so we got rid of them."

"Did you touch them?" asked Saliman sharply.

"No," said Zelika. "We thought they might be poisonous."

"Good. They are. Oslar has great fears about these deathcrows, and even now ponders what we are to do with them: he thinks they were sent not only to spread alarm and fear, and so weaken our resolve, but to spread disease in the city; and I fear he is right. For all our knowledge of the Black Army, we did not expect this, and I confess it has thrown our defenses. Nor do I think it will be the last attack: calculating that now our fighters will sicken and die, Imank will be patient and hold back the siege engines. I think that is why there has been no assault yet on the city walls, and why the Black Fleet holds back beyond our reach."

"So nothing has really happened yet?" asked Hem.

"Not yet. The Black Army now fills the Fesse of Turbansk, but they make no move. But that is not what I came to say. I am not happy that you stay in this house, and I want you to move to the Ernan, where you will be closer to where I spend most of my time. I want you to pack swiftly and come with me."

"But I want to fight!" said Zelika sulkily. "I don't want to be caged up in a palace so you know where I am, like a child."

"We are at war now, Zelika," said Saliman, in a tone that brooked no argument. "If you wish to be a fighter, you need to obey commands, as any fighter does."

Zelika met Saliman's gaze, but did not question him. "I don't even have a proper sword," she said, after a pause.

"That is more easily remedied in the armory of the Ernan than here," answered Saliman. "No one now is to venture into the street unarmored, in case the deathcrows come again; and I have in fact given thought to proper gear for you. Hem, are you all right? You look very pale."

Hem had been feeling dizzy since their arrival in the Bardhouse. The feeling had been getting steadily worse, particularly since he had been sick, but he thought it was just the aftershock of the morning's attack.

"I'm all right," he said. "I'll just get my things." He turned to run to his room, and found that his legs simply crumpled, as if they didn't belong to him. To his surprise, he found himself on the floor. Saliman leaped forward and caught him up, and then noticed the small wound on his neck where he had been struck by one of the deathcrows.

"Hem, what is this wound?"

"It's nothing, just a peck," said Hem, weakly trying to push Saliman away. He couldn't focus his eyes; he was seeing two of everything. "It doesn't hurt."

"He was hit by one of the crows, when we were running away," said Zelika. "Hem didn't tell you: we were caught in the street when they attacked, but Soron saved us."

Saliman cursed and lifted Hem onto a couch, looking anxiously into his face and feeling for his pulse. "Zelika, can you put Hem's belongings in a pack? There's not much, just what's in the chest in his chamber. We must hurry. I'll have to carry him to the Ernan. Just pray that the Light gives us safe passage . . ."

Zelika was out of the room before he finished speaking, and Saliman put his hand on Hem's brow. It was cold and clammy with sweat.

VII

THE BATTLE OF THE BIRDS

THE afternoon passed slowly, fading into night. Still more ranks of the Black Army poured into the Fesse of Turbansk, marching down the East Road, and where they marched were lines of moving torches, and where they camped were points of fire, and already they had dug long trenches, which had been filled with dull red flames. Inside the city walls all windows were shuttered and curtained: the city seemed like a dark island in a sea of fire. Tonight no houses were lit with lamps, and no musicians played in the perfumed gardens. The moonless sky stretched high above, a black expanse scattered with feverish stars.

Hem had no sense of where he was. Saliman had carried him to the Ernan that afternoon and laid him in a chamber near its western wall. Like every room in the Ernan, it was exquisitely decorated. Its cool blue walls were frescoed with dancing figures that moved through a vision of plenty—vines laden with grapes curled around their feet, and orange trees bowed low and offered the revelers their burdens of fruit. But by the time he was placed in his bed, Hem was oblivious to its beauty: he was already unconscious with a raging fever. His body was racked with savage tremors, and beads of sweat rolled off his face onto the bed sheets. A gentle breeze wandered through the window grille and caressed his forehead, and Hem shuddered as if he had been touched with ice.

Irc, who refused to leave Hem, perched on the back of a chair by the bed, but forewent his usual chatter. Zelika was frightened: Hem's illness had come over him so suddenly. It looked as if he were burning up from the inside. And she realized, for the first time, that Hem was her friend, her only friend, and she did not want him to die.

Saliman, who was a noted healer, had waved away the palace Bard, his brow heavy with worry.

"Will he live?" whispered Zelika, who had been allowed to stay when she had begged to help nurse him.

"I don't know," said Saliman. Zelika's heart shriveled with sudden dread. "I fear that many more will be like Hem by dawn. And this is an illness I do not recognize. But I swear to you, young Zelika: if I can save him, I will. He is precious to me, as well as to you." He smiled then, and Zelika began to understand why Hem loved Saliman. But it stirred other painful emotions. She pushed away the tears that threatened, brushed back her hair, and prepared to do whatever was required of her in the sickroom.

Saliman then took Hem's hand in his. Zelika watched with amazement—in Baladh she had not had much to do with Bards—as he began to glimmer with the light of magery, at first as gentle as starlight. The light slowly grew, until Zelika had to shade her eyes and Saliman seemed to be a figure of molten silver and all else beside him seemed dim and colorless. Saliman shut his eyes and said some words in the Speech. He called Hem's name, and then again; and the second time it sounded as if he spoke from a great distance. Then the light grew brighter still, and Saliman bowed his head, as if he were making some great effort. Zelika, unable to look away, felt tears of dazzlement run down her cheek. And then, as slowly as it had blossomed, the light began to fade.

Saliman looked up, and Zelika saw that his face was the color of wet ash. She dared not ask any questions, although they trembled on her lips. He met her eyes and smiled tiredly.

"It is a foul illness," he said. "But I have driven it from his blood, and called him back from the dark reaches." He drew a deep breath. "Ai! I can taste it on my teeth. Zelika, I am going now: there are other tasks that demand my care. Watch Hem, and tell me if he wakes, or does anything except sleep peacefully."

Zelika nodded fiercely, her eyes fixed on Hem. He did seem a better color than he had been before, when he had been the shade of bleached parchment. Saliman left, and Zelika sat by the bed, gnawing her lip, and held Hem's hand as the afternoon darkened to twilight and then to night.

Just before twilight, there was another attack of the deathcrows. It was not so frightening, as this time she was inside, and she watched the shadows of the birds plummeting outside with a cool curiosity. Why did they not care if they killed themselves? It was very strange. Some tried to force themselves through the metal grille over the window, but the holes were too small. One or two got their heads stuck and broke their necks. When the attack passed, Zelika got up and pushed the corpses out of the grille with a stick. Then she sat down next to Hem again.

By now it was night. It was very quiet in the palace, and there was no birdsong in the gardens. She hummed to herself, to pass the time and to dispel the silence: snatches of the long Suderain epics, childish rhymes, folk songs. After a while Irc came up to her and pulled her hair, cawing, and she guessed that he wanted something to eat.

"I have nothing to give you," she said impatiently. "Go and find Saliman!"

Irc peered at her, his head cocked sideways, and gently pecked her hand.

"Oh, you stupid creature! I don't have anything!"

Although Irc could not follow her words, he did understand her tone. He cawed sharply and pecked her quite hard—for revenge, she thought—and then flapped slowly out of the room. Zelika was left to herself. She was getting sore from sitting so still, and wriggled and stretched to relieve the stiffness, and then she yawned. She was more tired than she had thought. Finally, when she couldn't stop her eyelids from dropping, she crawled onto the huge cushioned bed, curled up next to Hem, and went to sleep. Irc swept back into the chamber a little later, landed on the pillow next to Hem, and gently pecked his face. When the boy did not wake, Irc took up his perch on the chair, tucked his head under his wing, and slept also.

Outside in the darkness, drums pulsed like a fever in the blood, and the archers on the city walls changed watch, and the guards in the Red Tower stared through their starglasses at the dark lines that separated sea and sky, searching always for ominous black sails, and fires leapt and spread in the shadowed Fesse of Turbansk. But the two children slept as deeply as if they had never heard of war.

Hem dreamed of birds.

He was one of the deathcrows, and he had three wings, one that grew out of his breast, and as he flew, black feathers dropped from his skin. If I lose any more I won't be able to fly and I'll fall out of the sky, he thought, but without fear. It seemed to him it would be a grace to lie on the ground, wrapped in darkness and silence. Then suddenly he was Hem again, but he sat on a white branch on a high tree, with Irc on his shoulder. Every branch of the tree was crowded with hundreds and hundreds of birds of all kinds—predators and prey next to each other, eagle next to finch, buzzard by bee-eater, kestrel by wren. Falcons, warblers, bulbuls, herons, crows, vultures, larks, robins, meenahs, ibises, ducks, egrets, and long lines of yet more birds, of yet more kinds, were flying toward the tree through a blue summer sky, out of the heart of a white brilliant sun.

A great happiness rose in Hem's heart. Now he knew what to do . . .

He opened his eyes to the first light of dawn. He sat up in bed, looking around with wonder at the magnificent room: he did not remember coming there. The last thing he remembered was falling down in Saliman's Bardhouse.

Irc was perched on a chair nearby, fixing him with a hungry stare. Zelika was fast asleep, her hands clasped together underneath her cheek, her hair tumbling over her face. He had never seen her sleeping before; it made her seem much younger. He slipped out of bed quietly, careful not to wake her, and only then noticed he was dressed in a nightshirt and didn't know where his clothes were. And he was starving.

I'm hungry, said Irc. He flapped to Hem's shoulder, but the boy pushed him off because Irc's claws scratched his skin.

I don't know where they keep food here, Hem said. He was almost hopping with impatience. *I've had an idea, Irc. Where's Saliman?*

Even as he spoke, Saliman entered the room. He pulled up short when he saw Hem.

"What are you doing out of bed?" he said.

"I'm starving," Hem answered. "And where are my clothes? And Saliman, I've had this idea—about the deathcrows."

"Hem, last sunset I was afraid you would not survive the night. I doubt you should be out of bed."

Hem looked surprised. "I feel as well as I've ever felt!" he protested. "No, listen, Saliman, this is important—I had this dream, and then I woke up, and I thought, where are the birds of Turbansk? Can't they help us fight the deathcrows?"

In his excitement, Hem's voice rose and he woke Zelika, who turned over and then sat up, rubbing her eyes.

"I'm sure the birds would help us. They've all had to hide. Where are they? Couldn't they help us? And there are at least as many of them as the deathcrows—"

"What are you talking about, Hem?" said Zelika.

"Even if the birds could help us," said Saliman, "there is no time to gather them. Already Imank is making the first move. The Black Fleet threatens us, as I feared, and the forces of Dén Raven move now on the city walls. And many people sicken from the plague the deathcrows brought with them; the healers are hard pressed—"

"I've got time!"

Zelika scrambled out of bed and stood next to Hem. "I think it's a good idea," she said. "I could help too, since you won't let me fight. You promised me armor," she said reproachfully. "And I haven't got any."

"You can't speak to birds," said Hem scornfully.

Zelika cast him a look of dislike. "So? I could still help. But it would make a difference, wouldn't it? Unless you think those deathcrows are all dead. They get in the way of the archers, don't they? How can anyone defend the city when they've got these horrible crows raining down on their heads? It's a really good idea."

"What is there to lose?" said Hem.

Both the children stared at Saliman, their eyes shining.

Saliman put up his hands to silence them. "All right, all right! Yes, you're quite correct, Zelika. The deathcrows impede us, and if we could stay their attacks it would help us considerably. But first, Hem, let me look at you. I can't believe that you have recovered so quickly."

Hem consented with bad grace to sit down on the bed while

Saliman felt his forehead and pulse and inspected his irises. When he had finished, he shook his head.

"I know I'm a good healer," he said. "But you must have some special strength, Hem. I can't see anything wrong. Unless this disease runs its course very quickly."

"I told you I was fine," said Hem crossly. Irc cawed sharply. "And we're hungry, and I don't know where my clothes are. But I should speak to the birds first. We don't have any time . . . But I can do that now!"

He ran to the window and wrenched open the metal grille, and, putting forth all his summoning power, called out in the Speech, *Where are you, birds of Turbansk? Come to me!* He paused, listening, and then called out again. Irc jumped from the chair and perched on his shoulder, but this time Hem did not shrug him off.

Saliman was shaking his head, but he was smiling. "I'll leave you to your summoning, Hem. Breakfast is on its way here, never fear. For you, too," he added, looking at Irc. "Your clothes are at the end of the bed, Hem, if you care to look. Many things call me now, and I cannot stay."

"What about my fighting gear?" said Zelika belligerently.

"That too is on its way. I have not been idle. Farewell! I will return soon."

He left the room hurriedly, and Zelika turned to watch Hem. Nothing happened for a long time, and she began to feel disappointed.

"What if they don't answer?" she said at last. "Maybe the deathcrows killed them all. Anyway, where could they have hidden?"

"Shhhh!" Hem turned from the window with his fingers on his lips.

"But—"

"Be quiet, I tell you!"

Hem's expression was so fierce, even though he whispered, that Zelika was immediately silenced. In the quiet she heard a small cheep, and Irc cocked his head and cawed inquiringly. Then there was a sudden rushing noise, and the window darkened. For a terrible moment Zelika thought the deathcrows had returned for another assault, but then she saw it was dozens of other kinds of birds. Those that could landed on Hem's arms and head, and the others hovered outside the window or perched in the courtyard outside or in the bedroom. She was confused by their variety: it seemed that every kind of bird she had ever seen was suddenly there, from tiny brown finches to magnificent white egrets, from hook-beaked buzzards to iridescent pigeons, from eagles to crows. But she saw enough to notice there was only one of every kind. A hubbub of birdcalls filled the room.

Zelika stared in awe; she hadn't known Hem possessed such powers. The boy spoke, and the birds listened, their eyes bright, and then there was another chaos of birdcalls. He spoke again, and the birds took off in another rush of wings, and were gone so suddenly that Zelika blinked.

Hem turned, his face shining.

"I told you! I knew they'd help!"

"So what did they say?" asked Zelika.

"They are frightened and angry." In his excitement, Hem had forgotten his modesty. He had thrown off his nightshirt and was hurriedly pulling on his clothes. "They fear the deathcrows greatly. They say the deathcrows are not birds at all. I told them that if they work together, they could keep the skies clear. They go now to speak to the other birds, and the falcons and eagles will spy out the deathcrows, to find out where they come from and how many they are. They'll return soon with their answers."

For once, Zelika couldn't think of anything to say. She had

never seen Hem so sure; usually he was a little boastful, a bright veneer of confidence that Zelika guessed sardonically was underlain by uncertainty.

When breakfast arrived soon after, hot honeyed dohl in silver bowls, and some raw meat for Irc, they all ate hungrily. Hem was restless, keeping one eye on the window, and when a pelican flapped heavily down and perched on the sill, he jumped up immediately to greet it. The huge bird filled the window, its yellow beak almost as long as Hem's arm. They spoke briefly, and the pelican departed, leaping off the sill and spreading its huge black wings. Hem came back to finish his breakfast, his face flushed.

"It's going to work," he said. "The pelican is the king of them, I think. He calls himself a name that means Feather of the Sun, *Ara-kin*. The birds gather now. He said the deathcrows are beyond the Black Army, on some hills near a forest and a small lake."

"That's probably the Jiela Hills," said Zelika, frowning. "I think."

"He says they prepare for another attack this morning. There are Hulls moving among them. Where's Saliman? He should know this." He waved his spoon impatiently. "The birds of Turbansk are gathering swiftly. I've told them to keep the carrion back from the walls. They can attack them from above, as they fly toward the city. They can't fight them where they are, on the ground, because the Hulls would blast them out of the sky."

Saliman arrived shortly afterward, followed by two palace aides who carried bundles wrapped carefully in cloth. Hem at once told him what he had done, and Saliman listened in silence. When Hem had finished he said nothing for a time, and simply stared at Hem with a mixture of amusement and admiration.

"You think like a general, Hem," he said finally. "Well done. It may yet work, the Light willing."

Hem flushed with pleasure at Saliman's praise.

"There is news," added Saliman. "The assault on the harbor is beginning, as I thought, even as it also begins on the outer walls. I am in haste: I am needed elsewhere. Here are your arms." He gestured, and the aides came forward and began to place their burdens on the bed. They carried arms and armor in the colors of Turbansk.

"It was not so hard as it might have been to find some your size," said Saliman. "But remember you bear royal arms— wear them with respect! These were made for the sons of Har-Ytan when they were your age."

Hem stared at the gear, his attention suddenly caught. The light through the window struck off the golden sun emblazoned on the shields, and he blinked, dazzled.

"Hem, Zelika, if you wish to see what is happening you can climb the Red Tower. I will be at the harbor, but do not seek me unless you have real need, and send Irc if you do. The aides here, Ja-Rel and Han, will show you the gates of the Ernan if you seek them. Remember which gate you enter by, or it will take you long to find your way back here . . . I must go. Remember what I say!"

Saliman gave Hem a hard, urgent stare, as if he wished to say more than words or time allowed. Hem blinked, feeling a sudden gathering of grief in his chest. With a sharp pang, he wondered if he would see Saliman again. Things seemed to be moving too quickly: there was not enough time for anything. The Bard hurriedly embraced the children, kissing each on the forehead, and departed almost at a run. Hem and Zelika stared at each other.

"I have never owned arms so fine!" Zelika said, her eyes sparkling. "Let's get dressed."

Hem knew how to arm himself from his swordcraft lessons, but the aides assisted him gravely as if he were a fine lord. He

found it a little disconcerting. And this time putting on battle
gear had a special significance; he was not about to attack a
classmate with a bamboo sword, but might soon find himself
fighting for his life. He shuddered involuntarily as the cold mail
met his skin. The corslet of blue ceramic scales was much
lighter than those he was used to, and the round shield was also
light. He looked at it closely; it was made of some very strong
metal he didn't recognize. He strapped on leather greaves and
vambraces, both dyed blue, and tied the blue-dyed sandals to
his bare feet. He refused the golden helm, and put the fine mail
gauntlets in a leather bag at his waist. Lastly he strapped on a
shortsword.

Zelika tried the balance of her sword. "It is a good weapon,"
she said, and she smiled. It was a smile that sent a chill down
Hem's spine; he had not seen this expression on Zelika's face
for some days, and had almost forgotten it. Now all her gentleness had gone, and in its place was a cold savagery. "Better than
a cooking knife, eh, Hem?" She slashed the air with the sword.
"I wager this edge will unstring some necks."

Hem studied his own sword. It was, he could see, a fine
weapon, with the steel folded and tempered by master metalsmiths to an edge that would cleave a hair. Swordcraft was a
skill that he enjoyed, the only classes at the Turbansk School for
which he had displayed talent and application. But he did not
feel the same bloodthirstiness as he saw in Zelika. He wondered why: the Dark had murdered and enslaved his family
too, and had destroyed his life. He hated the Dark as much as
he hated anything. All the same, he could not feel Zelika's
strange delight at the prospect of battle; when he saw that
gleam in her eyes, he believed that she was speaking truth
when she said she didn't care whether she died.

All of a sudden, he felt weighed down by a huge, inconsolable
sorrow. He looked dubiously at his sword, and sheathed it.

"We'd better move," he said. He turned to speak to Irc. *Can you be a messenger, my friend? Tell the birds where they can find me.*

Irc gave a sharp cry and flew out of the window.

"I wish I had the Speech," said Zelika. She strapped her shortsword to her waist and then stared at Hem. "What's wrong?"

Hem shrugged, and half turned away. "I don't know," he answered.

Zelika studied his face for a moment, and drew her lips into an impatient line. "We're all sad," she said. "Everybody has something to be sad about. But right now, I think it is better to be angry." She jammed her helm on her head, and strode out of the door.

Hem squared his shoulders and followed her more slowly, studying her straight, determined back. Even after days of spending almost all his time with Zelika, he still found her very hard to read.

The aides in the Ernan and the Red Tower guards told Hem and Zelika that Saliman had sent instructions that the two children were to be allowed the freedom of the city. Hem pondered this as they made the long climb up the stairs. He wondered what Saliman expected of him. Perhaps it was simply trust.

Saliman had made no secret of the fact that he disapproved of Zelika's desire to be a fighter, and Hem had expected a stand-up argument about it. Perhaps Saliman had wisely deduced that the only way to keep Zelika out of battle was to lock her up. Or maybe he thought that when it came to the point, Zelika would be more sensible than her words suggested. Hem himself wasn't very confident about that: he had seen the madness in Zelika's eyes when she spoke of the Black Army, and he thought no reasoning would hold her back from her desire for revenge.

Climbing the Red Tower was tiring at the best of times, but in full armor it was hot and exhausting. Long before they reached the top, Hem was wondering if his legs would hold out. Zelika was climbing steadily before him, and only pride stopped him from calling for a rest. Even pride didn't stop him from sitting down awkwardly when they finally reached the watch at the top, breathing hard and wiping away the sweat that sheeted down his face. His hair was soaked, as if he had jumped into a pond. It was still early, and although the day was already growing hot, this high up the air was cooled by a soft breeze. It wasn't long before Hem recovered his composure and was able to remember why he had climbed there.

The golden dome that topped the Red Tower gave a welcome shade. Beneath the dome was the watch, a square floor surrounded by low walls that permitted an unimpeded view in every direction. Four guards stood there, one at each wall, and two lightly armored messengers. They all turned to look when the children emerged from the stairs, but after nodding in greeting took no further notice of them.

As Hem stood up, Irc swooped into the shade, landed on his shoulder, and nibbled his ear.

I've told the pelican, Ara-kin, he said. *He says I am now his messenger.* Irc seemed inordinately pleased. *The birds will find you here.*

Thank you, my friend, said Hem, and stroked Irc's head with his finger. Then he asked a question that had been bothering him. *Do the crows harry you?*

Irc puffed out his feathers a little smugly. *They do not harry the messenger of the King,* he answered.

The King? repeated Hem, confused. *Did the birds mean him?* But then he realized Irc must mean Ara-kin. *Anyway, what is happening out there?*

Look, said Irc.

Even as Irc spoke, the guard looking west turned to one of the messengers and said sharply, "Deathcrows! Coming from the west!" The messenger leaped to her feet, preparing to run, but the guard put up his hand to stay her. "Something else. Flocks of birds . . . but they are not crows. I do not know what they are. They're very high up. Very strange—it is not the season for such flocking. And they are flying toward the deathcrows. What does this mean? Perhaps they prepare to attack the enemy, though I do not credit it. Report it, anyway."

The messenger nodded and vanished down the stairs to the Ernan, Hem supposed. But he and Zelika rushed eagerly to the west wall and stared hard into the distance, screwing up their eyes against the bright sunlight.

He could see that there was movement at the city walls: large siege engines were being wheeled toward the defending towers, and something was happening at the West Gate. Arrows flew through the air, catching the sunlight as if they were on fire, and he could see the occasional flash of magery or sorcery. But Hem stared impatiently beyond the walls, wanting to know what was happening farther afield.

It was a while before they spotted the deathcrows. The guard's starglasses meant he could see farther than Hem and Zelika could. But eventually, behind the mass of the army that filled the Turbansk Fesse, they made out a black, swirling mist rising up out of the hills and moving toward the city. Closer, but dwindling into the distance, they saw with a thrill in their hearts the birds of Turbansk. They were flying much higher than the deathcrows, well out of range of the Black Army's arrows. Irc was bobbing up and down on Hem's shoulder with excitement. Hem resisted the urge to tear the starglasses out of the guard's hands: it was very frustrating not to be able to see clearly.

As they watched, the two clouds of birds, one light, one dark, met in midair. It wasn't until they were close together that

Hem could see that the Turbansk birds outnumbered the deathcrows. He started to hop from one foot to another, biting his lip. As they neared their destination, the Turbansk flock divided into two, and then swiftly encircled the deathcrows. For a moment the two forces were clearly visible, and then they seemed to fuse into one.

"They *are* attacking the deathcrows!" said the soldier next to him, letting down his starglasses in astonishment. The other guards looked over from their watch.

"I don't believe it," said another, but looking west he confirmed it for himself. "By the Light!"

The first soldier put the starglasses to his eye again. "The Light willing, they will prevail. I cannot tell . . . it is just a confusion out there . . . no, it looks as if the other birds are retreating. No, they are high again, but the deathcrows seem fewer, they do not head this way, anyway . . ."

It was agonizing. Hem's eyes were watering with the strain of trying to see, and his heart hammered in his ears. Now that the two flocks were embroiled together, he couldn't see which was winning. He could see tiny red flashes arcing upward from the battlefield, and he thought that maybe Hulls were trying to drive off the birds that attacked the deathcrows.

Then he saw the lighter flock climb back into the air, withdrawing. And now there was no sign of a black mist beneath it.

"The deathcrows . . . the deathcrows have vanished!" said the soldier. "They've just gone!"

"They killed them. They killed the deathcrows!" said Zelika. "Hem, it worked! It really worked!"

Hem stared again into the distance. Now the flock of Turbansk birds was flying slowly back toward the city. It was smaller, he thought, than it had been. But the soldier was correct: there was no sign of the deathcrows behind them. He was filled with a wild elation, and turned to hug Zelika, who was dancing, whooping with joy, while Irc plunged through the air in his own celebration.

Now all the guards were staring at the children. "Do you know about this, *Lios Hlaf*?" the first soldier said, using Hem's nickname. He stared curiously at the boy.

"The birds of Turbansk fight with us," answered Hem, his face glowing. "They fear the deathcrows as much as we do."

"That is clever," said another guard. "But alas, it will not be enough."

"No. But each little bit helps, Inurdar," said the first guard. "You said yourself only yesterday that the deathcrows were a curse beyond the hurt they do us."

Hem and Zelika sobered, remembering that the defeat of the deathcrows was only a small part of the battle for Turbansk. For a moment they had felt as if they had won the war.

A sudden *boom* sounded from the harbor beneath them. They became aware that they could hear the cacophony of battle, faint at this distance, but still clear. He and Zelika exchanged swift glances, and ran to the south wall of the watch.

From this side, the Red Tower dropped sheer down to the Lamarsan Sea. To their right stretched the walls and towers of Turbansk Harbor. Looking down, Hem had an aerial view of a vicious sea battle.

The boom they had heard was from a ramming ship that had smashed into one of the walls of the harbor. It was driven by sorcery, Hem could see, not by wind or oars; it moved too nimbly in the water. Even as they watched, the ship backed swiftly from the wall and drove toward it again. This time they saw the wall give, and one of the smaller towers, newly built and not as solid as the others, half collapsed. Stones tumbled down the side of the wall and splashed into the water. Hem saw some tiny human figures fall with them, and with a sudden constriction of his throat remembered that Saliman was defending the harbor.

Those who fell had little hope of being rescued: he saw bowmen on the black ships shooting them in the water.

"That's what Saliman said Imank would do," said Zelika at his shoulder. "He said there would be attacks from sea and land. And Imank planned to send the deathcrows too, to make defense impossible. Well, there are no deathcrows to help them."

"It's bad enough," said Hem. He could not take his eyes off the harbor.

There were three ramming ships, protected by perhaps half a dozen fighting dromonds, one of which was already broken in two and floated directionlessly on the water, its front half in flames. Standing well back from the immediate battle was a fleet of ships with black sails and figureless black shields painted on their sides. On the deck of each dromond stood dozens of soldiers, so that each ship seemed to bristle with spears.

The dromonds nearest the harbor were in battle with ten Turbanskian ships, which were smaller than those of the Black Army, and more maneuverable; they also, Hem could see, were driven by magery. They were aiming to break the ramming ships, but these were well protected by the enemy dromonds. Then, with a deadly whistling noise, something catapulted from a tower by the harbor and one of the black ships burst into flame. The harbor walls seemed to be raining fire. The black ship blazed so suddenly, from its prow to its stern, that Hem blinked; he couldn't see where the fire came from. He could see people jumping from the deck of the burning ship into the water. Some missed their mark and fell into the sea, sending up great gouts of steam, but others hit three of the black dromonds and one of the ramming ships. The Turbansk ships broke through the line of dromonds and two of them attacked one of the remaining ramming ships, breaking its hull so that it began, with a strange slowness, to list and then sink.

The final ramming ship shot backward, away from the

harbor walls, and dodged the Turbansk dromonds. Hem could see that the remaining black ships were also withdrawing toward the waiting fleet. But this time he felt no elation: his eyes were fixed on dozens of figures he could see struggling in the water. He could not tell which were defenders and which were attackers. One of the Turbanskian dromonds was sending down ropes to pull survivors out of the water, but Hem could already see that most of those in the water were fated to drown. He looked away from the smoking wrecks up into the clear blue sky, feeling sick.

"We beat them back," said Zelika with satisfaction.

"A tithe of their strength is all," said the guard who had watched the battle with them. "And we cannot leave the harbor until we destroy the fleet. They wait like wolves for our ships to leave haven."

Hem didn't know how long he had been watching the sea battle; it felt like ages. But he squinted at the sun and realized it had hardly moved. It was still early in the day; the skirmish he had just witnessed had taken very little time at all.

"I don't like this battling much," he said to Zelika.

She looked at him with what he thought was a strange pity. "Whether you like it or not, it is on us," she said.

As she spoke, the air around them suddenly filled with the beating of wings, and the great pelican perched on the western wall, folding his wings and letting out a sharp cry. In the air a creature of grace, when he landed he seemed clumsy and heavy. He called for Hem, using the same nickname given him by the Turbanskians, White Crow. The guard jumped back, alarmed; this close up, the pelican's wildness and size were alarming. Hem strode forward and greeted the bird respectfully.

We destroyed the deathcrows that flew this way, said Ara-kin. *They fell like rain from the sky. They have no fast ties to life, and die easily.*

We saw, said Hem. *It was a brave sight.*

The black sorcerers sent up fire to scatter us, the pelican continued. *Many of our numbers died by beak and claw and flame. Yet we prevailed.*

Our thanks can never be enough, said Hem, bowing his head.

We fight for our nests, also. Ara-kin turned his head and looked west. *There are more of these evil creatures. My kin watch the skies, and will see when they stir.*

How many more? asked Hem, dismayed.

At least as many as those we killed, said the pelican. *But we are more.*

Will you fight them, also? Hem asked.

Ara-kin outspread his wings in a sudden flourish, and despite himself Hem stepped back; the bird's wings must have covered more than two spans. *We will fight them,* the pelican answered. *We fear the black sorcerers. But we will fight them and we will win. Your enemy is very great: I do not think you can kill them all.*

Maybe not, said Hem. *But we must try.*

Ara-kin turned his head and fixed Hem with his yellow eye. *Fight bravely, then, as we do. Farewell, White Crow. Send your messenger, if you want word of us.* Irc cawed in assent, and the pelican leaped off the parapet into the air.

Hem watched the bird until he was a tiny speck in the sky, and then turned around to find all the soldiers had momentarily abandoned their watch and were staring at him in undisguised amazement.

"Well, what did Ara-kin say?" asked Zelika.

"He said there are more deathcrows, and they watch them and will destroy them as they did the others," said Hem.

"By the Light, did you think of that?" said the soldier called Inurdar.

Hem blushed and stared at the ground. "It was just a thought in a dream," he said.

"*Lios Hlaf* is not the name for you," said another guard. "You should be named the Emperor of Wings. The General of Birds!" The other soldiers laughed, but there was nothing unkind in their laughter, just an amazed admiration.

Hem did not know how to respond to their banter, and suddenly felt very tired. He had had enough of watching battles.

"I'm hungry," he said to Zelika. "And I want to find out if Saliman is all right."

"Let's go back to the Ernan, then," she answered. "It's still early, but I know where the kitchens are."

"Eat while you can," said Inurdar. "These are but the first skirmishes. The real battle is yet to begin."

VIII

SIEGE

IT was strange, Hem thought, how quickly one could get
used to things. After only a day, being besieged by the Black
Army became almost routine. After two days, it was part of
the texture of everyday life. People ate and joked and made
music and went to defend their city. Most returned, but some
did not. There was no longer any such thing as a casual
farewell; each parting, no matter how minor, could always be
the last; anyone could be unlucky, and at any time. This lent life
a new, vivid urgency. Although no one spoke of it, Turbansk felt
like a doomed city, and against the darkness of its fate, its
beauty seemed to glow with a poignant intensity.

Only in the evenings—when by common consent minstrels
and Bards all over Turbansk would bring out their instruments
and sing the beautiful Suderain epics to those who were not
guarding the walls—would anyone permit this knowledge to
rise to the surface; otherwise it was too hard to face. Hem,
although he was not a native of Turbansk, felt this strange mixture of dread and love seeping into the marrow of his bones.

Imank's army could not as yet break through the city walls;
their siege towers were driven off by magery and missiles, and
the rams that aimed for the western gate had not yet pierced its
defenses. But, as it had at the Il Dara Wall, the enemy continued
to assault the walls of Turbansk in constant waves, all day and
all night. These were driven off, at greater cost to the Black
Army than to the defenders; but the Turbansk forces were so
greatly outnumbered that every loss to them told ten times

more than any of the enemy losses. Turbansk was slowly being worn down, and time was all on the other side. The enemy fleet still stood off from the harbor in the Lamarsan Sea, making minor attacks like the one Hem had seen, but no larger moves. For the moment the battle stood at a stalemate.

It gave the Turbanskians a chance to deal with the problems caused by the deathcrows. The streets had been cleared of the dead crows by people with cloths steeped in medicinal potions covering their mouths and noses, to keep out the stench and infection, and the corpses had either been burned or put into catapults and flung back over the walls onto the Black Army. It was an inexpressible relief to see the streets clean again, and to be able to walk under the sky, and the atmosphere in the city lightened perceptibly. It was true, as the soldier on the tower had said, that the deathcrows had been an assault beyond the actual harm they had caused.

The birds of Turbansk had completely destroyed the flocks of the deathcrows in two more forays. Ara-kin had come to Hem at the Ernan the evening of the next day to deliver the news, perching on the sill of his chamber window. Hem was still surprised by how big the bird was, how wild and fierce and alive it seemed against the confines of the room.

That is news beyond hope, Hem said. *How can we thank you?*

Destroy the wrongness, said the pelican. *That will be enough.*

Hem hesitated before he answered, thinking of the great army at the walls. What hope did they have? *That is all our desire,* he answered.

Ara-kin bowed his head, and then leaped into the air with a great beating of wings, and was gone.

Zelika and Saliman, who had come to share the evening meal, watched the boy and the pelican from inside the room. When Hem turned, his slim figure silhouetted against the golden light streaming through the window, he saw their eyes were fixed on him. He rejoined them at the cushions around the low table, suddenly feeling very self-conscious.

"That was well done, Hem," said Saliman quietly.

"It was just from a dream," Hem said awkwardly. He still found it difficult to accept praise with grace.

"But you had the idea. Anyone else would have dismissed it as mad. And it worked." Saliman reached for a fig, tore it open, and smiled, studying its rich color. "I heard a singer this afternoon, already making the Battle of the Birds into a song. Everyone now sings the praises of the White Crow."

"The birds did everything themselves," mumbled Hem. He wanted to change the subject.

"Nay, Hem, take praise where it is due," said Saliman. "I must tell you now, you and Zelika are summoned to the Ernani at the ninth bell. She will want to hear from your own lips how the deathcrows were defeated. Perhaps that was why the song was being composed."

Hem flushed, and bowed his head to hide his confusion. He would be expected to speak to the Ernani, he thought distractedly; he hoped his mouth would not be as dry as it was the last time.

After their meal, Saliman guided Hem and Zelika through the palace, leaving an indignant Irc behind. By the time they had passed through a dozen rooms, Hem was already hopelessly lost. This time they did not go to the throne room but to a smaller, if no less beautiful, chamber in Har-Ytan's living quarters. To Hem's astonishment, when Saliman knocked, the Ernani herself opened the door of her chamber, and welcomed them in.

Hem blinked. Har-Ytan seemed like a different being from the regal woman he had seen in the throne room; she was of more human dimensions, but even so she was very impressive. Her braided hair was tied back from her face, and she wore a thin tunic of plain golden damask over a white shirt and trousers. Her feet were bare, but she stood taller than Saliman. She smelled of musk and jasmine. Behind her Hem saw three or four people rising to greet them from low couches arranged around an ebony table set with a silver jug and cups.

"Welcome," said Har-Ytan, looking at Hem. "Forgive this informality; this is the only spare time I have."

Hem stared at Har-Ytan, and found to his dismay that his jaw seemed to be wired shut. Zelika glanced sideways at him with what he thought was scorn.

"We are sensible of the honor you pay us, my lady," said Saliman. "You have already met Cai of Pellinor." Hem bowed his head, his face scarlet with humiliation. "This is Zelika of the House of Il Aran, from Baladh."

"The House of Il Aran?" Har-Ytan turned her direct gaze on Zelika, who met it levelly.

"I am all that remains of that House, Fountain of the Light," she said. "My sword is yours, until I die." She knelt gracefully, and Har-Ytan lightly touched the top of her head.

"Rise, Zelika of the House of Il Aran, and forget your sorrows for this brief moment," she said. "I see that, however young you might be, you are by no means the least of your noble house. Come, there are fruits and sweetmeats here, and sweet wines."

Hem looked curiously at Zelika as they moved toward the couches. From the assurance of her movements, he could see that, unlike him, she knew how to behave in these circumstances. He felt as stiff and awkward as a puppet.

Leaning on one of the couches was a very handsome man considerably younger than the Ernani, who turned out to be Har-Ytan's consort, Mundar. Hem recognized also the captain of the Sun Guard, Il Hanedr, and Juriken, the First Bard of Turbansk. To his confusion, he also recognized Alimbar el Nad,

Har-Ytan's consul, whose garden he had plundered weeks ago, in another lifetime. Alimbar gave him a narrow, suspicious look, as he nodded a greeting. Besides the wines and sweet-meats, Hem saw that maps and reports were spread out on the broad table; they had clearly been discussing the siege.

"So, children are to show us the way forward?" said Juriken, coming forward to clasp Hem's hand. "I argued with Saliman, I confess, when he said that he had decided you were to stay in Turbansk. But he has already had the better of us!" He exchanged a friendly smile with Saliman, and looked down again at Hem.

Juriken's hair was white and cropped close to his dark head, and his face was lined with age, but the eyes that regarded Hem were full of a young laughter, wholly without malice. Hem swallowed, and involuntarily glanced across to Alimbar. The man had a sour look on his face, as if he were forced to be civil to a piece of dung. This made Hem feel momentarily outraged, which had the effect of unlocking his tongue.

"It wasn't me who did it," he said. "It was the birds of Turbansk. They defeated the deathcrows, not me."

"They say the greatest heroes are the most modest," said Mundar languidly from the couch. "This lad must be the great-est of them all. He can barely say his deeds." He stared at Hem mockingly.

Before Hem could react, Har-Ytan spoke. "It is not so strange. Most of the human race is more modest than you are, Mundar," she said. Mundar did not miss the edge in her voice and, despite himself, he flushed. He gave Hem a spiteful glance and turned his head pointedly away. "Now, Cai of Pellinor," she continued. "In the city they name you *Lios Hlaf*, the White Crow, after your pet. Is that what you prefer to be called?"

"My lady," said Hem. "My real name is Hem. And Irc is not my pet; he is my friend."

Har-Ytan smiled, and Hem's innards, which had suddenly clenched in panic at his rudeness in correcting the Ernani, relaxed. "Hem," she said. "That is a strange name. It is not Annaren, I think?" She handed him one of the silver cups, filled with a golden liquid. Hem took a nervous sip and felt the liquor shudder down his body to his toes, but to his eternal gratitude he did not splutter.

"No, my lady," he said. "It is a Pilanel name. It's what I've been called all my life."

"You are a Bard," she said. "But you do not prefer your Bardic name. Is that not strange? Have you yet been given your Truename?"

"No, my lady."

"And do you desire to have a Truename?"

"I do not know, my lady." Her questions, and the thoughtful gaze she turned on him, made him feel uncomfortable.

"Only a few Bards relinquish their Truenames," she said. "The best and the worst."

Hem did not know what the Ernani meant. The only Bard he knew of who had cast out his name was the Nameless One. Was she saying he was evil, somehow? He felt completely at sea with these people. He took another gulp from the silver cup, and looked pleadingly to Saliman.

"My lady, you forget the power of your presence," said Saliman, with the ghost of a smile quirking the edges of his mouth. "Hem is still very young."

"Yet he has solved a problem that baffled even Il Hanedr, the greatest captain of this city," said Har-Ytan.

At this comment, Il Hanedr grinned at Hem.

"We had not the arrows nor Bards enough to down them all out of the sky," he said. "And the truth is, we could not have coped with any more attacks: cleaning up the bodies that were already there took all the resources we could spare, and the disease they spread cost us many fighters. Yet no one thought of summoning creatures, although creatures were used against us."

"The birds of Turbansk said the deathcrows were not creatures," said Hem. "They did not know the Speech. Irc said they were mad." He shuddered, thinking of the two-headed corpse he had seen in Saliman's rooms, the way the feathers would fall out of the deathcrows' skin, as if they were not properly attached. "In a way, it was as if they just wanted to die."

"It would appeal to the Nameless One, to create beasts that long only for death," said Juriken thoughtfully. "For life is what animals can teach us: how the present moment is all, and past and future are illusion."

"Perhaps that was the wrongness the pelican king spoke of," said Zelika, looking over to Hem to prompt him; but again, he found himself floundering, and merely nodded. There was a short pause.

"I am curious how you thought of this, and why you have such authority among the birds of Turbansk," said Har-Ytan. "I am used to the ways of Bards, but still, it seems marvelous to me."

"I've always talked to birds. And I dreamed about the deathcrows," said Hem. "When I had the fever, I dreamed of the birds. And when I woke up, I knew what to do."

Har-Ytan kept her dark gaze on his face, and he looked down, discomfited by a sharpness of perception of which he had been unaware; Har-Ytan was not merely powerful, but subtle in ways he could not begin to guess. "A dreamer," said Har-Ytan at last. "Your sister, too, is a dreamer. Perhaps it is the dreams of our young that will lead the way through the shadows that beset us. I am glad to meet you, Hem. And I thank you for what you have done."

"I am honored, my lady," said Hem thickly. He suddenly

wished fiercely that Maerad were there, beside him; she would not be so overawed; she would look Har-Ytan in the face and answer her with her special straightness. His shoulders slumped.

Although people were being very kind to him, Hem didn't like being the focus of so much attention. Mundar was pointedly ignoring him, Alimbar still looked as if he were trying to conceal the fact that he had swallowed a fly, and otherwise Hem felt he was just making a fool of himself in front of the most important people in Turbansk. But Har-Ytan, aware of his discomfiture, began to chat to Saliman, and the conversation became more general. Hem breathed out in relief, like a small child, while he thought nobody was looking at him. He did not notice, as Zelika did, that Saliman glanced toward him and smiled to himself, as if he were well pleased. Zelika, who was sitting next to Hem, took his hand and squeezed it. Hem looked up at her in surprise. Her eyes were sparkling with what he suspected was suppressed laughter.

"Your face goes bright red," she whispered. "It is very strange, to have pale skin."

Hem smiled sheepishly, but said nothing. Normally he would have taken umbrage, but now Zelika's teasing made him feel a little better.

Before long, a minstrel bearing a dulcimer entered the room, and bowed.

"Welcome, Ikarun," said Har-Ytan. "Now," she said, turning to the others, "we shall hear something to lift our hearts."

The minstrel bowed. "By your leave, O Fountain of Light, and my lords and ladies," he said, "I wish to play for you a new song, for your pleasure." He inclined his head courteously to Hem, struck a chord, and began to sing in a rich, beautiful voice.

Hem thought of what Saliman had said earlier, about hearing a song being written about the Battle of the Birds, and his face grew hot. He felt Zelika beside him, and knew without looking that she was trying not to giggle.

> *"I sing of a boy who came from the north*
> *With a bird on his shoulder,* Lios Hlaf,
> *Balm in his hands and Speech on his tongue,*
> *He came at our darkest hour,*
> *At our darkest hour . . ."*

The song was, as Hem had guessed, about the Battle of the Birds. It was not entirely unpleasant to be praised as a great hero, although Hem knew he was pleased, rather than feeling it; the actual experience made him too self-conscious to really enjoy it. When the song ended everyone clapped, and the minstrel bowed again, and left the room.

"Any victory in these times is worthy of celebration," said Har-Ytan. "This is why we praise you, Hem, most modest and youngest of generals." Then, smiling in a most unqueenly fashion, she leaned forward and pinched his cheek as if he were a baby. Hem thought he would never stop blushing.

Now Zelika, unable to hold it in, did giggle. Har-Ytan glanced at her, her mouth twitching, and began to laugh as well, as freely as if she were not the queen of a city that might soon be trampled to rubble by the army at its gates.

Not everyone who had been attacked by the deathcrows had fared as well as Hem; some had been sick indeed, and a few had died. The day after Hem had been summoned to the Ernani, Oslar again asked for Hem's help in the Healing Houses, and in the ensuing days Hem and Zelika spent most of their time there. The Healing Houses seemed strangely untouched by the battles outside: an air of tranquillity filled the cool rooms, and the healers moved quietly between their patients, unhurried and grave.

There were many ill with the crow fever, and Hem was shocked when he saw how sick they were. He had recovered so completely that he hadn't given his own illness a second thought. Oslar had inspected Hem personally before he had permitted the boy to work, his brow furrowed, and Hem had submitted with a barely concealed sigh of impatience; but now he saw why Saliman had been so concerned.

"You are lucky, my boy," said Oslar, when he had felt Hem's pulse and temperature, examined his irises, tapped his elbows and knees, and been reassured that his appetite was normal. "You have a toughness beyond some of our hardiest fighters. Strong men have withered in this illness."

"Saliman cured me," said Hem.

"He is a great healer," Oslar said. "I could wish for his skills here, and I regret that he should be forced to spend his time killing rather than healing. But I am at least Saliman's equal, and I have been able to drive the sickness from the blood of only a few. And even so, they are bedridden for days."

"Are there many sick?" asked Hem.

"Not as many as there might be. You will find more wounded by arrows and fire than sickened by the deathcrows. But that is due to you, I hear." The old Bard smiled, and Hem blushed and stammered.

"Not me, the birds of the city . . ." he mumbled.

"There is more to you than meets the eye." Oslar stared into Hem's eyes and a gentle light bloomed in the boy's inner vision, as he felt the touch of the Bard's mind on his own. There was a short silence, and Oslar sighed. "I begin to understand why Saliman has kept you here, although he has his own Knowing, which is hidden from me. Is there any knowledge that does not sadden the knower? But many tasks call me. Come, Hem, I need you to care for those in the Room of Lanterns, which would free Urbika for me."

Hem followed Oslar, puzzling over what he had just said. What did Saliman think he could do in the war against the Nameless One? Now he had seen the scale of it, he didn't believe he could make any difference. But Saliman seemed to think he had some part to play. Perhaps he would tell him one day what it was.

In the Room of Lanterns, Hem tended patients with relatively minor wounds—fleshy lacerations or cleanly broken bones. Those who could walk did not stay in the Healing Houses, as there were not enough beds; instead, they were billeted out into the city, and came morning and evening to collect potions or salves or to have their dressings changed. It was peaceful in the Houses of Healing; the thick walls kept out the clamor of battle and the burning heat of the day. The wounded lay on their pallets without complaint, watching the sunlight that filtered through the grilled windows as it moved slowly around the pale blue walls, or talking quietly together. Most of the time Hem was on his own, and he walked confidently from bed to bed, attending to various needs—water here, a new dressing there, a salve or potion or charm to staunch pain somewhere else.

Hem had never been a boy much given to reflection, but in the cool, wide spaces of the Healing Houses, between one task and another, he found himself ruminating in a new way. It was a novel feeling to be placed in this position of trust, to be needed, and Hem decided that he liked it. The word had spread about the strange Annaren boy with a white bird who worked in the Healing Houses and had driven off the deathcrows. Strangers greeted him smilingly in the musical tongue of Turbansk, calling him by his nickname, *Lios Hlaf*, and they surrendered without question to his ministrations; no one caviled at his age. He liked the smiles of the warriors whose wounds he tended, their gentle thanks. He liked the feeling that he belonged.

He remembered himself when he first came to Turbansk: it was like thinking about a stranger. He felt no need now to be angry with the Bards; what had seemed to him in his initial ignorance to be patronizing and insulting, he now recognized as friendly respect.

Sometimes, despite the fact that he was treating wounded soldiers, Hem remembered that Turbansk was at war only when he left the Healing Houses for his evening meal and heard the faint noise of battle carried on the wind. The realization always came with a skin-tightening sense of shock, and induced a strange feeling of unreality: he was more at peace with himself than he had ever been, and yet he had never been in more danger. If only, Hem thought, he had not come here in time of war; if only he could stay here and learn the art of healing from Oslar.

At such times he thought of Maerad; he remembered a curious expression that had sometimes flashed across her face, when she looked at Nelac's students in Norloch. He thought he understood it now. Maerad had occasionally told him how much she wished she could stay in Norloch or in Innail or in Gent, where she could learn the scripts of Annar and the Seven Kingdoms, and study the lore of Barding. When she spoke of her desire to learn, her voice cracked slightly with emotion, since it seemed that it would never happen: instead of living the quiet, studious life of a scholar, she was fated to follow dark roads on a perilous quest.

To Hem, Maerad's regret had been mystifying: why would anyone want to work so hard on something that seemed so dry and dusty, when you could go off on an adventure? For Hem's mind was packed with heroic stories that he had made up to comfort himself in the darknesses of his childhood. But now he had encountered real danger, he found that, after all, Maerad was right. In the Healing Houses, a light kindled inside him: he had found something he wanted to do with his life, and he burned with the desire to learn its art. And yet, like Maerad, Hem had discovered what he wanted just as it seemed it was on the brink of being destroyed.

Now that the deathcrows no longer attacked Turbansk, he left his armor in his room, and looked at it askance when he came back to sleep. The thought that he might have to fight and kill someone filled him with a horror he dared not admit to Zelika. He hated the Black Army, and the terrible wounds he had seen in the children of Baladh had made his heart smolder with anger; he knew that the Dark had destroyed his family and blighted his life, but sometimes he wondered whether he could kill even a Hull. It made him feel ashamed. Even when the Hulls had threatened to cut his throat if he refused to murder a boy—long, long ago, it seemed now—he had not been able to lift his hand. He had no difficulty with breaking someone's nose, but extinguishing the life of another human being was different. He lacked Zelika's ruthlessness.

All the same, despite her vow to slay as many of the Black Army as she could, Zelika was working in the Healing Houses with Hem, and walked back with him to their rooms in the Ernan each night. He was slightly surprised that she had not demanded to go to the walls to fight alongside the soldiers there, but she had given him a mocking glance when he asked her why she had set aside her sword.

"I want to see their faces, when I kill them," she said. "I want them to see my face. Arrows are no good. And there will be plenty of time for killing, when the walls fail."

The cold confidence of her answer made Hem shiver, and he asked no further questions.

Over the following days, it couldn't escape even Hem's attention that the assault on Turbansk was increasing in ferocity.

The influx of wounded into the Healing Houses increased markedly, and the injuries were worse. Hem was called now to help Oslar with more serious cases in the room called the Chamber of Poppies—so called because the painkilling tincture distilled from poppies, madran, was used so often there. He saw soldiers with burns like those he had seen on the Baladh refugees, and heard, with a shiver of dismay, that the dogsoldiers were making their first assaults against the city. Each night now, as Hem wearily walked back to the Ernan for something to eat, he smelled burning on the soft evening air, and tasted a bitter grit of ash on his tongue. There were few nights of song anymore. Often he went back to the Healing Houses after the evening meal, since there were not enough healers to cope with the injuries, and worked long into the night. His fragile sense of peace popped like a bubble and disappeared altogether.

Zelika still came with him to work with Oslar, obediently and patiently plying the mortar and pestle to grind up medicinal herbs, or running errands. She too was looking strained and depressed, her mouth set in a grim line of exhaustion. She did not speak to Hem of fighting anymore, and in the few spare moments he had, Hem wondered whether the suffering she had seen had dulled her passion for revenge.

It could have been the heat, which was relentless. The days of late summer pounced on the city like a ravening lion. In times of peace, the streets of Turbansk would be empty after the morning dew had evaporated into the heat of the day, the population retreating to the inner rooms of their houses to sleep until the cool of the evening, when the city would again come to life. But now Turbansk was awake at all hours, pinned by the merciless sun as much as by the enemy at its gates.

Sometimes at night the city would take hours to cool down. Then those lucky enough to live in the inner city would sleep on the roofs of their houses, beneath the stars. Near the city walls it was too dangerous: the Black Army kept up a constant assault all night, every night, flinging into the city catapults laden with rocks or, more dangerously, liquid magefire—white-hot missiles with a red tail, which would sail through the night air with a strange and terrible beauty and land with a bloom of flame, setting alight everything around them.

Each successive day felt more grim, and a miasma of despair began to wind through the city like an evil mist. It was one thing to speak of fighting to the death against an enemy that could not be defeated, and quite another to stand, day after day, drained by the heat, while your friends were killed one by one around you, facing an army that remained, despite every small victory, as overwhelming as an ocean. If only the real assault would begin, some whispered, it might not be so bad—but the Black Captain waits and holds fire while the best of our strength is spent on minor skirmishes. The worst is yet to come.

Others called for a brave sortie against the enemy, to drive the army decisively back from the city walls, although anyone who looked could not but know this to be the most suicidal folly. And others still, in quiet voices, began to speak of leaving the city. Why die for a city that is already doomed? And they looked fearfully across the glittering surface of the Lamarsan Sea, where those with the sharpest sight could see a dark navy of ships grouped ominously in the distance. Perhaps we stay because we cannot get out, the whisperers said: the sea way is blocked, and we are trapped here, and will die whether we choose or no. It is too late, the whispers said, too late, too late . . .

Hem did not see Har-Ytan or Juriken again, and hardly saw Saliman. Underneath his every moment lay a dull dread that each brief conversation might be their last; he did not know what Saliman's duties were, but knew all the same that he was never far from danger. When he did see Saliman, the Bard was too tired to talk much, and he seldom smiled anymore. He would stare at Hem with dark inscrutable eyes, ask how he was, nod, and sink into silence.

Only Irc seemed untouched by the rising despair that pervaded Turbansk. He told Hem, with a hoarse chuckle, that it was a good time for him: he was building an impressive collection of shiny spoons, buttons, and other treasures filched from the palace, which he had hidden somewhere under the eaves of the roof. When Hem slept, he was comforted by Irc's presence, and often, as if he knew this, the bird did not sleep on his perch, but crouched on the boy's bed close to his body, crooning himself to sleep.

I X

THE EDGE OF DOOM

BECAUSE Hem was not a native of Turbansk or the Suderain, he did not know most of those he cared for. The men and women he tended were strangers to him, and he learned to steel his mind against their suffering, to do what had to be done to alleviate their hurts. If he had fully acknowledged the horror of everything he saw, he would have collapsed in distress, and been useless; so he turned his mind from that understanding, and concentrated instead on healing spells and salves, bone-setting and pain relief. It had not been so bad in the Room of Lanterns, where none of his patients had been in any danger of their lives; but now that he was helping Oslar again, he saw some terrible things.

On the fifth day a man was brought in on a litter. He had been above the West Gate, where the fighting was fiercest, and he had been hit by one of the evil projectiles that the Black Army was catapulting at the defenders on the walls. When these projectiles hit, they exploded in a deadly hail of spiked iron fragments and a form of magefire—liquid flames that burned into the skin of anyone luckless enough to be in the way. The man had taken the main force of the projectile on his right arm and shoulder, now a mess of ragged, burned flesh and barely recognizable as belonging to a human being. Another piece of metal had shattered into his stomach and, besides scores of lacerations over the rest of his body, his right thigh was smashed so badly that splinters of bone stuck out of the skin.

Hem took one look at the man and knew he was doomed; it was amazing that he was still alive. His skin had the gray, dusty hue of one who was already dead, and his breath was harsh and irregular. His face was spattered with blood, and around his mouth the saliva had dried into a white foam flecked with black. At least, Hem thought, he can feel nothing . . . But then, to the boy's astonishment and distress, the man turned his head and opened his eyes, looking straight at Hem. With a cold shock, which went down to the soles of his feet, Hem recognized Boran the coffee seller.

Hem was already holding the potion of madran, the poppy tincture that stayed pain, and gently he lifted Boran's head to drip it into his mouth. Boran stirred, and his blurred eyes suddenly became very clear and present. Even in his extremity, he tried to smile.

"It's the bird boy, isn't it?" Boran's eyes were fixed intensely on Hem, as if he were the only thing left in the world. Hem nodded.

"Hello, Boran," he whispered, leaning close to the man's face. "Drink this. It will help with the pain." He held the potion to Boran's lips, but he turned his mouth away.

"It will send me to sleep, huh? And I will not wake up." Boran winced, and struggled for breath.

"No, you will wake," said Hem, knowing he was lying. "It will be all right."

"Hey boy, I know the lies of healers." Boran swallowed convulsively, and his body shuddered. "Don't try to fool old Boran. I know I'm done for. I can't feel anything, anyway." He shut his eyes for a moment, and then stared intensely again at Hem, struggling to speak. Hem leaned closer to him. "I don't regret anything, boy," Boran said. "I fought with honor. I'm glad I sent my daughter away. But all the same . . ."

Boran shut his eyes, and, putting the potion to one side,

Hem wiped his forehead and mouth with a damp cloth, pity wringing his heart.

"All the same," said Boran, so quietly Hem could hardly hear what he said, "I would have liked to have seen her again. She is so lovely, my Amira, so lovely. She was lovely when she was born, and she is lovely now."

He lay very still, and Hem wondered for a moment if he were dead. But then Boran's eyes opened again. "If you see Amira, tell her that I love her," he said, in a voice that was suddenly clear and strong. "Tell her I will see her at the Gates, and that I thought of her when . . . I thought of her . . ." He trailed into silence, and Hem leaned over him, tears starting in his eyes.

"I'll tell her," he said fervently, taking Boran's hand, the one that was not shattered beyond recognition, in both of his own. "I'll tell her, I promise, I'll tell her." But Boran was already dead, his glazed eyes staring into nothing. A drop of water fell onto the still face, and Hem realized that he was crying.

Hem stayed bowed over Boran's corpse for a long time, until Oslar, who was attending another soldier with serious injuries, noticed him. The old Bard called another healer to take over his task, and came across to Hem and embraced him, saying nothing. Hem burst into convulsive sobs, and Oslar, with a strength that Hem had not suspected he possessed, lifted him up as if he were a small child and carried him next door into a tiny storeroom, where he put him down on a low bench and sat next to him, his arm around his shoulder.

"It was Boran, the coffee seller in the market," said Hem, when he could speak again. "He—he—he just—died."

Oslar nodded, staring at Hem with compassion and concern, and took his hand.

"I think, Hem, that I have been asking too much of you," he said at last. "You have such amazing untaught skill as a healer, and we have such need, I had forgotten that you are still a child."

Hem brushed the tears from his eyes with an impatient hand. "I'll be all right," he said gruffly. "I want to help. I'm not a baby."

"You are a child, Hem." Oslar looked at him soberly. "An unusual child, certainly. But a child, all the same."

"I hate war," said Hem, suddenly and passionately. "I hate all this killing. It doesn't mean anything. It's such a . . . waste. A terrible, terrible waste . . ." He felt the tears rising up inside him again, a whole sea of tears, which would still never be enough to express his grief.

"My dear, dear boy," said Oslar. He was too wise to give Hem any false comfort, and just held him close. They sat without speaking for a time. Then Hem remembered where they were and squared his shoulders.

"I'm taking you away from people who need you," he said. He looked up at Oslar, his face still swollen with tears, and the old Bard smiled, a sweet, gentle smile that held more sorrow than joy.

"There is no pain greater for a healer, than to be forced to tend wounds that he cannot heal," he said. "You are right, Hem. It is a terrible, terrible waste." There was a short silence.

"Well, back we go," said Hem.

"I think you should go home," Oslar said. "For a while."

"No," Hem answered. He stood up, and looked into Oslar's face, his whole body stiff with determination. "No, Oslar. You need me here; you said so. I couldn't go home, it would make me feel much worse. Let me stay."

Oslar studied Hem's face intently, as if measuring him, and smiled sadly again. "As you wish, my boy. You are right, I do need your help." He stood also, sighing heavily, and they walked without speaking back to the Chamber of Poppies, and started again on their work.

* * *

That night, Saliman joined Zelika and Hem for the evening meal. When he entered the room he looked at Hem sharply.

"What happened?" he asked, even before he greeted them. "Something happened today, yes?"

"Oh," said Hem unhappily. "The coffee seller in the market, Boran, he was brought in today, and he died." He didn't meet Saliman's eyes; he didn't feel like talking about it.

Saliman waited for Hem to say more, but when the boy remained silent he did not ask further. Zelika, who had been sitting quietly since they came home, glanced at Hem with a sudden quick sympathy.

They ate in silence. Halfway through their meal, Irc flapped in through the open window, landed heavily on the floor, walked over to Hem's foot, and gently pecked his ankle.

"Oh, go away," said Hem thickly, and kicked out at the bird. Irc flapped away with a caw of alarm and regarded the boy warily from a safe distance, ruffling his feathers.

Saliman leaned forward and clasped Hem's forearm. "Hem," he said.

Hem would not answer or look up.

"Hem, look at me."

Hem unwillingly lifted his eyes to meet Saliman's. What was he going to say? How sorry he was? Of course he was sorry. He saw sights as bad, or worse, every day. Everyone was sorry . . . But Saliman simply kissed the boy's forehead. Hem felt his lips warm on his skin, and from the kiss a light like a golden lotus opened and slowly flowered in Hem's chilled heart.

"Take care, Hem," said Saliman softly, letting go of his arm. "It is only the darkness in our own hearts that will defeat us, in the end."

Hem nodded wonderingly, feeling a new ease inside him.

He thought he began to understand why Oslar spoke of Saliman with such respect; healing was a matter of the mind as much as of the body. He looked across at Irc, who had turned his back on him and was preening his feathers huffily.

Irc, I'm sorry, he said.

Irc said the crow equivalent of "Hmmmph."

Come here, you silly bird. I have some torua for you.

Irc could never resist torua, a kind of spiced meat, and he swivelled his head over his shoulder and regarded Hem coldly, his yellow eyes unblinking. Hem held the meat out, and slowly, with exaggerated dignity, Irc stepped over to Hem and took it delicately in his beak. He was clearly very offended.

You're still not talking to me, said Hem. *Have it your way, then.*

You kicked me, said Irc, and fluffed out his feathers with indignation.

I said I was sorry.

Irc swallowed the torua and stropped his beak on Hem's sandal, which was the closest Hem was going to get to forgiveness. Hem lifted him onto his lap and scratched his neck, and Irc stretched out his head, his eyes slowly closing in bliss.

"Well, at least someone is happy," said Zelika sharply. "And all the rest of us can just sit around, waiting to be killed." And then she laid her head on her arms and burst into tears.

Hem stared at Zelika, astonished at her outburst. Zelika had certainly been quiet tonight, but he hadn't realized. . . . He put Irc down on the floor again and started up awkwardly, laying his hand on her back to comfort her, but she pushed him away and looked up, her face crumpled in woe.

"I—I'm not afraid of fighting," she said, hiccuping. "I *want* to fight. But this waiting, day after day after day . . . It's so horrible. I feel as if the whole city is slowly toppling down on top of me."

Saliman had watched the two children, his face unreadable.

"Sieges can go on for months," he said at last. "We have supplies enough to last through winter, if we can hold out."

"I know." Zelika sat up and pushed her damp hair out of her face. "I *know* that."

"But I do not believe that this siege will last that long," Saliman went on. "We hoped to hold off the Black Army for a couple of months, at least, to give Car Amdridh some breathing space. But Imank has only made two twists of the vice, and already the city trembles. And the Hull holds its major strength in hand. There is a main arrogance in these tactics, I would say: Imank is very sure of victory, and can wait for it, wait for us to crumble under our own weight; and then Imank will move."

"What does that mean?" asked Hem. During his days in the Healing Houses he had lost track of time, and of what was happening in the wider city. It seemed to him that Turbansk had been under siege forever; but when he thought back, he realized it was only about a month since the Black Army had arrived.

"It means that we are like a chicken on a chopping block, waiting for the blow to fall. It may come today, or next week, or not for weeks; but we all know it will come. And you must remember that Imank is not only a captain of soldiers, but also a mighty sorcerer; apart from the Nameless One, this Hull is the most powerful sorcerer in Edil-Amarandh. It is not just Imank's army that saps our will, steals the courage from our hearts and the strength from our arms, and sends evil dreams to plague our rest."

Zelika looked up, interested. "So Imank is magicking the whole city?"

"Something like that."

"Can't we magic back?"

"Of course we're magicking back," said Hem impatiently. He looked at Saliman's face, which had been gaunt with strain for weeks now, with a new understanding. "Isn't that so?"

"Aye," answered Saliman. "We fight on all fronts. And on all fronts, we are losing."

"We should do something else, then," said Zelika. Although her face was still damp with tears, a belligerent light flickered in her eyes. "Not just flap around while Imank the Hull does what it pleases. What have we got to lose?" She smiled. It was her frightening smile, reckless and fearless and more than a little mad, and Hem noticed Saliman staring at her curiously. He had not yet seen this side of her.

"Yes, Zelika, you are right," he said. "We have to wrest back the initiative from Imank. We have news today from Car Amdridh; they are ready, and our people have arrived there. We need not sacrifice ourselves to buy them more time. And so . . ."

Zelika's eyes sparkled. "And so?"

"We must first win back the sea route." Saliman leaned back. "Our people must be able to escape the city when it falls. For fall it will, and I think sooner rather than later. We must destroy the enemy fleet. But if Imank sees us coming, they will be ready for us; and so we are preparing an assault on the Black Army, to divert attention."

"Outside the gates?" said Hem, his eyes wide. "It's mad; everyone will be slaughtered."

"Yes," said Saliman shortly. "That is very likely. This is why those who fight in this battle will do so of their own free will. We are not Black Sorcerers like Imank, and we do not send our soldiers unwillingly to their certain death."

A terrible fear was building in Hem's chest.

"But you won't do that?" he asked, his voice cracking. "You're not going to—"

"Nay, Hem." Saliman smiled. "I am needed elsewhere. You

forget that I am a captain of the harbor forces. I will be sailing with the Turbansk fleet."

This was not much better. Hem bit his lip to stop himself saying anything.

"I'll go," said Zelika. "I'll volunteer."

"You will not." Saliman looked at her expressionlessly. "You will remain with Hem. I have other plans for you."

"I will go. They will not turn me away . . ."

Saliman stood up. "Zelika, I am not going to argue with you. If I need to lock you in a cage to keep you in the city, I will do so."

Zelika stood to face him, her lips drawn back from her teeth in a snarl, her nostrils quivering, and drew herself to her full height. Despite her slight figure, her rage made Hem quail. Irc discreetly retreated to the far wall; he was already familiar with Zelika's temper. "How dare you?" she said, with a quiet intensity that was more fearsome than shouting would have been. "How dare you speak to me like that? I will do as I like. You can't stop me."

The observing part of Hem watched Zelika with admiration, even as he warily got out of the way. She scarcely came up to Saliman's chest, yet she spoke with all the hauteur and arrogance of a queen.

"Zelika, of course I can stop you," said Saliman mildly. "I could pick you up with one hand, and I am not nearly so big as a dogsoldier. You would last outside the gates for about the space of three breaths, and before you died you would not make the smallest dint in the armor of the smallest warrior in Imank's ranks. You are not going."

For a moment, Zelika stood absolutely still. All her hauteur had fallen away, and her bottom lip trembled, as if she held back tears. Then something flashed in her eyes, and almost quicker than Hem's eye could follow, she had grabbed Saliman's arm. The Bard was too surprised to move, and with a strange twist, she seemed to pick him up bodily, and throw him across the table.

Irc cawed in alarm, as dishes and a carafe smashed on the floor and water splashed over the walls and furnishings. Saliman landed heavily on the floor and Zelika stood over him, breathing hard, crouched in a fighting pose. Hem backed against the wall, staring in mingled horror and astonishment. Saliman looked very angry indeed, and Hem wondered whether it might not be wiser to leave the room altogether. But before he could decide, Saliman had somehow leaped to his feet, as if he were pulled up by strings. Zelika whipped around to kick him, but he moved even more quickly than she did. She fell to the floor with a crash, and Saliman twisted her arm behind her back. Zelika writhed furiously, trying to loosen his grip, and he pulled her arm up savagely. She gasped in pain, and then seemed to collapse and lay without struggling further, her chest heaving.

"It is not wise," said Saliman evenly, "to try those tricks on me. Do not think, Zelika, that kindness equates to weakness. It does not."

A thick silence fell over the room, broken only by Zelika's panting.

"Will you attack me again?" Saliman asked.

Zelika shook her head. Slowly, he let go of her arm and she sat up, her curls straggling over her face, her black eyes bright with hate.

"Now, will you listen?"

Zelika stared at him. "You should not insult me," she said.

"I did no more than say truth. Did I not? You saw the dog-soldiers in Baladh, Zelika. If you so wanted revenge, why did you not attack them then? Why did you not harry the Black Army as they marched here? You had every chance: no one would have stopped you."

Now Zelika stared blankly at the floor, and Hem felt his heart constrict with pity. All her rage and hatred had evaporated as quickly as it had arrived, and she suddenly seemed like a small, very forlorn child.

"I was too afraid," she whispered. "And it made me ashamed."

"There is no shame in understanding what is the case." Saliman brushed some remnants of food off his robes. "You would have been swatted as easily as a fly, and your death would have made no difference at all. That is no way to seek revenge. So no more arguing; I do not wish to waste my time wrestling with a berserk child. I am your captain, and like a good soldier you will do what I command."

Zelika's bottom lip pushed out in a pout.

"Yes?"

"Yes," she said sulkily.

"Good. Well, first we ought to tidy up this mess. And after that, you will listen to what I have to say."

All three of them cleared up the remains of their meal—which had been flung all over the room—in silence. (Irc quietly stole the rest of the torua while no one was looking.) When the chamber was in some good order, if still a little damp, Saliman sat down on the cushions, waving the two children to do likewise.

"What an interesting evening we are having," he said pleasantly. "A change from our recent glum meals, anyway. All right, Zelika, I admit that you are not so bad at unarmed combat. You have given me a couple more bruises, which, frankly, I could do without. What you did not know is that I am counted among the best in the city, and if you had not surprised me, you would not have had a chance." He gave her a sly look. Zelika, uncertain whether he was mocking her, scowled down at her hands.

"You did land quite heavily," said Hem. He still felt a little stunned by the force of Zelika's temper, and watched her nervously, wondering if she was going to erupt again.

"I did," said Saliman. "Zelika is correct on one point: for those who are skilled in the arts of arbika-el, size is immaterial."

"I can fight," said Zelika, under her breath. Although she had been beaten, she didn't look in the least chastened. "I am the last of the House of Il Aran."

"The House of Il Aran is a family with many famed fighters, from a city that is a byword for warriors," said Saliman, glancing at Hem. "Most of Zelika's celebrated ancestors were a little bigger than she is, however, when they attained their fame."

Now Zelika was certain he was laughing at her, and her scowl deepened. Strangely, Hem thought, Saliman looked more cheerful than he had in days; the contretemps with Zelika seemed to have lifted his spirits.

"Nay, Zelika, don't frown so terribly." Saliman leaned forward and cupped her cheek in his hand. "You deserve a little teasing, after that display. I mean you no insult. Despite your skills in arbika-el—which I am very glad to know about—what I said earlier about how useful you would be in any foray outside the city remains true. I will not have you throwing away your life for no reason. I have other plans for you."

Despite herself, Zelika gave him a curious glance. "What plans?" she asked.

"It is now five nights from the full dark of the moon. We will make our assault from the walls and on Imank's navy three nights hence. We aim to win back the seaways, and gain some time in which all those who yet remain in the city can retreat over the Lamarsan Sea, back toward Car Amdridh. The retreat has been long planned, ever since we knew there would be a siege. But that is not the way I will go, and I think you two should come with me."

Hem's interest quickened. "Which way do you go?" he asked.

"North to Annar, eventually," said Saliman. "I think, Hem, that is your way; I do not feel I can give you to another's care, although I have thought of sending you to Car Amdridh with Oslar."

Hem gave an involuntary cry of protest.

"Hem, in many ways that would be the most sensible plan, and Oslar has asked for you to come with him," Saliman said. "But there are many strands of fate working now, and we must follow the right ones, and choose as well as we are able between one thing and the next. They are not easy choices; at the best of times it is very hard to know what is right. But nevertheless, I think that you must stay with me, and that we must find Cadvan and Maerad. You came south only so you would be safe; well, you are no safer here than in Annar, even if it is already ravaged by war. I see no reason for you to stay in the Suderain."

At the thought of seeing Maerad again, all the breath seemed to leave Hem's body.

"And what about me?" asked Zelika, her brows drawn together in a dark line. "Why should I go to Annar?"

"Because I say so," said Saliman quietly.

Zelika looked up and met his dark gaze. She said nothing for a moment, her face unreadable, and then, to Hem's amazement, slowly nodded.

"I will be a good soldier," she said. "For now."

In the coming days, the weather continued hot and breathless. The sun rose in a blue sky and sucked the moisture out of everything, and a punishing dry wind blew from the southern deserts. Night brought no relief, and even the cool interiors of the Healing Houses began to heat up, as the stone walls absorbed the sun during the day. If Hem went into the courtyard and stood in the fountain until he was dripping wet, he would be almost dry by the time he walked back inside.

His routine continued unchanged, in its strange parody of everydayness, but now he began to feel an increasing tension prickling the city. He still felt heavily depressed when he woke, and when he rested, exhausted after a day spent with the wounded, the dread that underlay everything would pounce on him. But he was too tired to remember his dreams, which was perhaps just as well.

On the second night the heat was unbearable. There was no escape anywhere, and despite his weariness he couldn't sleep and tossed restlessly in bed. At last he got up and walked into the courtyard outside his room, to look at the stars. There were no stars at all, but he was too tired and hot to wonder where they were; the blackness enclosed him with an oppressive languor. Not the smallest breeze stirred the black leaves of the trees, or cooled the sweat that made his skin slick and itchy.

Hem sat under a tree, listening to the cicadas, which were very loud tonight, the harsh cry of some night bird, the clicking and booming of the frogs, the night chatter of monkeys squabbling in the trees. It was deceptively peaceful, but his skin crawled with a strange restlessness, as if he were expecting something to happen any minute. If he listened hard, he could hear underneath the ordinary night noises the faint thunder and bray of battle noises, and he knew that as he sat there, people were struggling, that they were hurting and dying; but now it all seemed very far away. He leaned back against a tree, looked up, and swallowed. He would like some water. He would get some in a moment. He felt too heavy to move.

Then he sat up, sniffing, suddenly alert. Something had shifted, but he did not know what it was. Then a blessedly cool wind whispered against his naked chest, nuzzling him gently. He breathed out with inexpressible relief, stretching his arms and standing up, letting the wind play around his body and dry him off. For a time, the relief of that coolness was all he could think about.

The breeze swiftly picked up. Then there was a sudden gust of a stronger wind, ruffling his hair, and above him a rumble of thunder. Hem felt his hair prickle and stand on end. There was going to be a storm.

He wondered briefly if the Bards of Turbansk had planned this, or the Black Army, or if it was nothing to do with either of them, just the weather breaking in its natural pattern. He didn't know enough about the weather of Turbansk to be sure. Then he decided he didn't care. He stood in the garden, letting his skin drink in the delicious cool air, waiting for rain to fall. But there was no rain, and the cool breeze seemed to caress him in farewell and then disappeared. The heat sprang back, like a beast that had been lying in wait for its prey. Hem sighed with disappointment, and remembered how tired he was. He walked back to his chamber, fell on his bed, and slept.

The next day it seemed, if anything, even hotter, although the sun was hidden behind slate-gray battlements of cloud that stretched from one horizon to another. They bore down on Turbansk heavily, rumbling ominously with thunder. Every now and then a charge of sheet lightning would leap up from the south horizon, throwing a livid glare over the city.

Hem hadn't seen Saliman at all for the past two days, although he left daily messages at the Ernan, to let the children know that he was still alive. Zelika was still coming to the Healing Houses, patiently helping in the easier work, cleaning and making bandages and splints and medicines. She had been quiet and thoughtful after her confrontation with Saliman. The two children, as had become their recent custom, broke their fast silently together, yawning. They were preparing to leave the Ernan when Saliman entered the room. He was in full armor, and in a great hurry.

"Good, you're still here," he said shortly. "You will be needed at the Healing Houses today; Oslar has to arrange for all the wounded to be carried to the harbor. Then come back here and wait. I will come for you."

"Is it going to rain?" said Hem, stupidly he thought, once the words had left his mouth.

"Yes," said Saliman. "I doubt the clouds will break today, though. It will be a bad night. Oslar will send you back at the third bell, and there will be a supper set for you. I want you to wait until I come here."

"What if you don't?" said Zelika, her voice sharp and tight, as Saliman was leaving. It was the question on Hem's lips, but he did not dare to ask it. "What if something happens to you?"

"If I do not come for you, someone else will. Do not fear. Put on your armor, and pack anything you want to take with you. Be ready." He turned and looked intensely at Hem, his face stern, and said in the Speech, *Now it finally begins, Hem. There is no time for lament or sorrow or fear. If you love me, do as I wish, and remember that I love you and need you to be strong. If I do not come back, you will be taken care of. I will see you tonight, the Light willing. Expect me in the darkest hours.*

Hem nodded, his mouth suddenly dry. Saliman turned and vanished out of the door.

"What did he say?" said Zelika.

"He said that it begins, and that we have to do what he says," said Hem, staring after Saliman. Despite himself, his voice wavered. Maybe that's it, he was thinking; Saliman really thinks this time that he may go to his death. And he never said a proper good-bye . . .

Zelika pursed her lips. "About time," she said. And then, feeling as if his legs were made of water, Hem walked to the Healing Houses with her.

There was no sense of peace there today; the Houses were all ordered bustle. Wounded people were being lifted onto litters and carried down to the harbor through the alleys, even as others, newly wounded, were being carried in from the walls. Orderlies were loading huge baskets of supplies onto donkeys. Hem was immediately busy, dispensing madran or binding limbs so that they would not be damaged by movement. He noticed that the bandages he was given were made of strange materials, instead of undyed muslin.

"We are running short," he was told, when he questioned why he had bandages with flowers embroidered on them. "We go not a day too soon, I say." Hem nodded gloomily, and took the incongruously cheerful bandages back to the Chamber of Poppies. Here, he thought, there were many who should not be moved at all.

"Better that than being slaughtered here in their beds, Hem," said Urbika briskly, when Hem turned in dismay from a badly injured woman who was moaning with pain. He had already given her as much madran as he dared. Urbika gave Hem a tight smile. "There is no help for it, when the Black Army drives us."

"No, I suppose not," said Hem haltingly.

Urbika squeezed his arm, and moved on to the next soldier. Irc, who was perched as usual on Hem's shoulder, gently nibbled his ear. Hem scratched Irc's neck, obscurely comforted, and took a deep breath. He cast a sleep spell on the woman, hoping that it would not be too much with the madran, and supervised the orderlies who loaded her onto the litter. Then he moved on to the next task. He was feeling dizzy; things seemed to be moving too fast, after ages and ages when it felt like nothing was happening at all. And yet lots of things had been happening, he thought, confusedly. It was just all too strange, and too dreadful.

By evening, the Healing Houses had been emptied. Hem stood at the doorway looking forlornly down the road to the harbor, watching the last litters slowly wind their way through the evening shadows. It was already dark, with the clouds lowering overhead, and very hot; the air pressed on him with a stifling weight, and the setting sun lit everything with a strange, lurid glare. He felt stunned with weariness.

Oslar, who was to travel with the wounded, came to the door, a small cloth bag that held all his possessions slung over his shoulder.

"Well, Hem, we now go our different ways," he said.

Hem looked up at him miserably. "Yes," he said.

"I am sorry to leave you. Perhaps you do not know how much I have depended on you these past weeks, and how grateful I have been for your help. It was a heavy burden I laid on you."

Hem continued to stare down the road. "I don't want to go," he said at last. "I would have liked to stay with you."

Oslar put his arm around Hem's shoulders. "That is how it should be," he said. "Alas, things are seldom as they should be. I have only once had a student as naturally talented as you, and he too did not go the way of the healer."

"Who was that?" asked Hem curiously, twisting his neck to look up into Oslar's face.

"Saliman, of course," said Oslar, smiling. "He was my apprentice when he was not much older than you. But his burning desire was to understand the High Lore, and he traveled to Norloch to study with Nelac of Lirigon. It is, perhaps, possible to be too talented."

"Oh," said Hem, surprised. "I suppose that's how he knows Cadvan."

"Yes, he and Cadvan of Lirigon are very old friends," said Oslar. "He came back here, of course, since he is Turbanskian to the bone. I thought once he would be my successor. He travels other roads, alas; I shall always regret it. Our fates do not always unwind as we expect."

"No," said Hem, with an edge of resentment.

"Nay, do not be bitter, Hem, although these are bitter times." Oslar bent and kissed Hem's forehead. "I expect to see you again, the Light willing, when all this is over."

Hem looked up gravely into his face. "I've got a lot to learn," he said, although that was not at all what he wanted to say to this wise, gentle Bard, who had been so kind to him and whom he might never see again.

Oslar smiled, as if he understood what it was that Hem was unable to say. "Aye, my boy. All you need for learning is desire, and you have that. May the Light shine on your path."

"And on yours," said Hem fervently. Without saying anything more, Oslar stepped out onto the darkening road, and Hem watched him until he disappeared into the gloom. He felt bereft, as if a brief, shining chapter of his short life had closed forever.

X

THE WEST GATE

HEM waited for Zelika for some time at the doors to the Healing Houses, but she didn't come. At last, thinking she had probably gone ahead of him to the Ernan, he wandered moodily back to the palace.

The city lay deserted under the crushing heat, and the flags of the awnings in the marketplace hung sad and limp, rags of former joy. Irc had disappeared on one of his mysterious forays, probably to thieve some shiny object or other. Hem was worried; he did not know what was going to happen, and he did not want to lose Irc. On the way he bumped into Soron, and poured out his worries about Irc's absence.

"I *told* him," he said. "I told him to be here at sunset."

"He always turns up," said Soron. "If not now, he'll definitely be there for supper. And I'm sure Zelika will be at the Ernan. I'll come with you; I was going that way anyway."

Hem was grateful for the Bard's company. Busy at the Healing Houses all day, he had not had a chance to find out what was happening in the rest of Turbansk, and Soron was full of news. The diversionary force that was to attack the Black Army was, he told Hem, to be led by Har-Ytan herself.

"How do you know?" asked Hem, amazed. "I thought the attack was a secret. Does everyone know about it?"

Soron laughed. "No, not everyone. All the same, Turbansk is a town that loves rumor and gossip, and it would not surprise me if word had got out that something was to happen tonight."

But another thought had struck Hem. "Saliman said that everyone who went on that attack would be killed."

Soron looked somber. "Their chances are small, that is for sure; but I am certain that not all will die. They attack only to retreat. You see, when Baladh fell, Har-Ytan said that she would stand or fall with Turbansk. And she has chosen, if need be, to fall. But she will lead a stern fellowship of warriors, many of the flower of our ranks. And even among them, Har-Ytan is a mighty warrior in her own right. They will not be beaten easily, even by such forces as assail us."

Hem, thinking of Har-Ytan's statuesque figure, had no trouble believing that she was a mighty warrior. "But you haven't said how you know," he said. "Were you there at the planning of it?"

"Nay, I am not so important," Soron answered, with a deprecating smile. "No, I know for other reasons." He paused, and looked sideways at Hem. "When Har-Ytan said she was to lead the ranks, she called her sons and gave to her heir, Ir-Ytan, the ruby of the Ernani, which is the emblem of her power. He is to be the new Ernani, if ever Turbansk shines again after this darkest of nights."

Hem remembered his first sight of Har-Ytan in the magnificent throne room in the Ernan, standing as if she were sheathed in living flame, the great ruby ablaze on her brow. He breathed in sharply, feeling a great sorrow well up inside him.

"Then she believes she will die," he said flatly.

"She is as brave an Ernani as ever ruled this city," said Soron. "She faces death without fear. When I first came to Turbansk from Til-Amon and was presented to the Ernani, I thought I had never seen a woman at once so beautiful and so frightening. Yes, the thought of her passing breaks my heart. I am glad I have seen such a woman." He was silent for a few moments, and then continued. "Well, as I was saying. She gave the ruby to Ir-Ytan, and Mundar, her consort, became hysterical."

"Hysterical?" said Hem with interest, thinking of the languid, spoiled young man he had briefly met and disliked.

"He did not know that Har-Ytan planned to do this, I believe. And for all his faults—for I do not rank Mundar as among my favorites—he loves Har-Ytan with all his heart and soul. Unlike some who have been in his position, it is not mere self-interest that keeps him there. He rent his clothes and his hair, and smashed his head against the walls until blood ran down into his eyes. I've never seen anything like that—not even Har-Ytan could calm him."

Hem stared at Soron in astonishment; he could not imagine it. "By the Light! He didn't seem . . . I mean, I would have thought . . ."

Soron smiled a little sadly. "You are yet very young, Hem. But I hope you never have the occasion to feel such grief." Hem gave Soron a questioning glance that the Bard didn't notice; the boy thought privately that, however young he was, he knew quite enough of grief. But he said nothing.

"Anyway," Soron continued. "You healers were too busy to be disturbed, and so I was called to help. I brought my strongest teas and potions, and at last he quieted down. Har-Ytan stood there, in full battle gear, the Sun of Turbansk blazing on her breast, a sight to strike terror into any Hull: and yet there were tears in her eyes, as she kissed him farewell. She left the room without looking back."

Soron shook his head, remembering, and they walked for a time without speaking.

"Do you know what will happen tonight?" asked Hem at last.

"I know a little," said Soron, giving Hem a measuring look,

as if weighing whether to tell him more. "The world will be a sadder place by the end of this night, I wager. Turbansk will not stand. I go with you and Saliman, after the seaway is cleared."

"You're coming to Annar?" Hem said, pleased. He liked Soron.

"The Light willing. It is my home, after all, and in dark times one longs for home. I wish to fight there. But we do not head there first; we must meet up with some friends of Saliman's. There is yet work to do."

The palace was strangely empty; apart from the guards at the gate, they had seen no one. When they reached Hem's chamber, neither Zelika nor Irc were there, but a substantial meal was waiting on the low table in covered dishes. To Hem's relief, Soron stayed with him and shared his meal.

They ate in silence, and Hem stared at the bundles laid against the wall—his and Zelika's, packed and ready for their departure. Each moment he felt tension twist higher inside him; he wished he knew where everyone was. He put some food aside for Irc, and walked restlessly about the room, trying to calm down.

Outside, it was growing darker and darker. There was a sudden flash of lightning, throwing an ominous glare briefly over the room, and then a low rumble of thunder. Why wouldn't it rain? The pressure of the unburdened storm was almost as bad as everything else. Not far from Hem's room, in the Western Chamber, there was a huge water clock, which at every hour struck a silver bell. It struck now, and Hem jumped.

Soron, lying listlessly on a couch in the corner, watched Hem walking up and down.

"Sit down, Hem," he said.

Hem sat down, but in a short time he was up again, pacing the room. "I hope Zelika hasn't done anything stupid," he said. He was reflecting that her uncharacteristic obedience over the past few days had really been too good to be true. "And it's unlike Irc, not to be here for dinner."

"Irc will turn up. As for Zelika . . . well, if she has done anything stupid, as you say, there's nothing you can do about it. Have you tried to call your bird?"

"I did, and he did not answer. I hope nothing has happened to him. And what if he comes back here and we're already gone?" Hem went to the window and looked out into the breathless evening. It was not yet completely dark. "He won't be able to find us. I don't know where Saliman is taking us. And what's going on out there? I can't stand it, this waiting." He plumped down on some cushions, biting his nails, and then started striding around the room again. "Why did Saliman want me to wait here, anyway? It's unbearable."

Hem didn't speak his greatest fear, that Saliman might not come back at all. Perhaps he now stood at the prow of one of the great fighting triremes, staring ahead through the lapping darkness of the Lamarsan Sea toward the fleet of black ships that gathered malignly on the horizon. Perhaps already one of the terrible missiles of magefire had landed on the deck, splintering the frail wood, setting fire and death about it, and the great ship was sliding beneath the black surface of the waves.

Hem had seen too many times what happened to flesh and bone when one of those missiles hit a human being. He could imagine all too clearly Saliman's body torn and broken—floating burned and abandoned in the water. For a moment the vision was so vivid he was almost convinced it was true, that Saliman was already dead. He shook himself, and remembered that very few Bards came to the Healing Houses; Bards had ways of protecting themselves, after all. But Saliman would be at the thickest of the fighting. "The Light protect Saliman," he breathed to himself. "Oh, the Light protect him . . ."

"You're making me nervous," Soron said. He was sitting

languidly on a cushion, wiping the sweat from his brow. "What will happen will happen, Hem. There's nothing we can do about it."

Soron was right, Hem knew, but nothing would stay his anxiety. Another flash of lightning and a huge clap of thunder made him jump; the thunder was so loud that for a moment he thought the walls of the Ernan were falling down. Almost instantly a great flash of sheet lightning lit up the room.

"It's going to start raining," said Soron.

"It's felt like that for ages," Hem said. "But nothing has happened."

"It will. When the wind changes."

"What wind?" asked Hem.

A heavy silence fell between them, and Hem decided to go out into the garden. It was no cooler outside than inside, but it made a change. He lay down on the glazed tiles and stared up into the darkening sky, which trembled with small lightnings. He emptied his mind and tried to call Irc, investing the summoning charm with all his power and love. He had already attempted this once that evening, but had received no response, and he feared to hear nothing again: it made him very afraid that Irc was dead. Perhaps, in his insatiable curiosity, the bird had ventured too close to the battlements and had been hit by a stray arrow.

But this time he thought he felt a faint pull in his mind, an echo of a voice that could only be Irc's. It seemed very far away. Hem sat up, puzzled, and tried the mindtouch once more: again that faint pull. *What is that bloody bird doing?* he growled to himself. *Is he hurt, and unable to come? What is it?*

And where was Zelika? It was most likely that she had stolen away to be part of Har-Ytan's force, and the thought made him so furious he felt like punching the wall with his bare hand. How could she be so selfish? How could she lie to

Saliman? And she would probably be killed, and that would be the end of her. At least he need never again listen to her endless strictures on how badly he pronounced Suderain . . . a lump rose in his throat, and impatiently he wiped away the sudden tears that welled in his eyes. If she died, it would serve her right. If he ever saw her again, he would throttle her.

A sudden lightening of the atmosphere made him look upward. It felt as if all the air had been twitched up by some giant hand. There was a pause, as if everything held its breath, and then a gust of wind, and a small pattering sound that Hem couldn't at first identify. Then he realized it was the noise of isolated raindrops falling to the ground. A big, fat drop of rain splashed warmly on his face, and then another.

"I told you!" called Soron, from indoors. "You'd better come back in; it will start hammering down soon."

"I would like to get wet," said Hem. "You should come out here."

"You'll drown," said Soron. "You don't know what it's like." He came out with a lamp that glowed phosphorescent against the hot darkness, to listen to the rustle of the leaves in the wind. He and Hem stood without talking, staring up into the sky, waiting, as the soft drops fell one by one, and steam rose from the warm tiles. Then, as gently as it began, the rain stopped.

"No chance of drowning in this," said Hem.

"You wait," said Soron, and turned to grin at Hem. "It won't be long."

At that moment, Hem heard the clear call of a trumpet. Not the harsh braying of the trumpets of the Black Army, but a trill of clear, melodious notes, which were almost immediately answered by another. As it died away, it seemed to resonate in his mind, as if it had been a flowing script written in silver over the dark sky. Soron cocked his head, listening, and drew a deep breath.

"Har-Ytan's flourish," he said. "Aye, well. May the Light be with her, and with all who fight with her."

Hem felt a cold dread, as if his insides had suddenly been replaced with empty space. He sharpened his Bard hearing, but he could make nothing of the noises he heard; a jumble of thunder, and confused rumblings.

After what seemed like ages, there was another long, loud peal of thunder, and then a crash that could have been thunder, but wasn't. Hem stared at Soron, his face harshly lit by sheet lightning that covered the entire sky.

"What was that?" he asked.

"I don't know," Soron said.

"It sounded like—like the gate falling," Hem said in a low voice. He stood in an agony of listening, his eyes dark and fearful.

"Maybe." Soron wiped his face again. He didn't like the heat, and sweated profusely and uncomfortably. "It's hard to tell."

"Do you think they have broken the West Gate?" Hem turned to Soron, his eyes large and liquid in the dark.

"It could be," said Soron steadily. "We will find out in due course."

"Where's that bird?" Hem said again, uselessly. The place on his shoulder where Irc usually sat seemed to ache with emptiness. As if to answer his question, the rain began again, a few large drops at first, making darker spots on the tiles by his bare feet, and then the spots joined together into one darkness and the pattering rose into a constant roar. It happened so quickly that he was drenched before he could react. The rain came down as heavily as a waterfall, striking back up from the ground in a spume about their feet. It poured in solid streams off the roof of the Ernan.

Hem and Soron stumbled back inside, dripping. They could hear nothing except the downpour, and, faintly above it, the rumble of thunder. Being indoors felt like being underwater. It was still warm, but the dreadful choking pressure had gone away.

"I told you what it was like," said Soron, blinking water out of his eyes.

"How will they fight in this?" asked Hem. "The rain's so heavy, you can scarce see a hand in front of your eyes."

"Saliman and Juriken knew the rain was coming," Soron answered. "I think they may have summoned it."

Momentarily, Hem brightened. "Yes, I'm sure you're right," he said. "It must have been part of their plans." But then he thought of Irc. "There's no way Irc can get back now," he said mournfully.

"He'll manage," Soron said kindly. "He's a very clever bird. I'm sure he'll find a way. As for Zelika—"

"If she ever gets back here, I'll throttle her with my bare hands," said Hem blackly, and started furiously gnawing his fingernails. "If she gets back . . ."

He stared out into the moving darkness.

As Hem had suspected, Irc had gone on an errand to filch a treasure, an earring he had spotted on the ground near the Healing Houses, sparkling in the dim light. Someone had obviously dropped it, and it stirred his covetousness. Late in the afternoon, while Hem was busy with the last of his patients, Irc had flapped off in search of his prize.

It was gone: although Irc searched the whole area diligently, he could find no sign of it. Disgruntled, he perched on a nearby tree and preened his feathers crossly. It was then that he saw Zelika stealing out of the Healing Houses, looking around cautiously to make sure that no one saw her. Furtively she stole down the street, and turned into one of the covered alleys.

Zelika's manner piqued Irc's curiosity, and he swooped

down and followed her. With unusual guile, he took great care to remain hidden; there were plenty of old awnings and trees to hide behind if Zelika, as she often did, turned to check whether she was being followed. She hurried to the Ernan, saluted the guards, and passed inside. To his frustration Irc couldn't follow her: the guards shooed him away.

Irc was now beside himself with curiosity about what Zelika was doing: he was quite certain she was bent on mischief, and although he was a little afraid of her, she attracted and charmed him. Impatiently he perched on a wall opposite the gate to the Ernan and waited to see if she would appear again, passing the time by squabbling with a couple of meenahs, the loud-voiced birds who usually spent their time scavenging the market for scraps. Since he had taken on the mantle of the King's messenger and not even the crows dared to harass him anymore, most of the local birds had begun to find Irc rather irritating. He took no notice of territorial boundaries and felt his status entitled him to be rude to anyone he chose.

His quarrel proceeded noisily, with satisfactory insults on both sides, until the meenahs gave it up and flew away, shrieking more abuse as they went. Irc fluffed his feathers and stropped his beak triumphantly on the wall. He was just wondering whether to fly back to the Healing Houses when Zelika emerged from the Ernan, dressed in full armor.

Irc almost didn't recognize her in her new attire: what gave her away was her caution. She looked carefully up and down the street, but didn't spot Irc. She began to walk quickly toward the West Gate.

It was now nearing twilight, so it was easier for Irc to remain unseen in the long shadows. He flapped slowly along, following her at a discreet distance, until they reached the huge square before the West Gate. It was thronged with ranks of soldiers, all in full Suderain battle dress. Nearer the gate were

ranks of horsemen, their heavy mounts standing patiently in
the heat.

Irc could count, but only up to five (a useful disability for
Hem, who regularly emptied Irc's treasure troves—as long as
he left five objects, the crow didn't notice anything was missing). The numbers here were well beyond his counting; it was a
flock of human beings, filling the entire square, swelling into
the broad roads that ran off it. Yet, for all their numbers, there
was very little noise. Among the press of people the air was
close and heavy, but a weight and tension lay over the soldiers
that was due to more than the heat; the somberness of this gathering impressed even Irc.

The soldiers stood or squatted in orderly rows, the golden
emblems on their breasts shining dimly in the gloom, or flashing
weirdly now and again in the dry lightnings that illuminated
the dark clouds. Some talked quietly together; others were
making last checks of their battle gear, testing the edges of their
blades, and throwing knives, while others merely sat, staring
silently at the ground.

Zelika stopped, and stood hesitantly at the edge of the
square. No one took any notice of her. Fearing to lose sight of
her among the crowd, Irc flew much closer than he had dared to
before, perching on an ancient lintel to keep his eye on her.

Irc was a very intelligent crow, but his understanding was
still that of a bird. He had no idea what Zelika was doing, as he
didn't understand the intricacies of the arguments that she had
had with Saliman. However, his crow cunning, honed in his
own thieving, told him that she was doing something wrong:
he thought it was likely that she was seeking to steal a treasure
of her own, which might be of interest to Irc himself. He was
puzzled by her being here among the soldiers, in the shadow of
the city walls: there could be nothing precious here.

Irc avoided the walls of Turbansk, as they were dangerous

places where burning things might appear out of nowhere and explode, and where the mind-destroying noise of the Black Army—the constant throb of the war drums and the scream of trumpets—became clear and terrible. Over everything rose the smell of blood and rotting flesh and burning, made pungent by the heat. Being a crow, Irc had no objection to carrion: but here the stench frightened him. It was at the walls that you knew Turbansk was at war; deeper inside the city, it was easier to ignore.

Out of habit, Irc idly scanned the closer soldiers in case there was something he could add to his treasure trove. In doing so, he inattentively hopped off his perch onto the ground, and he also took his eye off Zelika. This was a mistake, for Zelika turned and, for the first time, spotted him.

Zelika's response was immediate and violent. She launched herself at Irc and caught him, first by one wing, and then by his feet. Panting with rage, she scrambled up, holding him upside down. Flapping furiously, Irc hung from her hands, screaming with fright and anger, twisting his neck to try to peck her. She held him at arm's length to keep out of range of his beak.

"You scrawny piece of fish bait," she spat. "I might have known you'd be spying on me. I ought to wring your filthy neck!"

While Irc could not understand what she said, the general gist of it was clear enough. He doubled his cries of alarm.

"Shut up, or I'll *kill* you."

Swiftly she took a leather thong from her waist and tied Irc's feet together, so he was trussed like a chicken. Irc screamed crow obscenities the entire time. Now his fright was overtaken by his outrage: how dare she treat him, Irc, the King's messenger, like this?

The small scene was beginning to attract notice. Zelika, still holding Irc by his feet, looked around desperately, and tried to clamp his beak shut with her hand. He stabbed her viciously. He was a heavy, powerful bird, and at this point she let go of him. He fell to the ground on his back and twisted desperately, trying to get airborne. But Zelika grabbed him again, and held him so hard that she was really hurting his feet. Ignoring the blood that ran down her hand, she finally got hold of his beak and held it shut. It did not stop Irc's shrieks; they were merely muffled. Now he really did think she was going to wring his neck.

"So, what's going on here?"

Somebody lifted her helm from her head. Outraged, Zelika looked up into the hard, weather-beaten face of Inhulca of Baladh, the Bard she had briefly met weeks ago on the top of the Red Tower. She opened her mouth to answer, and then shut it again. He was regarding her with open amusement.

This stung Zelika's pride; she realized how ridiculous she must look holding an outraged bird, like a peasant woman at a market. She dared not let Irc go, because he would at once go back and tell Hem. So she hung on to the heavy bird, pretending that he was not there, and stared defiantly back at the Bard, who was studying her with lively interest.

"You're the little girl from Baladh, no?"

At "little girl," Zelika felt like spitting. She turned to walk away, almost in tears of anger. It was all going wrong. But Inhulca was too quick for her, and caught her arm in a grip that she could not shake off.

"And that bird you have there, that is *Lios Hlaf*'s crow, isn't it? I think you should not treat it so harshly; some here have reason to be grateful to this creature."

"He's just a little sneak," said Zelika hotly. "He followed me here. He's nothing better than a dirty spy."

"Perhaps." The amusement vanished from Inhulca's face as suddenly as if a light had been extinguished. "But I think the bird is probably correct to be suspicious. What are you doing here? You have no business at the gate."

Zelika drew herself up to her full height. "I have every right to avenge my family," she said. Even holding a squawking Irc, she achieved a surprising measure of dignity.

Inhulca regarded her with raised eyebrows. "And what family is that?" he asked.

"The House of Il Aran," said Zelika arrogantly. "You are Baladhian; you will understand my right."

Inhulca was silent for a moment. Then he looked at Irc and said in the Speech, *Hold your tongue, bird. She is not going to kill you. If she were, she would have already broken your neck.*

Irc was so surprised he stopped screaming at once, and twisted his head around to stare at the Bard who had spoken to him.

"You are in the ward of Saliman of Turbansk, if I remember rightly," Inhulca said. "I think that he would not be pleased to know that you are here."

"He's not my family," said Zelika. "You have no right . . ." She struggled against his grip, but could not loosen it.

"You are a child," he said.

"I'm not a child!" Zelika shouted.

"A child," Inhulca repeated coldly. "And despite your illustrious house, you very obviously have no idea what battle entails. An inexperienced soldier in a battle like this one can cost lives. Even one life at our own hands is too much." He glared at Zelika with such ferocity that even she quailed. "Do you understand?"

She gulped.

"Do you understand?" His grip tightened on Zelika's arm, and she nodded.

"And you are a nuisance. I cannot leave you here. And I do

not trust you." Inhulca contemplated her briefly and seemed to reach a decision.

"You will come with me. Quickly, time is running short, and the rains will soon begin, if I am any judge of weather."

He gave a couple of peremptory orders to the soldiers who stood nearby, and then led a resisting Zelika, who still carried Irc, at a trot through the crowd to a turret near the West Gate. Inside it was close and hot, and Zelika felt sweat trickling down her back as Inhulca pushed her up some dark, winding stairs to a room two floors up. Inside, grouped around a plain wooden table on which stood a jug and goblets, were the First Bard Juriken, Har-Ytan, and two others. They turned curiously when Inhulca entered with his strange charges.

"A couple of unexpected arrivals," said Inhulca shortly, casting Zelika's helm onto the table. "I must return to my rank. These are Saliman's, I believe; I leave them here, for your decision." He finally let go of Zelika's arm, and said to her: "Remember what I said."

Zelika scowled at him blackly. Irc, dangling forgotten and bruised by her side, gave a small caw, and unconsciously she lifted him up and cradled him in her arms.

"Very gracious," said Inhulca sardonically. "I hope we will both live to see the day that you will remember this, and thank me." He nodded to the others, and left swiftly.

Zelika stood awkwardly, feeling her anger drop away, to be replaced by something like shame. Juriken and Har-Ytan were staring at her in astonishment and irritation.

"Zelika of the House of Il Aran, why are you here?"

Har-Ytan's voice was not raised, but the force of her displeasure cowed Zelika like nothing else had. She bowed her head, suddenly overwhelmed by humiliation. She realized that they thought her exactly the same as a naughty child who unwittingly drops and breaks a precious object, because it knows no better.

"I came to fight, Your Brightness."

"To fight in this last desperate stand is not an honor we give to children." Har-Ytan's voice was cold and hard. "There are many great warriors who offered their services tonight, and who were assigned to duties elsewhere, where they are more needed. Each one of them was more worthy than you."

"Yes, Your Brightness." Zelika bowed her head, feeling her ears burning with shame.

Without speaking to her further, Har-Ytan turned away. Zelika felt about as big as a thumb. She looked around the room, wondering where she could sit. It was a very small, windowless room, probably a guardroom, and there was nowhere to hide. Nobody took any notice of her, and perversely it made her feel more in the way. She pressed herself against the wall, trying to make herself as small as possible.

"The weather will soon break, Fountain of the Light," said Juriken, with a gentleness in his tone that made Zelika look up.

"Yes." Har-Ytan stood very still, and for a moment it seemed to Zelika that her form was surrounded by a nimbus of light. She stood tall and stern and graceful, in the shining blue and gold of Turbansk battle dress, and Zelika thought she had never seen anyone look so beautiful, or so sad. Then slowly Har-Ytan drew her sword, and held it in front of her eyes so the blade gleamed in the dim lamplight.

"I go now, into the Dark," said Har-Ytan. "I shall not return. May my blade bite deep into its heart."

She met Juriken's eyes, and they exchanged a deep look. To Zelika's surprise, the Bard stepped forward and embraced the Ernani, and kissed her on the mouth. He stood back, and bowed his head.

"Go then, my Queen. May the Light go with you."

Har-Ytan was flanked by her two senior captains: the Captain of the Sun Guard, Il Hanedr, and Menika, the chief warrior of Har-Ytan's personal chamber. Menika was a tall, thin, very dark, very tough woman, whom Zelika had never heard speak. Il Hanedr knelt before Har-Ytan, and she briefly laid her hand on his head.

"My Queen," he said. "It pains me sore."

"Aye, it does, Il Hanedr," said Har-Ytan. "But would you have me countenance the slaughter of all the flower of my city? I must give thought to afterward, as must you, if we are not to lose for all time. You must guide my son, and lead my people hence."

Il Hanedr kissed her hand, and then wordlessly embraced Menika. Then the two women walked out of the guardroom and onto the inner wall, where a walkway ran over the top of the West Gate. Zelika heard a faint cheer rising from outside, which was drowned in a long rumble of thunder.

Il Hanedr and Juriken both sat without speaking for a time in a room that seemed much darker than it had before. Il Hanedr lifted his head and Zelika, glancing shyly over from the wall, saw that tears stood in his eyes. She was shocked and embarrassed that such a captain, to Zelika a real hero, should be seen in such a moment, and she stared down at Irc.

At least the crow had enough sense to be quiet here, she thought. Suddenly overcome by remorse for how she had treated him, and for her whole sorry, futile adventure, she sat down, crossing her legs, and gently untied the thong with which she had bound his feet.

To her surprise, Irc did not move at first. The truth was that she had tied his feet so tightly that he could hardly feel them and he was, in any case, bruised and sore. Then, finally realizing he was free, Irc hopped away from her lap, and fell over.

Biting her lip, Zelica reached out to catch him. She feared

she had broken his legs; Hem would never forgive her. Irc let out a sharp caw and stabbed at her hand, shuffling away from her.

I suppose I don't deserve any better, thought Zelika. *I am nothing. I am nothing but shame.* She hid her face in her hands.

Irc hobbled to the other side of the room, where he watched Zelika warily. Il Hanedr spoke to Juriken and also left the guardroom. Now there were only Zelika, Juriken, and Irc.

The Bard sat in silence for a time, and then sighed and stood up.

Now, White Crow, he said to Irc in the Speech. *Your friend will be waiting for you, fearing you are dead.*

I didn't want to come here, answered Irc sulkily. *She brought me. And now my wings hurt and my feet hurt.*

Juriken laughed. *I am sorry for that,* he said. *But nevertheless, we must leave here. I have business at the Ernan, and it will rain soon.*

Rain?

Juriken crossed the room, squatted next to Zelika, and put his hand on her head. She didn't look up, but a feeling of peace spread from his touch. She began to feel a little better.

"Zelika," said Juriken softly. "Forget your pride. This is no time for such things. You will have to come with me. No foolishness, now."

The girl nodded meekly, and stood up, her armor rattling too loudly in the small room. Juriken, she noticed, wore no armor, just the plain red robe he always wore.

Irc felt too bruised to fly, and did not dare to sit on Juriken's shoulder, so he had to swallow his pride and sit on Zelika's. She did not push him off, as he half expected she might.

Juriken led the girl along the inner walkway, away from the West Gate, and entered another tower. They climbed another small spiral stairway, until they emerged onto another inner wall, this one higher up. Panting, Zelika followed him up a short flight of steps and found she was in a small roofless lookout. Here it was quieter than at the West Gate, although the constant noise of the Black Army, the drums and trumpets and shouts that had underlain Zelika's life for weeks now, was still loud. Juriken glanced up into the sky, his face briefly illuminated by lightning, and Zelika involuntarily followed suit. The sun had vanished beneath the horizon, its last glow gilding the thick clouds that pressed down on them.

The archers in the lookout bowed their heads and moved aside for Juriken, and the Bard stepped up to the parapet and looked over it.

"We will watch from here, for a time," said Juriken. "Then I must return to the Ernan, where you are supposed to be already."

Irc flew up to the wall, and then flapped back in alarm as an arrow zipped over their heads with an unpleasant whirring sound. Juriken said something that Zelika couldn't understand, and the air seemed to change around her, gaining a brief, strange luminosity.

"The Black Army does not sleep. This will protect us from stray arrows," he said. Zelika looked at him dubiously; she was still a little suspicious of Bardic magery. Then she stood on her tiptoes, and found she could just see over the edge of the parapet.

Before the walls, there was an empty space for some two hundred spans. Then there was a thicket wall of tall, black shields and, behind them, a long row of tents. And then another row, and another, stretching back until they vanished into the thick dusk. Between the tents, Zelika could see figures walking. It all looked very still and orderly.

"Watch the West Gate," said Juriken. "And look also to the north."

Zelika stared to her right, and drew in her breath sharply. From here, they had a clear view to the gates. There, where the fighting had always been thickest, there were no tents. There was the same space before the gates, where the Black Army kept out of bowshot, and then the line of shields. As Zelika watched, a fiery missile arced into the sky, smashed into the city walls, slid down, and exploded on the ground outside in a red bloom of flame. A huge siege engine stood farther back, a sinister outline against the sky, and another behind it. The sky flashed, and in its livid light Zelika saw that the whole ground was a mass of moving figures, which seemed to seethe like a single, threatening creature under the heavy clouds. Now it was almost dark, and the fires behind the enemy lines flared bloodily.

There was another roll of thunder. Zelika's hair prickled all the way down her back; she was beginning to think that she would burst with tension. Why was nothing happening? Then she saw a sudden flurry of arrows and other missiles from above the West Gate.

"It's beginning," said Juriken. "Watch."

A long, high note rang out over the field: the flourish of a trumpet. Briefly its pure music sang defiantly against the darkness and fire, and then faded away. The trumpet call stirred Zelika's blood—not with the desire to kill, but with a sudden lifting of her heart that was entwined with an almost intolerable sadness. It was in that moment that she understood what it meant if Turbansk really was about to fall to the Black Army. She wondered why the fires had become blurred, and then realized that, despite herself, she was crying.

Then it seemed as if the trumpet was answered, as another flourish sounded to Zelika's left. Wondering, she looked along the walls toward the North Gate. She turned to Juriken, a question forming on her lips. He glanced at her, and smiled grimly.

"We do not attack only on one front," he said. "Imank might think it a trap."

As the trumpet notes died away, the North and West Gates began to open. And as they opened, the Turbanskian forces flooded out into the field with an amazing swiftness, illuminated by the almost constant flickering of the lightning: two seas of dull gold and blue and silver pushing against the somber darkness. Zelika saw the blue-and-gold banner of Turbansk standing out in the wind, and also the silver sword of Baladh, the crimson horse that was the symbol of the Alhadeans. First came the horses: ranks of Alhadean and Bilakean archers, and a rank of the mounted Sun Guard. After them marched the foot soldiers. They seemed so many that Zelika blinked. The Black Army seethed and swirled, as captains reacted to the attack and marshaled their forces to meet the two prongs of the Turbanskian ranks, and a faint shouting reached Zelika's ears. The front ranks of the riders crashed into the line of shields, and the Black Army shivered under the impact, and fell back.

It was hard to make out what was happening in the gathering darkness; Zelika followed the banners, which shone dully, the gold sun and the silver sword and the red horse, as their forces spread and met and began to fight on a single front. In the initial shock of their attack, the Turbansk forces pushed through to one of the siege engines, and as she watched, the huge machine slowly toppled over, crushing many people beneath it. The soldiers around Zelika cheered, but Zelika made no sound, biting her lip so hard that she drew blood. Where was the crimson horse? The sun banner had vanished; it had fallen. No, it was risen again; perhaps the herald had been killed, and another had picked it up. Zelika knew that Har-Ytan would not be far from the banner. The fighting was now very fierce, but it seemed that unbelievably, step by step, the Turbanskian forces were driving back the Black Army. It could only be sheer will: they were hopelessly outnumbered, and yet their line stood unbroken.

But even as she watched, Zelika saw great beasts coming from the back lines toward the Turbanskian forces, beasts that breathed gouts of flame and had huge blades jutting from shoulder and snout and knee joint, ridden by figures that were themselves wreathed with fire. They carelessly trampled the smaller figures of the Black Army as they forced their way forward to the front line. Zelika drew in her breath sharply; these were the irzuk, beasts made of iron and flame ridden by dogsoldiers. She had seen them at Baladh, and knew that no warrior, no matter how strong, could withstand them. But behind them marched things she could not name that froze her heart. These were dark manlike creatures that stood thirty spans tall or more, yet for all their size were hard to fix in the eye: they seemed to be woven out of shadow and vapor, and their movements were more sinisterly threatening than even the irzuk. They seemed to wade through the fighting soldiers as if through shallow water, and where they walked, all—foe or ally—fell to the ground. As they approached the front lines, the bright banners of Turbansk wavered and retreated.

"Mauls," said Juriken, watching closely at her elbow. "Haunts of shadow and mist and disease summoned by the sorcerers. We expected them: they are deadlier by far than dogsoldiers, and neither iron nor fire will hurt them. The Bards will keep them back for a time, if they can. But the mauls cannot withstand rain."

He stared up at the dark clouds, as if commanding them to burst, and as he spoke a warm drop of rain fell on Zelika's face. Then another. In a few moments, with a blinding suddenness, the rains came down.

She squinted desperately through the rain, but it was so

heavy that she could barely see a hundred spans. Irc squawked in protest and jumped onto Zelica's shoulder, trying to nestle in underneath her hair.

"We will not see anymore," said Juriken, shouting over the roar of the rain, although he too stared into the gray darkness, as if his sight could pierce its thick curtains by its sheer intensity. Then, with a sudden resolve, as if he had finally made his mind up about something that had been troubling him, he took her elbow and guided her back into the turret. The rain was not so loud inside. Zelika gasped with relief at being out of the downpour, and brushed her soaking hair out of her eyes.

"What's going to happen?" Zelika turned to Juriken, all her previous complaints forgotten. A thin stream of water poured down her face and off the end of her nose and chin.

"Many people will die, are dying now, on both sides. And most of them will not deserve such deaths as they will suffer." Juriken turned to look at Zelika, and for a moment it was as if he had forgotten that he was speaking to a young girl. His face was haggard, and his shoulders sagged with weariness or grief. "Tell me, Zelika, does a slave deserve to die? For Imank drives many slaves: those forces are not merely Hulls."

"They're attacking us," Zelika said, puzzled by Juriken's words. "I don't feel sorry for them. They want to *kill* us."

Juriken's gaze focused on Zelika, as if he returned from some inner distance.

"Aye, Zelika," he said gently. "Nevertheless, fear and lies and hatred and despair are all enslavements, and are to be pitied. Well. May the Light keep them all." Wiping away the water, he passed his hand over his face, and Zelika saw with astonishment that it was trembling.

Zelika suddenly wondered how old he really was: she had heard Bards were long-lived. Juriken suddenly seemed hundreds of years old. But he gave her no time to ponder.

"Now we must hurry," Juriken said. "We must go back to the Ernan, where you will wait with Hem, whom I assume has done what he has been told to do; and thence I will go to my own tasks."

As he spoke, there was a huge crash, and the tower walls shook. Irc flapped up in alarm, and settled shakily back onto Zelika's shoulder. Right now, he just wanted to get as far away from the city walls as he possibly could; being there was giving him a very bad feeling.

"What was that?" asked Zelika, her eyes huge and dark in the torchlight.

"Imank seizes the chance," said Juriken, "and will take it in claws of iron. The Hull thinks that we sought to drive its army off; and the gates are now open and the spell barriers can be broken. That was magefire that has been thrown against the walls. Imank brings in the big weapons now."

"What if the gates fall?" asked Zelika. As if a shield had fallen from her, all her pride and anger had vanished; and underneath she found she was afraid, terribly afraid, as she had not been before. She remembered the dogsoldiers in Baladh, the slaughter she had witnessed there, and her heart fluttered in her throat like a trapped butterfly.

"The gates will fall," said Juriken expressionlessly. "The wager is that they will not fall just yet. The Light willing, all will go well now. The Light willing . . . Now, we must go!"

XI

THE CAVES OF LAMARSAN

THEY hurried through the dark, empty streets. There was no wind; the rain fell straight and heavy, soaking them to the skin. Rivers ran in the stone gutters, and the trees drooped in the deluge, as if they were all weeping. They are mourning the city, Zelika thought, as if they know what is going to happen here.

There was a strangeness in Juriken's manner that filled Zelika with a dread beyond the fear she already felt. Even Irc was uncharacteristically quiet, and simply clung grimly to Zelika's hair, trying not to fall off her shoulder as he was bumped around in their haste. At last they reached the gate to the Ernan. To Zelika's disquiet, the gate was unguarded, and the Bard and his strange companions passed unchallenged through the spirals of atriums and courtyards and rooms into the wide Western Chamber of the palace. It was not far from there to Hem's room.

Zelika slowed down as they neared it. She had not thought of what she would say to Hem. He would be angry with her, and she did not like the idea. Since her dressing down by Har-Ytan, Zelika felt as if she had no skin, as if all her feelings were raw flesh. She could not bear it if Hem were angry with her too. She knew he had every right—she had lied to him, and she had nearly killed the bird who was his dearest friend. But, she reminded herself, lifting her chin, she was Zelika of the House of Il Aran. If she had acted with dishonor, she must take her punishment without complaint.

When they entered the room, Hem and Soron stood up, and Hem ran toward them, his face alight with relief. Irc cawed and flew to Hem's shoulder and gently pecked his ear. Hem tickled the crow's neck, his lips trembling.

"Greetings, Juriken," said Soron gravely, coming to meet the Bard. "I see you bring two who have been sorely missed."

"Aye," said Juriken. "I am glad to see that you and Hem, at least, are here. Forgive my shortness: I must meet Il Hanedr here, and then be gone to the School. The Light go with you!"

"And with you, Juriken," said Soron. He took Juriken's hand, and looked soberly into his face, and his expression changed. Quite suddenly, he embraced him. "It has been one of the joys of my life, knowing you, these past years. You have been a good friend to me. I fear we shall not meet again, this side of the Gates."

Juriken met his gaze. "I think not, brother. In these darkening times, many things will pass, never to come again. Farewell, Soron."

The two Bards stood in silence for a few moments longer, as if they spoke without words. Then Juriken turned to Hem and Zelika.

"Farewell, you two children," he said. "I think that perhaps Har-Ytan was right, when she said that the dreams of our young may lead the way through the shadows that beset us. If she is right, I deem that it will go hard with you. May fate be kind to you both."

Hem swallowed and nodded, and without saying anything further, Juriken left the room. Staring after him, Hem thought that the First Bard had aged since he had last seen him. Yet the Bard sense in him also perceived a strength in Juriken that he had not seen before, a great resolve wound to such a pitch that Hem felt something like awe. He wondered, not without a flicker of fear, what it was that Juriken was planning to do.

Soron returned to the couch where he had been waiting and turned his face away, looking through the open doorway into the rainy darkness. Hem stared at Zelika, who was standing humbly before him, her head bowed, her face hidden in her dripping, straggling hair, waiting resignedly for him to shout at her.

But Hem did not shout. As Zelika stood forlornly in her soaked battle dress, all her pride in tatters, Hem found that his anger had completely evaporated. There was an uncomfortable silence, while Hem waited for Zelika to speak. In the end, he realized that Zelika would not say anything because she felt too humiliated. Impulsively, he stepped forward and clumsily hugged her.

"I'm glad you're back," he said gruffly.

Zelika nodded, still not meeting Hem's eyes, but she held him tightly for a moment before she let him go.

She tied my legs up! Irc hissed in his ear. *She was bad to me!*

Maybe, Hem answered. *But she is sorry now.*

Now Irc was out of the rain, he was not so disposed to forgiveness. He ruffled his feathers. But there was something in Hem's voice that told him that he should not argue.

"What now?" said Hem restlessly.

Soron turned, his gentle face somber. "We wait," he said. "Perhaps Zelika could dry herself off. She is somewhat damp."

Zelika shook herself, and disappeared into an adjoining chamber, and Irc hopped down and inspected with interest the food that Hem had put aside, looking upward questioningly.

Go ahead, said Hem. *I saved it for you.*

The crow started gulping down the food, and Hem looked closely at Soron.

"It wasn't a coincidence that we met on the way here, was it?" he asked.

Soron smiled slowly. "Nay, Hem. I have instructions, like everyone else."

"And yours are to look after me?"

"In part." Soron stood up and went to the table, where a jug of wine stood still untouched after their meal. "I think some wine will not go astray, eh? Not enough to fuddle our wits, but enough to pass the time."

Hem shook his head. "Not for me," he said. "You know more than you are saying, Soron," he added.

"If I do, then I will tell you in good time."

"But now we wait for Saliman?"

"We do."

Hem gulped. He didn't want to ask his next question. "And—and what if Saliman does not come back?"

"I fully expect Saliman to return." Soron fiddled with his goblet. "I expect him in the dark hours, after the turn of midnight. Whatever happens, we must be well out of here by dawn."

"How do we get out?" asked Hem impatiently.

"There are ways," said Soron. "Your room was not chosen for you idly." But despite Hem's insistent questioning, he would say no more. At last Hem cast himself on a couch, and stared out glumly into the rain. It was completely dark outside now.

More waiting. He couldn't stand it.

Hem spent the next few hours on a knife-edge of anxiety, as time seemed to swell into an infinity of tedium. It was strange, he reflected, this feeling of being at once bored and terrified. The Ernan seemed to be empty; he could hear no movement at all. I suppose everyone has gone down to the ships, he thought, and maybe even now they have left the city. Maybe we're the only people left inside the walls.

He strained to listen for any hint of what was happening outside, but aside from some unidentifiably faint explosions or crashes, he could hear nothing above the steady pelting of the rain and the rare chimes of the water clock. The intervals between the hours seemed far too long; at one stage Hem went to check if there was something wrong with it.

Irc perched on the arm of a chair and, exhausted by his adventure and gorged with food, fell fast asleep. Zelika had emerged from her chamber, dry but still clad in her armor. Her sword was unsheathed, and she sat down and laid it across her knees. She looked at Hem.

"You should put on your fighting gear," she said.

"Why?" asked Hem irritably.

"Just in case. Unlike you, I've seen what is going to come through that gate."

Hem shrugged unenthusiastically. It would pass a bit of time, anyway. Turbanskian fighting gear was not, as armor went, especially heavy, but it was hardly comfortable clothing.

When the midnight bell rang out, Hem began to expect Saliman's return. It made the time pass even more slowly; now every moment dragged. Soron grew restless, and started to pace up and down the room.

The first bell after midnight struck, and still nothing had happened, except that the rain eased off slightly. Its sound was soporific. Hem yawned. He had had an exhausting day, and this nerve-fraying wait was no less tiring. Soron leaned across and offered him a flask.

"Medhyl," he said. "Both of you have some. It guards against weariness. Now we must be most awake."

Hem sipped the Bardic liquor, and felt his exhaustion lift. Then he tilted his head: surely that was the sound of running, far off? He glanced at Soron, and saw that he too was listening.

Yes, he was sure it was running. Many people. And, farther off still, the clash of metal against metal, and faint, confused shouting. Soron stood up, suddenly alert, and disappeared briefly, returning with a pack, which he slung over his shoulders. Zelika looked at them curiously; she did not have Bardic hearing, and did not know what they were listening to.

"Saliman isn't back yet," said Hem nervously.

Soron glanced over at Hem. "I expect him at any moment," he said. "I think now we should go to the Western Chamber. Hem, you had better wake up Irc."

Hem picked Irc up. He opened one eye and gave a soft, protesting caw. Soron took a lamp, and then the children followed him to the Western Chamber. It was a circular, domed room with plaster walls dyed a dull red and decorated with plain golden pilasters, and Soron's lamp threw strange shadows over the walls. Several doors opened from it. It seemed very large and empty after the intimacy of the room they had just left, and their feet echoed unsettlingly on the tiled floor.

In the center of the room, the tiles radiated in a curious pattern from a round black stone, which had a high polish. Soron dropped his bag by this stone, and sat cross-legged on the floor.

"We should have brought some cushions," said Hem.

"I doubt we will be here long," Soron answered.

Zelika said nothing, but looked wary. Now even she could hear noises in the city outside, above the steady fall of the rain.

"Will Saliman be here soon?" asked Hem, his voice cracking.

"I expect so," said Soron imperturbably, covering the lamp. "Whether he is or no, I judge that we cannot wait much longer."

There followed a long, heavy silence, as they sat in the dark chamber in the empty palace. Hem was close to tears; Soron was giving away nothing, but Hem was quite sure that Saliman should have been there by now. Zelika, who had hardly spoken a word all night, sat very still with her naked blade resting on her lap.

Not long afterward, they heard footsteps that sounded as if they were in the Ernan itself. Zelika started up, holding her weapon, followed more slowly by Soron and Hem, who were listening intently. Hem was sure it was one person, running toward the south door of the chamber. Saliman? He gulped, and wondered whether he should draw his sword. Soron looked equally uncertain. It was very unnerving, not knowing what approached them; Hem stood rigidly, his arms straight by his sides, torn between hope and fear. The steps were moving closer, echoing unnaturally loudly in the empty palace, but they seemed sure of where they were going; it could not be an enemy, surely, as an enemy would be lost . . .

At last a figure burst into the room. Even in the darkness, Hem knew at once it was Saliman, and he cried out in relief. The Bard paused by the doorway, squinting into the chamber, and walked toward them. As he approached them, Soron held up the lamp briefly, letting fall a little light, and Hem saw with horror that Saliman seemed to be covered with blood; his face was splashed with it, and his armor mired and blackened.

"Are you hurt?" he asked, running up to Saliman.

"Not much," said Saliman, and his teeth flashed in the gloom as he briefly smiled. "I am glad to see you, Hem. Is everyone here?"

"Palindi has not come. Nor Jerika," said Soron, naming Bards whom Hem knew only by sight.

"Palindi is dead," said Saliman shortly. "Jerika was fighting down by the harbor; she could not make it past the markets now. They are all on fire. I only just got through in time. I pray she is on one of the outward ships." He swayed, and passed his hand over his brow. "Soron, there is very little time. Can you begin the opening? I need to recover myself. Then I will help, if need be."

Soron, whose face had crumpled in distress at Saliman's news, nodded and took a deep breath. Zelika watched curiously as the Bard gathered his power and began to glow with magery.

Now the ugly noise of fighting was louder, and she looked up
swiftly, like a hunting wolf sniffing danger, and moved to guard
the west door. Hem remembered that he also had a sword. He
walked reluctantly to the door closest to Zelika, drawing his
weapon, and stared through into the gloom beyond, his nerves
humming with tension.

Soron began to chant in the Speech in a low, musical voice,
and as he did, the black stone in the center of the floor also
began to glow. Hem had never really thought of Soron as a
Bard; he had seen him in the kitchens, making the best seedcakes in the Suderain, stolid and dependable and friendly, as
different from the mercurial Saliman as it was possible to be.
But now he remembered that Soron was much more than a
cook; and the hair bristled on the back of Hem's neck as he
sensed the power the Bard was exerting.

Hem hoped the spell, whatever it was for, would not take
long. There were definitely people in the palace now, and coming from the Hilan Gate, not far from them, he could hear
fighting and shouting, and the sound of things being smashed.
No one was coming their way yet, but it was only a matter of
time . . . Saliman started up and began to chant with Soron,
melding their powers together. Almost at once the stone blazed
as bright as lightning, leaving an afterimage that made Hem
temporarily blind. Then it was dark again. Saliman stood up,
staggering.

"Hem, Zelika, here, quickly! This will not last long." They
ran to the center of the room. Where the polished stone had
been, a deep hole now opened in the center of the floor. Soron
had already dropped down, and they could see him below
them, carrying the lamp, which he had partly uncovered. It
was quite a long drop: maybe three spans. Hem hesitated for
the briefest moment, and Saliman said sharply, "Jump! Now!"
and pushed him down. He landed heavily, jarring his legs.

Irc leapt off Hem's shoulder in alarm, having a bird's dislike of enclosed spaces, but Saliman said so fiercely, *Down! Follow the boy!* that instead of fussing, as he would normally have done, he dived straight into the hole in the ground. He landed on Hem's shoulder and clung there, hiding his eyes under his wing. Zelika jumped after Hem, landing gracefully, and Saliman followed her.

They stood in a narrow stone passage, scarcely wide enough for the four of them. Their breathing echoed harshly from the walls. Hem looked up anxiously; there was a loud crash very near, and a hoarse scream. It would be easy to see where they had gone; it would be easy to follow them. But the moment the thoughts occurred to him, the hole above them sealed itself up. It wasn't like a stone door grinding shut: the stone, which had not been there, was suddenly there again, solid and immovable above their heads. Irc gave a faint caw of dismay. Soron uncovered the lamp a little more, and all four gazed at one another in the yellow light.

"That was a near thing," said Saliman. "Nearer than I'd have liked."

"We made it," Soron answered painfully. "Some of us."

Saliman clasped his shoulder. "Aye, some of us. Some of us. It has been a black night, Soron. As black as I'd feared it would be. Well, if we are to survive the night past this moment, we must be far from here by dawn. We have a long way to go."

For the first time in days, Hem began to feel cold. He wished he hadn't put his armor on; apart from being uncomfortable, it clanked noisily in the narrow passage. And he was so tired.

Saliman led them on without even a pause for rest. Soron walked beside him, carrying the lamp, and behind them came Hem and Zelika. They were in a narrow stone passage with a smooth floor and walls; every now and then they passed strange carvings, detailed pictures of lions and horses and men in chariots, which stood out in relief against the walls. Hem had no time to look at them, although they sparked his curiosity.

"What is this place?" he asked once.

"It is called the Passage of the Kings," said Saliman. "There are three entrances from the Ernan, and they lead to the Lamarsan Caves, where we will be soon. The knowledge of these entrances is secret, and only the First Bard and the Ernani know where they are, and how to open them. Har-Ytan gave the telling of it to Soron and myself, when we made the plans for this night. We will not go to the Caves of Light, which open to the Lamarsan Sea, but by darker ways that are known to few."

They didn't speak any further. Saliman was hurrying them as fast as they could go, and it took all their energy. Twice they passed the mouths of other passages that Hem presumed were from the other entrances in the Ernan, and there Saliman halted briefly, listening. Hem too sent out his hearing, wondering what Saliman was listening for, but he could hear nothing, apart from a faint rumble, very faint indeed, like a deep groan of rock.

Hem quickly lost all sense of time; he felt that he had been walking forever through this dark passage, with the shadows from the lamp ahead falling back around them, and his legs as heavy as stone. Zelika walked beside him, her mouth set in a straight, determined line. He knew she was as tired as he was, but she would not betray any sign of it.

After a long time, they left the carved passages and passed into natural caves. Here it was harder to walk, as the ground was uneven and sometimes the roof came down so low even Zelika had to stoop. Hem, Zelika, and Saliman stopped very briefly to take off their armor, and shove it into their packs; it was made so craftily that the scales folded up surprisingly small, and it was light to carry.

Now a thin layer of damp shone back from the walls in the lamplight, and Hem could hear the sound of running water, muffled through rock, in the distance. An underground river, he supposed. They were passing through a bewildering maze of rock: other caves ran into theirs at strange angles, from above or below, and icicles of limestone sometimes hung down from the roof, or tripped him up where the patient dripping of years had built a white column. Hem was now all but stumbling with weariness. Irc clung glumly to his shoulder, completely silent. This in itself was unusual; almost nothing could keep Irc quiet for long. But Hem could feel the rapid beat of Irc's heart where the bird pressed against his neck. Irc was terrified of the darkness, of this awful still place, where there was no sky and no wind.

Sometimes they came to a place where five or six passages branched off. Saliman chose his direction unerringly, as if he knew exactly where he was taking them. How could he know, if he had never been in these caves before? Could he make a mistake? Saliman was, after all, very tired. Hem began to worry what might happen if he made a wrong turn: they could wander through these caves forever, and never see the light again.

He was also concerned by the faint rumble that he had heard earlier. He was sure it was getting louder. He had no idea what it could be, but all his Bardic instincts were ringing little bells of alarm. Although Hem had never been underground before, he was almost certain that this noise was not right. The very rock seemed to be complaining. Like Irc, he began to think that all he wanted to do was to get out of the caves and see the sky again. Now his whole body was hurting, as if all his muscles were made of bruises, but the fear whispering at the back of his mind kept him moving: one step, and then another step, and then another . . .

The walls were running with water, a thin curtain of wetness that gathered into rivulets, and ran over the floor of the cave, over their feet. Sometimes they waded through water up to their knees. The caves were still leading downward, and the water was getting deeper, and it was becoming colder and colder; Hem was shivering constantly.

They had been walking for what seemed like hours when they were forced to crawl through a cave that was barely a span high, and that was almost filled with water: only a hand's breadth of air was between the black, cold surface and the roof of the cave. It was very difficult to move through, as the water current was quite strong. They had to walk awkwardly, crouching low, keeping their heads and packs above the surface of the water, which was too high to permit crawling on hands and knees. It was sheer torment. And then Soron dropped the lamp, and everything went completely black.

At this point Irc's nerve cracked: he had been close to panic as it was, and this was too much. He was clinging to Hem's head, trying to keep out of the water, but when the lamp dropped he took off, trying to fly back along the passageway, and fell squawking into the water. Hem grabbed for him in the darkness, and picked him up, soaked and terrified, his beak open, his chest palpitating, as Saliman made a magelight and its gentle bloom illuminated the rough walls of rock. Somehow, squatting in the freezing water with his thighs and knees burning with strain, Hem calmed Irc down, and dried his feathers with a gentle charm. And then, because there was nothing else they could do, they went on.

They scrambled out of that passage into a huge cavern, so high they could not see its roof. A wide expanse of black water glittered before them in the magelight, stretching farther than they could see. At its edge was a beach of coarse red sand. They sat on the beach, panting and massaging their legs, and gazed at each other in the wan magelight. They were not a prepossessing sight: smeared with mud all over, and wet through and shivering.

"There's not far to go now," said Saliman. His voice was hoarse.

Zelika looked up at him. Her hair was in witchlocks, falling over her face in tangles, and deep shadows cut beneath her eyes.

"I'm so tired and cold I think I will die," she said. "Can we rest for a little while?"

Hem had wanted to ask the same question. He looked yearningly at Saliman.

"We can rest once we are out of here," said Saliman. "We have come through the hardest part. But we cannot rest now."

Hem looked down at his trembling legs, and then took a deep breath and stood up. "All right, then," he said.

They each had a sip of medhyl. Then Soron relit the lamp, and they stumbled for a long time along the sand, the sound of their steps dull and strange in the wide space, until Saliman led them into another cave. To Hem's relief, for the first time since they had entered the Passage of the Kings they were heading upward. His relief didn't last very long, as the incline became steeper and steeper until they were almost climbing. Hem gritted his teeth and tried to ignore the pain in his body. He really didn't know how much longer he could keep going. Every now and then he thought the ground shuddered under his feet, and he was sure the deep groaning that troubled him was getting louder. But he was so dizzy with exhaustion that he wasn't sure of anything anymore.

At last they stopped climbing, and the roof of the cave drew away from their heads. Their way twisted and turned, still heading upward in a gentle incline. Hem struggled on with a surge of renewed strength. Surely they were on their way out now. But then the cave seemed to reach a blind end, and his heart sank.

They stopped by the wall, Zelika giving Hem a glance of dismay. Saliman pointed to a hole by their feet. "We have to crawl through here," he said. "One at a time; it is not far. Hem, explain to Irc, so he does not get too frightened. We're almost there."

Hem wondered briefly where "there" was, while he obediently told Irc that they were going through another small cave and that he was not to panic. Irc, silent with fear, pressed even closer to Hem's neck. The bird was exhausted, his legs hurt after what Zelika had done to them, and now he was living through a ceaseless nightmare that made him believe that he would never see the sky again. Soron had gone ahead with the lamp, and now it was completely black, so Hem made a magelight. He was so tired that even this small magery was a struggle. Then, sternly telling Irc to go ahead of him, he stooped and crawled into the hole.

Saliman was right: the hole was a tunnel scarcely longer than the length of a man, and when he scrambled to the end of it, Hem fell a short distance onto a surface of damp earth. He stood up slowly and saw he was in a rough, dimly lit cave.

Hem's eyes had been blurring in and out of focus for some time now, and at first he wasn't sure if he was imagining it: could it be daylight? But then he noticed that the air was fresher than the still, close air of underground. He didn't really believe that they had reached the end of their journey until Irc gave a little caw and leaped off his shoulder, flapping toward the light. The crow perched on a stone near the cave entrance, ruffling his feathers, and looked back.

Eagerly they followed Irc, and in a short time stood at the entrance. Long flowering vines hung down from above it,

stirring in a slight wind. All Hem could see were leaves, veil after
veil of leaves of every imaginable shade of green. After the lamp-
lit tunnel, he felt almost drunk with the color. The trees and
bushes were dripping, as if it had only just stopped raining, and
the earth was exhaling a damp, rich smell of rotting vegetation.

Looking up toward the sky, Hem saw that they were just
above the floor of a narrow gorge: red cliffs climbed high on
either side of them. He couldn't see the sun, but it felt as if it
were just after dawn: the air was still crisp and cool. He stood at
the cave entrance and gulped in the fresh air, too overcome to
speak.

None of them spoke, in fact, for a long time. In the filtered
light Hem could see how tired Saliman was: underneath the
grime and blood that smeared his face, his skin was ashen. He
sat down heavily, drew a flask of medhyl out of his pack, took a
gulp, and passed it around.

After the medhyl, Hem's limbs stopped shaking so much.
Soron sat with his back to the others, and did not answer when
Hem addressed him. Hem remembered that he had asked after
two Bards who were supposed to be with them and had not
come; they must have been friends of Soron's, and now he
grieved for them. Zelika leaned against the trunk of a tree and
gazed up at the small patches of blue that she could see through
the leaves.

The first thing Hem did was to change his wet clothes. He
sat beneath a tree and felt the deathly cold of the caves slowly
leaving his body. Irc, who had flown up into a tree out of sight,
came back and sat on his shoulder, nipping his ear.

I did not like that, he said. *Never take me back there.*

It was better than being cut to pieces, said Hem. *But I didn't like
it either.*

It is not over, said Irc. *Something is going to happen.*

What? asked Hem. *What's going to happen?*

I don't know, the bird answered. *The earth is crying out.* Irc restlessly jumped off his shoulder, and then hopped back on, and finally flapped up into the trees again.

Irc was making Hem jumpy; he remembered the rumbling he had heard underground. Trying to rid himself of his unease, he looked across at Saliman, who lay on his back staring up at the sky.

"Saliman," he said. "What happened, out there on the Lamarsan? Did you clear the seaways?"

Saliman did not answer for a time. Then he sighed heavily, and sat up.

"Aye, Hem, we did," he said. "The last defenders of Turbansk are, I hope, now well on their way to the Zimek Harbor, from which they can retreat to Car Amdridh. It is not an enviable journey, not with the Black Army on their heels; but their way is open, and I hope we have bought them some time."

As he spoke, he took off his tunic and inspected a nasty wound on his forearm. Hem stood up, searching in his pack for his healing balm and a spare bandage, and knelt down to help him.

Zelika's face lit up. "Then it worked," she said.

"Yes, it worked, but at a heavy cost. Of the two score ships that set out to destroy Imank's navy, less than half returned to harbor. And on each of those ships were no less than four score warriors and oarsmen."

"But we won," said Zelika, with a savage joyousness. "That's what matters."

Saliman caught her eye. "Zelika," he said, with a hard edge to his voice. "I am a warrior by necessity. I fight not because I love war or joy in arms, but because I must. We had the victory on the sea, but I cannot be glad of it; it is a bitter triumph. Many, many people died, so that many more could live. That is a harsh logic. I accept it, but I do not like it."

Zelika blinked with confusion and averted her gaze.

Saliman went on. "I believe that we were betrayed. We were expected, and in the darkness and rain our fleet was encircled. It was all too neat for comfort: someone knew our strategy intimately. For a time I thought that we had failed utterly. But we did not fail, even though when we came back to harbor, we found two black ships had come in over the boom chain, and soldiers were setting fires in some of the ships and in the markets. That was when Palindi was killed. He saved my life: but for him, I too would be lying cold in the Harbor of Turbansk. He was murdered by treachery." Saliman's voice hoarsened, and he stared down at the ground, his eyes hidden.

Soron, who had been listening intently, stirred but said nothing.

Before Hem's inner vision passed a series of images, brief but intolerably vivid, of burning ships moving through veils of rain over an expanse of black water, of broken corpses floating waterlogged between broken wreckage, of the desperate struggles of the drowning and the terrible fights on the decks of the triremes and on the quays. Darkness and water and fire and death. He shuddered.

"Betrayed?" said Zelika sharply, bringing him back to the present. "Who would betray Turbansk like that?"

"I do not know," said Saliman shortly, and would say no more. But into Hem's mind flashed an image of Alimbar. He had not trusted him; something had moved in his stomach whenever he had had to speak to him. He had put it down to his misadventure in the garden, but Hem knew in that moment, in some deep part of him, that Saliman suspected the same thing.

"Why would anyone do that?" Hem whispered, staring at Saliman. The idea that a Turbanskian, even a Turbanskian he distrusted, should even speak to the Black Army shocked him to the core.

"Fear, perhaps," Saliman shrugged. "Greed, no doubt. Hulls, after all, were all Bards once. Some people desire only power, and will do anything for it. I do not care why. If ever I meet the traitor, I will take my revenge, Balance or no Balance."

Hem had never heard such implacable hatred in Saliman's voice before. Even given everything that had happened, it surprised him; Saliman had always seemed to him somehow too noble for such emotions. He finished tying off Saliman's bandage in thoughtful silence.

As he did so, he suddenly realized that everything around them had gone still: he was sure he had heard birdcalls before, but now he could hear only the wind rustling through the leaves. Around them the air seemed thick with a dreadful, tense quietness. He looked at Saliman and opened his mouth to ask a question; but it was never asked. At that moment the earth shrugged, and Hem, taken by surprise, toppled over onto his face.

He scrambled up and looked around him wildly as a shower of small pebbles and soil rained onto his head from the rocks above. Zelika sat bolt upright, her eyes wide with alarm, and Soron put out his arms to steady himself, his face white. Saliman cried out to the others and ran for the middle of the gorge floor, between the swaying trees; stumbling in panic, they followed, afraid that the rock walls were about to collapse on top of them. A landslide of boulders crashed down on where they had been sitting only moments before, and stones bounced down the cliffs above them and landed around them. Before Hem, a great tree seemed to rise up in the ground like a living thing, and fell over, dragging smaller trees in its wake. There was nowhere to shelter: if they went back to the cave it might collapse on them.

The ground shuddered like a giant animal for what seemed an age. Hem, terrified, wondered if the gorge walls would fall on top of them, burying them beyond recall. When at last it stopped, all four cautiously looked up. There was another long silence and then, all at once, a chorus of birdcalls broke out, and far off Hem could hear the indignant chittering of a troop of monkeys. Irc, frightened witless, burst out of the trees and landed on Hem's shoulder, cawing in distress.

"What was that?" asked Hem shakily.

"An earthquake," said Zelika. "It sometimes happens."

"It was indeed an earthquake."

Saliman stood up, and Hem saw that his face, already haggard with strain and exhaustion, now seemed drawn with a dreadful grief.

"Juriken has done what he promised he would do," Saliman said. "No Bard in all the ages of Edil-Amarandh has done anything greater than Juriken's task this day."

Hem stared at Saliman. "You mean that Juriken made the earthquake happen?" he asked, his voice cracking. He thought of his last sight of the Bard, and how he had sensed that he was about to do something terrible. He had not imagined anything like this.

"Aye," said Saliman quietly. "Here we felt just the outer edges of his power: we are far enough away not to feel its full wrath. Turbansk now will be a wasteland of rubble. That was our plan: to attack and then retreat, so we would draw the Black Army into Turbansk—and once they were within the walls, to call up the slow anger of the earth and bring the city down upon the heads of Imank's forces. Juriken alone, of all of us, had the power to do such a thing. And now it is done, and he will be dead."

"I did not know," said Soron in a low voice. He was sitting with his hands clasping his knees, rocking from side to side. "I did not know what he was going to do, but I knew I would never see Juriken again."

"Alas for Juriken, whom I loved as a brother," said Saliman. He looked up to the sky, and Hem saw that tears were running down his cheeks. "I cannot speak his loss: it goes deeper than words, deeper even than song. I have no words for Juriken, my friend and my master; Juriken of Turbansk, greatest of Bards; Juriken, whom I loved."

He bowed his head and Hem, filled with wonder and awe, did the same, his heart cold with the thought of what Juriken had done: its courage and its utter ruthlessness.

After a long silence, Saliman spoke again. "Alas, alas for Turbansk! Turbansk, the city of my birth, the city where first I walked as a child, where I grew into a man—city of memory and song, ancient and beautiful and forever young. I will never again walk through the covered streets of the markets to buy persimmons, nor gaze down from the Red Tower onto the beauty of the Jiela cedars; nor will I eat and laugh with my friends in its fragrant gardens. All is gone, gone, gone: as the green grass withers on the hill, as the winds of spring kiss our cheeks and never return, so my city is shivered into ruin and all its loveliness shattered, never to come again . . ."

And as the Bard-born will, Saliman spoke his grief, turning it into song; and amid the bird-haunted greenery the others listened to his lament, in awe and fear and sorrow.

NAL-AK-BURAT

Before the shrine of Nyanar
Eribu bowed his head
And the Elidhu spoke to him:

Go forth from this city
Not in banishment but in hope.
Go forth though your tears stain your face.

Now I will go forth from this city,
Said Eribu.
Not in banishment but in hope,
Though tears stain my face.
I fear I will never see again
The light-filled palaces of Nal-Ak-Burat.
I fear that I will never again stand
In the Temple of Dreams.
I fear I will never touch again
My sons and my daughters.

And Nyanar said: I will not say
Do not fear.
Fear is the other face of hope.

Fragment from *The Epic of Eribu*,
Library of Turbansk

XII

THE THREE GATES

S ALIMAN drew a map in the sand with his forefinger.
"This is Turbansk," he said, making a dot. "This is the
Lamarsan Sea. Last night we went south, underneath the
sea itself, and then turned north. The Il Dara Wall is twenty or
so leagues northeast of here, and the Neera Marshes begin
about a league hence. We are now in Savitir and we need to get
here." He stabbed a point eastward on his makeshift map.
"Near to Nazar, just past the Undara River."

"So we're in conquered land," said Zelika, leaning forward
to see the rough diagram, frowning with concentration. "How
can we go from here? Won't we be seen by the spies of the Black
Army?"

"If we tried to move above ground, yes, we would almost
certainly be seen," Saliman said.

"More caves?" Hem shuddered. "Irc won't be very pleased."

"Yes, more caves." Saliman grinned mirthlessly. "Not so wet
nor so narrow as those we went through earlier, fortunately.
And, I hope, far enough away that they have not collapsed."

It was some hours after the earthquake. The sky had
gradually cleared of clouds, and as the day heated up, it had
begun to get warm even in the shade of the gorge. Earlier, Hem
and Zelika, followed by Irc, had cautiously made their way up
the gorge, pushing through the shrubs of thyme and worm-
wood that grew under groves of wild almond and fig trees.
Many of the larger trees had fallen, and the ground was littered
with broken branches and leaves. A little farther on they found

a pool of green water that was bordered on one side by flat, red
rocks and on the other by a narrow shore of sand. It might have
been designed for bathing.

They sent Irc back to tell Saliman and Soron where they
were, and then stripped to their underclothes and jumped into
the pool. The water was very cold, most likely because it was
spring-fed, and they stayed in just long enough to wash off the
mud and sweat of the previous days. The relief of having clean
skin was inexpressible. Hem washed his dirty clothes, and
stretched them out on the rocks to dry. Then he and Zelika lay
down side by side and idly watched the sunlight dancing on
the surface of the water. Occasionally a butterfly flew raggedly
across their field of vision, but otherwise all was still: a low hum
of insect life filled the air with soporific music. Before long they
had both fallen fast asleep.

They were woken by Soron, and found that a meal was laid
out on the rocks: dried dates and a hard honey-flavored biscuit
and smoked meat. Saliman and Soron had also bathed, and
they talked in low voices as they ate. By tacit consent, none of
them mentioned Turbansk, nor the ordeals they had so recently
undergone. After the strain of the past days, the past weeks, the
peace of this little gorge seemed dreamlike, something beyond
imagining even hours ago, and each of them was loathe to disturb it. Here, there was no trace of war; it was almost strange
not to hear the throb of the drums and the bray of trumpets,
which had underlain their every moment for weeks now.

When they finished eating, Soron, who had scarcely spoken
during their meal, moved away. He sat very still on a rock on
the other side of the pool, gazing into the water, his face averted
from them. Hem looked at him with concern, and Saliman
noticed the direction of Hem's gaze.

"Palindi and Soron were very great friends," said Saliman
softly. "Palindi too came to Turbansk from Til Amon. And

Jerika—she planned to come with Soron because she loved him. Now he does not know if she is dead or alive."

Hem nodded slowly. He had seen many people mourning in the past few weeks, but repetition didn't make it any easier. If anything, it made it worse; he understood something now about the dreadful isolation of grief. He stirred restlessly, plucking some grass and twisting it around his fingers. Was Maerad still alive? How could he know? And yet he felt that she was . . .

"So do we go straight north to Annar?" asked Hem at last. "Is there a way across the marshes?"

"The marsh people know how to cross the Neera," said Saliman. "And they have shown me some of their paths. But if we went that way we would have to cross the East Road, and it is too dangerous: I doubt now that even a hare could do so unseen. We will have to journey to Annar by more circuitous routes."

Hem looked down to conceal his disappointment. He had hoped that they might begin to search for Maerad straight away.

Saliman gave him a sympathetic glance, as if he understood what passed through Hem's mind. "There are some people I am hoping to meet who will help us, and some tasks to do before we make our way north, which have been long planned," he said. "And I do not know what is happening in Annar now; there has been no news in Turbansk for weeks. I do not like the idea of walking into the fire without at least some foreknowledge of what to expect."

"And we have to find Maerad." Hem spoke as if this were the most straightforward of tasks, and despite himself Saliman smiled.

"Yes, we must. Though you do realize, Hem, that to find Maerad is the whole desire of the Nameless One: and if Maerad and Cadvan are in Annar, they will be in hiding. Annar is a very

big place, you know. In any case, when we last spoke, she and
Cadvan were planning to go north, to Zmarkan."

Hem's heart sank slightly at Saliman's words.

"But we will still look for them? I know we can find them."

Saliman hesitated, and then nodded. "Yes, Hem. There are
many things that we must do, and that is one of them. And we
have business in Annar."

"What other things do we have to do?" Hem looked at
Saliman reproachfully. "Isn't finding Maerad more important
than anything else?"

"More important for you, maybe," said Zelika, who had
been listening impatiently. "What I want to know is, what do
we do *now*?"

"Well, that is easy to answer," said Saliman. "For the
moment we can rest and recover our strength a little. We'll wait
until nightfall before we move. The caves we must find are a
couple of leagues northeast of here."

"More caves," Hem said again, glumly.

"It's not so bad," said Saliman. "We could be flitting from
bush to bush, terrified that at any moment we would be spotted
by some spy of Imank's. Be grateful. The land around here is
like a honeycomb, and even with its best efforts the Dark has
not been able to find all of our hiding places. The caves may be
cold and uncomfortable, but we will be safer there than anywhere else in the whole Suderain."

Hem stared gloomily at the ground. "All the same, I don't
know if I can persuade Irc back underground. He told me he
never wanted to go back there again."

"There's no choice," said Saliman. "If he wishes to stay with
you, he will have to."

When dusk began to fall, Hem moodily gathered up his dried
clothes from the rocks and called Irc back from the trees, where

he had spent his time boasting to the local birds. Remembering how cold he had been the previous night, Hem put on an extra layer. He was still very tired; more than anything, he would have liked a long sleep in a comfortable bed. But, as Saliman said, it was not a question of choice.

They set off down the gorge. There was no path, and the ground was rocky and uneven with the tumbled detritus of the earthquake, so their going was slow. A smell of crushed thyme rose as the air cooled in the evening, and through the branches of the trees above, Hem could see the twinkle of white stars.

Hem felt as if he were drinking in the peace through his skin. He remembered his journey with Saliman through the tranquil mountains of the Osidh Am. That seemed so long ago now; when he thought of himself then, it was like thinking about a stranger. So many things had happened to him since: he had found Irc; he had met Oslar, and had found that he was himself a healer; he had spoken to the King of the Birds and driven off the deathcrows from Turbansk; he had seen Har-Ytan, the Ernani of the city; and someone had written a song about him. And he had seen more death and suffering than he wanted to think about.

He felt as if he didn't know the edges of himself anymore. He was taller, maybe a hand taller, than he had been when he arrived in Turbansk, which had made him uncharacteristically clumsy, knocking things over because he couldn't judge anymore how long his arms and legs were. He no longer felt like a boy of twelve years. His voice was breaking, and he had noticed also that the hair on his body was getting thicker and darker. All this was disconcerting enough, but on the inside, it was even worse: all the unseen parts of him had changed out of recognition. His time in the Healing Houses had taught him more than how to bind limbs and mend torn skin; he had learned how to be patient with those in pain, how to read another person's needs without speaking. But the changes inside him were more than those skills could account for.

Even thinking like this was new: Hem had never been particularly introspective. His brutal childhood had taught him always to look mistrustfully in front of him, to react to whatever his present situation was, without reflection or regret. But now, as he followed Saliman and Soron through the darkness of the trees, thoughts seemed to drift up of their own accord. For weeks he had hardly had time to do anything except sleep, eat, and work, and it was as if a host of thoughts had lined up in his mind and were now demanding his attention.

For one thing, he hadn't had a nightmare for several days now. For almost as long as he could remember, he had suffered from nightmares every night. He had thought that they had disappeared because he was so tired and slept too deeply to remember any dreams. But it could be, he thought blackly, that what he had been facing every day in Turbansk was actually worse than his nightmares. Maybe, Hem thought, I'm not so afraid anymore—or at least, not so afraid of the things that used to frighten me.

But in another way, he knew he was more afraid than he had ever been. He was afraid for those he loved, afraid for Maerad and Zelika and Saliman; but he was also afraid for the world. It sounded foolish, put that way, but it was true. He had seen the forces of the Dark outside Turbansk, their ruthlessness and destructiveness, and now he could imagine them everywhere. The memory of the deathcrows, their deep wrongness, still made him shudder: what if the whole world were like that, poisoned by the same sickness?

He studied Saliman's back, a span or so in front of him, as the Bard steadily made his way through the shadowy undergrowth. His gait betrayed nothing of the weariness that must have been afflicting him; like Cadvan, who could push himself past the limits of exhaustion, Saliman seemed to be made of iron. In contrast, Soron's shoulders betrayed his tiredness, and he sometimes stumbled. And yet Saliman had been fighting for hours, before he led them through the caves.

Hem thought of what Saliman had said earlier: *I fight not because I love war or joy in arms, but because I must.* Saliman might be a great warrior, but he did not like war. Like Hem, he was a healer. Maybe that was the real reason they had liked each other on sight.

When Hem had first met Saliman, in Nelac's rooms in Norloch, he had seemed like a figure out of his daydreams. Hem had no memory of his own father, and for as long as he could remember, lying on his meager pallet in the orphanage, he had dreamed of having a father who was like Saliman: heroic, handsome, witty . . . So when Saliman had offered to bring him to Turbansk, it had seemed as if his dreams were coming true; even if it meant that he had to leave his sister, he was gaining someone who could be, in some way, the father he had never had. But, Hem thought now, *Saliman is not my father, and he has never pretended that he is. I never had the chance to know my father; I know only that he is dead. And I don't really know Saliman very well at all.*

Hem had admired Saliman with the idealistic passion a young boy might feel for a mighty captain, but now it dawned on him that Saliman was both less and more than he had imagined. For all his courage and strength and ability, Saliman the Bard was also a man, and ordinary like other men: he was as prone to doubt and error and pain as anyone else. He was himself, as Hem was himself, and he existed outside anybody's desires and expectations.

As these thoughts passed through his mind, Hem realized that he loved Saliman more than he knew, and differently than he had thought. The realization pained him; it was as if he were giving up some cherished dream, and turning instead to face a strange and challenging reality.

Saliman was right: the caves weren't as bad as those they had negotiated the night before. They could walk through them without having to stoop, and the walls did not drip with water. Even so, they were bad enough: certainly Irc thought so. Hem very quickly lost any sense of time. Their journey seemed to go on forever and ever.

No one spoke unless it was necessary, and the only sound was the harsh echo of their breathing and the scuffle of their feet on the ground. Hem began to feel he had always been in these caves—blinking in the yellow lamplight, breathing the stale, cold air—and that he would always be there. He felt there had never been anything else: the sky, the trees, the wind, the colors of flowers were all lovely visions he had merely dreamed.

The entrance had been hidden by a spell; until Saliman revealed it with a word, it had looked like blank rock. They had entered it silently, braced for a long sojourn below ground; Saliman warned them that these caves would take them much farther from Turbansk. Irc, as Hem had expected, objected violently; it was probably the sternest test of loyalty he had faced. The boy had spoken to him quietly, and at last Irc, shivering, had agreed to come. He clung to Hem's shoulder, hiding his head in Hem's hair, and refused to move off, even though the farther they went, the heavier Irc seemed to become. And Hem's pack, bulging with his fighting gear, was heavy enough.

They stopped for a meal, slept on the stone floor, then rose and went on; they stopped and ate and walked and ate and slept. Every now and then they would strike underground streams, from which they could refresh their water bags. The Caves of Lamarsan . . . Hem thought of how, months before in Norloch, he had been promised the sight of the Hallows, where the caves opened onto the Sea of Lamarsan. It was the center of the Light in Turbansk. Saliman had said the Hallows were one of the wonders of Edil-Amarandh and had spoken of the way the waters of the Lamar River trickled in a waterfall into the Sacred Pool, and sparkled like a curtain of pearls in the moonlight. And yet, when Hem finally had seen the caves, it was not light he found, but impenetrable darkness. It was his bad luck, he thought, that he had been forced to see their other side. Perhaps he would never see the Caves of Light that Saliman had spoken of; perhaps they had been destroyed, as Turbansk must have been destroyed, by Juriken's summoning of the earthquake.

On some profound level, Hem could not understand that Turbansk must lie in ruins. It was as if it were too big an idea to imagine. How could those high, proud walls have fallen? How could the Ernan be merely broken walls and rubble, overrun by the Black Army? It didn't seem possible; somewhere deep inside himself he couldn't believe it, although his rational mind told him that was what had happened. When he tried to visualize Turbansk, a strange, dulled grief rose inside him. He would probably never know what had happened to the people he had cared for with such diligence in the Houses of Healing; perhaps they had managed to escape, but equally their ships might have foundered and sunk to the bottom of the Lamarsan Sea.

And among all the many things that had been lost in the chaos of war, among the broken toys and burned homes, the families divided forever, the lives snuffed out—among all these things that Hem couldn't grasp in his tired mind because there were too many of them, too many tragedies, too many losses, too many tears—among all these things, a young girl called Amira would never know that her father, Boran, the coffee seller, had thought of her as he was dying.

As he wandered through the dark maze, this caused Hem

more grief than anything else. It was a task he had taken upon himself, a bitter gift with which he had been entrusted. When he had promised to tell Amira of Boran's last words, Hem had not known how he could pass the message on. Even so, he had believed that somehow, someday, he would be able to find the girl and tell her about her father. But now he understood the futility of his hope. How could he find her now? Perhaps Amira, too, was dead; how would he ever know? His promise, made with such passion, such sorrow, was one he could never keep. A great bitterness swelled in Hem's chest, so strong he felt as if he might be sick. He set his jaw, drove the memory of Boran from his mind, and focused on making his feet move, one foot in front of the other, again and again, through the endless, flickering shadows.

Saliman led them unfalteringly through the maze of stone, and Hem wondered how often the Bard had been through these same caves. He remembered Saliman's many absences from Turbansk, how he said he had been to Dén Raven itself. Maybe he had used these very passages. Perhaps these paths wound all the way to the Iron Tower.

After several meals, Hem stopped thinking altogether; it took all his mental energy just to keep going. Sleep was merely a blank interruption in the endless tunnels, which Hem began to hate. Soron's lamp eventually burned out, and they continued with magelights, which were steadier but fainter than the yellow lamplight. Increasingly, the four humans moved as if through a dream. Irc remained almost completely silent. He would take his share at mealtimes, since not even the skyless darkness could depress his bottomless appetite, but his normal ebullience had completely vanished. Like all of them, he simply endured.

At last Saliman stopped before a rocky wall, on which, Hem saw, were inscribed some runes in a style he could not recognize. He watched passively, expecting that Saliman was counting his

way through his memories, remembering where their next turning would be; but instead Saliman raised his arm, and the light
of magery glowed around him.

"*Lirean!*" he said, and suddenly the wall was not there.

Before them stood a wide-arched entrance, and behind that
opened a huge cavern, its far end lit by a solitary torch. Saliman
turned to his companions, and smiled.

"We are here, at last," he said.

"Where are we?" asked Zelika, looking confused.

"We have come to the entrance of Nal-Ak-Burat," said
Saliman. "This was once an ancient city that was made beneath
the desert so long ago that the people who made it are now forgotten. But the city is not entirely forgotten; some use it even
now. Come. Stay close to me as we cross the cavern."

They followed Saliman silently through the arch and into
the wide cavern, and walked across flags of dressed stone
toward the torch that flickered on its other side. The cavern was
so high that its ceiling vanished in the darkness, and on either
side of them they could not see the walls.

It felt strangely unsettling, after an unmeasured time in the
small confines of the caves, to be in so wide a space; but as they
walked on, Hem began to think his sense of disquiet was to do
with more than the sudden emptiness around them. Zelika
glanced at Hem, her eyes wide and dark with unspoken apprehension, and Hem felt a shiver run down his spine, as if cold,
unseen fingers were touching his neck. Saliman and Soron
marched steadily before them, over the level ground; the small
magelight drifted in front of them, casting a circle of silver light,
and Hem squared his shoulders and trudged on.

The silence around their footsteps was so intense it seemed
to have its own quality. Was there such a thing as a loud silence?
Hem began to feel a chill dread, although he didn't know why.
There was nothing, he told himself, to be afraid of; but all the

same, he felt fear creeping through his scalp, down his back, raising all the hairs on his head. Halfway across the expanse Zelika reached out and took his hand, and he gripped her fingers tightly, taking comfort in her touch.

As they neared the torch, they saw it was placed in a bracket next to what seemed to be a door carved out of stone. Hem eyed the torch narrowly: it didn't seem to burn with any ordinary flame. It was a little like the lights the Bards used in Norloch, but its light was sulphurously yellow. Saliman put his hand on the door, muttering beneath his breath, and it swung wide open. Then he shepherded the rest of them inside, and they felt the heavy door swing shut behind them, with scarcely a sound. The magelight was extinguished as the door shut, leaving them in complete darkness.

"A magelight, Soron, if you will," said Saliman, his voice steady and strong. There was a slight pause, and then a silver light grew and bloomed near Soron. In that bloodless light, Hem thought they all looked like ghosts.

"Why did the light go out?" asked Hem, his voice wavering. "Did you do that on purpose?"

"I did not," said Soron.

"Then why did it go out?" Magelights should not go out, thought Hem, unless the Bard intends it so. Someone *put* it out. He could feel his pulse running jerkily through his body, and a cold sweat on his brow.

"Don't be afraid," said Saliman. "Stay steady. We have done well: we have passed the first gate."

"The first?" said Zelika. She had walked for days through the darkness without one sign of complaint or fear, but now her voice trembled.

"Aye. That was the Gate of the Dead. Now there are two more."

"Oh." Zelika swallowed hard, but said nothing further.

"The Gate of the Dead?" Hem's voice was higher than he wished. "I thought—it felt as if someone were there. I thought . . ." He faltered into silence.

"It is said the dead of the city guard this gate," said Soron. "And that they do not permit any with evil intent to pass."

Hem didn't want to know any more; he had a sudden creeping memory of feeling that he was being touched by cold fingers. "So, what's the next one?"

"This is the second. The Gate of Dreams."

Hem looked around. It didn't look like a gate at all, but the last one hadn't looked like a gate, either. It was a short passage of stone that led to a dead end. The walls and ceiling were covered with intricate carvings, but they were not, when he squinted at them, carvings of anything he could recognize. They looked like the same strange runes that had been carved over the entrance to the great cavern. He could feel, in the prickling of his skin, that the air was thick with magery; but it was somehow unlike the magery of Bards.

"So, how do we get through the Gate of Dreams?" he asked warily.

"We dream," said Saliman. Hem stared back at him with blank incomprehension. Saliman smiled, in a way Hem had not seen him smile for a long time, with a spark of pure fun. "We dream of a gate."

Zelika's eyebrows were drawn together in a black line. "We dream of a gate?" she repeated fiercely. "That is nonsense."

"Nevertheless, that is what each of us must do. Dream of a gate. Preferably, a gate you love."

Zelika drew in a sudden, sharp breath, as if something had hurt her. Saliman glanced at her.

"I warn you all: now we must be careful. Nothing will harm us here, save what we bring with us. So have a care of what you dream. Now," Saliman closed his eyes, "I remember, when I was a small boy, and like you, Hem, loved sweet fruits: sometimes I was allowed to go and stay with my grandmother. My grandmother lived in a house about twenty leagues from Turbansk, past the Jiela Hills. It was a little white stone house enclosed by a whitewashed stone wall, and around it were groves of almond and cherry trees, and a great stand of date palms.

"My grandmother was a famous gardener, and in her private garden she grew many aromatic plants for the herbalists and perfumers. There were frankincense trees, with their strange fleshy branches and fragrant sap, and galbanum and spikenard and camphor; and at the feet of the trees grew narcissi and geraniums and roses. I loved nothing better than to enter that garden of perfumes, to gather the white tears of the sap of galbanum, or to lie on the flagstones by the pond and close my eyes and let the scents drift over me."

Saliman's warm voice resonated through the stone passage, and the others listened, enchanted by the lovely vision. Hem could see the house and garden vividly with his inner eye, as if it stood before him.

"The gate to that garden was wrought of black iron," said Saliman. "It was shaped to fit the archway, and through its grille you could see the trees and flowers, and the breeze would bring you faint wafts of perfume. The iron was fashioned as little six-sided flowers, each fitting ingeniously into the other, and it was never locked. When you pushed it with your hand, it groaned faintly, and swung open. And then, you stepped through into my grandmother's garden."

There was a short silence, and Saliman lifted his head and stared toward the end of the passage. For the briefest moment it seemed to Hem that a white wall glimmered there, and a wrought-iron gate, and through it a sifting vision of sunlight and green leaves, which vanished to bare stone.

"Soron, you go last, and guide these children," said Saliman.

"Remember what I have said. Each of us must make our own gate." Then he walked to the end of the passage, and seemed to pass straight through the blank wall.

Hem blinked and Zelika gasped. Soron looked at the children. He had hardly spoken at all in their long wending through the caves, and now it seemed to Hem that he had changed: there was a toughness in his voice that the boy had not heard before.

"Zelika, Hem; Saliman just showed you what to do. Now you must do it."

"But I'm not a Bard like you," said Zelika, her voice wavering. "I can't do magery."

"The magery does not come from you, but from this place," Soron answered. "Come, have faith. There is no other way."

There was a short pause, and Hem heard Zelika swallow.

"Do I have to say it out loud, like Saliman did?" she asked.

"No," said Soron. "You must just see it in your mind. The walls will hear, and shape themselves. Now, Zelika: you first."

Zelika shut her eyes, concentrating hard. There was a long silence, and she opened them.

"It won't work," she said flatly. "I told you."

"Zelika," said Soron patiently. "There is no other way. Think of a gate. Think of what it feels like. What it is like to open it. What lies beyond it."

She stared at Soron, her mouth a straight line. Then she shut her eyes again.

This time the darkness shimmered at the end of the passage, and Hem briefly glimpsed a nimbus of golden light and a hint of waving green and white, like a tree in flower. Zelika's eyes snapped open. An expression of wonder and delight flickered over her face, and she ran to the end of the passage and vanished through the wall.

Soron turned to Hem. "That was the hard one," he said. "Now you, Hem."

Hem sorted through his memories, wondering what it was that Zelika had seen. As he did so, he felt a small stab of envy: his memories had not the beauty of Saliman's. He could remember best the gate of the orphanage. It was made of thick, weathered wood, and it was always bolted fast. There was the gate of the house in Edinur, where he had briefly stayed with the Hulls, but that memory filled him with horror, and he dismissed it.

He shut his eyes, and summoned the orphanage gate to his mind's eye. It was of silver wood, so hardened and polished with age it was impossible to tell of what kind, and almost completely plain. It had once been washed with lime, and near the top was a crack. If you looked closely, you could see, very faintly, the patterns of knotholes in the wood. To the side was a tarnished brass handle, which turned and lifted a latch. When you opened it . . .

Irc gave a soft caw. A breath of cool air, like the air of a street in far-off Edinur, buffeted Hem's cheek. He opened his eyes, and he gasped. He was standing in a tunnel of stone, but at the far end, bathed in shifting sunlight, stood the gate to the orphanage.

"Quick, go through," whispered Soron, who was watching Hem closely. "There is not much time."

Hesitantly, Hem walked to the end of the passage. He knew the gate was not real, he knew he stood deep inside the earth, hundreds of leagues from Edinur; and yet he walked in cool, silver sunlight down an Annaren street. He put out his hand and touched the latch; the gate opened, and he passed through.

The gate shut behind him, and the sunlight vanished. Irc, who had been standing on Hem's shoulder trembling with joy, made a small, woeful noise and hid his eyes again. They were in another rocky passage, stretching forward into the dark, and behind Hem was an unpassable wall of stone. Nearby, he could hear the sound of running water. After his brief vision of the outside world, it seemed even colder and darker than before.

Saliman and Zelika stood nearby, in the unwavering magelight. Zelika, Hem saw, was in tears, and Saliman's hand was on her shoulder; neither of them spoke when they saw Hem, but merely nodded in greeting.

Shortly afterward, as Hem watched, fascinated, the blank stone seemed to shimmer, and Soron emerged through the wall.

"Now for the final gate," said Soron softly.

"What is this one?" asked Hem.

"The Gate of Water," said Saliman. "Come."

Saliman led them briskly down the tunnel. The roof now ran lower, so Saliman and Soron both had to stoop. In the confined space the sound of running water became louder and louder, its echo bouncing around the walls so that it was impossible to tell where it came from. It could have been a river running behind a wall of rock next to them, or even above them.

Before long the passage widened again, the walls drawing away from them, and the ground changed beneath their feet from rock to pale sand. The sound of running water grew louder still. At last they reached a fall of water, sparkling silver in the magelight, that blocked their way. Hem realized that an underground river must run high over their heads, and now plunged down into a deep abyss in front of them. He could not see how far the water fell, or what was beyond it, and the spray struck up a fine mist, wetting his face.

The roar of the river was so loud that he could not at first hear what Saliman said, and knew he was speaking only because his mouth moved. Saliman gestured them close to him, shouting into their ears.

"This will take some time," he said. "We cannot make a

magelight here: once past the water, there is a force that blocks all magery. Follow me closely, one by one. Soron, you come last. Hem, you first: stay very close to me, and step where I tell you. Take care that you do not slip; some of the rocks are slimy."

Hem nodded, and followed Saliman. He saw that a path curved around the extreme side of the tunnel, around the edge of the waterfall; it was certainly made by human hands. Saliman went cautiously, testing each step as he went, and Hem concentrated on placing his feet exactly where Saliman placed his. Saliman was right: the rock was in places very slippery.

Carefully and slowly they rounded the edge of the cave, and soon were almost underneath the waterfall, protected from being washed away only by an overhanging lip of rock. The path here was very narrow, scarcely wider than a man's foot was long, and there was nothing to hold on to. Saliman's magelight went out; and, his heart in his mouth, Hem leaned into the wall and tried to ignore the noise to his left, where massive volumes of water plunged down unseen—who knew how far—into some unimaginable gulf. Irc clung to his accustomed place on Hem's shoulder, hating the roar of the water and the utter blackness. It seemed to take an age, but at last the path widened, and then ran out onto a broader ledge.

Saliman paused here, breathing heavily. "The first part is over," he said. "We can rest here a short time."

Hem nodded and gingerly sat down, feeling the space with his hands. He felt more exhausted than their progress along the path, in truth a short way, seemed to warrant.

After too brief a break, they resumed their journey. This was challenging in a different way; they carefully made their way up a path as narrow as that which had skirted the waterfall, and so steep it was nearly vertical. Hem scrambled behind Saliman, feeling for each foot- and handhold, listening to Saliman's instructions, while Irc, night-blind, hung on painfully to his hair. The roar of the river gradually subsided behind them.

Despite the chill, Hem was dripping with sweat when they at last clambered over a lip of stone and fell onto level ground. He lay like a stranded fish, gulping in the air, dizzy with relief. Irc celebrated by pecking his face. Hem pushed the bird away.

It's all right for some, he said to Irc. *Some creatures didn't have to climb.*

Irc cawed complacently. He was more at ease now that they were no longer in an enclosed space.

"We're almost there, Hem," said Saliman. "I'll show you where you have come."

Saliman spread his hands, and a silver light filled the cavern. Hem blinked, and then crawled to the edge of the rock. What he saw made his whole body go cold. He was looking over the edge of a high cliff. He could see the dark line of the path he had just climbed, which plunged down some hundred spans and then turned sharply right onto the ledge where he and Saliman had rested. Then, if he squinted, he could see the narrow path that skirted the waterfall, until it disappeared into the spray of water and the darkness.

For the first time he realized what would have happened if he had slipped and fallen. The waterfall plunged down, long past the tiny path, into an abyss so deep he could not see the bottom. If he had known the full extent of the risk, he would have been almost paralyzed with fear. His blindness had been a mercy.

The illumination dimmed back to the tiny magelight, and Hem sat on the ledge, his heart hammering against his ribs with delayed terror.

"And you're going to do that four times?" he asked, sitting up and staring at Saliman with his mouth open.

"Five, there and back, actually." Saliman smiled at him tiredly. "Make a magelight, Hem, and wait for me. It will seem a long time, waiting here. But I will come back. Zelika is next."

Impulsively, Hem leaned forward and embraced Saliman. "May the Light guide your feet," he said, his mouth dry.

Saliman returned Hem's embrace, with a sudden, surprised tenderness. Then he opened his pack and took out a length of rope. He tied it around an outcrop of rock, carefully testing the knot, and threw it down the path.

"Going down won't be as hard as coming up," he said, grinning. "I'll return. Be patient." Then he grabbed the rope in his hands and let himself down the side of the cliff, into the darkness. His magelight went out. Hem remembered Saliman's instruction to make his own, and swiftly conjured one. He drank a couple of mouthfuls of water, nibbled some dried dates from his pack, and gave Irc a bit of dried meat. Then he composed himself to wait, trying not to think of what might happen if something went wrong.

As Saliman had warned, it seemed a very long time before he appeared again with Zelika. Hem felt very alone and very small, sitting in the dim, unchanging light above that terrifying abyss, with nothing to mark the passing of time. He tried to rest, but anxieties kept running through his mind like little mice: what if? what if? what if? He couldn't rid himself of them. At last he saw the rope tighten, and he scrambled to the edge of the cliff, carefully looking down to see Zelika and Saliman clambering up the final steep path and, as Hem had, climbing over the edge and collapsing. For a time, Saliman lay on his back, his chest heaving.

"It's bad enough having to do this once," he said. "Well, I can't keep Soron waiting too long." Then he disappeared again.

With Zelika's company, the waiting was not so bad. The children whiled away the time playing an old Annaren game—

knife, cloth, stone—that Hem had taught Zelika back in Turbansk. The rhythm of their chanting was soothing, and it seemed much quicker this time before Saliman reappeared with Soron.

Saliman simply lay down and didn't move for a while. Soron collapsed to the ground, his limbs trembling. After a short time he sat up and looked at the children. He reached for his pack and took out a flask of medhyl.

"By the Light, I hope I never have to journey that way ever again," he said. "That is the worst thing I have ever had to do."

"It was pretty bad," said Hem. "Saliman showed me what it looks like out there."

Soron shuddered. "I don't have to look," he said. "I could *feel* it." He took another gulp of the medhyl. "I do not like heights. And I almost fell."

"You slipped?" said Zelika.

"Aye, my feet are not so nimble as yours," said Soron. "I stumbled on that horrible narrow path. It felt like a very bad nightmare. I do not know how Saliman stopped me."

"Neither do I," said Saliman, from the ground. His chest was still heaving. "It was a near thing. But I did, and that is all that matters. Give me some of that medhyl, my friend; I need it too."

Soron shuddered again, and handed Saliman the flask. "I thank you, Saliman, from the bottom of my heart. Though my gratitude seems a poor return for my life."

"It will do." Saliman's teeth flashed white as he grinned, and took a deep draught of medhyl. "Come, the worst is over. We are almost there."

XIII

NEWS FROM ANNAR

A FTER running the gauntlet of the entrance to Nal-Ak-Burat, the last thing Hem expected to see was an actual gate. But there it was, right in front of him: a plain gate of brass glimmering dully in the magelight, stretching up to twice his height.

It was not far from the Gate of Water. They had walked away from the cliff, and the roof of the huge cavern had gradually become lower until once again they were walking through a cave, although this one was broad and high. Soon they had reached a wall that had clearly been made by human hands, and set into the wall was the brass gate.

Saliman reached out his hand and pushed the gate, and slowly it opened. A warm, flickering rush light spilled out into the cold darkness. From behind Saliman's shoulder, Hem peered through curiously, but could see nothing, apart from a torch flaming in a bracket by the gate.

Saliman quickly ushered them through, and soundlessly the brass gate closed behind them. They were in what appeared to be a broad thoroughfare, flagged with stone. It was lined on either side by windowless walls that were pierced irregularly with carved portals blocked by doors of the same dull brass as the gate they had just passed through. Others opened onto black passageways. The hair prickled on Hem's neck; perhaps someone stood in those black doorways and watched them.

"How strange!" said Zelika, and jumped. Her voice sounded unexpectedly loud. Aside from the faint crackle of the burning torch and their own breathing, the street was utterly silent, and her voice bounced disconcertingly.

"Yes, it is strange," said Saliman, taking the torch from its bracket and leading them down the street. "Strange and beautiful and sad. But let's find Hared. He won't be far from here."

With more eagerness than he had felt since they had entered the caves, Hem followed hard on Saliman's heels, down the empty, dark streets. Sometimes they saw flights of steps between the walls, leading into darkness, and far off, on heights and gulfs they could only dimly perceive, the outlines of more buildings. Sheltered from the scouring of wind and sun, the stone looked as if it might have been carved yesterday; every now and then he saw a crack in a wall, where the earth might have shifted, but that was all.

"What is this place?" Hem asked Saliman, as he hurried after him. "Who lived here?"

"Nobody knows," said Saliman. "Once this city must have been fair and populous; it stretches a league at least from end to end. And yet scarcely anything remains in memory of those who lived here—a line in a song here, a child's rhyme there . . ."

"Then how did you know about the Gates?" asked Zelika. "Somebody must have known."

"Bards have long memories," Saliman answered. "The site of this city, and how to enter it, has been passed down through the ages, from Bard to Bard. So, Hem and Zelika, count yourselves fortunate! Not many alive have seen this city. In the Great Silence, after the Nameless One overran the Eastern Suderain, Nal-Ak-Burat was used as a base from which to harry his forces. Alas, we were stronger then than we are now: for neither Baladh nor Turbansk fell to the Nameless One in those dark times. It was wise to keep this place secret, against the time we might need it again."

At this, they turned out of the street into a massive square, and Hem gasped. Here the roof of the cavern leaped away, out of sight, so it was almost as if they stood in the open air. Irc gave a hopeful caw; for a brief moment he had thought they were outside under a night sky. Nearby was a Bard lamp, and its pure, steady light falling onto the pale stone made Hem blink. They still could not see any sign of people. Hem wondered briefly why there were no guards or watchmen, but then thought of the Three Gates. They were surely guard enough.

Carved into the rock wall to their left was a wide doorway, its lintel surrounded by the same strange runes they had seen by the Three Gates. Saliman led them inside, into a huge, well-illuminated chamber. The walls were covered in murals that must once have been bright, but now the colors were so faint it was hard to make them out; he saw the shape of an ibis, and a strange beast with the head of a lion and the body of a woman. There was an incongruous smell, faint but unmistakable, of cooking: spices and meat. Hem's mouth started to water.

Saliman stood by the door and shouted Hared's name, making the children jump. It sounded much too loud in that silent place.

"If I'm not mistaken, it is time for dinner," said Saliman, turning with a smile. "Or breakfast. Who knows what time it is in the upper world? A meal, anyway."

"Something hot would be right welcome," said Soron. "I am sick to my back teeth of dried dates."

But now they heard footsteps, and a man entered the chamber from the far end and came toward them. He was very tall, and his skin was very black, darker even than Saliman's, and he was dressed simply in a tunic and loose trousers. He looked older than Saliman, and tougher. Unconsciously Hem drew closer to Saliman as he approached them.

"Greetings, Saliman," the man said soberly, taking his hand and embracing him. "I should be more glad to see you, if it were not for the news your presence brings. So Turbansk has fallen?"

"Alas, it is so, Hared. You have not heard?"

The man dropped his eyes, and was briefly silent.

"News has been hard to come by, the past week," he said at last. "These are evil days. Alas, for my home! We must skulk in the heart of the earth, and struggle for better times. But tell me, who are your companions? You bring children here?" He stared with undisguised curiosity and a touch of disapproval at Hem and Zelika. Irc, who was recovering some of his normal equilibrium, gave a defiant caw.

"You know Soron of Til Amon," said Saliman shortly. "Hared of Turbansk, this is Hem of Turbansk, and our friend Zelika of the House of Il Aran, of Baladh. Now, my friend, we have traveled far, and we are hungry: we can smell your dinner. Is there enough to share?"

Hared nodded courteously in greeting, although the look of disapproval on his face did not fade. "There is plenty to share. Plain food, but good. Though now a famous cook has joined us, eh? Perhaps things are looking up."

"Are the others inside?"

"A few of us," said Hared. "Come."

He strode to the far end of the room, and disappeared into a wide hallway, also well-lit. Zelika and Hem trailed after the others, feeling awkward and shy; Hared was rather intimidating. As they neared the end of the passage, they began to hear the murmur of people talking. It made Hem realize that he had not heard other people for days on end. They entered a small chamber, decorated like the larger room with faded murals, and warmed by a brazier of glowing coals. In the middle was a low table of polished stone, and around it were, surprisingly, a number of comfortable cushions, covered in brightly colored silks. The table itself was set for a meal, with many small brass

dishes of sauces and even a jug of wine. Around it sat four
people: a man and three women. Hem saw immediately that
they were all Bards, but he didn't recognize any of them. The
tallest woman stood up and greeted them.

Saliman spread out his hands, smiling. "Do not get up,
Narbila," he said. "Sufficient courtesy if we are permitted to
double your guests, and to rest on those wonderfully soft cushions. My body is bruised from sleeping on rocks."

"It is a hard journey from Turbansk," she said. "But, as
always, you time your arrival well, Saliman. Unidan is just
bringing dinner. But tell us, who are your friends?"

While Soron and the children were seated and introduced,
one of the Bards brought in various dishes from the adjoining
room. There were meats in thick sauces, smelling of cardamom
and coriander and garlic, and a basket of freshly baked unleav-
ened bread, and a dish of spiced pulses, all served in shallow
bowls of intricately engraved brass. Hem was so intent upon the
food—he felt as if he had not eaten a solid meal for weeks—
that he failed to catch anyone's name; suddenly it was as if a
wild animal were clawing at his vitals. Zelika nudged him in his
ribs.

"It's rude to glare at food like a starving tiger," she muttered.
"You must wash."

Hem started, and cleansed his hands in a dish of water that
was being passed around the table. Then, without further formality, they began eating. Irc was being very polite—for him, at
least—and remained demurely on Hem's lap while he fed him
titbits of meat. Although all the Bards eyed Hem's bird with
wonder, they were too courteous to comment on Irc's presence.

Soron tasted the food, and nodded approvingly.

"Very good," he said. "How do you get goat meat down
here? And wild duck? I see no farmlands!"

"Fresh meat is rare, so you are lucky," said Hared, smiling.

Hem noticed that his smile did not reach his eyes. "The northern entrance to Nal-Ak-Burat is not so forbidding as the Three Gates, if arduous in other ways, and supplies are more easily brought through there, if we can get them. And at a pinch— though we are not so desperate at present—there are fish in the lake and bats in the upper caves."

Hem wrinkled his nose at the thought of eating bats.

"Strange fish we find here," said Narbila. "Some do not have eyes. But good to eat, if cooked well."

Hem's whole attention was on food for some time. He thought he had never had so delicious a meal. But once his initial hunger was allayed, he began to take notice of the Bards, and to sort out who was who. Narbila, the tall woman, and Hared seemed to bear the most authority, although there was little sense of a hierarchy. They were, Hem found out later, both members of Turbansk's Second Circle. The other three Bards— Orona, Nimikera, and Irisanu—had the paler skin of those from farther east; Nimikera originally hailed from Jerr-Niken, a School that had been razed by the Nameless One shortly after Pellinor had been destroyed, and Irisanu was from Baladh. Orona did not say where she came from.

None of the Bards mentioned Turbansk until their guests had finished eating. Hem realized that this was out of courtesy, and not lack of interest; when Narbila asked Saliman for news of Turbansk, her voice trembled.

Saliman told what had happened to the city, and the Bards listened attentively without interrupting, their eyes downcast. When he spoke of Juriken summoning the earthquake, the Bards gasped, and Hem saw that even Hared's eyes clouded. When Saliman finished his story, there was a long, heavy silence.

"It is good to have news," said Hared at last. "Even such sorrowful news as that you bring. I thank you. We have heard

nothing from Turbansk since Imank besieged it. Even our birds
could not get past the Black Army."

"Aye, well," said Soron. "It is a heavy grief, to live in such
times as these, and to tell such things. It will get darker, I trow,
before the end. But Hared, have you news yourself? Do you
know what is happening in Annar? I confess, my heart hungers
to hear of my old home, Til Amon."

"Yes, we have news. I will speak of it later." Hared shot a
swift glance at Hem and Zelika, which spoke plainly of his mistrust. Zelika opened her mouth to protest indignantly, but
Saliman put his hand on her arm to silence her.

"Speak now what you know," he said calmly. "There are
none here who have not proven their trustworthiness."

Hared's lips tightened, but he met Saliman's eyes and nodded.

"If you say so, Saliman, then it must be so." He paused, as if
gathering his thoughts. "It is a complex tale. Annar, we hear, is
on the brink of civil war. Enkir has sent out orders for men-at-
arms to all Schools and cities, and those who refuse to supply
them are considered to be traitors and enemies of the Light.
We believe that Enkir plans an assault, probably on Lanorial,
Ileadh, and Culain, and that it is likely that he plans it for when
Imank establishes a base in the Suderain and pushes north into
Annar. We expect, from what little we have found out about
how he moves his forces, that might happen sooner rather than
later."

"It depends whether Imank decides to attack Amdridh,"
said Saliman, frowning. "It will not be nearly so easy to take as
Baladh or Turbansk: the defenses are stout, and protected by
both mountain and sea. And we do not know how dearly the
siege of Turbansk has cost the Black Army; the earthquake must
have had some effect, and if they wish to use Turbansk as a
base, they will now have to rebuild some of the city. That will
delay them, surely? And I judge that even the Nameless One

cannot muster enough soldiers to attack both the north and west at once."

"We are not so sure," said Narbila, leaning forward. "We suspect that the forces set upon Baladh and Turbansk are but a tithe of his strength. There are rumors that the Plains before the Kulkilhirien are black with soldiers, and yet more gather from within Dén Raven. They could, of course, be rumors spread by Hulls, to make us despair. . . . We need to be sure one way or another, but our activities have been curtailed of late—"

"But what of civil war?" interrupted Soron eagerly. "What of Til Amon? Do you mean that Schools in Annar are now rebelling against Enkir?"

"It is hard to know," said Hared. "You must understand, Soron, that much of the news from Annar is very uncertain, and comes through perilous routes. Our most reliable sources are the Pilanel messengers, who ride through all Annar, but in many places the Pilanel are persecuted now, and it is difficult for them to range as widely as once they did. We know that the Seven Kingdoms prepare for war; none of them believes any longer that Enkir will stay his fist."

"What of the Schools of Annar? Do they stand back and say nothing? Has no one heard of the Balance?" Soron leaned over the table, his face flushed with anger.

"It does not all go Enkir's way," Hared answered. "Since the rumors that he plans to invade the Seven Kingdoms, some Schools are rousing: not since the Long Wars has the alliance been threatened so. We hear that some Schools have lodged emissaries of protest with Norloch: Elevé, Lok, Innail, Lirigon, and Arnocen for certain. Enkir is not yet sure in his power, and must still woo the Bards of Annar. Til Amon and Eledh, we hear, say neither yea nor nay: they are two weeks' straight march from Norloch, and have neither mountain nor distance to protect them, should the hammer fall there first. And I think they are right to be afraid: Norloch is powerful and Enkir is likely to make an example of them, so that others will be afraid and follow."

Soron's face had darkened as Hared spoke. "Even with those Schools you name, that leaves precious few to side with Norloch," he growled. "Ettinor, Desor . . . I can think of no others. The rest are all in the Seven Kingdoms, or abandoned, like Zimek; or destroyed by fire and war, like Jerr-Niken and Pellinor and Baladh and Turbansk."

Without warning, Soron's face crumpled, and he hid his face in his hands. He made no sound, but his shoulders shook. Hem, who was sitting next to him, tentatively put his hand on his arm, wanting to comfort him. By a great effort of will, Soron collected himself; he looked up at Hared, his eyes damp and red. The other Bards watched him gravely.

"Forgive me," he said. "There are too many losses. And this dark night has scarce begun."

"There is nothing to forgive, my friend," said Orona. She spoke Suderain with a strange accent that Hem could not place. "The betrayal is not yours."

"None should be ashamed of grief," said Hared, his face hard. "But now we have our backs to the wall. It is fighting we should be thinking of now."

"If the Annaren Schools are against Enkir—" began Soron.

"Some are," Hared answered. "But we do not know how deep corruption runs within them."

"Innail stands firm," said Saliman.

"I believe you," Hared said. "But in others—even those who protest war against the Seven Kingdoms—there are many who are reluctant to see that Enkir has allied himself with the Nameless One, and stretches out a greedy claw for his share of the Seven Kingdoms. They listen to his blandishments, and reckon those who speak against him as rebels. We do not know in many places how the dice will fall."

"But can't they see?" said Zelika impatiently. She had been listening intently to the conversation, but this was the first thing she had said since they had sat down. "Aren't Bards supposed to be wise?"

"Wisdom oft trips itself," said Nimikera. "And you must remember, people are afraid. Enkir promises that he alone can defend the Light against the Dark. And as things worsen in Annar, they turn to him as their hope. The defeat of Baladh and Turbansk only strengthens his hand."

Zelika looked as if she might spit, but said nothing further. Hem knew how she felt. After what he had seen in Turbansk, the thought of Bards working with the Dark made him feel sick in the pit of his stomach.

"The other thing is, you must not forget the Stewards," Nimikera continued. "In many places in Annar, even where the Schools hold firm, there is much distrust of Bards, and the people have turned against them."

"That is not always the fault of the people," said Saliman, with a note of disgust. "I do not know if you have seen Ettinor Bards in action—they do not deserve the name."

"That is true, I admit," said Nimikera. "Arrogance and complacency have done much to damage the cause of Barding, and we all know the Light has been in retreat for many decades, dozing in the sun as the Nameless One gathered his strength. But neither is it always the fault of the Bards. The Nameless One has taken great care to sow suspicion of Bards and the Lore, these past decades. And now it is clear how well he has set his seed; malice and suspicion grow everywhere, and no man trusts his neighbor. Most of Annar now is traversed by armies of brigands, which kidnap children, we hear, as well as forcing farmers and others to be soldiers. Some say they are led by Hulls, but it seems not all of them are. Enkir claims these are armies of rebel Bards, though we are certain that they roam under his orders."

"So my friend, dark news, as ever," said Narbila. "It is hard to see hope anywhere. All goes the way of the Nameless, and the Light darkens. To fight what we face is to court despair. But to bow our heads and submit to the Nameless One is beyond thinking; we must fight, even if we know there is no hope for us. And we must remember, we are not alone."

A gloomy silence settled over the table. At last Hared stirred, and looked at Saliman.

"But tell me, Saliman: what of your own plans? Who are these children you brought with you? Do you plan to stay with us, to help us in our work, or are other things afoot that we know nothing of?"

Saliman grinned at Hared. "You are perceptive, as always, Hared," he said.

"I'd be a dead man, else," answered the other Bard, studying Saliman narrowly.

"It is true. Well, my answer to your last question is both yes and no. I think we must spy out the extent of the forces arraigned against Annar, and take that knowledge north. And there are those plans we spoke of a month ago, which I wish to discuss with you. Once those duties are fulfilled, I plan to go to Annar."

"To find Maerad," Hem said, interrupting.

"Maerad?" said Hared.

"My sister."

"Do you mean Maerad of Pellinor?"

Hem nodded, and Hared looked at him properly for the first time.

"She's your sister? Yes, I have heard of Maerad of Pellinor, and that some say the Fated One has been found. To be honest, I do not put great faith in prophecies. And it seems to me very unlikely that a young girl could be the hero foretold in song and legend."

"But she is, anyway." Hem's bottom lip stuck out. "Whether you believe it or not, she will bring down the Nameless One, in his darkest rising." He had decided that he did not like Hared.

"In any case," said Saliman, giving Hem a warning look. "North we will go."

Hem woke and stretched luxuriously, thinking for a moment he was in Turbansk: he lay on a palliasse stuffed with rushes and some sweet-smelling herb, and was covered with a warm blanket. For days he had been sleeping on stone, with only a pack for a pillow; this was comfort beyond belief. But then, with a start, he remembered that he was in Nal-Ak-Burat.

He sat up and looked around. Irc, who had snuggled up next to Hem, gave a sleepy caw of protest at being disturbed. Hem was in a tiny chamber, scarcely larger than the palliasse he lay on, with a low door covered with a length of heavy woven fabric. Light spilled through the door, and outside he could hear a low hubbub of voices. He began to listen; surely they were little children? He shook his head. He was who knows how far underground, in a city of stone; there could be no children here . . . There was a faint crash, as if something had been dropped on the floor, and someone started crying.

Consumed by curiosity, Hem pulled back the cloth over the doorway and peered into the next room, a fair-sized chamber that opened into about a dozen of these sleeping rooms. He had indeed heard children, at least half a dozen of them. None looked older than five years old, and some wore bandages: one on her head, and another little boy had both his arms wrapped. They were playing with some carved blocks of wood: the crying

Hem had heard had erupted after a squabble over a particularly desirable block.

Zelika was sitting at a table watching them, with a child scarcely more than a baby on her lap. When she noticed Hem, she looked up and smiled.

"What are they doing here?" Hem asked in wonder.

"They were all rescued after the Black Army overran Savitir," she said, speaking in Annaren so the children could not understand them. "Probably their parents were murdered. And there was nowhere else for them to go, so Irisanu brought them here, where at least they'll be safe."

"So who else lives in this benighted place, then?" Hem stepped out, rubbing the sleep out of his eyes. "I don't remember these last night."

"They were probably all asleep when we went to bed." Zelika gently jogged the baby on her lap, stroking his hair, while the others played about her feet. "This one is Banu, the others say. Nobody knows where he is from. He's sweet, no? What we call a sunchild."

Disconcerted by Zelika's sudden motherliness, Hem stared at Banu. He was the color of dark honey, with black curls like Zelika's, and big brown eyes. He was chewing on a piece of bone, and dribbling profusely.

"He's teething, poor baby," said Zelika. She rubbed his gums hard with her fingers and Banu bit down on her knuckle.

"So they put us in with the babies last night?" said Hem. He sat down with Zelika. "That would be Hared, I suppose. He didn't like us much."

"Oh, Nimikera said not to worry about that. It's just his way."

"So, what are they going to do with us now? Keep us locked up here?"

"We're not locked up. Anyway, it's nice to play with babies

again." Zelika pushed her hair out of her eyes. "All their
families are dead or missing, poor chicks. No, Mutir, give that
to Asra." She carefully put Banu down on the ground and
firmly took a block away from a little boy with thunderously
drawn eyebrows. "She had it first."

Instead of howling, as Hem had expected, the little boy
meekly gave up the block and began to play quite happily with
another toy. Hem watched Zelika in wonder for a little longer.
This was a side of her he had not suspected. Not for the first
time, he wondered about Zelika's family; she must have had
little brothers or sisters, or maybe small cousins. If so, she never
spoke about them.

"Where's Saliman?" he asked restlessly.

"If you go through that door and down the passage, you'll
find the room we ate in last night. I think Saliman's around
there somewhere," Zelika said vaguely. She had picked Banu
up again and he had grabbed a lock of her hair in his fist and
was trying to eat it.

Hem walked down the short passage to the room they had
been in the night before—at least, he supposed it was the
night before. It was so long since he had seen day and night
that he no longer had any idea what time it might be in the
upper world. He heard voices, one of which he was sure was
Saliman's, and he hesitantly looked through the doorway.
Hared and Saliman were deep in conversation at the stone
table, but no one else was there. Saliman looked up when he
heard Hem's footsteps.

"Hem! Come in. I suppose you are looking to break your
fast?"

Hared said nothing, but kept his eyes fixed on Hem as he
walked toward them.

"Er—yes, I was wondering if there was anything to eat."
Despite himself, Hem blushed with awkwardness.

"There's some dohl in the next room, I believe," said Saliman. "See for yourself. It might be a bit cold: you slept long."

Hem walked across the chamber, conscious all the time of Hared's gaze drilling into his back. Next door was a large galley, with a stone trough still full of water for washing dishes, and an iron oven. On the oven, as Saliman had promised, was a covered pot of dohl. Hem found a clean bowl and spoon, and some honey, on a shelf nearby. After he had helped himself, he took a deep breath and went back into the next room. He sat down with his meal at the far end of the table, trying to look as if he weren't there.

"Fifteen, at least," Hared was saying. "It is hard to know who was captured and who was killed. We haven't been able to get out there since."

Saliman whistled. "And from Nuk Caves?"

"Another six killed. Munira saw them blasted before she got away. But we are being hunted like vermin."

Saliman stared down at the table. "I suppose you have considered whether there is an informant in our midst."

"Aye." Hem couldn't see Hared's face, but his tone sent chills down his back. He would not like to be the traitor Hared uncovered, he thought; there would be no mercy. "But I trust all those in Nal-Ak-Burat, at least."

Despite himself, Hem was listening hard, and now Hared looked up at him. He busied himself with his breakfast, trying to look as if he had not been eavesdropping.

"Good morrow, lad," said Hared. "Saliman has told me of some of your adventures. We have seen those deathcrows, but only far off. We need someone with birdlore here: our chief birdmaster was killed only two days ago."

Scarlet, Hem nodded. "I like birds," he blurted out.

"Don't mind Hared," said Saliman. He seemed to be amused by Hem's awkwardness, which only made the boy feel more embarrassed. "He is as tough and twisted as an old olive tree, but you could not have a better man at your back in a tight spot."

"Oh. I'm sure," said Hem. An awkward silence fell, and he spooned up the rest of his dohl as quickly as he could.

"The dogsoldiers don't seem to be able to smell children," said Hared thoughtfully. "Our soldiers have noticed that much. And young Hem seems a smart lad. Perhaps the boy could spy for us. I have been wondering about those child armies—"

"Hem will do no such thing," said Saliman sharply. "Do not think of it, Hared. He has not the skills."

"Skill can be taught."

Hem looked up into Hared's cold gaze, his heart quickening.

"I wouldn't mind doing something like that," he said slowly. "I would like to do something. Zelika would, too. I mean, if you think I could help . . ."

"I do not wish you to walk into harm's way, Hem," said Saliman.

"There's nowhere out of harm's way," Hem answered bitterly. "Except here, maybe. And I can't live underground for the rest of my life." Suddenly he was overwhelmed by a longing to feel the warmth of the sun on his skin, to breathe wind that smelled of grass and trees, rather than the cold, unchanging air of underground. "I haven't seen the sunlight for so long."

Saliman looked displeased, but said nothing further, and the conversation moved on to other topics. Hem, feeling a little more at ease now that Hared wasn't treating him as a potential traitor, furtively took the opportunity to study him. He found the Bard both fascinating and repellent; there was something in his face, a pitilessness edging to cruelty, that chilled him. It was difficult to work out Saliman's attitude toward him; he clearly trusted him, but Hem thought that he did not regard him as a friend.

Hem learned that the network of caves beneath Savitir

extended through Nazar almost to Dén Raven, and were used by the Bards to gain information that was sent on to trusted Bards in Annar, or used to mount minor attacks on the Black Army behind their front lines. A resistance was gathering shape even as the Nameless One consolidated his power in the Suderain.

"Our only power is in knowledge," Hared explained. "We are not many, but among our numbers we count some of the most skillful Bards in Edil-Amarandh; we may lose now, but we struggle so there is hope for the future. We are entering an age like the Great Silence, when the Nameless One held sway over all our world, and the Light was kept in just such places as these. All the same, our recent losses hit hard."

Saliman nodded abstractedly. "There are many levels to this struggle," he said. "Remember Maerad's foredream, Hem? The voice that spoke to her out of the Shadow, and said: *I live in every human heart?*" He shot a piercing glance at Hared. "The time has come for every person to choose where they place their faith: and that choosing may be more difficult than it seems."

"What do you mean?" asked Hem, bewildered by the sudden change of tack.

"It may be a question of whether to use the weapons of the Dark in order to worst the Dark, or whether it is better to be defeated, with all that defeat means."

"Your riddles are meaningless, my friend," growled Hared. "This is the problem with most Bards. It's so easy to debate right and wrong, while our house collapses around us. I do not think in such terms."

"I know that, Hared," said Saliman softly. "Our situation is desperate indeed: I understand that as well as you do. But how can we say that we fight for the Light, if we show ourselves no better than the Dark?"

Hared's lips tightened into a thin, unforgiving line, and an expression of mortal offense flashed over his face. In the accompanying silence, Hem looked from Bard to Bard, feeling suddenly alarmed. For a moment the tension that flared between them made him wonder if knives would be drawn. They seemed to be arguing, but he had no idea what about: perhaps earlier, before he came into the room, they had been debating some tactic of which Saliman deeply disapproved.

Hared laughed, and the moment passed as if it had never been. "You ask difficult questions," he said. "I suppose that is your special gift. I respect you for it, Saliman. But I tell you, there are times when choice is beyond us, and we must do what we must."

Saliman smiled, but with an underlying grimness. "There is always a choice, my friend," he said heavily. "There is always a choice."

XIV

THE SKYLESS CITY

IT was some time before Hem breathed open air again. By then, living underground seemed almost normal; even Irc had regained his usual insouciance, and had become a favorite of the Bards at Nal-Ak-Burat, despite the almost immediate resumption of his bad habit of thieving bright objects.

Within a day, Hem had met everyone in the small community that based themselves in the underground city. There were about sixteen Bards, as well as the six small children, who were kept there, as Zelika had said, because there was nowhere else to go. The children were mainly cared for by a Bard called Nimikera of Jerr-Niken, a silent woman who had been injured in some recent incident; the top of a vicious, barely healed scar was visible on her neck, running down toward her breast, and she walked with a bad limp.

The Bards in Nal-Ak-Burat were only a small part of a network working behind the lines of the Black Army; most of them hid in the honeycomb of caves that ran beneath Savitir and Nazar. Saliman told Hem that their true number was kept secret; only the leaders—the five Bards they had met on their first encounter—knew the true extent of the resistance. This was to protect the network if any were captured by Imank's forces.

"There is a chance that Hulls could scry them against their will, and find everything they know," Saliman explained. "So it is politic that the left hand does not know what the right hand is doing, lest we lose both."

Hem had been scried during his short stay in Norloch, voluntarily opening his mind to that of another Bard's. The thought of such an invasion, made without permission, made him shudder. "But what if Hared or someone were captured?" he asked. "Wouldn't the same thing happen?"

"Do you remember how Dernhil killed himself, rather than be scried by Hulls and betray Maerad?" said Saliman. "That is the last defense. And Hared or any of the other Bards would do exactly that, if they were captured. But still, it is easier to keep a secret if you don't know it in the first place."

Hared had again raised the question of Hem working for the Bards, and Hem, both excited and daunted by the prospect, had talked it over with Zelika. Initially, to his surprise, she was dubious.

"I don't know, Hem," she said. "What could we do? Perhaps it is better to do as Saliman says, and to stay out of danger."

Hem was so taken aback by Zelika's change of heart that he didn't know what to say. "But you want to fight the Black Army, don't you? Don't you want revenge for your family? To help the Light? You're the one who went to join the attack in Turbansk, not me—"

Zelika avoided Hem's eye as she answered. "Yes, I did," she said. "And I learned my lesson. I am probably more use here, helping with the babies." Even as they spoke, she was dandling Banu on her lap.

"But Hared says this is a way we might help," said Hem.

"And what does Saliman say?"

Hem was silent. Saliman was against the idea, and angry with Hared for speaking to Hem about it without his consent; as Zelika knew very well, it had been a subject of contentious argument between the Bards.

"But if we can help . . ." said Hem, waving his arms around with frustration. "If we could do something—Hared says we can help in ways that others can't."

Zelika put Banu down and looked soberly at Hem, her head on one side.

"That may well be true, but I don't trust Hared," she said. "I mean, it's not like he's a traitor or anything. It's just that he doesn't care about us; if we died, he would think it perfectly fine as long as he got the information he wanted. And even Hared admits it's dangerous work."

"But there's nowhere that's not dangerous—" Hem began to argue, but Zelika interrupted.

"Hem, I don't feel anymore that I want to die. Saliman wouldn't get so cross about it if he thought we would be all right. And it's not as if he exactly coddles us. After all, he let us stay in Turbansk, which was hardly safe."

"Yes, I know." Hem pushed his fingers through his hair. He didn't understand why he was so attracted to the idea of helping the Bards in their perilous work against the Black Army. He just knew that when Hared had suggested the idea, his heart had jumped in his breast with a mixture of fear and excitement. Somehow, he felt he could do this work, and do it well. He was tired of feeling useless in the struggle against the Dark.

But aside from that, a deep anger had begun to smolder inside him. He thought of how the Dark had blighted his life, almost from the moment he had been born; how the School that should have been his home had been burned to the ground, his family captured and slaughtered; and how he had been kidnapped by Hulls and put in the orphanage. His childhood had been stolen by the Nameless One, as surely as if he had burned the School and murdered his father with his own hands. And now his second home, Turbansk, lay in ruins like the first. He had no prospect of any other, apart from refuges like Nal-Ak-Burat.

Nightmares had begun to torment him again. He would wake in his small room gasping and drenched in sweat, fending off half-remembered visions of the ceremony the Hulls had held to turn him into one of them, when they had ordered him to murder another boy from the orphanage called Mark. Hem hadn't known him well, but he quite liked him. His anguished, terrified, despairing face haunted Hem's waking hours. This was the Dark, he thought. This was its essence: the terror that stamped the faces of the innocent, the wanton cruelty that joyed in this terror, the horrifying indifference. He hated it with all his heart; and he wanted to do what he could to defeat it.

He looked up and saw that Zelika was contemplating him with what he felt was an uncomfortably sharp perception. "I don't want to die, either," he mumbled. "But I can't stay here, doing nothing. I'll go mad."

"Help me with the babies, then," said Zelika. "It's time for them to eat."

"That's not what I meant," he said petulantly. But all the same, he followed her to the galley and ladled food out into bowls, puzzling over this new Zelika. She glanced at him as she fed Banu.

"I know what you're thinking," she said.

"Do you?" said Hem, with a touch of belligerence.

"You're wondering why I don't want to fight."

"Well, yes . . ."

"It was the Second Gate. The Gate of Dreams, when we had to remember to get through."

Hem nodded.

"I saw the gate to my home, in Baladh. And you know, for a

little while I really thought it was there." A longing woke in her voice. "I thought that if I ran through, I would be in Baladh again, with my little brother, Arlian, running up to me so I could pick him up. I thought I could sit with him by the pool of water lilies, and look down at the golden fish. We had a lot of fish, and they were so beautiful . . ."

Zelika's voice wavered, and she wiped Banu's face briskly before she continued. "I'm not used to magery," she said. "I didn't understand that it would just vanish when I passed through. Saliman explained it all. But, I don't know, after that . . . I felt a bit different."

Hem thought of the orphanage gate he had passed through in the Gate of Dreams, and then of Saliman's warning that he should choose his memory carefully. Perhaps he had chosen badly. Perhaps he had unwittingly brought into the city of Nal-Ak-Burat something of the anger and despair he had felt in Edinur, just as Zelika had found a fleeting vision of the peace of her lost home. Maybe that was why he felt such a desire to avenge himself against the Dark. But the thought did nothing to dispel his restlessness.

Over the next few days, Hem and Zelika spent their spare time exploring Nal-Ak-Burat. Saliman reluctantly gave them permission, but told them to stay away from the northern and southern Gates, and to be careful—it was easy to get lost, and to end up wandering for hours through a maze of stone. And some places were perilous: there were stairways that wound up great cliffs that, if they had ever had handrails, now lacked them. A careless step could mean a fall of thirty spans or more.

At first they confined their forays to the huge square and its surrounding alleys, which covered a large flat area that made up the heart of the city. It was easy to see why the Bards had chosen their current building—it had obviously been some kind of palace, where many people had lived, and was built to a human scale. The other buildings that flanked the south side of the square, some of them carved deep into the rocky walls, made the children feel like ants. They walked through rooms so high that the ceilings—if they existed at all, for there was little need for roofs underground—vanished into shadow high above their heads, while before them columns marched in unvarying rows, dwindling into the distance.

The walls were most often decorated with murals similar to those they had seen in the entrance room to the palace, and they spent hours examining them. Some, in the inner rooms, were astoundingly well preserved, with colors almost as bright as they must have been when they were first painted. They told inscrutable stories: here a king was bowing to a giant heron, offering the bird what seemed to be a platter of fruit; there a line of men were chained together, being led by the same king in a war chariot, while behind them walked a giant cat plumed with feathers. Another picture showed what seemed to be the same prisoners being killed: a figure in a robe held a long knife, with which he was cutting the throat of one, while the others stood in a row behind him, as if they were next. Hem and Zelika passed by that scene quickly. In the next picture, a man stood with his arms outspread, and leaves grew from his limbs, as if he were transforming into a tree. Fascinated, Hem and Zelika traced the outlines of the runes that interleaved the pictures, wondering what they meant.

"Perhaps that one," said Hem, indicating the tree man, "is an Elidhu. A wood Elidhu. Maerad says they can change their form."

"I thought Bards could change, if they wanted to," said Zelika, looking curiously at Hem.

"No. They can *seem* to change—that's easy."

"Can you do that?" asked Zelika. She had never been very

interested in Bardic magery, but her experience at the Gate of
Dreams had sparked her curiosity.

"Of course I can!" said Hem, slightly indignantly. Glimmerspells were the least of enchantments, and even though he had
paid small attention at the School of Turbansk, he could do illu-
sions. He thought for a moment, then looked down at his
hands. As Zelika watched, she gasped: green tendrils shot out
of the ends of his fingers, and out of his arms and legs. As she
watched, Hem burst into leaf before her eyes.

"I didn't know you could do that," said Zelika, with a new
respect in her voice.

Hem lifted his hands, and the leaves vanished. "Any Bard
can," he said dismissively. "The only problem is, it doesn't
work on other Bards, unless they agree, of course. Or Hulls. So
you can't fool Bard eyes."

"Well, maybe the tree man is a Bard."

"Maybe. Some kind of Bardic people lived here, for sure.
This place is stiff with magery; you can feel it everywhere. It's
woven into the very walls. But it's strange. You can feel it's very
old, and it's like those pictures—you can't read it."

"Might it be dangerous, do you think?" asked Zelika in a
low voice. "They killed people. And who were the dead, in the
First Gate?"

Hem remembered the First Gate with a shudder. "All
magery can be dangerous," he said, after a pause. "That's why
Bards go on and on about the Balance. You don't have to be a
Hull to do things that you might regret. But I'm not sure Bards
could use this magic; it's too strange. Maybe if we could read
the runes, they might explain something. I wonder what this
place was for?"

They looked around at the massive chamber. It was
impossible to guess its use; maybe it had been some kind of
throne room, or a meeting place for the people of the city. At

one end there was a dais, raised the height of a man above the rest of the room; but like everything else, it revealed nothing, resonant with a massive significance that no one now could understand.

"Maybe it was a temple of some kind," said Zelika.

"A temple?" Hem looked inquiringly at Zelika; such things were unknown in Annar.

"A place where people came to worship their gods."

"You mean, like Elidhu? But people don't worship Elidhu . . ." began Hem.

"In some places, people make shrines," said Zelika. "And they pray to their gods for help, if they need something."

Hem looked confused. "Why don't they ask a Bard for a charm, then?" he asked. "That's what people usually do. When Bards are around, that is."

"It's not like that. They believe in their gods, and they worship them. It's kind of . . . how they explain the world. And how they work out good and bad."

"Do you know anyone who does this?" asked Hem, astonished.

Zelika looked at him slyly. "It's not so strange. Don't Bards worship the Light?"

"Well, they . . . they don't exactly *worship* it," said Hem carefully. "It's more about the Balance, and things like that—about how you act." He shook his head; this conversation made him feel slightly dizzy. "Do you know anyone who does it?"

"I knew some who worshipped the Light, in Baladh," said Zelika.

"But that doesn't make any sense. How can you worship the Light? It's not there to be worshipped."

"They did, all the same. Just because it doesn't make any sense to you doesn't mean that it didn't make any sense to *them*. Bards don't know everything."

"They don't say they do," said Hem hotly. "No one does."

"Well, then."

Irc nibbled Hem's ear to calm him down. Zelika was getting annoyed, and Irc still had vivid memories of what happened when Zelika became angry. So they dropped the subject by mutual consent, and walked from one end of the huge hall to another, Hem's magelight seeming small and fragile in the echoing darkness. It took them a long time. The stone flags of the floor were covered with a fine layer of sandy dust, which their feet kicked into the air, so their mouths became dry and gritty. The place possessed a melancholy grandeur that became more oppressive the farther they went.

"I wonder who the people were who lived here?" said Zelika, as they stared at the dais. They had thought of climbing up, but there were no steps; and they both felt that they were somehow intruding, and were eager to leave.

"I don't know," said Hem. "But they're all dead now. I wonder if the place misses them?"

Zelika didn't answer. Thoughtfully they retraced their steps, and went back to the palace, where it was a relief to see homely firelight and to hear the hubbub of ordinary conversation.

Away from the square they found smaller buildings that had clearly once been homes. These were of much humbler dimensions, often built one on top of the other and linked by precarious stairways cut into the rock. Many of them lacked roofs—not because they had fallen in, but because they had never been there in the first place. This seemed strange, until they remembered that it never rained in Nal-Ak-Burat. The eating and sleeping rooms were small and all were roofed, Hem supposed, to keep the warmth in. They found hearths still black with ashes that had been cold for countless years, and in these places they found other signs that human beings had lived there—crumbling bones; the remains of some long-since-eaten meal; clay pots decorated with patterns pressed in by a stick; or iron pots so pitted with rust they fell to pieces as soon as they were touched. In one house they discovered a wooden chest, painted with strange designs; and when they opened it, they saw that it contained cloths of embroidered crimson silk. Zelika gasped with wonder: but even as they stared, the silks, preserved in the airless chest, lost color and crumbled, leaving behind only dust that exhaled an elusive perfume, the remains, perhaps, of frankincense or nard that had once impregnated the cloth.

The more they saw of the city, the more mysterious it became. Its riddles multiplied under their fascinated eyes: the stories told by the murals, which they could only guess at, or the strange objects they sometimes found, the uses of which had vanished with the people who made them. But perhaps what made it most mysterious were the intimate belongings they sometimes found in the houses: an intricately carved ivory hair comb, pitted with age, worn perhaps by some beauty of the city; or a little horse on wheels carved of hardwood, which must have been the toy of a child. Here they had lain in darkness, lost perhaps in the final abandonment of Nal-Ak-Burat—maybe a child had cried for her toy, maybe a woman had frowned when she found her favorite comb was missing. Why had they left? Were they driven out by some plague? Or did the city's people tire of never feeling the wind on their cheeks and, hungering for sunshine, turn their backs on their marvelous city of stone and climb out, blinking, into the light?

That night (the Bards still divided the time between day and night, despite the unchanging darkness, using a water clock to measure the hours) they gathered as usual in the palace for the evening meal. The Bards took turns cooking, and tonight Soron, with Hem's help, prepared the meal. He grumbled as he kneaded dough for the flat bread, which would be cooked in the bottom of the oven.

"I could do with some greens, my boy," he said. "But it seems supplies of fresh foodstuffs are rather depleted at the moment."

Hem, who was always grateful to get anything to eat—his days of hunger were, after all, not far behind him, and his future was anything but certain—looked up in surprise.

"But it all smells delicious," he said. "Anyway, I'm amazed they can bring any food in at all. But I suppose the other way in doesn't have a Gate of Water."

Soron glanced at him humorously. "I'll wager it doesn't. And thank the Light for that, else I'd have to stay here forever. But I tell you, someone has prepared well here for thin times— back in the storerooms there are more grains and dried fruits and pickled foods than I have ever seen in one place, and stacks of dried and salted fish, and even sides of cured deer. All packed into barrels or hung, neat and dry, so it won't spoil. And as wide a range of spices as in the Ernan's kitchens, and a cellar of wines to rival those of the Bards of Turbansk—typical Bards! Well, this is the perfect place to store things, I'll say: dry and cool and dark, like a giant cellar. I'm not ungrateful; but I do hunger for fresh meat and vegetables, all the same."

Hem suddenly thought of a delicious salad of herbs he had eaten once in Turbansk, and for a moment he stopped slicing the dried fish that Soron was preparing for a stew. His mouth filled with water; he could almost taste it.

"Greens would be good," he said. "But more than that, I'd like to see the sun."

"Aye," Soron answered. "But who knows what is happening up there, Hem, while we skulk down here?"

Hem fell silent. He knew Bards here had ways of gathering news. Hared was much better informed about what was happening in Annar than the Bards had been in Turbansk where, as he had said, even bird messengers had trouble getting past the besieging army. But he remembered that Soron did not know what had happened to Jelika, the woman he loved, who was supposed to be with them, but had been torn away by war. Perhaps, Hem thought, he would never know; such things happened. Soron never mentioned Jelika, and most of the time seemed the same kind and patient man he had been in Turbansk; but sometimes, as now, Hem perceived the deep sadness that lived inside him.

It was, Hem thought, a bit like how he missed Maerad. He, too, had no way of knowing that she was still alive; and perhaps he would never see her again. She might have died on her quest, and he would never know. The thought hurt, so he pushed it aside and concentrated on cutting the dried fish, which was tricky, even with a sharp knife.

At dinner there was a new face—a grim-faced Bard called Til-Naga. He spoke with the same accent as Orona, one that was unfamiliar to Hem—his ear was now becoming good enough to pick up variations in the Suderain language—and for some of the meal Til-Naga sat next to Orona speaking to her in a language that Hem did not know. They spoke quickly and intimately; Hem glanced over toward them curiously, since Orona was usually very taciturn, and he had never seen her so animated. It seemed to Hem that Orona was asking after mutual friends, and that not all she heard was good. Once she gasped, and sat looking down at her bowl without moving, an expression on her face of terrible sadness, and Til-Naga took her hand and held it tightly without speaking.

Nobody asked Til-Naga any questions until after the meal, when mint tea was served, with some of Soron's seedcake.

"That was a famous meal, Soron," said Narbila, sighing. "I had forgotten your skills with food—it's been a long time since

I sat at the tables of Turbansk. I swear, you could make a feast out of old boot leather."

"I thank you for your faith," said Soron, bowing his head. "But boot leather might defeat even my skills. A cook is only as good as his ingredients; and I must say, despite the shortage of fresh meat, that the quality of food here is high indeed. I salute you for your foresight!" He lifted his cup in a toast.

Narbila laughed. "We have had long to prepare, and some of us foresaw how bad things were going to be. But it is, indeed, our pleasure." She solemnly returned his toast.

Hared was frowning; not with irritation, Hem thought, but with concentration. "So, Til-Naga," he said. "It is good to see you back, though you are later than we expected."

"There were problems," the Bard answered, "as you have no doubt worked out for yourself. I thought I would not get back at all: I was followed by dogsoldiers past Jerr-Niken, and had to ride all the way to the Malinau Forests to throw them off my trail. Jared"—here he named a region north of Dén Raven— "has been cleared of all its trees, so it is blank as a table; not a mouse may stir but Sharma, the Nameless One, will know of it. I dared not set foot there, and so I had to go through the Glandugir Hills, which are full of monstrous beasts that do not hear the Speech, and trees that eat men. But at last I made it to Dén Raven."

At the mention of Dén Raven, Zelika sat up and began to pay attention.

"Did you manage to meet with Ranik?" asked Narbila, leaning forward over the table.

"Who's Ranik?" asked Zelika.

Saliman glanced at her briefly. "Ranik is not his real name. But the man Til-Naga speaks of is a Bard of Dén Raven, of more courage than any of us here," he said briefly. "He works in Dagra."

Zelika's eyes opened wide with shock. "A Hull, you mean?" she said.

"Not a Hull," said Hared. "Though most people believe that he is."

Zelika's face darkened. "Then how can we trust him?" she muttered quietly to the table, but only Hem heard her.

"I did meet Ranik." Til-Naga was silent for some time, but the other Bards waited patiently for him to speak again, forbearing to prompt him. "He came to the meeting place at great risk to himself. The Eyes in Dén Raven are more numerous now, and the slightest transgression is punishable by imprisonment, at the very least. And they are, as always, very eager to deal out death. Even Ranik now feels that he is watched."

Hem remembered that the Eyes were Hulls employed by the Nameless One to oversee the people of Dén Raven.

"Nevertheless, he came. He told me he cannot come again; he was very afraid. It seems that certain rivalries are breaking out between those forces loyal to Imank, and others who pledge their allegiance to Sharma, the Nameless One, and this makes it doubly perilous to travel through Dén Raven."

"Those rivalries have always been there," growled Hared.

"Aye. Sharma owes Imank much, and I doubt that Imank would be slow to remind him of it. It is possible that Sharma fears Imank more than he fears any captain of Annar."

Hared chuckled sourly, but Til-Naga stared soberly at the table. "Be not quick to construe any advantage to us, in such a conflict," he said. "I can see little: if they war between each other, you can be sure that whoever wins will be the stronger for it. But that is not the chief of what Ranik told me. He said that the siege of Turbansk has stretched Sharma's forces more than we guessed: Imank did not expect the resistance found there, and the enemy's supply lines are now very thin indeed. It seems that he expected it would fall before the sword as Baladh did, and that the Black Army would then move swiftly to Car Amdridh."

Saliman thumped the table, smiling savagely, and Hem jumped. "I knew it!" Saliman said. "I knew that if we could only hold out—"

"It worked," said Til-Naga softly. "I salute you, Saliman, and all those who defended your city so bravely. And Juriken, too. I hear that he is dead. I wish I could have met him; he sounds like a very great Bard. Ranik said that maybe ten ranks of the Black Army were killed in the earthquake of Turbansk, and many more injured. For the moment, Sharma cannot contemplate letting Imank open another front in his war, and nor will he take the Black Army into Annar."

Soron breathed out with relief. "Til Amon is safe, then, for the meantime."

"Unless it's attacked by its own, my friend," said Saliman. "But I think that is not all Til-Naga's news."

"There was something else. You will have heard of the child armies?"

The other Bards nodded.

"Ranik believes that Sharma plans to use these armies more. He has rounded up ranks of children from the Nazar and Savitir regions, as well as every child over ten in Dén Raven, and Ranik has heard that they are being trained in special camps. It is hard to find out more; it seems this is one of Sharma's own pet projects."

Beside Hem, Zelika gasped quietly. He knew she was thinking of her brothers and sisters, who may not have been killed, after all.

"Trained?" said Saliman. "For what?"

"It seems they were very useful on the Wall of Il Dara," Til-Naga said expressionlessly. "Utterly without mercy. This awoke Sharma's interest. He is collecting his child armies near Dagra, and seeks yet more children to swell their ranks. Ranik judges, and perhaps he is right, that maybe Sharma is toying with the idea of sending child armies into Annar, so that he does not have to deplete his other forces. No one knows for certain. It is certainly possible. But finding out anything about these children is especially difficult."

There was a short silence, while the other Bards digested the news.

"Til-Naga, this is grim news, but nevertheless it gives me hope," said Saliman.

"Aye." Til-Naga's face hardened, as if he struggled to conceal emotion. "But I cannot feel glad of it. My dearest friend was killed at Turbansk, Saliman; he could not escape the Eyes. He was a good man who tried to act with honor in the very worst of circumstances. I feared for him, when I heard he was part of those forces; and I mourn him now."

"I don't feel sorry for him," said Zelika suddenly, her voice hard and taut. "What kind of friend would he be, who would be part of the Black Army? Or do you come from Dén Raven?"

There was an embarrassed silence, which was broken by Orona.

"I am a Bard of Dén Raven, and yes, so is Til-Naga," she said quietly. "There are such things."

Zelika stared at Orona, her lips set in a tight line. Hem put a warning hand on her arm, but she shook it off.

"Then we have spies in our midst? Just openly, like that?"

"Zelika, do not speak of things you do not understand." Though he spoke quietly, Saliman's eyes blazed with anger. "You dare to insult these Bards? They have done more to help us than you ever have. You apologize, now."

Til-Naga waved his hand, indicating an apology was not necessary, but Zelika stood up, trembling with rage. Hem tried to pull her down onto the cushion, but she would not heed him.

She looked crazed again; her eyes glittered dangerously, and her mouth trembled at the edges. He had not seen that expression since Turbansk fell. He stood up also, and tried to drag her from the room, but she would not be moved.

"Apologize? To this scum?" Zelika spat. "I suppose I should apologize for having my baby brother murdered in front of my eyes. I should apologize for Baladh being in ruins. I should—"

Hared moved so swiftly that Hem had no time to react. The Bard stood up and slapped Zelika across the face with his open hand, knocking her over. She lay on the floor, her hair tumbling over her face, while Hem stared down at her, appalled.

"That was not necessary," said Orona coldly. "She is only a child."

"If Saliman insists on bringing children to this table," said Hared, breathing heavily, "then he should also insist that they behave with some decorum." He returned to his place, as Hem knelt by Zelika, gently stroking the hair back from her face. A dark bruise was spreading on her cheek.

"Zelika," he whispered. "Get up, now."

Painfully, she sat up. The crazed look had left her face, but she glared at Hared with hatred.

"Zelika," said Saliman gently. "These Bards are from Dén Raven, yes; that does not mean that they are your enemy. You must remember that the Nameless One has made his own people suffer first, and they too have reason to work for his downfall. Now, you have gravely embarrassed me by insulting those I consider my dear friends, and I would have you apologize to them."

Zelika stared at Orona and Til-Naga, who steadily returned her gaze. Her face was unreadable.

"I'm sorry I insulted you," she said at last, bowing her head gracefully. "It is true, I did not understand. Sometimes I get so angry I feel I could kill someone, but I see that was wrong of me."

They nodded, accepting her apology.

"But I think Hared should also apologize to me," Zelika added, staring at the Bard with her chin in the air. Hem noticed that she did not deign to touch the bruise on her face, although it must have been hurting badly. Hared met her eyes, and grinned wolfishly.

"I apologize, then," he said. "But I hope you will refrain from entertaining us in such ways in future."

Zelika nodded with chilly dignity.

"More mint tea?" said Soron, breaking the uncomfortable pause that followed Hared's comment. "I think that will have a calming effect." And he hurried out into the galley to put a pot of water on the fire.

Just before he woke the next morning, Hem had a brief, vivid dream of Maerad. Unlike the last time he had dreamed of her, this had no taint of nightmare. They were in Saliman's garden, in bright sunshine, and Irc was perched on Hem's shoulder. Maerad sat cross-legged on the grass, looking up at her brother, creasing her eyes against the sunlight. Hem leaned against a tree, and he was eating a mango, cutting it with his clasp knife. Maerad looked paler than when he had last seen her, and the skin beneath her eyes was bruised blue; but both of them were laughing, although Hem couldn't remember why.

He woke with a lightness in his soul that he had not felt for a long time. Maerad was all right, he thought; she was alive, and she was thinking of him. He got out of bed and went to the meal room for breakfast. Zelika was already there, spooning dohl into her mouth.

"You're right, Hem," she said, as Hem settled onto the cushion next to her. "We must do something. And there are things that we might do better than the others here."

Only the two children were at the table: everyone else had

eaten earlier. Hem looked up swiftly from his dohl, which he had begun to devour with single-minded attention.

"Good," he said. "I didn't want to do it by myself."

"I spoke to Hared already," said Zelika. "He said he could train us. But he also said that he would not, unless Saliman gave his permission."

"Oh." Hem gloomily contemplated his bowl, absently waving Irc, who was trying to steal some of his breakfast, away. He thought that it was very unlikely that Saliman would allow them to work for Hared. Hem had not pressed the point, although Saliman knew how he felt.

"And why shouldn't we help?" said Zelika. She brushed her hair out of her eyes. "If we do nothing, we can still be killed. And I don't want to stay down here for the rest of my life."

Hem finished his meal without speaking. He carried their bowls to the galley, washed the utensils in the stone trough, and set them to dry with special care.

"Well, then," he said, turning to Zelika. "I suppose we should find Saliman, and persuade him to let Hared train us."

"I was looking for him earlier, but no one knew where he was. Or if they knew, they weren't saying."

"Do you have to care for the babies now?"

"No. Nimikera said she would need no help today. She has been sick with her wound, but she says she is getting better."

Hem nodded absently. He felt a determination hardening in his breast; he would *make* Saliman give his permission. And if he wouldn't . . .

Hem didn't finish that thought. He had never openly defied Saliman; but for the first time he felt that the Bard's judgment was awry. He was perfectly aware that to Hared, he and Zelika were merely useful tools, but he also knew, from the conversation the previous night, that the Bards were very anxious to find out more about the armies of children. And it seemed, from what had been said, children themselves were best placed to do so. It was simply not enough to say that he and Zelika must be kept out of danger.

There's work to be done, he thought. It was a thought that gave him a good feeling as he held it in his mind, like a smooth, hard stone that fitted satisfyingly in the palm. Work for me and Zelika.

He called Irc to his shoulder, and the two children started to search the palace. They found Saliman at last in a small room the Bards called the meeting chamber. Here, Hem noticed, were more paintings of the strange tree man they had seen in the huge throne room or temple. Saliman was seated on a cushion, huddled in his cloak to cheat the chill of the unheated room, reading with deep concentration a parchment scratched with spidery writing.

He looked up and frowned when the children entered. Hem hesitated at the threshold, stammering an apology for disturbing him. Saliman sighed, and then smiled.

"Come in, come in," he said. "It's all right, Hem, I am not cross at your being here. It's only more bad news." He folded the parchment and put it in his tunic pocket. "You are seeking me?"

"Yes." Now that it had come to the point, Hem felt his resolution waver. He had never known Saliman to be anything but wise and farsighted, and he knew much more than Hem did about the ways of the world.

"We wanted to ask you if you would give Hared permission to train us," said Zelika. "Because both Hem and I want to work for him, and he won't train us unless you agree."

Saliman glanced from one to the other, his face expressionless.

"Sit down," he said.

Hem and Zelika sat down next to Saliman, and Irc hopped

onto the table and gently pecked Saliman's hand in greeting. Hem swallowed nervously, and then wondered why he was nervous. Saliman did not look angry, and Hem was not a little boy anymore. Soon he would be a man.

"You both know that Hared has spoken of this with me, and you know I do not like the idea," said Saliman. Zelika opened her mouth to say something, but Saliman raised his hand. "Wait until I finish, Zelika. The work of which Hared speaks is very dangerous. I know how dangerous, because I have done it myself."

"But we can't stay underground forever!" Hem burst out. "I've done nothing! When Turbansk was under siege, I was inside the walls, being safe. I've never been in battle, and Maerad is out there with Cadvan, facing who knows what perils, and you would—"

"Hem, I have not forbidden anything. Is that not true?"

Hem met Saliman's eyes, which were dark and sad, and bit his lip. "It's true," he said.

"Then hear me out. The work Hared speaks of is, as I said, very dangerous. And I would not be a good mentor to you, Hem, nor responsible for Zelika, if I heedlessly let you do something so perilous." Irc gave a quiet caw, as if in agreement, and Saliman began to scratch the bird's neck as he talked. Irc sank down on the table, crooning with delight. "Hem, I remember when I first saw you. Do you recall?"

Hem nodded.

"You walked into Nelac's rooms in Norloch, a scrawny, hungry young boy with huge eyes, trying to hide behind your sister. And I tell you, you moved my heart. I have loved you since, although I have not been able to care for you as I would have wished."

Despite himself, tears sprang into Hem's eyes. "You have

always been good to me," he said roughly. "I didn't always deserve it, either."

"Hem, love has nothing to do with deserving. One gives one's heart, and that is all. But that is not the point. In Norloch, I saw a lost child. Standing before me, I see that you are a child no longer; if you were of the Neera Marsh people, they would have made the ceremonies already to welcome you into manhood. But you are a Bard, and you are, in our counting, still not quite a man. You have grown much, though, Hem. You are thoughtful, where once you never thought. You are patient, where once you were a tangle of rages. And," he added, with a teasing smile, "you have grown much taller. You will soon overtop me, and I am not a small man."

Zelika had turned slightly away from them, and was staring at the wall. Hem could not see her face, but he guessed she was feeling shy and left out. She turned back to face them, as Saliman had stopped speaking, and Hem was surprised by how troubled her face was; she looked for a moment haunted by loneliness.

"I am not your father, Zelika, as you once pointed out," said Saliman gently, turning toward her. "It is the sheerest accident that you came to be under my roof. But since you have been in my care, I have been responsible for you." He smiled, and leaning forward, cupped her cheek with his hand. "And I have grown to love you too, Zelika. You are Baladhian, and like all Baladhians you are cross-grained to the core, but true and honest; I have seen that, too. And I like the idea of your going into danger as little as I like it for Hem."

Zelika blinked, and then stared at the floor. No one spoke for a moment.

"But is that a good enough reason for us not to work for Hared?" said Hem at last. "It's our world that the Nameless

One is destroying. And we are in danger whether we help
or no."

"Aye, Hem. I have thought these things. And it is a hard
choice, but it is one that I must make. I will say that Hared can
train you to spy for him. I know what it is that he wishes you to
do, and it troubles me; but I do not feel I have the right to prevent you from helping the Light."

Zelika looked delighted, and Saliman glanced at her somberly. "I have one caveat: you can only work for him after you
have finished your training, if Hared says that your skills are of
the highest standard. Anything less, and I will not contemplate
your doing any dangerous work. And Hared is the hardest of
taskmasters; he will demand more of you than you now realize."

"I will be brilliant," said Zelika, without a hint of modesty.
"I have no doubt of it."

Hem felt nothing like the same confidence, but thanked
Saliman.

"Now," said Saliman. "I am here because I have some thinking to do, and I wish to be undisturbed. Just let me finish what I
am doing and I'll speak to Hared later."

Hem put his hand out for Irc, who climbed lazily onto his
forearm, and they followed Zelika out of the room. Hem could
see by the jaunty way she walked that she was very pleased.

Hem didn't feel at all glad. There was a grim satisfaction
that at last he would be helping the Light, but he felt no pleasure in it. He had seen Saliman's eyes as he had given his
permission, and they had been dark with pain.

XV

THE TREE MAN

THE next day Hem dragged his Turbanskian armor out of his pack, where it had been carefully put away since their time in the Passage of the Kings. He stared at the dull gold sun on the ceramic breastplate with a sudden piquant sadness, remembering that this gear had been made for the children of Har-Ytan, when they had been his age. He had never met her sons, he realized now; he wondered what kind of people they were. They must be fierce and brave, he thought, with the blood of Har-Ytan in their veins.

And what of the Ernani? Had she lived through the hopeless battle in front of the gates of Turbansk? Hem thought it unlikely. Har-Ytan had not expected to. After all, she had passed on the Ernani's ruby to her son. She had said she would stand and fall with her city, and then had walked clear-eyed to her death. Hem shivered; there was something about the people of the Suderain, an unwavering purity of purpose, which made him feel small. He saw it most dramatically in Zelika, but Saliman possessed that same determination, if more subtly inflected. Once an action was decided, there was no flinching, no excuses, no regrets. Hem didn't feel nearly so certain about anything.

He thoughtfully buckled the shortsword to his belt, and, Irc clinging complainingly to his shoulder, went to meet Zelika, whose eyes gleamed with suppressed excitement. Hared was waiting there. He looked the children over sternly and led them out of the palace and through the square to a part of the city they had not seen—a large courtyard surrounded by sinister-looking low buildings, which was only accessible through a locked gate. Here the stone roof of the cave swept down to a mere few spans above their heads. It felt claustrophobic and somehow hostile in a way the rest of Nal-Ak-Burat did not.

Hared's training was as hard as the children had expected, but everything else about it confounded their expectations. Hem had thought he would concentrate on swordcraft and unarmed combat, and in that first session Hared put Zelika and Hem through their paces. He made them use their weapons instead of wooden substitutes, as Hem was used to in the School in Turbansk, and pressed each of them hard. By the end, Zelika had disarmed Hared, and Hem had resisted being disarmed himself, although Hared told him that, had they really been fighting, he could have killed him, as he'd let down his guard at a crucial moment. But their mentor professed himself satisfied with their levels of skill.

"You can hold your own, mostly," he said, leaning on his sword and breathing heavily. "Zelika, I'll even say that you creditably carry on the tradition of your great House. Being small can be an advantage—remember that, if you end up fighting for your life against someone twice your size. But if you are clever, you should not have to fight at all. The most canny warrior is he who never draws his sword."

Zelika could not conceal her pleasure at his words, which were a balm to her wounded pride. From Hared, this was high praise indeed. "You should work further with Zelika," said Hared to Hem. "You're quick, and you are not afraid of fighting dirty. But you are out of practice, I think. I expect both of you to work each day together, to make sure you are fit. There's nothing more I can teach you in a short time. The rest is luck."

Hem nodded.

"Now," said Hared. "I want you to wait here." He lifted up the lamp he had carried to the courtyard, bowed his head briefly in farewell, and walked off through the gate, locking it behind him.

Hared left so quickly that Hem and Zelika had no time to ask when he would be back. They were left in absolute darkness, in the strange square, and the unchallenged silence of the underground city—undiluted as it was in the palace by noise and human busyness—opened around them.

Hem summoned a magelight, and the two children stared at each other in its dim glow.

"He's locked us in!" said Zelika indignantly.

"Yes," Hem answered. Part of him wanted to laugh; he should, he thought, have expected something like this, and have come prepared. "I suppose it's a test. And I'm thirsty. Did you bring anything to drink?"

Zelika shook her head.

"Me neither. Nor any food. Perhaps there's one of those small rivers around here somewhere. Can you hear anything?"

They listened hard, but there was no running water nearby.

"How dare he lock us in!" said Zelika, her eyes blazing. "That son of a mangy dog!" She called him a few other, less complimentary names, before subsiding into a brooding silence.

"Of course he would dare," Hem said. "He won't put us in any real danger, I don't think . . ."

"Hmmpff." Zelika squatted on the ground. "Well, he said to wait. Maybe that's the test—to see how patient we are."

Hared could be back at any time. He might leave them there for hours. Days? Surely not; he would know that they needed water. Hem swallowed, already feeling how dry his throat was, and pushed thoughts of drinking out of his mind. He glanced at the buildings surrounding the courtyard. They gave him an eerie feeling; most of them had empty doorways that yawned like black mouths in the pale magelight.

"Did you notice how we got here?" asked Hem.

"Not really," said Zelika. "I was just following Hared, so I didn't really look." She hunched up gloomily. "And Soron is cooking today. I hope he doesn't leave us too long; I don't want to miss dinner."

"Maybe he wants us to escape from here."

"Maybe he wants us to obey his orders."

Hem weighed the possibilities. "I think we should wait, at least to begin with. And, after a while, if Hared doesn't come back, then we should try to get out of here. Do you want to have a look around?"

Zelika agreed; it wasn't as if there were anything else to do. Glumly—thirst was really beginning to bother them—they looked around at the empty doorways, feeling none of the curiosity that had pushed them to explore so much of Nal-Ak-Burat. Maybe there was a way out, but it was very clear that if there were, it was not from the courtyard. The rocky roof came down to meet the walls of the buildings, effectively enclosing them in a big cavern. And the gate was locked. Hem tried a few opening spells, without much hope; he was sure the magery in this place would not respond to anything he said and that, in any case, Hared would not lock them in if a simple opening charm would be enough to release them. He was right, of course.

Next, they peered unenthusiastically through some of the doorways. They led into blank, tiny rooms that felt like tombs. In the corners of some glimmered strange, luminous fungi that Hem had not seen elsewhere in Nal-Ak-Burat; they looked disconcertingly like pale hands growing out of the stone, and insects scuttled under them, away from the light. All the walls

were covered with paintings of sinister half-men with the heads
of birds or frogs, or the legs of lizards or goats. They seemed to
stare back, with blank, unwavering eyes that made the hair
creep on Hem's neck.

"We're stuck, then," said Zelika. She called Hared some
more names, and then bit her lip. "He'd better be back soon."

The children took off their armor—even though it was not
heavy, it was uncomfortable—and sat on the stone ground.
They took some time to find the right place, not too near to the
doorways, and not too far away, either. Although neither of
them said so, they had the uncomfortable feeling that one of the
birdmen might come flapping out of a doorway while they
weren't looking. They fixed their eyes on the gate through
which Hared had disappeared. Surely he would be back soon?
He couldn't leave them there all night, surely?

The stone was very cold and very hard, and it grew colder
and harder the longer they sat there. Their lips began to burn
with thirst, and Irc, who had settled disconsolately on the
ground nearby, began to nag Hem for some food, irritably pecking at his sandals.

They waited a long time. How long it was impossible to
know: in the changeless air, each moment seemed to stretch
endlessly. Apart from their own breathing and occasional restless movements, it was so silent that Hem could hear the blood
rushing through his ears. All he could think about was that he
was thirsty. Finally he stood up.

"Hared's played a nice trick on us," he said darkly. "But I'm
not going to sit here like a baby waiting for him to let us out.
This place makes my skin crawl. There has to be a way to get
out of here."

"Let's look around again," said Zelika. "It will be better than
sitting here, anyway. I'm going numb."

The children stamped their feet and waved their arms

around to get the blood moving, and then began a meticulous exploration of the strange cavern. It was, as Zelika said, better than doing nothing; but as they continued, Hem thought it was only marginally better. The more he looked around this place, the less he liked it.

There were about a dozen doors around the square where they had been training. They started with the one nearest the gate, and moved methodically to their left. This time they entered the rooms they had only peered into previously, examining the walls closely for any sign of an exit.

Neither of them could shake the growing feeling that they were being watched, although they didn't mention it. It was, Hem thought, the eyes of the creatures painted on the walls; they seemed to stare, as if they were living eyes, though when he looked at them closely they were just paint, faded and damp, with patches missing altogether.

They worked their way to the room opposite the gate without finding anything interesting. This chamber was the largest, and it had a stone slab, like a table, in the middle, which was covered with intricate relief carvings of runes and tiny human figures. Hem and Zelika stopped involuntarily at the threshold and unconsciously reached out and clasped hands.

Here the sense of watchfulness was almost overwhelming; it seemed to emanate from the very stone, as if something had been woken to alertness and now focused all its attention upon them. Hem gulped, and sent the magelight into the chamber ahead of them. Its silver light bloomed softly on the walls. There was nothing in there: just ancient dust, the white fungi in the corners of the room, the crumbling paintings.

The children stepped slowly inside, poised to turn and run. The silence and stillness were themselves unnerving; their footsteps sounded too loud. Even the beating of their hearts seemed amplified. At the far end, they saw a huge mural of a half-man half-tree, like the one they had seen a few days earlier in the great hall and elsewhere in the city.

"It's that tree man again," said Zelika, whispering.

Hem nodded, swallowing hard. The figure took up the entire wall, and unlike the other paintings, was not surrounded by runes or other pictures. It just stood by itself, its arms spread, its face blank of expression, its black-rimmed eyes seeming to stare straight at them.

"We'll just have a quick look," said Hem, pulling his gaze from the tree man with an effort. Zelika nodded, and they hurriedly turned to inspect the walls, as they had in the other smaller chambers. They immediately found they didn't want to stand with their backs to the figure in the mural. They tacitly agreed that Hem would keep watch, while Zelika inspected the walls. Irc had not wanted to come with Hem, but did not want to be left outside on his own, either, and clung to Hem's shoulder, with his eyes hidden in Hem's hair. They kept as far away as they could from the stone table; it was made of white, veined marble, and it was stained by a blackish red patch that looked like ancient blood. It seemed sinister.

In her desire to get out of the room, Zelika was giving the walls very little more than a perfunctory examination. Hem had to turn occasionally, to move the magelight for her. The third time, when he turned back to look at the tree man, he jumped. Surely its arms were higher than when he had last looked at it, moments before? No, it must be his nerves. He set himself to watching it again, studying its position, trying to still a panicky voice that was urging him to leave the chamber. The next time he took his eyes off the painting, he was quite sure it had moved. Now its arms were almost level with its shoulders.

"Zelika . . ." he said, keeping his eyes fixed on the mural.

"Yes?"

"Let's get away from here."

"In a moment—there's something there, don't you think, high up? Can you put the light up there? Maybe that's what Hared wanted us to find—it looks like a tunnel."

To Hem, it sounded as if Zelika were speaking underwater; her voice was muffled, and his ears filled with a roaring sound. Now he was staring at the tree man as if he were a rabbit transfixed by a snake; he was no longer conscious of the rest of room. Every moment the figure seemed more and more real, and less and less like a painting.

The tree man blinked, lowered his arms to his sides, and stepped out of the wall.

Hem felt a scream gathering in his throat but, as if he were in one of his nightmares, he found that he couldn't move or speak. The figure walked silently toward him, its eyes fixed on his. Hem had never been so wholly terrified as he was in that moment, but it wasn't really a fear that he would be hurt or killed. It was more akin to awe: the kind of feeling one might have at the edge of a huge precipice, on the brink of falling over it. The tree man was more than twice Hem's height, and his eyes were yellow like an owl's, with no white around the iris, and cleft with a vertical pupil. Branches, heavy with dark, narrow leaves, grew from his head like antlers and smaller leafy branches pushed out of the tendons of his arms and from his shoulders. The face was white-skinned, as white as the petals of a magnolia, and as blank of expression.

When he reached the stone table, which stood between them, the tree man halted. Then, to Hem's amazement, he spoke to him; he used some variant of the Speech, which Hem could only just understand. He wasn't sure if the tree man spoke aloud; his voice resonated inside Hem's skull, low and rich and melodious.

Songboy, he said. *At last, out of the foretimes, you come. I have waited for thee long.*

It was the last thing Hem had expected, and his mouth fell open with astonishment. After a few moments he realized he was standing like a gawping fool, and shut it with a snap. The tree man stood utterly still, as if he were waiting for Hem to answer. Hem struggled to gather his thoughts, which were whirling inside his head like panicked birds.

Me? he said. *I . . . I think there's some mistake—*

The tree man's expression did not change, but it seemed to Hem that a cold laughter lit his yellow eyes.

There is no gainsaying the Speech of the earth, Songboy. There is no mistake. Thou art but a spring leaf in the ages of the world, and there are many wisdoms that those such as thou—who pass like a ripple on a lake, like a ray of sunlight on a hill—will never understand. The knowing is sure. Thou art foretold.

Hem blinked. *You mean my sister, I think,* he said at last. *Not me. I'm not important. My sister's the Fated One. She's the one you mean. There have been mistakes before, when I was a baby . . .* He suddenly became conscious that he was babbling, and fell silent.

Yes, a sister and a brother. Out of the foretimes.

Hem didn't know what to say to that, and licked his lips. His mouth was so dry he could barely swallow.

Out of the foretimes, said the tree man softly. *To unchain the song.*

The Treesong? said Hem uncertainly. *But that's what Maerad is looking for—*

One for the singing and one for the music. Listen well, Songboy. Listen with the sinews of your heart, with the marrow of your bones, with the sap of your mind. The tree man leaned forward: to Hem's perception it seemed that his upper body stretched impossibly over the stone table across the entire distance of the chamber, so that now the tree man spoke into his ear. *Listen and remember.*

The tree man breathed into Hem's ear; and the world changed.

Afterward, trying to make sense of what had happened, Hem thought it was as if he had suddenly been tossed into an ocean of music, and he was a fish made of light, swaying in currents of pure sound. Or it was as if he were suddenly no longer flesh, as if his muscles and bones and organs were woven of melody, a harmony that contained all dissonance, trembling on the edge of silence. It was unbearable, a beauty so extreme that comprehending it was beyond his human capacity, but he wanted it never to end; and he felt it never would end, that the single moment of the tree man's breath caught him into eternity, that his body pulsed in time with the slow music of the stars, and beyond the stars, a pure, infinite darkness, the source and end of all beauty and all life.

The next thing he was aware of was a piercing pain in his left ear, and someone shaking his shoulder, saying his name. He tried to brush away whatever was hurting his ear, and his hand touched feathers: Irc. For some reason, he was lying on the ground. It was completely dark, so he lit a magelight and sat up.

Zelika was seated next to him, her face tense in the pale light. "Are you all right?" she said. "I thought . . ." She shook her head, as if she were trying to clear it. "Did you faint or something? You just fell over, and then the magelight went out and it was so dark."

"Didn't you see the tree man?" said Hem, looking at her curiously.

"What? The one on the wall?"

"He spoke to me."

"Spoke to you?"

Hem realized that Zelika thought he was delirious. And in any case, he wasn't sure that he felt like talking about what had just happened.

"It doesn't matter. Something happened, that's all. Maybe I imagined it." He looked around the room; the sense of a watch-

ful presence had vanished completely. Now it was just an
empty room. "Did you find anything?"

"No."

At that moment, they heard Hared outside, calling them.
Zelika met Hem's eyes.

"He's back," she said. "That weasel. Well, I suppose we can't
throttle him or complain, or we'll fail the test."

Hem laughed and stood up. His knees were wobbly, but
otherwise he felt no ill effects. He could almost believe that he
had suffered some kind of hallucination; he remembered how
fevered children in the orphanage saw all sorts of terrible
visions. But somehow, it didn't seem like that to him. They
walked out into the courtyard, where Hared waited for them,
holding a leather bottle of water.

After that day, Hem and Zelika didn't need to be told to come
prepared for anything. They always brought a water flask each
and, at the very least, a hunk of flatbread and some dried fruit.
Hem also asked if Irc could train as well, since, he argued, Irc
would be an invaluable help; to his surprise, after at first
demurring, Hared agreed. Irc was unusually well behaved
when he accompanied the children, which was a sure measure
of Hared's authority.

They finished each day exhausted, not necessarily because
they were doing physically punishing work, but because Hared
demanded nothing less than their complete attention, all the
time. They never knew what to expect, nor what would be
expected of them. Several times they spent the entire day on
memory games. Hared would place a number of objects on
a table, let them study them for a short time, and then cover
them with a cloth. The children were then expected to list all
the objects they had seen, in the order in which they had been
placed on the table, running from left to right. Hared would

not allow them to go until their recall was completely accurate more than three times in a row; and naturally, the more tired they became, the worse their results. But their teacher was pitiless.

Another day he took them into a room deep in the palace, shut the door, and extinguished the lamp, so they all stood in complete darkness. This was another, more sinister game, which Hared called "shadow hunting." The aim was to creep up behind one of the others without being sensed. Hem was not permitted to use his Bard hearing: the point was to be as silent as possible, while opening one's physical senses to their maximum sensitivity. If one of them managed to place his or her hands around another's neck, they won.

Hem found that shadow hunting was surprisingly nerve-racking. He would stand in the dark, rigid with alertness, hearing perhaps the smallest breath here, sensing a shift of air there, catching maybe the whiff of Hared's sweat or Zelika's musky smell. He had not realized that he knew their scents until he played this game. He learned how to stand absolutely still, how to control his breathing to make it soundless, how to step slowly and surely in the dark, using all the muscles in his feet to feel out the floor, how to minimize the air's movement around him. He would creep in the dark for what seemed like ages, sure that he had pinpointed a body a step or so away, only to find that somehow he had imagined its presence. And whenever, as happened most often, Hared slipped his cold hands around his neck, Hem leaped out of his skin with fright.

The first time he managed to catch Hared, he could see the Bard was grimly pleased. After that, he began to find it easier; he became aware that he had an intuitive feeling for bodily presence, which he could hone into a sense almost as good as sight. He was much better than Zelika at this game, and once, after Hem caught her three times in a row, she accused him of

cheating. Hem was outraged, and only Hared's sharp repri-
mand stopped them from coming to blows.

There were also lessons that Hem had alone, which he found
himself enjoying most of all, not least because he was free of
Zelika's relentless competitiveness. In these sessions, Hared
taught him the major charms of concealment and disguise:
the glimveil that glances aside a watching eye; the art of
shadowmazing that confuses tracks and makes them difficult to
follow; various kinds of mageshields, to hide the telltale glow of
Bardic magery from Hulls; and the skill of semblance making,
the creation of likenesses that can be used to fool an enemy.
Hem was quick and adept at these spells, and actually surprised Hared when he demonstrated the difficult disguising
spell that Saliman had taught him, long ago, in Turbansk; it was
the one time Hem saw Hared genuinely impressed.

But what Hem was really waiting for was the chance to go
above ground. He had begun to hunger for sunlight and wind
with a passion; at night before he went to sleep, he tried to
remember what it was like to walk beneath an open sky. It felt
like years since he had seen stars. But Hared continued to train
them in the underground city, with no word of leaving. They
worked long, boring, monotonous hours, repeating the same
exercises over and over again until they began to feel entirely
meaningless. Remembering Saliman's stricture that if Hared's
report was less than excellent they would not work for him,
they bit back any complaints. Irc was even more bored than the
children, but he continued his unusually good behavior,
although this required a lot of bribery on Hem's part. All of
them had had their fill of darkness.

Hem didn't speak to anyone about the tree man for some days.
Partly it was because their training took up most of their time:
Hared was devoting all his attention to the children. He clearly

thought the work they were doing was important, as important as his many other duties—for Hared was busy, and Bards from Nal-Ak-Burat were always leaving and reappearing. Also, as the days passed and the memory of his encounter with the tree man receded behind his daily activities, Hem became less sure that he hadn't had some kind of fit and, overcome by the strange atmosphere in the cavern, imagined the whole incident. In any case, he wasn't sure how to put the experience into words. So much of it, especially when the tree man had breathed in his ear, escaped his language. Sometimes he woke in an anguish of loss from dreams in which he was again in the breath of that music, tossed in that infinite, intolerably beautiful harmony; but he had no words for that, either.

He didn't attempt to speak of it to Zelika, who simply assumed that Hem had fainted and had been raving when he came to. He was too afraid that she would laugh. The only person he could trust enough to talk to was Saliman, and it was difficult to find time alone with him without Zelika becoming curious. But he found himself constantly dwelling on the tree man; there were, he noticed now, paintings of him all over Nal-Ak-Burat. When he had the chance, he examined them curiously. Who was he? What was his name? Was he some kind of Elemental, an Elidhu? Had the people of Nal-Ak-Burat perhaps worshipped him, as Zelika had said some people in the south worshipped the Light?

Maerad had told Hem that they had Elemental blood; she said she had even spoken to Ardina, a wood Elidhu, although Maerad's description of that Elidhu did not sound anything like the creature Hem had seen. Nelac had seemed to think that the Treesong, which Maerad had gone north with Cadvan to find, was something to do with the Elidhu. It was difficult not to think that the Treesong might have something to do with the tree man. And, after all, Saliman had said that Hem had some part in Maerad's quest; that was why he had kept him in Turbansk for the siege, instead of sending him away with the other students. Perhaps this was what Saliman had meant? *One for the singing and one for the music.* But then Hem would wonder again if he had imagined the whole thing; it seemed too like a dream.

Hem's chance came when Hared gave the children a rare day off. Nimikera asked Zelika for some help with the children, as she had sickened again from her wound. Zelika disappeared to the children's room, and Hem helped Saliman prepare the herbs to treat Nimikera's fever. Nimikera gave Hem a surprised glance when he entered her bed chamber with Saliman, but she did not object to his presence. She drew back her robe from her breast, and Hem and Saliman (accompanied by interested peeps from Irc) gravely examined her wound; it was a red slash running down from her throat almost to her stomach. But although it looked nasty, Hem saw straight away that it was a flesh wound, which miraculously had not pierced any vital organs. Another scar ran across her stomach, a white line, long healed, and Hem wondered about Nimikera's history.

"It looks as though the blade was poisoned," he said to her. "We had many such at Turbansk. The edges of the wound fester, and there is fever. But this must be a slow poison, I think; otherwise you would already be dead."

"It comes and goes," said Nimikera. "I curse it; each time I think I am recovering, I find myself abed again. This was done to me nigh on three months ago, and still it will not heal."

"You have no ill effects from that previous wound?" asked Hem. He had fallen easily into the role of healer again; here he felt at home, sure of where to place his hands, of how to speak, of what his instincts told him. Nimikera again gave him a curious glance—Hem was still a boy, and to the long-lived Bards he was considered very young indeed. Yet he was speaking like one of the wise, an equal to Saliman.

"I was left for dead after the sack of Jerr-Niken," she said. "Which might be counted as an ill effect—both the sack and the sword."

"I meant, now," Hem said gently, meeting her eyes. *Jerr-Niken?* he thought, remembering that, like Pellinor, that School had been razed to the ground and its Bards massacred by the Dark some years before. That no doubt explained Nimikera's grimness. "Sometimes wounds like this one can inflame old injuries." There was a short pause.

"No. No ill effects."

"You have a living sickness in your blood, I think." He turned to Saliman inquiringly. "What do you think, Saliman? If it comes and goes, it is not a simple poison."

"Aye, it seems so to me. To cleanse it thoroughly will take some magery. Hem, I can deal with this one; you look tired."

Hem nodded; he *was* tired. He left the tiny bed chamber and went back to the meal room, which was empty. While he waited for Saliman, he prepared some mint tea and sipped it morosely, thinking of Oslar. This was the first time Hem had been called on to do any healing since he had left Turbansk; it made him reflect on the training he was doing with Hared. It was difficult to imagine anyone more different from Oslar than Hared. Where Oslar emanated the kind of gentleness that comes from great strength, Hared had not a trace of gentleness. All the same, Hem thought, Hared was not weak; the past days of training had made him respect Hared's sternness, which he applied as unsparingly to himself as to others. But perhaps it was a kind of blindness. For the first time since he had decided to work for Hared, he wondered if he was really doing the right thing.

Saliman entered, interrupting Hem's musings. His face was gray with exhaustion.

"I'll have some of that," he said, pointing to the mint tea. Hem poured some into a little tin cup and handed it to him as Saliman sat down, sighing.

"She sleeps," he said. "But that was a hard one. You were right, Hem, it was not an ordinary poison. That's why the healings hadn't worked on her earlier. They don't have any real healers here; it is the one thing they lack."

"Irisanu isn't bad," said Hem.

"Aye. But she is a healer in the way that most Bards are; it is not her especial gift. There are some things she cannot do."

They sat in companionable silence for a time, pursuing their own thoughts. Then Hem roused himself.

"Saliman, something happened, that first day of training," he said.

"Hmm?" Saliman looked up. "I've been meaning to ask how you're finding Hared's tuition. He seems quite pleased with your progress, even though he won't say so."

"Well, this wasn't really anything to do with the training. And, you know, I'm not quite sure what happened. Maybe I had some kind of—I don't know, some kind of fit . . ." Hem hesitated, and then started to tell what had happened in the cavern. When he mentioned the tree man, Saliman sat up and began to pay real attention.

". . . and then he leaned over to me, and he *breathed*. Into my ear. And there was this music . . ." Hem stumbled to a halt, and Saliman waited patiently for him to find the words. "I don't know how to describe it—it was like I was *in* the music, and I *was* the music at the same time. It was so beautiful I couldn't bear it, but I never wanted it to stop. It was like . . . everything. Like the whole sky, all the stars, the whole earth, rock and tree and river, were all music. And something happened to me,

Saliman, I don't know, it's like the music changed me. It went into me and now I'm different, it's part of me somehow. The music is always there now, not just when I dream it. Like that poison in Nimikera's blood, only it's not harmful."

Silence fell between them, and Saliman thoughtfully finished his tea.

"I am quite sure it was not a fit," he said slowly. "I don't understand what happened, Hem. I can't pretend I do. But I think you are right that it was an Elidhu who spoke with you. Once the Elementals were very present in the Suderain. I wonder which Elidhu it was."

He pondered deeply for a time, and Hem watched his face. Saliman, he thought suddenly, is a very beautiful man. Why have I never thought this before? He carries a light inside him, even when he is somber and sad; it is like a joyous melody that is always there, that shines all the more brightly and poignantly for the darker chords that play around it. Sometimes it is laughter, because he loves making people laugh, but that is only its outer garment. People begin to glow when he is around. *I* glow.

He shook himself. He wasn't used to thoughts like that.

"And the tree man said, *a sister and brother?*" said Saliman at last. "Well, Hem, my Knowing told me that there is a part you must play in this story. A Bard's Knowing is a difficult thing; it will not always present itself in words, and sometimes it seems to run against the grain of common sense. But it seems that the Dark was not so misled as we thought, in kidnapping you. Yes, they were arrogant and ignorant in their dismissal of Maerad; but it seems that this riddle has two halves."

He gave Hem a penetrating glance, and then studied his hands. "I cannot be sure, but I think this Elemental is a being who was called Nyanar. He is mentioned in the chronicles, and he is linked with this area; but like most Elidhu, he withdrew during the Great Silence, and there has been no report of his

kind for hundreds of years. And now there is so much that is
lost and impossible to understand."

"So he was on our side?" said Hem.

"The Elidhu are not on any side, Hem. Our affairs are
meaningless to them, and theirs to us: except, perhaps, in this
one question of the Treesong—I wish I knew what it meant.
But you must remember that the Elementals are beyond our
Knowing and our bidding, and are perilous, as fire is
perilous. But, somehow, they need you; and that is interesting. There is some old grudge against the Nameless One. The
Elidhu are held by many Bards to be in league with Sharma,
and so are feared and distrusted. And it is certainly true some
came under his dominance: the Landrost, whom Maerad
spoke of, is one. But I for one have never believed they were
all his slaves."

Hem nodded slowly. What Saliman was saying made him
feel edgy.

"If the Treesong is to be played, it needs music, no?" added
Saliman, looking up and smiling. "Don't look so glum, Hem.
You and Maerad, you must travel dark paths, but few can avoid
such paths now. And it seems that we are not alone in our
struggle against the Dark. There is a great hope in that."

"Yes, but hope for what?" said Hem.

"For an end to this present darkness," Saliman answered.
"That something of the Light will survive our time, even if it is
but the tiniest seed lodged in the deepest crevice. Sometimes,
Hem, hope is a very small thing."

The two fell into silence again. Then Saliman laughed.
"Remember this?" he said, and, to Hem's surprise, began to
chant in a singsong voice:

"One is the singer, hidden from sunlight
Two is the seeker, fleeing from shadows

Three is the journey, taken in danger
Four are the riddles, answered in Treesong . . ."

Despite himself, Hem smiled: he hadn't heard that chant
since he was about six years old. "It's only an old rhyme," he
said. "We used it in games."

"Many forgotten wisdoms are preserved in those old rhymes.
Which are you, I wonder? Singer or seeker? Seeker, perhaps?"

"But I'm not looking for anything," said Hem. "Maerad is,
though; she's looking for the Treesong."

"True, though one can seek without knowing it. Well, I'm
glad you told me of this, Hem. It does give me hope. But you're
right: I'm not quite sure what the hope is for."

Hem remembered the Elidhu's wildness, its inhuman slitted
eyes. It was difficult to believe that such a creature could want
the same things he did. But any hope was better than none.

"Hem, before I forget," said Saliman suddenly, reaching
inside his robes. "There's something I have to give you." He
brought out a sealed letter.

"A letter?" Hem stared at Saliman in disbelief. "For me?"

"A Pilanel messenger brought it this morning," said
Saliman. "It comes from the north, from the Pilanel. They have
a very efficient network that stretches to the Suderain, and the
resistance keeps in touch with them as much as possible; they
are staunch allies."

Hem was still staring at the letter, his mouth open.

"Go on," said Saliman. "Open it. It has the highest mark of
urgency on it." He pointed to a strange rune, inked in red, by
the seal.

His hands trembling, Hem broke the seal and unfolded it.

"It's from Maerad," he said.

"Can you read it, Hem?" asked Saliman. "Or do you want
me to read it to you?"

"No, I can read it." He looked at the letters, which made some sense to him now, and began, slowly, to read it out loud, stumbling over some of the more difficult words:

My dear brother,
I am writing this letter in Murask, a Pilanel settlement in Zmarkan. I hope this finds you well, and that Saliman (greetings, Saliman!) has taught you enough script for you to be able to read this on your own. I am full of sad news: Cadvan, our dear friend, perished in the Gwalhain Pass on our journey here, with Darsor and Imi.

Saliman gasped, and covered his face with his hands.

"I'm—I'm sorry . . ." Hem stammered, looking up.

Saliman said nothing for a long time, and Hem watched him awkwardly, wanting to comfort him, and not knowing how.

"Ah, Hem." Saliman looked up at last, his eyes shining with tears. "Loss after loss after loss. Is there no end to sorrow? Cadvan! My friend! First Dernhil, and then Cadvan. Am I the only one left? We will be mourning forever."

He breathed in sharply, like one in deep pain, and then said more steadily, "Indeed, there will be time for such a grief. But that time, Hem, is not now. Tell me, what else does Maerad say?"

Taken aback, Hem looked down at the letter, which had been lying forgotten in his hand. It took a little time for the words to swim into focus, but he read on slowly.

There are no words to express my sorrow. I reached Murask on my own and am now about to travel farther north with a Pilanel guide to find a people called the Wise Kindred, who may be able to tell me something about the Treesong. I hope I am right, and that this is not a mistake. I may not return, and there are some things that I want you to know, in case I

am not able to tell you of them myself.
I have found our father's family here.

Hem stopped and looked up. Saliman was regarding him steadily. "I can't read the next bit," he said, offering the letter to Saliman. "There are some words I don't understand."

Saliman took the letter, and read that Maerad had met their Pilanel cousin, and the twin sister of their father, who was also a Bard.

If the School of Turbansk does not suit you, perhaps you
might find a place among them. Whether you find yourself
being a Turbansk Bard or no, I believe that you must one
day journey to Murask and speak to your kin here.

I write this with terrible sadness. I miss you more than I
can say and every day I wish that we were together, and not
separated by so many leagues. I have heard of war marching
on Turbansk, and I fear for you. We are born into such dark
times. But I also write this with hope and love, until one day
I embrace you again, my dear brother.

Your sister,
Maerad

"Thank you, Saliman," said Hem. His voice was muffled.

Hem couldn't say anything else for a while; his head was whirling with conflicting emotions. He was stunned by the news of Cadvan's death; it didn't seem possible. And yet he was so happy to have some word of his sister, and the news that he had kin in the north filled him with a surprised delight. But Maerad's letter sharpened his fears for her to a new and bitter edge. Was Maerad dead too? For a moment he was certain that she must be, by now—she was on a desperate quest, and Cadvan was no longer there to guide her.

"How are we to find Maerad now?" asked Hem despairingly.

"The simple answer is that I do not know," answered Saliman. "We don't know when she wrote this letter; it could be weeks old now, and she could have already returned from the north. The Pilanel can travel swiftly if need presses them. We don't even know when she and Cadvan left Busk." His voice cracked as he said his friend's name.

Hem sighed. "Perhaps she is in Annar." He didn't say the rest of his sentence, though they both thought it: *if she is alive*.

"We go north and seek her, I guess," said Saliman, after a pause. "We might be able to trace news of her. We will think about that when the time comes. First, there are tasks for both of us." He sounded very tired.

"I'm so sorry, about Cadvan," said Hem, and shyly he reached out for Saliman's hand. Saliman clenched it hard, and Hem could feel the profound emotion shaking within him.

"Hem, if you will excuse me, I wish to be alone for a time," he said at last. "There's something I must do."

Saliman stood up and walked out of the chamber. Hem watched him leave, wanting to follow him, but knowing he could not. He guessed that he went to make a lament for Cadvan, in the way of Bards. Hem knew that such sorrow could only be endured alone.

XVI

THE PLAINS OF NAZAR

IT was unbearably bright. Although it was dusk and Hem
and Zelika stood in the filtered light of trees, Hem's vision
blurred and swam. He was so overwhelmed he almost
retreated into the cave.

He felt as if he were drinking sweet, delicious water after a
time of great thirst. During his long sojourn in the shadows, he
had forgotten the opulence of color. It hit him in a great wave of
sensation: he had never realized there were so many shades of
green, from delicate, luminous lime to the dark, almost black
needles of conifers. Waxy crimson flowers, fading to a faint rose
in the center, dotted the forest floor like little red suns, where a
few caught the dying light; and elsewhere late orchids speared
through the undergrowth, the deep blue of an evening sky in
summer; and jasmine vines, their blossoms long withered,
wound over rotting logs, themselves adorned with emerald
mosses. Nearby a tree burdened with long, dry seed cases
rattled in the faint breeze. Through the tracery of leaves Hem
could see the faint gray of cloud, but even this seemed rich and
strange, and all the green breathed dampness, as if it had
recently rained and would soon rain again.

After the colors, what struck him were the smells: the rich
scents of loam and rotting vegetation; fresh droppings left by
some animal; the perfumes of the flowers. At first they made
him feel dizzy, as if he had drunk a goblet of wine. Irc gave an
ecstatic caw and flapped up into the branches that hung low

above them, and began to pull seedpods off the branches and
throw them down onto the children.

Irc looked a little strange: he was now in disguise, as his
white plumage was far too noticeable. The Bards had given
him, over his loud protests, a bath in tannin made from oak
galls. It hadn't given him the glossy blue-black of a crow; rather,
his feathers had taken the dye in a kind of mottle, so he was
now a dusty gray-black. For the same reasons, Hem and Zelika
were wearing the mail coat and gauntlets that went beneath
their Turbansk armor, but had left the blue ceramic armor
behind; instead they wore tunics of tough leather and dark-
dyed cloth and, over all, dark cloaks of greasy wool. It was
nearing winter, and the Suderain nights were cold.

Hem glanced over at Zelika's enraptured face, and knew she
felt the same delight at being out of the caves at last. It was like
being born again, he thought: everything seemed fresh and
newly alive, as if it had just been created, for their eyes alone, a
moment before. Saliman, standing behind Zelika with Soron,
gave Hem one of his sunny smiles, as if he knew what Hem was
feeling. As always, Saliman's smile made Hem's heart lift; it
gave him the feeling that all was right with the world, and they
were doing nothing more alarming than sauntering to meet
friends for a feast, to a warm house where the air would be
thick with merry talk and laughter.

Hared, who had crept noiselessly through the vegetation
ahead of them to scout out the area, suddenly reappeared, jerk-
ing his head for the others to follow. Cautiously the small party
crept through the undergrowth, placing their feet exactly where
Hared put his. Once Hem trod on a stick, and its snap as it
broke seemed as loud as a whiplash. Hared glanced back,
frowning, and Hem blushed. He put aside his joy at being in the
free air and began to concentrate. They were now in the territory of the Black Army, and any mistake could mean death.

*　　*　　*

They had left only that morning, winding again through endless tunnels, Hem with a glum and silent Irc clutching his
shoulder. Irc had mostly overcome his detestation of being
underground, but he still hated caves. The northern entrance to
Nal-Ak-Burat was protected by one enchanted barrier, similar
to the Gate of Dreams they had passed through on their way
there, but otherwise its main defense was the labyrinth of caves,
which were much more bewildering than those they had been
through earlier.

"One wrong turn, and you would be lost forever," Hared
had said, as he stooped, scowling, to read a cluster of runes at a
place where five caves forked from one.

"How do you remember where to go, then?" asked Hem
nervously. He had lost all sense of direction hours before.

"It's like learning a long piece of music," said Hared.
"Difficult music, with only a few notes. Left, right, straight
ahead . . . But there is a pattern to it. It changes every now and
then. Whenever you see these runes, they act as reminders that
it changes, but you have to know then what the next pattern is.
There's a pattern to the patterns, also."

Zelika looked confused.

"Like a change in tone?" Hem asked.

"Kind of like that." Hared had been almost chatty; he
seemed to become less grim the farther they were from Nal-Ak-
Burat. "Only much more complicated. I have been walking
these paths nigh on one hundred years, but I would never venture into them carelessly."

Zelika gasped. "One hundred years?" she said.

Hared gave her an amused glance. "Aye, my little fox," he
said. "I have wandered these caves since your grandfather was
a child. And yet it is a short time in the annals of the world."

Zelika had not liked the feeling that Hared was mocking

her. "You Bards are always boasting," she said, flashing him a dark look. "So what, if you live for ages? Does it make you any better than other people?"

Hared's smile widened. "Did I say it did?" he asked. "Nay, Zelika, I do not boast; I simply say what is the case. I think it is you who thinks that Bards are better than other people, but you can't admit it."

"Bards just think they're special, because of all that magic," said Zelika, scowling. "But they're not; they're just the same. They're just people, like everyone else."

She glanced at Hem, who was discomfited by the conversation, and her eyes were black and hostile. He opened his mouth to say something, and then thought better of it.

"You're right, Zelika," said Soron lightly. "Bards are no better or worse than any other people. Perhaps we can be forgiven for that, all the same."

Zelika bit her lip, but said nothing in reply.

"You are walking through fabled caves," said Saliman, breaking the silence that followed. "Even those who find them will seldom survive to tell the tale, unless they have a guide like Hared to tell the tune of the labyrinth."

"I hear that it's common in these parts to say of a tricky fellow that he has more twists than the Caves of Burat," added Soron. "But most people are quite unaware that it refers to a place they might walk over every day. Like many old sayings, it holds a kernel of knowledge, but the meaning is worn away."

After that, Hem had tried to discern the pattern Hared had spoken of in their endless turnings, but it was difficult; every time he thought he had caught a repetition, it varied slightly. Whoever devised this system, he thought, had a mind of unfathomable deviousness. He could no more discern the strange rhythm that Hared spoke of than he could fly.

The cave entrance was hidden by magery; as soon as they

had stumbled out into the dusk, it seemed to vanish into the rock wall. At last, Hem thought; at last we can begin.

They walked along the gorge for a time, a light, cool rain pattering through the leaves, until they found a place where the walls sloped rather than falling sheer. Here they paused and ate their evening meal, whispering when they had to speak, and Hem watched the sky clearing slowly above them. It was a moonless night, and the stars were cold and distant, caught in a faint haze. Hared frowned; he disliked even this much light. A chill settled over them. Hem shivered inside his cloak, and Irc fluffed out his feathers and crept close, snuggling into Hem's legs.

Then, tacitly agreeing it was time to move on, they gathered up their packs and slowly and laboriously climbed the steep slope out of the gorge. It was hot work, and after the hours spent in the Caves of Burat they were all very tired; but they had a long way to go before they could rest, so Hem gritted his teeth and ignored his complaining muscles. Hared led them, and when they reached the top of the cliff he cautiously examined the landscape before he heaved himself over the edge, signaling the others to follow.

Hem blinked as he sat, panting, on the edge of the gorge. His first instinct was a panicked impulse to go back down the way they had come; he was now on a level plain of grasses punctuated by low shrubs and trees, and the starry sky stretched infinitely high above him, filled only by drifts of vapor. He felt totally exposed.

"The Plains of Nazar," said Saliman quietly in his ear. "This is herder country. The Alhadeans once lived here, with their horses and cattle. They are not valley people, though there are gorges everywhere through Nazar, like cracks in an old face, where there is always running water." Saliman smiled.

Hem nodded, swallowing down his panic. Saliman's words

made him think of tears, of the land itself weeping. No one lived here anymore.

They began to walk, Hared guiding them by the stars. Hem knew, from what Hared had told them before they left, that they were now around sixty leagues northwest of Dén Raven. The land around them seemed silent and huge, stretching away into the haze farther than their eyes could see. The horizons were marked by irregular clots of red fire: the campsites, Hared said, of the guard the Black Army had left behind to keep watch over this empty land. Every now and then they disturbed some night animal that scuttled away into the grasses and made them tense in sudden alarm, reaching for their swords.

Hared had warned that more than human eyes watched these empty places, that Imank's Hulls set vigilances, ensorcelled snares that their steps might trigger from a distance of a hundred spans, and as they went they sensed out the landscape for any hint of sorcery. Saliman and Hared hid all their movements with muffling charms—shadowmazes, glimveils, mageshields, footwards—some little more than glimmerspells, but most of them deeper mageries to fox the cunning of Hulls.

Toward midnight they passed what had once been a village, and here, for the first time, they saw the scars of the war that had passed through this region. They could smell the burn and rot from a distance, almost before they saw the edges of wrecked walls jutting out of the plains. Hem's skin became clammy as he sensed old sorcery; it was like the smell of scorched metal, a bitter taste on the wind that dried his tongue. Hulls had been here, but even Hem could tell that what he smelled was only the remains of their presence, a cold scent. Irc, sleepily riding on Hem's shoulder, shuddered and drew closer into his neck.

It had been prosperous, a village called Inil-Han-Atar, the Place of Six Herds, and the low mud brick houses had been lined, walls and floors, with brightly dyed carpets made from the wool of the goats its people herded. The belongings of the people who had lived here were scattered outside their homes: broken instruments, cooking pots, splintered weapons. There was no sign of the people themselves. Around the remains of the houses were some ruined corrals, and inside them the dried and skeletal carcasses of animals—goats, kine, a horse— humped, distorted shapes in the darkness, limned faintly by starlight. The travelers passed by the houses warily, fearing they might trigger a vigilance.

"Do you know what happened here?" whispered Zelika. She was staring at the ruins, her nose wrinkled against the smell of death and burned wool. "Did everyone die?"

"Here they had little warning," said Hared flatly. "Inil-Han-Atar was unlucky; they were attacked by Hulls. Some stayed to defend their homes. Others fled toward Turbansk. Those who lingered or were too slow had no chance." He paused and then said, "We managed to bury those killed here, although it was risky. They lie beyond the village, under the clean stars. In many other villages in Nazar and Savitir, the bodies are left to rot like carrion, and we can do nothing for them."

Hem looked curiously at Hared, who had turned his face away. There had been a slight catch in his voice, which surprised Hem; he had thought the Bard beyond such feeling. Perhaps he had known this village well; perhaps friends of his had lived here. But if so, he did not say.

They walked on and on into the cold night, until the village disappeared behind them. By now Hem was so weary he could barely lift his feet, and he felt cold to his very bones, colder than even the night could explain; what he had seen under the faint starlight at Inil-Han-Atar had chilled his soul. He thought of Cadvan, killed in the mountains; had he been buried, or did he too lie abandoned under the stars?

Saliman had not mentioned Cadvan since they had received the news of his death, but Hem had seen how a sadness now lived inside him, as it lived unspoken in Soron. This, thought Hem, was the way of the Dark: this wanton destruction, this murder of love, this endless mourning. He felt a deep anger stir and harden inside him.

They reached their destination in the dark hours before dawn, scrambling down the sides of yet another gorge, which had opened before their feet without warning, and into another cave hidden in the walls.

This was a simple cavern, hollowed into the rock face, and inside were several Bards and others—dark-faced people who welcomed them with soft voices and bade them rest on beds of skin and straw. Hem was too tired to register any names; he knew this was one of the Light's outposts, a camp deep inside the territory of the Nameless One. All he understood was that here he was hidden from hostile eyes, and that at last he could stop walking. He fell asleep instantly, and dreamed of nothing.

The next day Hem woke late, his limbs still heavy and aching with weariness. Around him people were astir, busy examining equipment or eating or talking quietly. Zelika was still fast asleep on a pallet next to him. He swung his legs out from under the skins and rubbed his eyes. They would not leave today, Hared had said; the plan was to rest before setting off on the next part of their journey, toward the Glandugir Hills where there was reportedly a camp of child soldiers.

A young man who said his name was Infalla brought Hem some dohl and dried fruit. He was not a Bard. Hem thanked him and ate his breakfast slowly, looking around him curiously. He had been too tired the night before to absorb anything of his surroundings. This refuge was very different from Nal-Ak-Burat: everything here was plain and practical, with little

thought given to comfort. There were, thought Hem sardonically, no silk cushions in this place.

Sacks of grains and pulses were stacked on stone shelves at
the rear of the cavern, in between bunches of medicinal herbs
and smoked goat ribs. The makings of sleeping pallets were
piled next to them, to be dragged out as they were needed.
Weapons, all freshly oiled, were stacked against one wall. Hem
saw shortswords, bows, arrows, maces, and throwing knives,
all plain weapons made for killing rather than show. Next to
them was armor of various kinds. Mostly he saw the hardened
ceramic plate of the Suderain, enameled in the reddish color of
the earth and bearing no emblem. But there were some made of
metal plates like Annaren armor, again painted in earth colors,
and some that were simply hardened leather.

Besides the five newcomers, there were about eight other
people present, and the space was crowded. As Hem ate his
breakfast, two left cautiously through the narrow entrance,
wordlessly embracing those they left before disappearing
through the spelled wall. The cavern was clearly a stopping
place where no one stayed very long: a place of fragile safety
where those of the Light could hide between dangerous
missions against the Black Army.

Zelika stirred and sat up, rubbing her eyes and yawning.
"By the Light, I'm tired," she said.

"It was a long day yesterday," said Hem, turning toward
her.

"And another long day today, I suppose. *Aieee!*"

"Hared said we would rest today."

"That's unusually kind of him. Where did you get that dohl?
My innards are eating me alive."

Infalla brought Zelika a bowl of dohl, and she ate hungrily,
looking around with bright eyes, her nostrils flaring. Hem

watched her warily, wondering what she was thinking. He could not predict Zelika's mood from one moment to the next; just now she seemed to be excited, as if they might rush out and attack the Black Army.

Soron came over and sat next to them on the rocky floor, his legs crossed. "A quiet day today," he said. "For which I am personally grateful." He stretched and smiled. "I might even do some cooking!"

During the idle hours that followed, Hem and Zelika chatted with the strangers in the cavern, who asked no questions of the newcomers, although they studied them curiously, and themselves would not speak of anything specific, not even their real names. But they did tell Hem what some of their tasks were.

Some of the Bards spent most of their time disabling the vigilances the Hulls had left scattered across the Nazar Plains, to permit freer movement for the Light. Finding and negating these sorceries was dangerous and delicate work, and a mistake meant almost certain capture by Hulls or dogsoldiers. Some watched the movements of the Black Army in Nazar and passed on word to other encampments and to Nal-Ak-Burat, from which it went to certain places in Annar; their main task was to provide warning of the expected attack on South Annar. Still others launched attacks or ambushes on the guard camps scattered through the plains, or destroyed bridges and roads in order to disrupt supplies to the armies farther west.

The most dangerous missions were to Dén Raven itself; not many of those who ventured there returned. But merely entering the plains was full of peril. The fighters said that the plains were infested with mauls—the vaporous beings Zelika had seen at Turbansk—and worse: there were rumors of wights leading bands of Hulls and wers, and flocks of deathcrows combed the skies regularly. Listening, Hem wondered how they had got as far as they had the night before without incident.

There was much talk of the continuing assaults led by dog-soldiers on the cave networks. One woman, a dark wiry warrior with a scar across her nose, estimated that at least ten of their havens had been discovered and smashed by the Dark, and many of their fighters slaughtered or captured. "Treachery," she said, casting a narrow look at Hem and Zelika. "There are spies in our midst."

Hem instantly felt self-conscious; but a man nearby laughed. "You need not suspect these ones," he said. "Nothing gets past Hared. He is a soulreader, if anyone is. Anyway, you forget the subtleties of the black sorceries they use against us."

"Maybe," said the woman. "But I smell treachery. Someone knows how to break our concealment charms. Someone knows a lot about our affairs—"

"But not everything," the man answered. "Else all of us would be dead."

The woman sniffed. "We'll be dead soon enough, I expect, the way things are going."

They left the next day late in the evening, and after creeping for a league or so along the relative safety of the gorge, which was, nevertheless, scarred now and then by some sorcery that stripped the trees of their leaves and poisoned the plants beneath them, they climbed up and pressed cautiously south over the plains. Tonight the sky was overcast, and soon a steady rain began falling. It was almost completely dark, and Hared was much happier. They moved noiselessly through the grasses, shadows flitting from tree to tree, but even so they felt as visible as black marks on a white sheet. The ground itself seemed to be aware of their passing, a sense that grew stronger the closer they came to Dén Raven. As they walked, the Bards wove charms of concealment to fool or turn aside any hostile eyes, and sleep spells to lull any awarenesses, and spread their own senses as widely about them as they could, alert for any sign of sorcery.

Hared was nervous about their number—even with the charms, five people were much easier to track and harder to hide than one—and he had to balance their need for swiftness with the equal necessity of caution. The fires of guard camps burned in the distance, a dim and baleful red. Hared skirted these as widely as possible. He was practiced, Hem realized, at traversing these lands, and found even in those flat plains lower ground and sheltered spaces where they had a better chance of traveling unseen. They passed several burned villages, but did not go through them, for which Hem was grateful; even at a distance he could smell the death in them.

The constant anxiety made the journey exhausting. Hem's skin was slicked with an icy film of sweat, so he shivered even under the layers he was wearing. After the conversation of the previous day, he felt more nervous than he had the first time. But something else bothered him: since his strange encounter with the Elidhu in Nal-Ak-Burat, he felt as if another sense had opened in his mind. He couldn't give it a name, but it was an awareness that ran through his entire body, as if he were attuned to the earth itself, as if he were part of it, or it was part of him.

He felt that the earth burned with violation, as if it were poisoned; an increasing sense of wrongness seeped up from the soles of his feet, afflicting him with a constant, faint nausea. It was particularly strong in places where plants had been killed—in the gorge he had retched as they passed through the skeletal trees—but it never completely went away.

The farther they walked, the more the huge, surrounding

silence bothered him. Even the animals seemed to have abandoned this forsaken land. Irc took little flights from his shoulder, and came back to whisper what he had seen or heard: he told of strange things Hem didn't understand, of clouds weeping blood, of a fear or a shadow that drove even the birds away.

They reached another underground haven later that night, much smaller than the last. Inside was a man with terrible burns. Despite their weariness, greater than could be accounted for by their journey, Hem and Saliman did what they could to relieve his agony; but both of them saw at once that he had no chance. He had been caught in the liquid fire of the dogsoldiers, and most of his skin was burned away. He died in the night.

His companion, a slight woman from Baladh with startling gray eyes shrouded with sorrow, told them his birth name as she closed his eyelids. "He was called Lanik," she said. "He was a good man."

Hem repeated Lanik's name, and bowed his head, feeling the futility of the gesture. He had not been able to save him, and all he could do for him now was to repeat his name. What was the use of that? What else could he do?

The woman thanked them for their help, and offered to share her meager food. It would have offended her to refuse, so they did not; but the travelers brought out their own food as well to ensure that she would not be left without supplies. Her trembling thanks made Hem feel much worse; he thought he might have preferred it if she had shouted at them for their failure to save her friend.

So they went, always by night, flitting furtively from haven to haven, until Hem began to wonder if he would ever see daylight again. Hared's skill kept them hidden from the Black Army guards, although they had a couple of close shaves. Once they almost tripped over a cunningly hidden vigilance, and only Soron's quick reaction and counterspell prevented their discovery; once the luck of a sudden rain shower saved them from the deadly vapor of a maul that rose without warning from the grasslands.

They had traveled in this way for several nights through increasingly heavy weather when they reached a hiding place Hared called, with grim humor, The Pit. They were now reaching the edges of Nazar, and could see in the distance the gray hills of the Glandugir at the borders of Dén Raven. The Pit, two days' journey from the Glandugir Hills, was the closest haven to Dén Raven that yet remained undiscovered; five others nearer had been attacked and destroyed.

The haven was aptly named. The gorges that hid most of the Bards' caves petered out toward Dén Raven, and The Pit was little more than a stone-lined hole dug straight down into the ground, protected by a complicated weave of concealment charms and a wardlock, which could only be opened by a Bard who possessed both the necessary spell and an iron key. It seemed to take a long time for Hared to find and open the haven, while the others shivered in the rain, fearfully keeping watch.

The Pit was the grimmest place Hem had experienced: it lacked even the rough coziness of the previous havens he had seen. It smelled of stale air and mold and damp, and was as cold as a tomb. The haven was empty: no one stayed here long, unless they were forced to. The only positive thing about it, Hem thought gloomily, was that it had good supplies of food, which took up roughly half the cave space. There were no means of cooking—a stove here was forbidden. Cold, miserable, and tired, Hem pulled out a moldy pallet of straw and sat down, throwing thin blankets from the stores over his shoulders.

The following day their party was to split. Saliman and

Soron were to strike north on a quest that Saliman would not speak of, but that Hem suspected lay within Dén Raven itself. Hem had privately thought Soron, the Bard whose heart lay with the art of eating, was too soft for such a mission, but the past few nights had disabused him of such an easy judgment. There were depths and strengths in Soron he had not suspected, and he could see why Saliman might choose such a companion.

Soron smiled tiredly at him across the narrow space, and Hem tried to smile back.

"Not quite Nal-Ak-Burat, eh, Hem?" said Soron. "The ventilation leaves something to be desired."

"And the heating," Hem said fervently.

Soron reached inside his pack. "Medhyl is the thing, I think," he said. He took a swig from his flask and passed it to Hem. The liquor coursed down Hem's throat, leaving a trail of heat behind it. He passed it on, and each of the travelers drank some. Hem stopped shivering, but his depression lingered.

"I thought the south was supposed to be warm," he said.

"It's almost winter," said Zelika crossly. She was damp and cold, and not in the best of moods. "What makes you think that winter comes only to Annar? I should be sitting on cushions by my grandmother's hearth, with servants bringing me hot drinks. That's what everyone here does in winter."

"Everyone with servants, you mean," said Hem, with a sudden stab of malice. "Anyway, you don't have servants anymore; they're probably dead, and your house is a heap of ashes. You're as poor as me."

Zelika gasped as if he had slapped her. "Only stupid urchins say things like that," she said. "Stupid ignorant boys like you who don't know anything."

"It's not me who's ignorant . . ." Hem began hotly, but Zelika had turned her back on him. Hem faltered into an embarrassed silence, suddenly aware that Hared, Saliman, and Soron were watching him narrowly.

He took a deep breath and realized that he regretted what he had said. Zelika's occasional pulling of rank was very irritating, and she was sometimes callously ignorant of how most people lived, but that was no reason to so brutally remind her of everything she had lost. He remembered that Saliman had asked him to be strong. Squabbling with Zelika probably wasn't what he had meant.

"I'm sorry, Zelika," he said. "I'm really sorry. It's just . . . it's just . . ."

Zelika did not turn around, but after a while she spoke in a muffled voice, which told Hem she had been crying.

"I know. I'm sorry too. Just don't be so nasty. Things are bad enough."

An exhausted silence fell over the whole group, and they all glumly watched Irc attempting to break open a bundle of dried strips of meat, without trying to stop him.

"This place is sick," Hem said vehemently, at last. "You can feel it in the bones of the earth."

"Aye." Saliman glanced at him soberly. "You say rightly, Hem. The very stones are ill. You sense the touch of the Nameless One, his ill will to all living things. It reaches deep into the earth."

Hem looked down at his hands. "I wish that things were different," he said.

"Aye, that we all do." Hared, who had been silently gathering together some dried fruits, bread, and smoked meat for their meal, turned and gave Hem the wolfish smile that never quite reached his eyes. "But they are not. They are as they are, Hem, and the only way things will get any better is through what we do." He waved his hands at Irc, who had given up on the meat strips and was now eyeing a date. "Keep that bird under control, Hem. I don't want his beak in our supper."

"But what difference can we make?" Hem absently picked up Irc, who pecked his hand in token protest. Tonight he felt numbed and helpless in the face of all the suffering he had witnessed. He thought of Boran, who liked nothing better than to sit in the marketplace, drinking bitter coffee out of his little silver cups and gossiping with his friends. He should not be dead, a man so generously alive, and yet he was. The little girl from Baladh with the terrible burns. Lanik in the small haven a few days ago, in an agony only death could alleviate. Mark, whom the Hulls had wanted him to murder on that terrible night so long ago. His father, whom he could not remember. Cadvan. Countless others, whose names he did not know, who had cried out and whom Hem had tried to help, and could not.

"It is not given to us to know what difference we can make, and perhaps we can make no difference at all. But that is no reason not to make the attempt," said Saliman quietly. "The Light shines more brightly in the darkness."

"Hard words, my friend," said Soron. "For all that they seem gentle."

"Not so hard, when you consider the alternative." Saliman looked up, meeting Hem's eyes, and his glance was clear and dark. "No act is without meaning. Even if the darkness swallows us utterly, I will brook no despair."

"Despair!" said Zelika bitterly, turning around. "What else is there? I don't have any hope; I don't think we have a chance. But I'm not going to lie down and die quietly—no matter how many mauls and dogsoldiers and Hulls there are. And even if they end up killing me, I'll die cursing them."

Her bottom lip was pushed out pugnaciously, and her eyes flashed; and with a leap of his heart Hem realized, for the first time since he had seen Zelika come out of the bathing room in

Saliman's house in Turbansk, how pretty she was. He flushed and looked away, afraid he had betrayed himself, but Zelika was frowning at the floor and did not notice.

Saliman smiled. "Spoken like a true Baladhian," he said, his voice warm and amused. "Though that's not quite what I meant."

They ate their cold meal, and then bedded down to sleep on damp pallets. There was only just room for the five of them to lie on the floor.

Despite his deep tiredness, Hem lay awake for a while listening to the steady breathing of his companions. Saliman had not spoken of their imminent parting, although Hem knew that the knowledge of it lay unsaid behind all his words that night. The thought of their separation weighed more heavily on Hem than anything else. It was as bad as having to leave Maerad; worse, because he knew more now than he did then, and could deceive himself less. It was, he thought, very likely he would never see Saliman again.

Saliman and Soron rose to leave soon after they had broken their fast. They made their farewells swiftly, wishing each other good fortune. Hem hung back, made shy by the intensity of his emotion, and Saliman farewelled him last of all. He took Hem's face between his hands and kissed his forehead; as once before, his kiss lit a golden flower in the chill that numbed Hem's soul, and the boy looked into Saliman's face with a wild, despairing gratitude.

"Go well, Hem," said Saliman in the Speech, standing back and regarding him gravely. "May the Light shine on your path."

"And on yours," said Hem, feeling a stiff formality paralyzing his body. He took a breath, wanting to say more. Hem found there were no words: he wanted to say too much, and so could say nothing. With a sudden clumsy rush of love he embraced the Bard, clutching him hard, breathing in the spicy smell of his skin. With surprise, he realized he was almost as tall as Saliman.

Saliman returned the embrace, holding him close, and then gently disengaged himself. He stroked Hem's cheek lightly with the back of his fingers.

"Come, Hem! Courage, my heart." He smiled, and for a moment his expression held no trace of sadness. Hem stared at him hungrily, wanting to fix in his memory his last sight of this man he loved so much. "All is not yet lost, and hope is not dead. I say to you, Hem, we will meet hereafter, through all these shadows."

Hem nodded, unable to speak for fear he would start sobbing and wouldn't be able to stop; and Saliman and Soron turned swiftly and climbed the iron ladder out of The Pit, vanishing strangely in the shadows as the charms embedded in the entrance began to weave themselves around their forms.

The others were to wait until Saliman and Soron were well clear of the area before they would leave on their own mission. Hem sat on the ground, covering his face with the hood of his cloak. Zelika and Hared busied themselves, making sure the haven was left as tidy as they had found it, and double-checking their own supplies. Irc pecked around Hem's feet, searching for stray crumbs of food, but did not try to speak to him. Even he knew that Hem wanted to be left alone.

When it was time, Hem hefted his pack onto his back and followed Zelika and Hared up the ladder and out onto the plains.

XVII

THE GLANDUGIR HILLS

NOW began the most dangerous part of their journey. The camp of child soldiers was reported to be several leagues southeast of The Pit, in the shadow of the Glandugir Hills, which lay before them, humped ominously against the horizon, dark purple under the haze of night sky.

They moved on through an increasingly heavy rain, Hem's sandals slipping on the wet tufts of grass, Irc clinging damply to his shoulder. At least they didn't have to worry about mauls in these conditions, Hem thought; it was hard to keep all his senses alert, though, when he was soaked through and continuously hammered by the rain. There was no prospect, either, of even such shelter as The Pit offered; from now on they camped in the open, relying on their magery and campcraft to keep hidden.

As they approached the hills, the vegetation thickened, and they began to make a better pace; the feathery grasses and shrubs of the Nazar were giving way to larger trees—wild almonds with bitter black fruits, shrunken, deformed cedars, and stands of twisted oak. They encountered a road of beaten earth, churned to mud by the recent passage of carts and feet. Hared paused a long time before he permitted them to go across, questing through the rain for any scent of vigilances or other sorceries.

Hem mentally kicked himself awake, reminding himself that now they were deep in Black Army territory, and tomorrow he and Zelika would have to go on without Hared, depending wholly on their own skills. Hared had been preparing them for this all through their journey from the Caves of Burat, sending each of them in turn ahead of the group to scout for signs of danger and constantly drilling them in their responses; but, even so, the thought of being without Hared to guide them filled Hem with an apprehension he couldn't shake off. As Hared kept reminding them, one mistake could mean death; there was no room for error.

As the sky began to lighten to gray, they found a grove of wild almonds huddled at the base of a large rock shaped almost like a ship. Underneath the low trees was a tangle of thorn-bushes, and they made their camp within the thicket. Beneath the dense outer leaves were thick leafless stems, which gave them a surprising amount of space, and it was comparatively dry, although the ground was covered by prickles. Lit by the ghostly glow of dawn as it filtered through the thick leaves, they ate a melancholy meal. Hem tried not to think of one of Soron's magnificent feasts as he chewed the salty meat. As they ate they spoke together in low voices, and Hared ran them through their plans for the hundredth time.

From this point, Zelika and Hem had to scout southward a league or so, getting as close to the camp as they could. Hared wanted to find out, if possible, how big the camp was, how the Hulls were training the captured children, and where they were being taken.

"If you can find any evidence of other camps, that would be good. But anything you see will be useful," he said. "Do nothing foolhardy; I want you to come back. The dead might not betray anyone, but they can't tell you anything useful either." He grinned, and Hem supposed Hared was making some kind of grim joke. "Remember what I've taught you. You've been good students, I'll give you that; make sure it doesn't all fly out of your heads the instant you meet real danger."

Zelika, who had barely said a word since they left The Pit, nodded seriously. It was as if she were sharpening herself, Hem thought, focusing her will with an iron discipline that impressed him. He knew how single-minded she could be, but he had never seen her so contained.

"I'll meet you back here in three nights' time, and we'll decide our next move from there, depending what you've discovered. If you can't get back yourselves for some reason, send Irc." He looked at the crow and spoke to him: *Remember this place, crow. If the others get lost, you guide them here.*

I never get lost, said Irc, and cawed complacently. *I am the King's Messenger.*

You're the messenger of a pretty poor king, if your livery's anything to go by. Hared looked over Irc's mottled feathers with sly amusement. *Well, make sure you don't get lost,* he said. *Three nights—I'll meet you here.*

Irc ruffled his wings in indignation, but didn't answer back. Hared was one of the few human beings who intimidated him.

After their meal, they prepared for sleep on the prickly ground. Even through Hem's thick cloak the thorns stuck into his skin, and he shifted around restlessly, trying to find a comfortable spot. They were taking watch in shifts; Hared was first. Hem lay on his back and stared upward into the gray tangle of thorns.

With a pang, he thought of Saliman and wondered how he and Soron were faring. Well, there was no time for regret now. He had decided on this course, he had chosen it against Saliman's advice, and now there was no turning back. He simply had to do the best he could. And then his thoughts moved to Maerad, now guideless on her own quest. Where was she? Was she still alive? He found himself suddenly listening with all his strength, as if he could catch through the hundreds of leagues that separated them some faint echo of her voice; but he heard nothing except the dry whisper of the wind in the trees.

*　*　*

They left the thorn thicket as soon as darkness fell the following
night. Hared bid them leave without ceremony. "Good luck,"
he said. "I'll see you soon." Hem was grateful for his brusque-
ness; it somehow made everything more ordinary, as if they
were simply about to perform some mundane task. Hem and
Zelika glanced at each other, took deep breaths, and stole out
into the night.

Tonight there was no rain, and a thin new moon threw
tangled shadows over their path. The children planned to head
south through the edges of the Glandugir Hills. They had been
warned not to go too deeply into the hills, as they were perilous
with weird, halfmade creatures—beasts that, like the deathcrows, had been twisted awry by the poison in the land. They
crept along under the cover of the trees, checking and recheck-
ing their surroundings. Irc flew overhead, hopping from tree to
tree and acting as a lookout. Hem kept in mindtouch with him,
so they were in continual silent conversation.

They made good progress through the first half of the night,
and when they paused for a quick meal, Hem said as much
to Zelika. She frowned at him. "Don't test our luck," she
whispered. "We have a long way to go yet."

Zelika's caution was borne out a little later when a winged
creature crashed out of a tree in front of them with a hoarse
scream, knocking Hem to the ground. Irc screeched as Hem
rolled instinctively, somehow drawing his sword. He sprang
back to his feet, his heart hammering, but before he could do
anything, Zelika had slashed its head off, and the thing
collapsed to the ground in a twitching tangle of limbs and dry,
insectile wings. It was the size of a large dog and its naked skin
glowed slightly, emanating an eerie reddish light. Hem saw
with a shudder that it had long, savage teeth, and it seemed to
have too many legs.

He didn't have time to register anything else, as another appeared out of nowhere, suddenly filling the blank air in front of him. It snapped at his face and Hem felt its teeth clash together, almost grazing his ear, as he ducked and thrust out his shortsword. It reared backward and fell to the ground with a scream, transparent matter spraying from one of its eyes, and Hem brought his sword whistling down through the air and split its head in two as Irc burst out of the leaves above, ready to defend his friend. The thing made horrible slobbering noises as it twitched in its death agony, but Hem took no notice; he was looking into the dark trees, wondering if anymore were coming. The woods were ominously silent.

After a while Zelika wiped her blade and put it back in her scabbard.

"Are you all right?" she said.

Hem nodded. He was only bruised.

"We'd better get away, then. That made a terrible noise; who knows what heard us."

"I wonder what they were?"

"Some filth. Hared warned us. Come *on*."

They went swiftly, without looking back. Hem took a deep breath, trying to settle his jangling nerves; he was beginning to feel a delayed shock. Zelika's mouth was set in a firm line, and she seemed unshaken; Hem wished he felt as steady.

That was no beast, said Irc scornfully into his mind. *That was an unbeast. Twisty and nasty.*

Keep your eye out for more, Hem said. *It's your watch, the trees. You should have seen that.*

It hid itself, Irc answered. *It twists the shadows.*

Doubling his alertness, Hem thought about what Irc had said. He was troubled that he hadn't had any sense of the creatures before they were attacked, and even more by how the second one had so suddenly appeared in front of him. Whatever they were, these creatures had strong powers of concealment: glimveils, probably, from what Irc had said. The hair on his neck bristled, as if they were being watched by something unseen, but, he thought, it could also be simple fear. He didn't like these woods. He thought that the trees moved when there was no wind.

His nausea became much worse after that encounter, but he pushed it away by sheer will. He scented sorcery, but not close by; and the sound of footsteps marching some way off made them hide for a long time, fearing their skirmish had been heard by guards. But, slowly and steadily, they made progress.

When the sky began to lighten, they stopped. They found a camp like the one they had slept in the night before. Once they stopped walking, Hem dropped to his knees and was overwhelmed by a bout of dry retching. Zelika watched him with concern, saying nothing.

"It's all right," he said at last, sitting up. "It's just that this place makes me feel sick. It's poisoned here."

"You have to eat," said Zelika. "Otherwise you won't be able to walk."

"I'm not hungry."

"Eat."

Zelika put some plain biscuit into his limp hands. Hem met her unrelenting stare, swallowed, and began slowly to chew.

After an uncomfortable sleep interrupted by false alarms, they continued their journey. Both Hem and Zelika were very tense. Fearing more attacks by the Glandugir creatures, they stayed as close to the edge of the tree line as they dared, keeping in sight the lighter strip of the dirt road that ran parallel to their course. Twice that night patrols of dogsoldiers marched past, close enough for Hem to smell them—a mixture of iron, fire, sorcery, and stale sweat that made him flinch. There was no rain to cover them, but the night was chill, and clouds hurried over the waxing moon, which rode high in the sky. Once a lone rider, perhaps a Hull messenger, galloped south, its black cloak billowing behind. At each sighting the children hid in foliage that seemed pathetically inadequate cover, trembling for fear that their presence would be sensed.

According to Hared's instructions they were to come across the camp soon, and should be able to overlook it from the hills. They had been told not to approach it too closely, nor take any risks; whatever they saw from their vantage point would have to be enough. "No heroics," he had said. "Heroes tend not to return."

Hem noticed that the clearings they crept through now were not natural: once he stumbled over a tree stump, almost completely covered by brambles and evergreen creepers. Trees here had been cut down to build something. And at the darkest hour of the night they came over a rise and saw a spot of red fire on the plains beneath them. They squinted and made out the darker outlines of a camp against the black landscape. They had reached their destination. If it hadn't been for the single guard fire, they might have passed it altogether in the dark.

Now they needed to make a hide, so they could watch unobserved. Hem found a thicket on a small hillock that he thought was perfect for their needs, but Zelika said it was too close to the road. They had a brief but furious argument, conducted entirely in whispers, before they settled on another thicket without such a good view of the camp, but a bit farther back toward the trees.

They spent a bit of time arranging their hide—fussily placing water bags where they were most convenient and pushing back bramble branches—before they had something to eat. Hem tiredly cast a strong glimveil, the magery draining the remains of his strength. He could feel the tension thrilling through Zelika: now that they had reached their goal, her body was pulsing with excitement. Hem felt no excitement at all, only a dull dread that seeped through his exhaustion. He didn't argue when Zelika said she would keep first watch, and simply lay down to sleep with Irc in his usual place at his neck.

When Zelika woke him the sun had just risen, flooding the hills with a bleak, pale light. Hem blinked, feeling that it had been days since he had walked openly in daylight. Irc gave a sleepy peep and flew up into a tree above their heads. Hem pushed himself on his elbows to the front of the hide and peered through the narrow opening. Now he could see the camp properly, he was shocked by its size; it was much bigger than he had imagined. Long huts stood in rows inside what seemed to be a roughly built stockade with a high spiked fence. Dogsoldiers stood guard on high platforms above the fences. Inside, he could see groups of figures forming complicated patterns; he thought they were probably practicing battle maneuvers. Faint shouts floated toward them on the still air.

"Training," whispered Zelika. "They've been marching since before dawn."

"You can't really see from here," said Hem.

"We can see well enough," Zelika answered tartly. "Remember what Hared said about heroes. It's good that it's not raining; the light's very clear. I'm tired; wake me up if anything happens."

She crawled back into their hide and Hem stayed where he was, watching the camp, thinking that he would feel much safer if it were raining. Despite his glimveil, the clear light made him feel very exposed. He spent his time trying to count how many people might be in the camp, and mentally noting everything he saw, storing it in his memory. It was hard to tell if the figures he saw were children; he could tell dogsoldiers from humans at this distance, but not much else. The games that Hared had forced them to play in Nal-Ak-Burat did not seem so pointless now; he knew he would remember everything accurately.

At midmorning he saw the gates open, and a file of people left the camp led by a lone rider. To Hem's alarm they began to march up the hills, toward their hiding place. He watched them for a time, and then noiselessly crept back into the brambles to wake Zelika.

By the time she wriggled out to their watch point, the line had disappeared behind a low hill to their left. Hem silently ordered Irc, who, despite all warnings, had been squabbling with some local meenahs, to be quiet and to hide.

When the file reappeared from behind the hill, they were much closer. Now Hem could see them more clearly. They were definitely children, perhaps a hundred of them, all of them pitifully thin. Their hair was cropped short, close to their heads, and it was hard to tell their sex. They were mostly, Hem guessed by their skin color, from the eastern parts of the Suderain; none had the black skin of Turbanskians. They wore an assortment of armor, from dusty ceramic plate to oddments of hardened leather and chain jammed over ragged tunics and trousers. A couple of them seemed tiny, and were probably around ten years old. Some were as tall as Hem, but none looked older than about fifteen. They were led by a cloaked figure on horseback, which Hem could tell, from a chill that made his skin creep even at this distance, was a Hull.

Despite their motley appearance, the children marched in an eerie lockstep, which made the hair rise on the back of Hem's neck. It was unnaturally precise. There was none of the usual fooling of the young; they walked with a wholly focused deliberation. Hem could feel Zelika trembling beside him, although he couldn't tell whether it was with fear or excitement.

The group halted on a barked command only a few hundred spans from Hem and Zelika's hide. The children rapidly formed groups of about half a dozen each and then headed in different directions into the forest. Hem held his breath as one group passed within a dozen paces of them. This close he could see their faces, looking from side to side, as they marched. Although he was very afraid of being sighted, this frightened Hem more than anything else. They had the soft, unformed features of children, but their faces were expressionless masks, their eyes glazed and somehow implacable. As they neared them, bile seared Hem's throat, and his whole body throbbed with sickness.

The group passed them and disappeared into the wooded hills, where Hem and Zelika could hear the sound of their marching retreat into the trees. Irc told Hem he was going to follow them; and when, with a pang of anxiety, Hem agreed it was a good idea, he flapped away through the trees. As Hem felt the touch of Irc's mind dwindle into the distance, he suddenly felt achingly lonely.

He listened to the squawking of disturbed birdlife as the bands of children pushed into the hills and then, not long after the sound of footsteps had sunk beneath the rustle of the leaves, he heard what sounded like an affray—the faint clash of weapons and a hoarse scream. No doubt the children's sword skills were being tested against the nameless creatures of the Glandugir Hills.

Hem shuddered and drew a deep, trembling breath. He turned to Zelika, not yet daring to speak, not sure if he had the words to say what he felt. Zelika's eyes were very bright, and her face was full of horror.

"What have they done to them?" she whispered. "What have they done?"

Hem shrugged. He didn't know.

"Medhyl," he whispered. "I think we need some."

He wriggled back into the hide and returned with his flask

of the precious liquor. It was more than half empty, but he took a long gulp before handing it to Zelika. It made him feel a little better, but not much.

Neither of them slept after that; they couldn't. They lay on their stomachs peering through from their hiding place, their eyes gritty with tiredness. The sun slowly climbed into the sky and hid behind some thick clouds, and it began to drizzle. They gloomily watched the camp, where dozens of children were performing drills in a large open yard in the center. Hem sent his hearing into the hills, trying to gauge what the bands of children there were doing and whether they were coming back, but something baffled his senses, as if a web of thick mist was woven between the trees. He hoped that Irc had not run into trouble; he dared not try to summon him. At least, he thought, their cover seemed effective; no one had made so much as a glance toward their hiding place.

At midday Hem crawled back into the midst of the thicket and dozed restlessly, sliding into fragmentary dreams in which the winged creature snapped out of nowhere and woke him with an unpleasant jolt. He sipped some more medhyl, and crawled forward again, lying next to Zelika. He gazed out over the rocky slopes before him, his eyes watering, thinking that he never wanted to see this particular landscape again in his life. All they had to do was to wait until nightfall and then leave the way they had come, making for their tryst with Hared.

And after that, thought Hem, we should just meet Saliman and Soron and go to Annar and find Maerad; even if it's at war, it can't be worse than this place here. He pushed down the fear that Maerad might be dead, or that Saliman might not return from his own quest.

Toward dusk the bands of children began to emerge from the Glandugir Hills. To Hem's relief they gathered some distance away from the hide. They moved with the same discipline that had so unnerved him earlier, but even from this distance he could see that some of them were wounded, and some bands seemed smaller than before. Many carried the corpses of deer or pigs slung between two of them from pikes or spears, and Hem realized that these were hunting parties, sent out to catch food for the camp.   .

One very small boy was carried by two others, his body limp. The smaller unit reached the larger group and laid the injured one on the ground. Hem saw the Hull bend over him, as if examining his wounds; there was the brief flash of a sword in the dying sunlight, and then the other children took the small body away from the group and flung it into some nearby bushes.

"They killed that boy," breathed Zelika in disbelief. "They just killed him. Just like that!"

"He must . . . he must have been too hurt to heal . . ." said Hem wretchedly.

At that moment, Irc called gently into Hem's mind. He had landed silently in the tree above their hide, and Hem had had no idea he was so close; normally he would have called as soon as he came within range. This bespoke an unusual caution.

Are you all right? asked Hem, relief flooding his body.

Yes, said the crow shortly. *But I'm not going back there. Never again. Be quiet. There are more coming.*

They heard nearing footsteps and the crackling of branches and grass and then, only a few paces away, four children came into view. Their faces were scratched and bloody, and the arm of one—a boy, Hem thought, of about eleven—hung uselessly by his side.

Zelika gasped and then, before Hem could do anything sensible, she sprang out of their hiding place into the open. He grabbed her as she lunged out, but her cloak ripped out of his hand. Hem reeled, feeling his glimveil shudder to the point of breaking, and frantically whispered a word to steady it as he lifted himself into a crouch, as if to follow Zelika. But something stopped him. Instead, frozen with shock, he watched as Zelika pounced into the small clearing to the side of the four children, her shortsword drawn.

The children turned with an eerie simultaneity, instantly hefting their weapons. From their point of view, it would have seemed that she burst out of the air itself; they would not have been able to sense her until she broke through the limits of the glimveil. But none of them seemed to register any surprise; their faces were calm and unruffled.

She's gone braintwisted, Irc hissed into his mind. *Get her back. Those humans are not right; they will rip her to bits.*

How can I get her back now? said Hem. He cursed out loud, feeling an icy sweat of fear break out all over him.

"Nisrah!" Zelika cried. She reached the wounded boy and shook him violently, but instead of wincing he just stared at her blankly. "Nisrah, it's me, Zelika!"

The other children surrounded her, brandishing their weapons, but for the moment did not attack her. Zelika grabbed the boy to her breast and kept the others at bay with her sword. She muttered into the boy's ear, eyeing the others warily and drawing back.

"Come with me, Nis. Now. We'll get away from here."

"That's not my name. I don't know who you are." The boy's voice was a hoarse monotone, but something like recognition flickered in the depths of his eyes.

"Your name is Nisrah, and you're my brother, and you're witched. Stop it, stop it now. And you—" Zelika thrust her sword toward the other children, "you're all witched too. Stop there. *Now.*"

Zelika was speaking with such furious intensity that the other children halted and, for the space of a heartbeat, their faces blurred with a sudden wash of feeling—of an unendurable pain. For a wild moment, Hem, watching in horror from his hiding place, thought that Zelika might actually break through the horrible sorcery that held them: she was afire with a kind of madness that was as compelling as any magery.

She pulled Nisrah back another step. He stumbled and cried out as she wrenched his wounded arm, and the moment passed. The feeling that Zelika had roused within the children focused into expressions of murderous fury. Roughly Nisrah tore himself from Zelika's grasp, and she nearly fell over. Nisrah had no weapon; his sword arm was wounded. He punched Zelika in the face with his unhurt fist, and she buckled; not so much from its force, Hem thought, as it wasn't very hard, but from the fact of it. The boy stepped away from her, and when Zelika started toward him, to grab him again, he raised his fist.

"Nisrah!" The cry held such despairing anguish that Hem closed his eyes; he couldn't bear it. "No!"

"She's a spy," hissed a girl. Her filthy hair stood up in spikes, and she held a spear that looked too heavy for her to carry, although she seemed to heft it without effort.

With a menacing slowness, the children began to circle Zelika. Now their faces were expressionless again, and their movements spoke only of merciless intent. They all had long weapons—a sword, a pike, a spear—double Zelika's reach with a shortsword. She backed away toward a tree, breathing hard.

"You were always an idiot, Nisrah," she said, her voice hard. "Do what I tell you. Get behind me. We'll get away."

"You're not a snout." Nisrah spat on the ground.

Zelika spoke without looking at him, her eyes fixed on the other children. "Don't pretend you don't remember me," she said. "Of course you do."

She did not seem at all afraid: when the tallest boy lunged

forward with a pike she leaped past his thrust with a deceptive, dangerous grace and stabbed him in the throat. He fell, gurgling blood, and she whipped around and parried a blow from the other boy, while the girl drew back, eyeing her warily. Nisrah did nothing, neither attacking her nor hindering the others. He seemed dazed.

"Get behind me, Nisrah. *Now*."

Nisrah made a step toward Zelika and halted, suddenly looking uncertain. Zelika whipped the long sword out of the girl's hand and she flung up her hands, wringing them with pain, and threw herself at Zelika, dodging her sword. Zelika twisted so fast that Hem hardly saw the movement, and the girl landed hard on the ground, winded.

With increasing panic, Hem heard people running toward them, although no one had shouted for help and there had, so far, been very little noise. He gripped his sword until his knuckles whitened, remembering Hared's admonition: *No heroics. Heroes tend not to return.* What should he do now? To leap out and fight alongside Zelika would be sheer suicide; and yet he could not stay where he was and simply watch her die. For several agonizing moments he wavered, unable to decide what to do; and then he took a deep breath and started to creep out of the hide.

Just before he broke cover, Irc screeched and flew into his face, all claws and beak, scratching and swearing, tearing at his cheeks. Hem fell over backward, his sword tangling itself in the brambles overhead.

You can't help her now, the bird hissed. *It's too late. She's wildered, gone.*

Hem scrambled forward, cursing and sobbing, but Irc reared in front of him, his feathers bristling around his neck, his wings raised, his yellow eyes blazing. *You can't help her,* he said again.

Others had reached the skirmish. Hem couldn't see what was happening; he could hear cries and grunts and screams and the horrible noise of weapons breaking bone. Then his stomach twisted, and he knew the Hull was very close. He doubled over in mingled terror and sickness. He could feel, like a chill blade in his mind, the direction of the Hull's gaze; it was hunting through the undergrowth, it was studying the bramble patch and its inadequate cover; any moment it would break his glimveil, it would find him, and haul him out . . .

Irc flapped upward and then gave a hoarse shriek and burst out of the top of the thicket. The eye of the Hull faltered, distracted by the crow's noise, and passed over Hem's hiding place. Hem cringed into the ground, too afraid to move. Zelika was screaming imprecations at the Hull: she was now, thought Hem, completely berserk. Her curses were cut off with a stunning abruptness, midword, and Hem thought that she must have been killed. Recklessly he sent out his senses and touched for a moment her warm, breathing presence: she was not dead, nor even wounded. She must have been gagged by a spell.

"Bind her," the Hull said. Its voice seemed to come from a far and terrible distance, although it stood only a few paces from Hem. "She may be useful. Leave the others."

Hem lay as if he were paralyzed, his whole body shuddering, his mouth gritty with dirt and leaves. A trickle of blood slowly ran down his face where Irc had pecked him. He heard the iron scrape of swords being pushed back into scabbards, the clink of weapons lifted from the ground, a grunt as someone picked up something heavy, the uniform tramp of feet vanishing into the dusk.

He couldn't open his eyes; he couldn't even cry.

Zelika was gone.

DÉN RAVEN

The river is dark and deep and wide
The shore is far away
And I must swim this heavy tide
Every night and every day

The lights are warm that beckon me
The shore is far away
And I know where I'd rather be
Every night and every day

The chains are heavy on my feet
The shore is far away
They give me dust and ash to eat
Every night and every day

One day I'll see my dead ones there
The shore is far away
And then I'll rest from work and care
Every night and every day

Dén Raven slave song,
Library of Turbansk

XVIII

DISGUISE

A RED half-moon, rising through pestilential vapors. Blurred stars bleeding into a mottled sky. Earth a purple stain.

He is lying on the ground, and its sickness reaches into his body and makes him retch in his sleep. He can feel its wounds as if they are snagged in his own body. The earth cries to him, a slow vibration of pain, cut, maimed, poisoned, gashed, marred.

Far below him, reaching up into his being, he feels a slow fire, a writhing of bright, liquid rock. He is possessed by a voice with no mouth, a language with no words, a raging music that twists him, distorts his bones, desiccates his lips, erases his eyes, warps his flesh to wisps of ash.

There is no healing here.

He opens his eyes. He watches the stars fade into the slowly lightening sky. His bones are scattered over the earth's brittle surface, a skein of dust with no purpose. The wind rises to a scream, boiling clouds swallow the horizons, lightnings punish his sight. The earth folds and climbs up to meet the sky: but no, it is a wave, here, leagues from the sea, a single wave, crested with white foam. It is completely silent. More than anything, it is silent, and its silence terrifies him. He watches as the impossible wave surges inexorably toward him, swallowing the earth in its path. It will devour everything, even the clouds. Mercy is a human vice; the wave knows nothing of it. Soon everything will be silent.

*　　*　　*

Hem woke up and lay shivering, clutching his thin cloak around himself. *There is no healing here.* The dream voice resonated through his skull as the terror of the dream receded. He bit his lip, wishing he could summon Irc. He struggled with himself, cursing his weakness, but he couldn't stand it; at last he cautiously reached out and felt for Irc's presence. Faint, too far off, but still perceptible. Perversely, that brief contact made him even more lonely.

It was completely dark. He lay on the naked floor of a small room, thick with the acrid smell of urine and old food, but the stench lent no warmth; the air was freezing. His skin itched as small vermin nibbled him.

What have I done? he thought to himself. *There's no way out of this nightmare, except death. I don't want to die.*

There is no healing here. The voice mocked him.

With a jolt, he felt the tiny vigilance outside the doorway stir, alerted perhaps by his brief mindtouch. Hem pushed his thinking down into the secret depths of himself, holding his breath; the thing sniffed around briefly, and then subsided without sending an alarm. Hem heaved a low breath of relief.

Sleep, he thought, I need to sleep. He hurt all over with tiredness, but sleep would not come. He lay on his back and stared open-eyed into the darkness.

After Zelika had been taken, Hem had lain in a stupor as the dusk deepened into night. Irc had returned to the hide sometime after the last footsteps had retreated, but he said nothing, not even nagging for something to eat. He crawled close to Hem, leaning into the center of his chest, crooning in sympathy with the boy's speechless misery.

Around midnight, Hem sat up. He opened his pack and took out some food and shared it with Irc, who ate listlessly and then found a perch and went to sleep. Hem was beyond sleep. He stared into space for hours, thinking.

It was possible, he thought coldly, that Zelika was dead. Unlikely, though: if they thought she was a spy, which she was, they would want to glean whatever information she had. And Zelika, he realized now, knew quite a lot. The full scale of the disaster of her capture began to unroll in his mind. A Hull could pick her memories like a vulture picking a carcass. They would know about Nal-Ak-Burat, about Hared, about the hopes and fears of the resistance. They'll know about *me*, Hem thought, with a clutch of panic. There was no way of keeping anything hidden if you were scried. Hem shuddered at the thought of such a violation, of what it would feel like to have a Hull inside his head, picking through his most intimate shames; but he pushed the thought aside. He was done with grieving and regret: the question was what to do now.

He should report back to Hared and tell him what had happened. But he could not leave here without Zelika. The thought formed coolly, like a decision he had already reached without being conscious of it. He had to get Zelika back. He had to find out what the Hull had discovered.

They'll know about me. If I show up, they'll know who I am.

He looked at his arms. With his dark hair and olive Pilanel skin, Hem might have conceivably passed for a Baladhian if he had not spent the past few weeks underground. His skin was sallow and pale, too pale for the Suderain. His language skills were good enough now to pass without comment, but would not survive any deep probing.

He thought of the disguising spell that Saliman had taught him during some idle hours in Turbansk. It was, Saliman had said, a speciality of Cadvan's, and it fooled Bard eyes. It was not a well-known technique, as few Bards could master it. It was time-consuming and exhausting, and it had a limited duration, so if he were to be disguised for several days it would have to be renewed regularly. But perhaps, thought Hem, he could manage a limited version of it that wasn't so tiring, rather than a complete transformation of himself: a few subtle shifts in his facial features, changing his blue eyes to brown, refining his cheekbones and darkening his skin. He was thin, but he could make himself slightly thinner so he looked as if he had been half-starved for weeks. It might work.

He knew how to shield himself, so the telltale glow by which Bards recognized each other was hidden. If he were to pass as an ordinary Suderain child, he would have to shield himself so deeply that no one would suspect the smallest glimmer of Barding within him, and he would have to keep the shield up all the time. That would be very tiring, but maybe not impossible. He had learned self-discipline and wariness in his years in the orphanage.

Slowly, methodically, he thought through the details of what he might do and weighed the risks of his plan. If he were caught, the consequences didn't bear thinking about. But he knew, with a fierce certainty, that he could not abandon Zelika to the Hulls. A complex shame that he had simply watched as she was captured—that, despite everything, despite Irc's astounding attack on him, despite the impossibility that he could have helped her at all, he had somehow allowed it—swirled beneath all his thoughts. He felt that now he could begin to understand a little of Zelika's madness: she had watched her family captured and killed, and could not exorcise the shame that she had survived.

Hem knew that Hared would be furious; he would think he was being "heroic." *I am not a hero*, thought Hem, *but I can't leave my friend behind, not knowing whether she is dead or alive, without even trying to rescue her.* He flinched away from thinking about what Saliman might say.

He began to prepare himself. If the Hulls had found out

about his existence, they would be hunting for him; before he did anything, he had to move his base. Apart from anything else, there were three pathetic corpses nearby that he dared not bury, in case someone noticed; he tried not to look at them as he left the thicket. He arranged his pack carefully, taking Zelika's food but leaving her other belongings where they were. The glimveil would wear off in a few hours, so he didn't bother to dismantle it. Then he woke Irc and hunted for a new hide, as far as possible from their previous one, but with the same advantages as a lookout over the camp.

He then told Irc to meet Hared, and coached him in his message: a plain statement of what had happened, and what he had observed of the training methods of the child soldiers. He did not mention what he planned to do, simply that he would stay where he was to observe further developments and would send further news. He took a tiny cloth bag from his pack and placed inside it three twigs, to signify the three ranks of children he estimated that the camp held, a pebble to represent the Hull, and sixteen seed cases, which was the number of dogsoldiers he had counted. He tied it to Irc's leg.

If he tells me to come back, Hem said, *tell him I can't.*

He'll be angry, said Irc.

He can't make me.

Irc didn't comment or ask any questions, which was unusual for him; perhaps he half guessed Hem's intention. He gave Hem a gentle peck on the nose in farewell, and flew off at once. It was only a few hours' flight, as opposed to the day and a half it would have taken Hem to walk that far. Hem was gambling that Hared would not come to get him. He doubted that the Bard would risk himself.

Once Hem had set up the hide to his satisfaction, the sun was lighting the early morning clouds. He was now so exhausted his eyelids kept shutting of their own accord. He lay down, making himself as comfortable as he could on the prickly ground, and fell into a dead sleep.

Irc was back the next day. Hared had sent back a curt message: *Don't be a fool,* and ordered that Hem come back to the base in three days' time. It was less incendiary than Hem had expected.

He waited for three days, resting as much as he could, trying to control the nausea that constantly afflicted him in this place. He practiced holding it within him, willing his body to ignore it. He could do nothing properly if he were sick all the time. After a day, he found a way to suppress it; the sickness was still there, but he could live with it.

That three-day wait was one of the hardest things he had ever done. Every moment he was tormented by the fear of what might be happening to Zelika; terrible images rose unbidden in his mind. But he knew he had to leave a gap between Zelika's appearance and his own if his plan was to have any chance of succeeding.

Again and again he went over the sequence of events that had led to Zelika's capture, wondering if there was something he could have done to prevent it. He realized now that the main reason Zelika had agreed to come with him was that she hoped to find out what had happened to her brothers and sisters; he knew that she suspected that they had been captured rather than killed. He blamed himself: he should have guessed. Now that he thought about it, it was obvious; and yet the possibility that she might see one of her family hadn't even entered his head. Of course, she had lost all self-control when she had seen her brother. Uselessly, Hem cursed that cruel chance.

Worst of all, he remembered it was his fault that she had come at all. It was Hem's cajoling that had made her agree to work with Hared. If it hadn't been for him, none of this would have happened.

He allayed his misery by observing the camp with ferocious concentration, taking careful note of everything he saw. To his surprise, there were no more sorties into the forest. No one came looking for him and nothing moved on the road. He thought this was encouraging; if they had discovered something important, they would surely have sent a message to Dén Raven.

He watched the little figures training all day, from the moment the pale sun emerged in the morning to last light, and noted what they were doing. He decided that his initial estimate of around three ranks of children—just under one thousand— was fairly accurate. Then he sent Irc back to Hared with his latest observations, and said he was staying where he was.

Irc returned a little flustered, with direct orders that Hem return to Hared. Hem nodded, smiling grimly, and began to prepare his disguising spell. Irc watched him in silent alarm for a time, and then asked him what he was doing.

I'm going into the camp, he said. *You'll have to tell Hared.*

You're as braintwisted as the girl, hissed Irc, in sudden anger. *You'll never get out. Not even birds fly over that place.*

Hem paused, and studied Irc. *I need your help, Irc,* he said. *I need you to tell Hared what I'm doing, and then to stay close to the camp, so I can get messages to you. I'll work out how—there'll be a way. It will have to be mindtouching.*

On my own? You want me to stay on my own? Irc flapped his wings in sudden alarm.

I'll be on my own, too. But I have to find Zelika, and get her out.

You're mad.

Maybe. But I have to. I can't leave her here. Hem looked at Irc; the crow had turned his head so he could fix Hem with one unblinking yellow eye. He could feel Irc's anxiety. *I'm sorry, Irc. I want to go back more than anything, but I have to do this first. Help me.*

Irc turned his back on Hem, and preened his feathers.

Please, Irc.

The crow looked up, and then moved close. Hem stroked Irc's crisp, cool feathers, regretting the loss of his whiteness: the motley dye was practical, but it marred Irc's usual smooth beauty.

I'll help, Irc said. *I understand that you do not want to leave your friend. And I do not want to leave you.*

Sudden tears pricked Hem's eyes. *Thank you,* he said. He picked Irc up, put him on his lap and gently scratched his neck.

I'm going to go in tomorrow. I've worked out how to get in, but after that I'll have to see what happens. Stay as close as you can, so I can reach you if I need to.

Irc was silent for some time, his eyes half-closed with pleasure as Hem tickled his neck.

What if they make you dead? he asked at last.

Then you go back to Hared, said Hem. *But they won't make me dead.*

He returned to his disguising spell. He had been correct: it wasn't so hard to manage a partial change. He made himself gaunt and starveling. He would look like a Suderain version of himself; it would last five days. With any luck he would not have to renew it. The magery left him utterly drained.

Irc examined him sharply. *You are not Hem anymore,* he said at last. *Who are you?*

With a dropping of his heart, Hem realized that although he had thought of everything else, he hadn't given himself a new name. *I'm Bared,* he said, after a pause. *I am a simple boy from a village, and I can't speak too good. My village burned down, and I ran away and lived in the plains by myself. I'm hungry.*

Irc made the throaty sound that meant he was laughing.

Hem examined his strangely dark hands as he ate his midday meal. He was very afraid of what he had decided to do, but at the same time, he knew his decision was irrevocable.

After he finished eating he carefully went through his pack, putting aside most of its contents. He drank the remaining medhyl and put the flask on the ground. His mail and battered leather armor went with it, and the remains of his food, which he wrapped carefully against damp. He debated for some time whether to take his shortsword; he was fond of it and it weighed well in his hand, but its hilt was plated with gold and enameled with Turbanskian blue. It was too grand a weapon for a ragged boy fleeing war. In the end, he put it aside. He unpinned the sun-shaped brooch, the token that showed he was a Turbanskian Bard, and put it with his sword. Lastly, with a wrench, he took the Pellinor medallion from around his neck. He tipped it out of its cloth bag, and stroked it with his fingers before he put it with the rest. It was still his most precious possession, and he did not like to leave it. He kept a spare jerkin, and his water bag. His pack was now very empty.

He dug a shallow hole and put all his possessions inside it. He stamped down the red soil and covered it with brush and a glimveil, wondering as he did so whether he would ever return to dig them up. Irc watched his preparations curiously, without saying anything.

Then Hem took a deep breath. Strangely, despite his fear, he felt very calm and sure.

Right, he said. *I'm going now. Tell Hared what I'm doing, and then come back as soon as you can.*

It's a long way, the crow complained. *And I just flew there yesterday and there are nasty things in the air.*

I know. But you are a King's messenger, Irc, the bravest of birds. You can do it.

Irc puffed up his chest feathers. His vanity, thought Hem with sudden fondness, was always reliable.

Go well, Irc, he said. *I will try to touch you when I can, but do not panic if it takes a while.*

The crow brushed Hem's face with his beak, and launched himself into the air. Hem watched until he couldn't see him anymore.

He waited until sunset, but before it was completely dark. Then he shielded himself, locking fast his inner self. He was Bared now, not Hem. He straightened his shoulders, and walked slowly down the hill, toward the camp.

After days of shadowmazing and creeping from tree to tree, he felt horribly visible. As he drew closer, he saw with a shudder that dogsoldiers were keeping watch from the high wooden platforms that rose above the fences. For a moment panic clutched him, and he almost turned and ran. He thought of Zelika, and forced himself to continue, his pulse fluttering in his throat.

He walked with a stumbling gait, like someone tired and half-starved. His hair was matted from days of traveling rough, and he stank of old sweat. He had rubbed his clothes in the dust to make them more ragged and filthy. His sandals were scuffed and worn, and although they were well-made, of good leather, he had not discarded them, reckoning they looked poor enough to pass muster; he had no desire to go barefoot. As he approached the camp, he triple-checked his shielding. He did not have to counterfeit his nervousness.

Even with his Bard senses hidden, he felt the shock of vigilances silently triggering alarms in the darkening air. He braced himself and shambled steadily on, expecting any moment to feel an arrow in his breast. Nothing stirred.

When he reached the gate he stopped, momentarily baffled. He had expected to be challenged by now. He examined it closely, wondering what to do. Its planks were lashed together with rough iron bands, and the wood was so recently hewn it was still raw. It was broad enough to permit a dozen people to walk through, but fitted inside it was a smaller, iron-bound door. Hem tried banging his fists on the door, feeling foolish, but the solid wood absorbed the sound. He stood back and recklessly waved at the nearest dogsoldier. It didn't move or respond in any way.

In the end, he sat down on the churned dirt of the road, leaning his back on the gate, and simply waited. He couldn't think of anything else to do, aside from walking away. It was now almost full night. Why didn't someone come and get him? A faint hunting howl echoed in the distance and he looked fearfully out into the night: he didn't know what beasts roamed out there, nor how close they might come to the stockade. It occurred to him that the walls were intended to keep things out, as well as in. Without any magery to protect him, he would rather be inside.

He had almost given up hope of being noticed and was weighing his alternatives when the small door in the gate rattled and opened. He scrambled up nervously. Inside stood a tall woman dressed in a robe of rough, undyed wool, who dragged him inside and bolted the door behind her. She was not a Hull, as he had half expected.

"What are you doing outside?" she hissed. "It's the Blind House for you, at least. Which block are you?"

Hem stared at her in incomprehension. "I'm—I'm hungry," he stammered. "I've walked a long long way, and there's beasties out there, and I ran —"

The woman halted and examined his face; her lips pursed. "You're not one of the curs," she said sharply. "Who are you? Where are you from?"

Hem was standing with his mouth open, trying to look as imbecilic and frightened as possible. The woman slapped him across the face, and he stumbled and almost fell. "Answer me!" she snapped. "Don't waste my time."

Hem clutched his stinging cheek, beginning to whimper. "My name is Bared," he said. "I'm hungry. I got lost."

"Hmmm." The woman paused, looking at him sideways with her eyes screwed almost shut. "Well, then, Bared. You must come to our welcoming chamber, and we will see. Follow me."

"Eat?" asked Hem pathetically.

"Yes, yes, you'll be given something to eat. Now shut up."

Hem followed her, surreptitiously looking around him as they went. On either side of him were rows of low windowless buildings, arranged around a huge square of beaten earth. The woman led him across the square to one of the few places with lighted windows. They entered a small, mean room off a hallway. It was, at least, warm. Along one wall was a bench, but otherwise it was empty and featureless. The woman pointed.

"Wait here," she said peremptorily, and disappeared through a door into another room.

Hem sat down heavily on the bench, grateful to be out of the cold. Now came the part that had made him most apprehensive: there was sure to be some kind of examination. And, his heart hammering, he wondered if they might connect his appearance with Zelika's, if they might suspect that he was a spy. He wasn't sure how well his disguise would hold up under close scrutiny. How deeply could he shield himself? Would he be scried? Scrying was his only real fear: not even Bards could protect themselves against that cruel examination.

He had thought long on this question and he knew he was gambling his luck. He was hoping that to scry him would be too much trouble. Bards were very reluctant to use scrying, in part because it was a deep intrusion into another's mind, but also because it was an extremely difficult and exhausting process. Hem was sure it would be the same for Hulls who were, after all, a kind of Bard; perhaps it would be worse for them, because they scried without assent, and would have to battle past the other's resistance. Surely Hulls were subject to mortal tiredness, even if they did not die in the usual way? Would a hungry, exhausted child be worth scrying? He gnawed his fingernails viciously, fighting to keep his anxiety under control.

He was Bared. He was lost and frightened and exhausted. His family was dead.

Hem emptied his mind of everything except the desire for something to eat. His mouth fell slack and he began to drool slightly.

The woman was gone a long time.

Hem heard returning footsteps. Even before they entered the room, he knew that the woman was accompanied by a Hull. He fought his instinctive horror. Bared would not be able to sense a Hull. What would Bared think? Bared would wonder immediately if he was about to be given supper. Hem looked up, a starveling hope stamped on his face, and when he saw their hands were empty, he stared down again in dull disappointment.

"Stand up when a master enters the room!" barked the woman.

Hem stood up with dull obedience. Where was his dinner?

"Tell the master your name and your story."

Hem licked his lips nervously. "My name is Bared," he said, and stopped, flicking nervous glances at the two figures before him.

"And how came you here?"

"I-I don't know."

The woman lifted her hand to slap him again, and he cringed away and started babbling.

"My people are gone, my da, my ma—a terrible thing, fire and dead people, blood, all the screams. . . . I run away. I been running and running. I couldn't find anyone. There are bad things in the dark and I'm lost and I'm so hungry . . ."

Cramps of nausea were ripping his stomach; they were very like the pangs of tearing hunger he had often felt when he was a young child. For the first time he glanced at the Hull, and momentarily his sickness doubled and a cold sweat broke on his skin. He shifted his gaze so it was indirect, trying to see in his peripheral vision what form the Hull was assuming; his Bard eyes could see through the glimmerspell that cloaked the living horror of its face. Red-lit eyes glared from an undead skull, hairless parchment skin drawn tightly over bone. He dared not betray his visceral revulsion; to do so was tantamount to admitting that he was a Bard. He doubted that the Hull would come before a terrified child without a glamour to hide itself.

To his relief, Hem finally caught a glimpse of the Hull's glimmerspelled form out of the corner of his eye. What he saw made him catch his breath with shock, as he focused his upper mind fiercely on his cramps. The Hull seemed a beautiful woman, dressed in a long, red robe, her dark hair falling freely down her back. She was tall and full-breasted, with a warm and gentle face.

"You will be given food when you answer some questions," said the first woman in a softer voice. "Now, tell the nice lady where you are from."

He looked up, steeling himself not to flinch at the Hull's masklike countenance, and smiled ingratiatingly through his tears. The woman Bared could see was kind, she would help him, she would feed him . . .

"I was at Inil-Han-Atar," said Hem. He remembered the carnage at that village and let the sobs well up again inside him. "It's all gone—no one left, no food left. I ate beetles . . ." He sniffed and wiped his nose with the back of his hand.

"And what is your name?" The Hull spoke for the first time. Hem knew that Bared would hear a mild tone, rather than the hollow, sexless voice he otherwise heard, and he let himself imagine it. He leaned forward eagerly, like a beaten dog craving a kind word.

"Bared, miss." He sniffed again. "My name is Bared."

"And what did you do in Inil-Han-Atar, Bared?"

"Miss, I helped with the goats. Tanshun said I was no good, but I was good with them, I looked after them, and now they're all dead . . ." His face creased and he started again to blubber, hoping against hope that neither of the beings in front of him was familiar with Inil-Han-Atar.

A chill shivered down his spine as he felt the Hull's mind probing his. It felt disgusting, as if slimy tentacles were caressing him intimately with a loathly gentleness. Hem was prepared for this: it was not scrying, but the mindtouching by which Bards sometimes communicated and which would reveal his conscious feelings. He had no idea if Bared would be aware of a Hull examining him this way, but he expected that he would sense something. Fortunately, Hem's nausea was so bad now it dominated everything; and he did not have to fake most of what Bared would be feeling. He was truly lost and frightened and alone.

The Hull withdrew its attention, and turned to the woman. "He's a simpleton," it said. "A pup in a yearling's skin. They are often the best."

The woman nodded. "No interrogation?"

"No interrogation," said the Hull with a trace of distaste, and Hem's insides went watery with relief. "Give him something to eat. I wonder that you bothered me with such a trifle."

A flicker of fear passed over the woman's face. "Forgive me," she said. "I just wanted to be sure."

The Hull nodded and left the room. The woman took a deep breath, and turned to Hem, who was staring at her pleadingly, thinking voraciously of food. "Come with me," she said.

She took Hem to a huge, squalid kitchen and ladled him some cold dohl out of a rusty pot. He took the bowl, his guts churning; the last thing he felt like at the moment was food.

"Eat," said the woman, pointing to a bench. "I will find where to place you tonight. You're one of the curs, now." There was no welcome in her voice, just a statement of fact. "You'll be assigned a block in the morning."

Hem spooned the dohl into his mouth with simulated ravenousness until, to his intense relief, the woman left the room. When he was sure she had gone, he hastily scraped the dohl back into the pot, and then vomited up the little he had eaten onto the floor. He scraped it under the bench; the kitchen was so filthy he doubted anyone would notice. When he had finished, he sat dully, waiting for the woman to return.

He was too tired to feel any flicker of triumph. But he'd done it. He'd gotten into the camp.

XIX

SJUG'HAKAR IM

THE camp, crudely made and temporary as it was, had a
name: Sjug'hakar Im. Hem didn't know what it meant
until later, when the strange, clicking language of Dén
Raven began, slowly and clumsily, to form itself into words and
then into short sentences; and when he worked it out, it scarcely
seemed worth the puzzling. It meant, approximately, "Cur
Camp One," or "The First Camp of Mongrels."

As just another lost cur, Hem had been swallowed into the
routines of the camp with scarcely a ripple. That first night,
when he had dreamed of the monstrous wave, he had slept in
the same building where he had been examined by the Hull,
shoved into a room the size of a grave with no blanket or bed to
soften the dirt floor, and told he would be collected in the morning. Despite the sick apprehension that gnawed at him all night,
the fear that perhaps his cover had not held and the interview
had been a charade that would be exposed the next day, he
slept. He woke bruised and itching with small parasites, and
was given boiled pulses and some nameless dried meat he
dared not identify. By now he was seriously hungry, and ate
despite the foul greasiness of the food; but it was too much for
him, and he vomited it up in the latrine. He spent the whole of
that first day light-headed with hunger.

His hair was cropped close to his head with a pair of shears
and he was given a plain brown tunic and trousers. These, he
was to discover, were the standard dress of every child in the
camp. He was told, also, that he would no longer be called

Bared: from now on his name was Slasher Blood. He nodded dumbly.

He was shown to his block—a group of around a hundred children who shared three of the long, low, windowless huts that surrounded the training ground. There were ten blocks in the camp, each holding around one hundred children. His was the Blood Block, and the children there marked their foreheads with a vertical smear of blood to indicate their place. If they fought and killed, they would smear a horizontal line across it with the blood of the kill. In other blocks, some scarred their faces, or made primitive tattoos from berry juices and dirt. One, the Knife Block, cut off the little finger of their left hand to the first knuckle. The Blood Block considered themselves the elite corps of the camp and scorned such crude devices: each morning they would make a small incision in their forearms, squeeze out some blood and freshen their marks, continuously renewing their pledge.

But pledge to what? Hem asked himself, watching wide-eyed from deep inside the war-stunned, imbecilic husk called Bared that was his disguise. That morning Bared, or Slasher, did as he was bid, and cut his arm with a sharp knife given him by a tall, dark boy. There was no ritual of initiation into the block, as he had half expected: the tall boy who seemed to be the hut leader—Reaver—gave him an indifferent glance and asked his name, but that was all.

He was taken to the armory and fitted with armor and a weapon: to his relief, he was given a shortsword, vastly inferior to the one he had buried, its blade pitted and spotted with age, but still sharp and deadly. He hid his skill, and picked it up warily, with the awkwardness of one unused to weapons. He was examined briefly by the storeman and handed a strange motley of armor—hardened leather and ceramic plates and a sleeveless jerkin of heavy mail and thick, greasy cloth to wind around his forearms as vambraces. He was allowed to keep his sandals and his spare jerkin and pack, but first they were closely examined. He watched as the storeman hunted methodically through it, a worm of anxiety wriggling in his stomach, fearing irrationally that perhaps he had overlooked something, that some trace of his Barding might remain to betray him. But the pack was returned without comment.

Reaver gave him a mirthless grin when he returned to the Blood Block. "Now you're a real snout," he said. Hem didn't know what he meant until later. The child soldiers always referred to themselves as *snouts*; it was not a name that came from the Hulls, so far as Hem could tell, but one they made up for themselves.

Reaver showed him a pallet of straw and a blanket, which now belonged to him. It was crowded and stuffy inside the hut, but no one spilled through the door: instead each snout squatted on their pallet, busy with various inscrutable activities. It was hard to tell the boys from the girls; in their identical tunics, with their roughly cut, short hair, they seemed curiously sexless.

They did not have the blank faces that had frightened him so much when he had seen them on their mission into the Glandugir Hills. They chattered and bickered as much as any children their ages, and pursued the usual internecine fights and rivalries. But there was something wrong with their eyes, a kind of glaze that made Hem retreat into Slasher's supposed dumbness, instead of talking, as he had planned, in order to find out information. He stared uncomprehendingly at any overtures from those next to him, his mouth open, dribbling slightly, and they shrugged their shoulders, exchanged mocking glances, and left him alone.

It was a rest day, Hem learned as he listened to their talk, which was why they weren't training in the yard. They sprawled at their leisure; some lay on their backs, staring up at the ceiling, throwing obscene comments now and again into the ceaseless chat that flowed about the room; others sharpened their knives or swords, or counted things they kept in rough bags patched together from scraps of leather and cloth. They gossiped about incidents at training or mocked the abilities of other blocks, or spoke of their commanders with a strange mixture of swagger and fear.

After a while, Hem began to feel a huge boredom crushing him. It was more than tedium; it was like an active force that pushed his body heavily down on the pallet and made his bones feel like lead, something like a monstrous despair. There were around thirty children in the hut, and they jabbered all the time like monkeys; but not one of them was saying anything at all. One would make an observation, and another would respond; but it was somehow as if neither heard what the other was saying, or forgot it as soon as it had died on the air. It was as if they only made noises out of habit, to engorge the silence that would otherwise fill the hut.

Hem listened hard for anything that might give him a clue about Zelika; any loose words about the foray into the Glandugir Hills five days before, or about a prisoner. As his boredom gradually shaded to an almost unbearable disgust, he felt his eyelids closing despite himself. He battled to keep awake, fearing to miss some glancing comment, some throwaway line that might give him an idea of where she was. Perhaps the foul sorcery of this place had already ensnared her, he thought; perhaps she was in another block, swapping obscene jokes with other bewitched snouts. But he heard nothing, only an endless litany of the same things, said over and over again—the same jokes, the same empty laughter, the same boasts, the same curses.

At dusk a gong was struck, the harsh sound hanging in the

darkening air, and the snouts filed out of their hut, signing for Hem to follow. They stood in orderly lines of about thirty each, row upon row of them pouring out of the huts and standing on the beaten red earth of the training ground. Everyone else seemed to know where to go: Hem just followed his block, and stood where he could find space. A Hull came out of the Prime Hut, the building where Hem had spent the previous night, and made an announcement that he could not hear. Then came a roll call. Three Hulls moved from block to block, a scroll in the hands of the tallest of them, and called out their names. Hem was now "Slasher, Blood Block Two"; when his name was called he didn't respond at first, and was nudged by his neighbors. The roll call took at least an hour, and the stars were shining fitfully through scudding clouds in the dark sky before they were summoned to the mess hall and their dinner. Nobody seemed to mind standing stiff and silent while the Hulls checked their lists, although Hem found his legs aching.

Hem vomited up his dinner again; he held it down only long enough to make it to the latrines. Now he had not eaten since before the previous night, and a hollow ache was opening inside him. He thought it was probably the sorcery in the camp, the deep imbalance he felt there, which increased his constant, underlying nausea to the point where he could no longer control it. But maybe it was simply the greasy, gristly stew, and the soggy mess of pulses that accompanied it, or the memory it called up of the kitchen he had briefly seen the previous night. Part of him began to worry. If he could not eat even such poor food as this, before long he would lose his strength; and he had never had such need of strength.

He could go three days without eating, he knew, with no ill effects, and for the moment his hunger made him feel uncommonly alert. As surreptitiously as he could, he studied his surroundings, fixing details in his memory to sort out later, when he could think. One thing puzzled him: the burned-iron stench of sorcery around the camp was enough to make him feel sick, but it was not the kind of power he had expected to find there. If his estimate of close to a thousand children was correct, the Hulls would have to tap huge reserves of magery to keep each of them enslaved.

Hem didn't know much about Hull sorcery, but he knew that Hulls were twisted Bards who swapped their Bardic Names for immortality. It seemed logical to assume that sorcery was kin to magery, that however twisted it might be from the ethics of Barding, its laws would at base be similar. He remembered uneasily how he had dreamed, long ago in Turbansk, that Light and Dark were somehow the same.

The sorceries he furtively sniffed—vigilances at each doorway, sensate wooden walls, tricks of mind control and surveillance—were minor. They were not enough to account for the spellbinding of the snouts. Moreover, no one had tried to do anything to him. He was just one of the many others, ignored: nobody had tried to bewitch him or even tried any kind of mass mindcharm. As he lay on his thin pallet later, turning over his thoughts while the children around him snored and twitched and cried out in their sleep, he puzzled over what bound them. It was not bewitchment, or not the kind of bewitchment he had assumed. They must be using something else.

He tried to mindtouch Irc that night. He waited until the small hours before he dared to begin. First, just to be sure that his magery would not be detectable, he wove another shield; this one, unlike the shield he used to hide his Bardic nature, was an external shield, a bubble around his body. Then he sent out the summoning, the vibration that only Irc could hear, that only Irc would respond to. It was a while before he got any response, long enough to make him anxious that some accident or worse had befallen his friend; but eventually, faint and sleepy, he felt Irc's voice.

You woke me up, you featherless witling, he grumbled. *You all right?*

Yes, said Hem, grinning despite himself. *As all right as I can be in this foul place. Did you see Hared?*

Aye, answered Irc. *He was very angry. He wants to wring your neck. I have to report back in three days.*

Good idea, said Hem. *Is he going to stay where he is?*

He'll move around. It isn't safe. And he has to go back to The Pit to meet Saliman. But he won't go back to Nal-Ak-Burat until he gets you back, he said.

Hem breathed out in relief: he had feared that Hared, in his wrath, might abandon him. *Good.*

Have you found the girl?

No. Saying so hurt; it seemed to drive home the folly of what he was doing, of what he hoped to do. *No, not yet.*

You'd better hurry.

I'm trying. A sudden tired despair washed over Hem. He hated what he was doing. It was worse than he had imagined; it corroded his very soul. *The sooner I get out of here, the happier I'll be.*

I miss you. I'm lonely, you braintwister.

Hem was silent. He knew what he was asking of Irc. He was only a crow, however clever, and yet he was relying on him as much as on any Bard.

I'm lonely too, he said at last, his mindvoice awash with feeling. *I miss you something fierce, Irc. When we get out of this, I'll buy you a special spoon.*

Lots of spoons, said Irc. *And some nice pretty gems. And even then—*

Hem sensed a vigilance begin to stir; perhaps the depth of his feeling had unsettled his shielding.

I've got to go, Irc, he said hurriedly. *Something's waking. I'll come when I can.*

He flickered their tenuous connection shut. The darkness suddenly seemed much darker.

He had never felt so alone in his life.

When he vomited up his dohl again the next morning, Hem began to suspect that the sorcery might be in the food. As with all southern cooking, it was spiced; but the spices tasted cruder and were administered with a heavier hand than Hem had been used to. He wondered where the food was stored, and whether he could bypass the vigilances and guards that would undoubtedly protect it. A casual question to Reaver revealed there were gardens behind the huts, dug by the snouts themselves, where much of their food was grown.

"Don't think you can thieve any, Slasher, boy, even when you're hoeing the weeds," said Reaver, looking at him narrowly. For some reason, Reaver seemed to like him, and had appointed himself his guide and protector in the block. "There's been others thought they could, and they got the spike."

"The spike?"

"It's pretty funny," said Reaver. "They take the kid and tie him up and skewer him on a sharpened stick in the middle of the yard. But only partway, see; then they stake him in the middle of the yard. He slides down very slowly, you see. You can hear the yelling a league off; it goes on for hours. It's been a while since we had one of those," he added, with macabre regret. "It's been a bit bloody boring lately."

Hem sniggered, as if he were pushing down a sudden fearfulness; inside he was appalled, as much by Reaver's reaction as by the brutal punishment. But he was careful not to let any of his real responses show. He was getting good at this double life, he thought sardonically. Hem was inside Bared, who was inside Slasher. How well hidden could he be?

If the food was ensorcelled, he could not eat it. And if he could not eat it, he would have to steal food from somewhere else, or face starving to death. Spike or no spike.

He would have to go raiding.

That day Hem began training with the snouts. After weeks of working with Zelika and Hared he was fit and skilled, but he took care to smother his abilities with a certain clumsiness. His hunger was beginning to bite and he did not have to pretend his tiredness.

All the blocks trained separately, under different commanders, some of whom were Hulls. The dogsoldiers remained at a distance; it seemed they were there simply to guard the compound. The Blood Block toiled for punishing hours under a slate-gray sky, marching up and down the huge, bare yard in the center of the camp, learning how to move in formation to shouted orders. After a break at midday, their training shifted to combat skills: they were divided into groups of ten, and then six, and then into pairs. As all of them possessed different weapons, this was challenging; moreover, the snouts took their training very seriously and, unlike the swordcraft lessons in Turbansk, if Hem didn't pay attention, there was a real chance that he might get hurt.

When they were fighting in pairs, he found himself eye to eye with a girl of about twelve. She had the almost painful thinness of all the snouts in Sjug'hakar Im, but this had no effect on her strength or endurance; she carried a spiked mace that seemed far too big for her, but she wielded it without difficulty.

Hem was taken aback by the hail of blows she directed at him and, despite himself, shouted at her as she came for him, her face empty of anything except enmity.

"Are you trying to kill me, you fishbrain?" he hissed, as he backed away, trying to parry her blows. He feared his short-sword might shatter, and a good blow from the mace might well break his arm.

The girl didn't answer and Hem was forced to fight her to defend himself. She swung a massive blow at him and he dodged the weapon and came in under her guard, tripping her with his foot and knocking the mace from her hand. She sprawled forward on the ground, scrambling to get up, and Hem put his foot on her neck and leaned down to her ear.

"Don't bloody try that again," he whispered hoarsely.

The girl rolled her eyes at him, twisting to get away. Hem pressed harder, so her face was pushed painfully against the hard earth. He was shaking with fury.

"I'll make you eat dirt," he said. "You stupid muckhead. You could have killed me."

"Let her up." The voice came cold over his shoulder. Hem shuddered, realizing that he had just made a dreadful mistake. Slowly, thinking fast while his face was turned to the ground, he took his foot from the girl's neck, and turned around.

"She could have killed me!" he shouted, his voice high with outrage.

"Then," said the Hull, staring at him intently, "you would not deserve your place in the Blood Block. Slitter was quite cor-rect. Only death blows are not permitted."

Hem swallowed. He could not read the Hull's expression; its voice was soft, with an edge of menace. "You are new here, yes? Your name?"

"Slasher, your—your—" Hem realized he had no idea how to address the Hull.

"Captain will do," said the Hull, with a flicker of cold amusement. "Slasher. Ah yes, the simpleton." It examined Hem closely, and his guts clenched with panic at the Hull's ironic tone. The last thing he needed to do was draw attention to himself.

The Hull's attention snapped to the girl, who was still on the ground. It gave her a kick and she groaned and stood up, rubbing her neck and directing glances of pure hatred at Hem.

"Continue," said the Hull, and strolled over to another pair of fighters.

It was a hard afternoon; Hem spent his time fending off Slitter's attempts to avenge her humiliation. He let her knock him down when the blow coming his way was not life-threatening, but rolled away when she tried to stamp on him. By twilight he was exhausted and famished.

Nobody noticed whether or not he ate his dinner; the snouts ate like ravening animals, shoveling as much food into their mouths as they could. Hem curled his nose at the thin stew in his clay bowl; the smell was disgusting. He pretended to spoon it into his mouth with enthusiasm, spilling much of it. While he did so he glanced around the huge mess hall, trying to see whether Zelika was present. It was impossible; there were too many people, and with their shorn hair and identical clothing, they all looked the same.

That night he made a heavy shield and conjured a rough semblance of himself to lie in his pallet breathing softly, to cover his absence. Then he cloaked himself with shadowmazes and glimveils and stole out of the hut, dreading lest the vigilance should sense his concealments. It was not a very sophisticated vigilance; it was designed merely to detect children who sneaked out of the huts, no doubt on errands similar to his own. But a strong magery could still trigger its alarm, and he was very cautious.

The camp was deserted, lit by a dull red glare. A gibbous

moon was heaving itself above the horizon, barred by dark clouds. He could hear the cries of unfamiliar night birds and animals in the distance, and wondered briefly how Irc was surviving. On the platforms above the high fence he could see the dark outlines of dogsoldiers, clanking faintly as they moved. Swiftly he made his way to the gardens, alert for any sign of Hulls, giving the Prime Hut a very wide berth. He easily skirted the vigilances that bordered the gardens, and soon found himself among orderly rows of aubergine and pumpkin vines, turnips and sweet potatoes, and rows and rows of beans. The domestic smell of cultivated greenery was incongruous; there was nothing wrong with these plants, even though they grew in wounded soil, and the breath of them was like a balm.

Carefully he pulled a turnip from the ground, brushed off the earth, and ate it. It was hard and its fibers caught in his teeth, but he was so hungry it tasted delicious. Then he moved from plant to plant, taking a bean here, an aubergine there, putting the rinds in his pocket. It was not the best of meals, but it filled his belly. He gathered a few extra supplies for later, plucking vegetables where his thieving would be least noticed. When he had finished, he crept out of the garden and stood, undecided, at the edge of the training ground in the shadow of one of the huts.

After his meal, he felt revived. His semblance would last another hour or so; he ought to use the time to explore the camp. He moved warily from hut to hut, listening, unsure what he was looking for. It was eerily quiet, dark, and deserted; but a feeling of watchfulness made him nervous, and he flitted through shadows, frightened that at any moment he might be detected by some vigilance he had not sensed.

He had made his way to the opposite side of the compound, far from the Blood Block, when a sudden scream made him jump. It sounded like someone in an extremity of terror—

desolate and hopeless. There was a pregnant silence, and then followed a chaotic babble of complaints and sobbing and wails. It barely sounded human, but it was torn from human throats.

When his heart stopped pounding, he sharpened his hearing and traced the noise to a hut that stood by itself behind a fence. It was guarded by a strong vigilance, and he dared not go too near. He listened as the terrible noise died down and then, heavy with a sudden deep depression, went back to Blood Block Two. He slipped noiselessly through the door and into his own pallet. He was now so tired all his limbs trembled. He emptied his pockets of the stolen vegetables, hiding them under his pallet with a glimveil, and dropped asleep almost at once.

Hem blinked awake to find the pale sunlight of an early summer morning shining straight into his eyes. He squirmed sleepily aside from it for a moment, jamming his eyelids shut. Sunlight? he thought to himself, jolting suddenly awake, and sat bolt upright.

He was sitting on soft grass underneath an enormous tree that stretched some hundred spans above his head, spreading a dappled shade around him. In front of him, in the east, the sun was just overtopping some densely forested hills, from which lazy mists curled upward and vanished. The sky above him was a clear, pale blue, and the air was fresh and cold, as if it had never been breathed before.

I must be dreaming, Hem thought to himself. But this seemed more real than any dream he had ever had. He stood up, banging his arms against his sides for warmth, and on an impulse touched the tree's broad bole, wondering what kind the tree was: he didn't recognize it. Its trunk was a papery white, and its leaves were small and dark, densely gathered on graceful branches. He felt a sudden thrill as he touched the bark: the tree seemed deeply alive underneath his fingers, and for a dizzying moment he thought he almost heard the music the tree man had breathed into his ear in the city of Nal-Ak-Burat.

Wondering, Hem walked around the tree's enormous girth and looked west. Plains swept before him, as far as he could see, alive with delicate pink-and-yellow grasses that trembled in the slight breezes. Far in the distance he could see what seemed to be huge herds of animals moving slowly, like dark clouds, across the plains.

Hem shook his head. He had fallen asleep in a dark hut, noisome with the fusty smells of thirty sleeping bodies; it was impossible that he could be in a place like this. He pinched himself so hard he bruised the skin of his arm, but nothing changed. He circled the tree again, and then sat down and breathed deeply, his body light with a feeling of relief.

After a while, he realized what the relief was. For the first time in days, he did not feel nauseous. His earth sense reached deep into the ground with a profound, contented joy.

Where am I? he asked himself. He didn't know that he had spoken aloud, but he must have, because someone answered him.

It is not where, a voice said, *but when.*

Hem jumped, his skin tightening with shock, and he looked wildly around. He couldn't see who spoke.

Do not fear, said the voice. *Here is no harm. Breathe the good air.*

Hem stared at the tree. Perhaps the voice came from there: it had felt so alive. *Are you speaking to me?* he asked, feeling foolish.

There was a pause, and then, as he watched, the air before him twitched, as if it were a curtain, and a naked man was suddenly standing in front of him. If standing was the right word, thought Hem; he floated above the ground, in an orb that seemed to ripple with waves of shimmering light. His hair was long and dark, lapping down his back, and he was pale-skinned; but what caught Hem's attention were his eyes, golden and cleft with a vertical pupil. An Elidhu . . .

We have met before, Songboy, said the Elidhu. *Or was it after? It is sometimes hard to tell.*

Hem nodded, his mouth suddenly dry. He knew that this was the same Elidhu he had seen in Nal-Ak-Burat, although he bore no resemblance to the half-tree, half-man he had seen then. He was not as frightening in this semblance, but Hem's heart hammered in his chest; here in the open air he seemed more wild, more untamed, more beautiful.

Does my home please you? asked the Elidhu. *This is myself.*

Hem nodded fervently, not quite understanding and, in any case, finding himself unable to speak. The Elidhu laughed, then he reached forward and touched Hem's forehead. His hand was dry and cool. Hem shivered, not with fear, but with a deep delight, and a pleasant warmth spread through his body.

Ah, you are weary, said the Elidhu. *So weary. Rest, my child.*

As he spoke, the Elidhu was becoming less substantial, as if he were made of mist; Hem could see through him to the hills beyond. He watched as the Elidhu slowly faded until he had vanished altogether. His voice lingered in the air after him. *Rest in my home . . .*

Home, Hem thought; ah, I know what he means. Here was no lintel, no door, no roof, and yet he was suffused with a sweet sense of homeliness, of belonging in some indefinable way to his surroundings. All at once he felt no fear or confusion, just a voluptuous sleepiness. He yawned, lay down on the soft grass in the shade of the tree, and fell fast asleep.

When he woke again, back in the hut with the snouts, he felt completely refreshed, as if he had slept for hours and hours. He lay for a time on his pallet, thinking about his strange dream. Could it have been real, after all? Given that he had kept himself awake in order to raid the garden, he could not have had more than a couple of hours of sleep; but he didn't feel tired. He lifted his arms above his head, stretching, and saw with a tiny shock a green bruise on his forearm, where he had tried to pinch himself awake during the night.

Once Hem had solved the pressing problem of food, he began to settle into the camp's routine. It was very simple: training all day, meals morning and night, a lighter meal at noon. The snouts were certainly not starved, which made him wonder at their emaciated appearances. To his relief, the counting didn't occur every night: it was a tedious ritual that seemed to bore even the Hulls and other commanders.

Saliman had told Hem about the rigid caste distinctions in Dén Raven, and Hem studied the Hulls cautiously, trying to guess where they fitted in the rankings. Unlike the other snouts, he found it difficult to tell the Hulls apart: they all used glimmerspells, glamouring themselves as noble men and women, but the disguises didn't fool Hem's eyes. Those at the camp were not on the whole, Hem reckoned, especially important. However, there was one Hull, universally referred to as "the Spider," that really frightened him; Hem took care to evade the Spider's notice, as he could feel the aura of its sorcery even from the other end of the training ground. He was glad that he had not met the Spider on his first night; he thought he would almost certainly have been discovered. The other Hulls—he counted six—had less native power than Hem did, although they used it prodigally. After his short training in the ethics of the Balance, Hem was shocked when he saw one Hull weathercalling, tearing a rent in the clouds to let sunshine fall on the vegetable garden, and then, just as casually, causing a local rainstorm. No Bard would use their magery so wantonly.

Hem found that life as a snout was, more than anything,

intensely boring. No one except him seemed to be bored, but Hem sometimes thought he would suffocate with it. Disobedience scarcely existed: when snouts were given orders they obeyed immediately, without question. At night they went to sleep early and did not stir. There were none of the midnight cruelties that Hem had occasionally witnessed during his time in the orphanage: no sly, vengeful beatings or murders of weaker children. He found it uncanny.

Occasionally Hem saw children collapse under the training. They were taken away, and at first he thought that they would be treated for exhaustion. When he questioned Reaver about it, however, he was told that if it happened more than three times, they were not seen again.

"Only the best stay at Sjug'hakar Im," Reaver said, with a pride that made Hem's stomach curdle. "All the weaklings are vanished."

"Where do they go?" asked Hem. Reaver gave him a swift, contemptuous glance, and Hem realized that he had broken a code. He covered it up with an imbecilic giggle. In Sjug'hakar Im, you did not ask any questions if a snout suddenly disappeared, just as you never asked any questions about anyone's past life.

Retribution for transgressions, real or imagined, was severe. Hem had not been there long before he began to suspect that punishment was doled out randomly, with no thought for even the crudest justice. Snouts were punished as examples to the others, to reinforce with fear the bewitchment that kept them enslaved. It was also what passed in the camp for entertainment.

Reaver had already told him about the spike, but there were other savage punishments. One of the more merciful—because it was, at least, quick—was the cur kill, which Hem witnessed on his third day. The blocks were ordered out for their usual morning drill, but instead of breaking for the midday meal an announcement was made by one of the Hulls. The snouts roared and whooped, waving their weapons over their heads, and then began to chant. It was too far away for Hem to hear, and he turned to Reaver to ask what was happening.

Reaver, his face distorted with a lust that made Hem recoil, was shouting with the others. Together they were making a massive noise: "Cur kill! Cur kill!" He took no notice of Hem's question. Not wanting to seem conspicuous, Hem joined in the chanting.

Still chanting, the different blocks arranged themselves in a long line, one or two deep, which stretched all around the perimeter of the square training ground. They put their weapons down behind them and punched their fists into the air. Then the Spider led a small figure into the center of the ground. Even from this distance, Hem could see that it was shaking so much it could hardly walk.

For a horrible moment Hem thought it was Zelika. But then he saw it was too tall: it looked like a boy, his hands and feet shackled by chains. As the boy shambled to the center of the ground, the chanting raggedly ceased, and the huge crowd of snouts became completely, menacingly silent.

The Spider put up its hand and spoke. Although it hadn't lifted its voice, by some sorcery Hem could hear it perfectly, as if it spoke next to his ear.

"Here is one who has broken the rules of the pack," the Spider said. There was a growl from the snouts, and the boy whimpered. A dark stain spread over the ground where he was standing: he had wet himself. Hem had never seen anybody so afraid.

"What happens to traitors?" hissed the Spider.

"Kill!" The word rumbled over the square, and then silence fell again. The Hull walked, with a painful slowness, back to the Prime Hut. The boy stood in the center—a small, broken figure, utterly alone. Even from this distance, Hem could see him shaking.

When the Spider reached the Prime Hut, it hit a gong. It was the signal for sudden madness; the crowd of children started yelling and running to the center of the training ground. Hem yelled and ran with them, sick with fear. Very slightly he hung back, not enough to be noticed, but just enough so that he would not be among the first to reach the boy. As he neared him, he had a brief glimpse of the boy's face, his mouth stretched in a scream that no one could hear, and then he was overwhelmed by a surge of punching, biting, kicking figures, transformed into frenzied demons. Someone elbowed Hem aside, almost knocking him over, in their frantic desire to get their blow in.

It was over very quickly. The snouts, their bloodlust sated as quickly as it had been summoned, began to walk toward the mess hall, joking and laughing. Many were splattered with blood; some were even wiping blood from their mouths. A latecomer kicked the pathetic remains of what had been, only a few short moments before, a human being. It was scarcely recognizable, a broken carcass on the ground, still pathetically shackled. Hem's belly roiled with disgust and terror and pity: he had never seen anything so horrible and grotesque. He forced himself to grin as Reaver came up to him, his eyes shining with a glazed ecstasy.

"Whoo! About time we had one of those!" said Reaver, clapping his hands together in a horrible parody of glee. "Did you see how he wet himself? And look!" He held up a shred of flesh. "I got his ear!"

Hem gave a coarse laugh, and followed Reaver into the mess hall.

That night, Hem seriously considered escaping. He didn't think he could bear it. He thought about the mob, slavering and glassy-eyed in its lethal frenzy. He couldn't forget the look on the boy's face, his abject despair and terror, as the maddened children ran toward him.

Perhaps Zelika had been cur-killed? Hem dismissed the thought at once; it was too unbearable to think of. He refused to believe she was dead; and in any case, even if there were only the smallest chance that Zelika was alive, he would continue until he found her. He was going to rescue her, and that was that.

He wondered who the snouts had been before they were captured into brutalizing slavery, what families they had been torn from. Very occasionally he had seen flickerings of those former lives in vagrant expressions that chased across their faces: ghosts of gentler feelings, which were always followed by a brief dazed puzzlement, the same expression he had seen on Nisrah's face when Zelika had pleaded with him to escape. Who would the snouts be, if they survived the camp? How could they live with what they had been?

Hem was no innocent: he knew what children could do to each other. He had thought himself prepared for anything he might encounter. Now he realized that he had been wrong. The forces in the camp were much more toxic than the mindless, vicious pettiness of damaged children: the violence was controlled, focused, and deadly. It was *intelligent*.

It made him deeply afraid.

But underneath Hem's fear lay a horrified pity. Murderer or murdered, every snout was a victim.

Hem had not thought about Maerad for a long time. His sister had slipped to the back of his mind, an anxiety and grief that lay among many others: his fears for Saliman and Soron; his sorrow at being forced to leave Oslar and his vocation for healing; his mourning for the destruction of the great city of

Turbansk, a destruction he still could not fully imagine or comprehend. But this night her face sprang vividly into his mind, as if she had called him across the dark, empty leagues that separated them. He realized with a pang of guilt how long it had been since he had thought of her, and his longing for her broke open inside him like a fresh wound. He missed her so badly. He had missed her all his life.

The nightmare that surrounded him was no phantom shadow of dream; nothing could take its stain off his soul. Yet right now, more than anything else in the world, Hem wanted Maerad's small, cool hands on his forehead to wipe away the bad dreams. He wanted the comfort of her breathing body next to him as he slept, the complex spice of the smell that was hers alone. A grieving love filled his body, a sweet, unassuagable ache that seeped through him from the marrow of his very bones. *Maerad, my sister . . .*

When at last he slipped into an uneasy sleep, the dream of the silent wave came back and made him cry out, although he did not wake. In his dream, he realized the earth's slow, molten anger was part of the music the tree man had whispered to him — its violent bass notes.

Even in his sleep, Hem found himself wondering what an Elidhu really was; such beings were so outside his ken they were almost unimaginable. They did not fear death, because they did not die. The implications of this seeped through Hem's dreams, infecting him with awe and horror. The music of the Elidhu was shot with darkness, which both deepened its mystery and beauty, and drew it far beyond Hem's grasp. The Elidhu were neither good nor evil; such words were invented by human beings to explain human actions. They did not apply to the Elementals. He could not understand them; yet somehow, since the tree man had spoken to him, that music had become part of him.

The voice of his dream, the Elidhu's voice, sounded in his mind, and Hem's fear began to ebb away, leaving behind it, like a gentle residue, the peace he had felt a few nights earlier in the Elidhu's home. *There is no healing here,* the Elidhu had said. But also, giving Hem a mysterious sense of hope: *It is not where, but when.*

X X

THE BLIND HOUSE

THE longer Hem stayed at the camp, the more difficult he found his double life. He had secret tasks almost every night, so he was often short of sleep. On his fifth day there he had to renew his disguise, which required him to make a very strong mageshield and then perform the demanding spell, and the following day he could barely get through the training. The continuous fear that he might be exposed at any moment only added to his weariness.

Perhaps the worst thing he felt was loneliness. He spoke to Irc as often as he could manage, but their mindtouchings were always hurried and brief. Irc told him that he had established a territory for himself, throwing out rival birds from an almond tree, and was foraging without too much difficulty; but he was bored and missed Hem. He had flown off to meet Hared on the day that Hem was supposed to return, taking the information Hem had passed on about the structures of the camp. He came back with a curt message: if Hem were caught, he was to kill himself at once.

I know that already, Hem thought impatiently. For a moment he felt angry that Hared had not seen fit to praise him for what he was finding out about the child army; it was more than the Bards could have possibly known before. But, he realized resignedly, that was really asking too much: after all, he had expressly disobeyed Hared's orders. Still, he was sure that Hared would find his information very useful.

* * *

After the exhausting business of renewing his disguise, Hem found that his weariness was beginning to be a real problem. He didn't have to pretend that he was as dull as Slasher: his mind was thick with exhaustion. The only thing that kept him alert was terror at the thought of being unmasked.

The following night he decided to go out spying again, despite his tiredness; he felt that he didn't have much time, and that he had to discover as much as he could about Sjug'hakar Im and find Zelika. As he lay in bed, listening to the snores and muffled cries of the sleeping snouts, he wondered about his dream of the Elidhu—if it was a dream—three nights before. He remembered that Saliman had taken his vision of the tree man in Nal-Ak-Burat very seriously, and had not dismissed it as the fancy of a disordered mind. So why shouldn't this vision also be real? Hem remembered that Saliman had given the tree man a name, and groped around in his mind before he recalled it: Nyanar. That was it.

Who was this Nyanar? And what did he want with Hem? He seemed nothing like Maerad's descriptions of Ardina, who sounded almost human; this Elidhu, even when he took human form, did not seem human at all. And yet, despite his prickling awareness of the Elidhu's strangeness, an awareness that was only this side of fear, Hem felt an intimacy, as if the Elidhu plucked some deep chord of kinship inside him. Perhaps that odd feeling of familiarity was part of the music that Nyanar had breathed into him, which had opened his senses to a new, uncomfortable awakening.

He wondered why he had felt so at home in a wild place he had never seen before. This seemed an even deeper mystery. What did Nyanar mean by *home*, after all? Hem had not had a home since he could remember; almost his entire life he had been alone and ophaned, abandoned in a cruel world. Turbansk had been a home for him, almost—especially when he had found that he was a healer, when he had found work that he could do. But Turbansk was gone. And when he imagined a home for himself, a real home, Maerad was always there. This was a different feeling, and he didn't understand it at all.

He was too tired to think further. Whether it was true or not, he could do with some of that enchanted sleep; his whole body ached, remembering the sheer luxury of that rest. His longing for sleep was so intense it overshadowed even his need for food. He battled to stay awake, but his eyelids kept shutting of their own accord, and at last he gave up the struggle and drifted into the blank sleep of utter exhaustion . . .

. . . and woke, after an unmeasurable, dreamless time, under the high tree, in a clear, unstained landscape.

Again it was just after dawn, and the beams of the rising sun stretched over the trembling grasses, turning individual drops of dew into prisms of unbearable brightness. Hem blinked and stared, his belly taut with a sudden anticipation: would Nyanar step into the air again and speak with him? He sat up and waited for what seemed like a long time, trembling with a strange, inexpressible delight, but no one appeared. Oddly, it didn't disappoint him, and the sweet tautness seemed to gather and grow stronger inside him, until he thought he might burst.

I am here, said a voice into his mind. *I am all that is here. There is no here that is not me.*

It was almost as if Hem were thinking these words himself, and yet he knew they did not come from his own mind. They fell into his hearing as gently as petals falling onto a stream. Hem nodded, suddenly understanding, and relaxed. Yes, Nyanar *was* this place; he was not in this place. He did not need to make a home here; he *was* that home. Hem breathed out slowly. He thought he could begin to understand what an Elidhu was.

The sun lifted itself over the tree-darkened hills, pouring its

warmth onto his back, and Hem's shoulders relaxed as he
remembered his weariness. He had longed to be in this place,
he had longed to lie down on this soft grass, to restore himself.
Unquestioningly, like a small baby nestling into the arms of its
mother, he curled up and fell asleep.

Over the next few days, Hem kept alert for any scraps of information, finding that Slasher's simplicity was a useful mask.
Because the snouts thought Slasher was stupid, their talk
around him was often unguarded; it was as if he were invisible.
On the other hand, his food supplies were becoming his major
difficulty: his raids on the vegetable garden were more and
more risky.

On his final raid, Hem almost ran into a dogsoldier on guard
in the darkness. He retreated in confusion, his heart hammering,
but he had been so hungry he had overcome his fear and stolen
into the garden anyway. He realized that his thefts must have
been noticed, and it was only a matter of time before he was
caught. When a snout was sentenced to the spike for stealing
vegetables a couple of days later, Hem was stricken by guilt. It
was, as Reaver had told him with such macabre relish, a
particularly horrible way to die; and the child was being punished for Hem's crime.

He joined a small group of snouts who had the lowest status
in their blocks, and who sometimes didn't get enough to sate
their ravenous appetites. They lingered by the kitchen after
meals, begging for more to eat, until they were chased away to
their blocks. Sometimes, for the amusement of the cooks, the
snouts were thrown scraps, for which they would fight like
starving dogs.

These gatherings were always chaotic, but Hem used his
Bard hearing and eavesdropped on the cooks' casual conversations. He was very cautious in his listening, as the cooking was

done by low-ranking Hulls and he feared they might sense him. Once he thought he had betrayed himself when two Hulls looked up and swept their blank eyes toward the snouts. But in this way, he discovered how the children were ensorcelled.

It was, as he had suspected, something that was put in the food: a drug the cooks called morralin, made of the crushed shells of snails and the powdered root of some plant that Hem didn't know. There were three kinds, of differing strengths: one for the morning meal and one for the night, and another—a more potent mixture, Hem assumed—that was given before battle.

One nerve-racking night, Hem covered himself with several layers of glimveil and raided the kitchen. This was his most dangerous mission so far, as the kitchens were next to the Prime Hut and there was a real risk he might be sensed. Wrinkling his nose at the smell of rotting peelings and other refuse, he found the three clay pots where the morralin was kept. He stole a small spoonful of each, careful not to touch it with his naked skin, and bound them in scraps of cloth. He could feel the sorcery in the drug even through the cloth, as if it burned his hand. When he got a chance, he would give the bundles to Irc to send to Hared.

His eavesdropping also solved his pressing hunger. He discovered that the morralin was cooked only with the pulses that made up the major part of the snouts' meals. Hem thought that he could perhaps eat the other foods without harm, and tried some cautious experiments. He was dubious about the meat, remembering that it was hunted from the Glandugir Hills: what poisons might it hold? But sometimes the training left him so famished that he ate the meat anyway. He found his body was a good guide: he simply could not keep down anything tainted with morralin.

He had been finding mealtimes increasingly difficult. When

one of the Blood Block snouts made a derisive comment on his strange eating habits, he panicked. Even with the chaos at meal-times, when the snouts gobbled their food with an almost insane appetite, it was sometimes difficult to avoid eating with-out being noticed. He had developed an especially messy way of devouring his food that permitted him to spill much of it and scrape it off the table and into his sleeves with a bit of shielded illusion. At the worst, he would eat his meal and heave it up later, but he could not continue to vomit in the latrines without someone beginning to notice, and perhaps even reporting it to a Hull. Now he could eat at least some of the food he was given. Vile though the meals were, they were enough to stop him starving.

With the edge taken off his hunger, Hem began seriously to search for Zelika. It was much more difficult than he had expected.

Part of the problem was that the snouts, with their cropped hair and dull uniform dress, all looked the same from a dis-tance. In the long hours of the counting, Hem would scan all the other blocks, trying to discern her face, but it was hopeless. There was no communication between the different blocks: they kept to themselves, and ate always at the same tables. Every few days during training, one block might be assigned to fight another, and Hem took advantage of this to examine furtively the faces of the snouts; but he realized, with an increasing sense of despair, that there were some blocks he would never have a chance to see close up, and if he did not, he would never be sure if Zelika were there.

After two days of increasing desperation, he decided to try to feel for her with his mind. If she were there, even if she were bewitched, surely he would know. This was magery even more difficult than the disguising spell, and much more dangerous: because he would be touching minds, there was a real risk that a Hull might become aware of him. He permitted himself an unbroken night's sleep before he attempted it.

When the snouts were snoring quietly, he made his shield and then summoned the image of Zelika to his memory. Like everyone else, she had her own unique mental vibration: it was like a particular music, a particular smell, a particular glow. Even if she were bewitched, it would still be there, however blurred, and he knew he would recognize it if he felt it. Cautiously and delicately, Hem sent out his magesense into the camp, searching for any trace of her presence.

He tried to work methodically. He started from the south end of the camp and moved in a spiral, sniffing each mind he encountered until he was sure it was not Zelika. But very soon he found himself getting confused; some dreams were louder than others, some minds more pungent, and his skills were not precise enough to be able to sort one clearly from another, or to keep track of his direction. The dreams of the snouts bled into his head, dreams of violence and terror, or vagrant memories of other lives that even the morralin could not erase entirely. There were too many. Once, his scalp tightening with fear, he almost touched a Hull.

He knew that the vigilance by the hut was beginning to stir, and he hadn't finished. Desperately, he scouted over some dark places he had not been—not bothering with each individual mind, just searching for some sign, some scent. And just at the last minute, he thought he felt her. He touched a particularly bad knot of several minds tangled together, a jangle of nightmarish emotions that made him flinch. But somewhere inside it there was surely something: a tiny, familiar glow in the teeming darknesses, a faint perfume that recalled Zelika, smeared and unclear, fogged by sorcery, darkened and twisted with terrible pain. Eagerly he reached forward, trying to get closer, to be absolutely sure; but the sense vanished, and he could feel the vigilance tensing, on the verge of triggering, and he had to withdraw. He lay on his thin, lumpy pallet, his heart pounding, utterly drained by what he had done. He felt the vigilance slowly relax, and breathed out with relief.

He had sensed Zelika, he was sure of it. She was somewhere in the camp. Perhaps in a prison? The minds were so much darker where she was. She was bewitched, he was sure, and that would be a problem. He thought of how she had tried to persuade her brother to come with her, and how Nisrah had not recognized her. The sorcery was powerful, and he could not expect Zelika to have resisted it. Perhaps she would not come voluntarily. He would have to find where she was, and most probably he would have to disable her somehow and carry her out of Sjug'hakar Im. She was a skilled warrior, and he could not be sure that he would beat her in a fight, especially if the madness took her; he would have to use a sleep charm of some kind. And then he would have to bind her until the sorcery wore off, in case she tried to kill him. He would have to steal some leather thongs or rope for the job; he thought he knew where to find some.

It would be difficult, but not impossible. But first he had to find out where she was.

He still listened to as many conversations as he could, trying to find some word that might tell him where Zelika was. It was frustrating; the camp was awash with constant rumors, stories whispered from one ear to another about this bloody exploit, that punishment, the war for which they were all being trained. But there was no mention of a girl who had been recently captured, and where she might have been placed. It was as if she had vanished into thin air. He dared not ask any pointed questions, for fear someone might think them odd or treacherous. So he had to listen to hours of talk, fighting his boredom, his ears pricked for any detail that might tell him where she was being kept.

This was how Hem heard of the Blind House.

On his seventh day at the camp, a new girl appeared in Blood Block Two. Her face was so drawn it was almost skeletal, her skin ashen, and regular tremors shook her body. Hem stared at her curiously, wondering if she had, like him, just turned up at the gates; but eavesdropping on a whispered conversation she had with Slitter, when the snouts were settling into their beds, he heard where she had been: in the Blind House. The name went around the hut almost at once, sending a shudder through every snout who heard it.

It was, the children said, where the weakest were taken if they collapsed too often at training. And others were taken there too, it was said in low voices—those who were disloyal, or broke rules. It was feared much more than the dire punishments Hem had witnessed, although he did not understand why; those cruelties were the subject of foul jokes, but nobody jested about the Blind House. And anyone could be sent there: the last leader of the Blood Block, a girl called Hate whom everyone thought as loyal a snout as any who drew breath, had been sent there for three days and had come back changed beyond recognition. She had tried to escape Sjug'hakar Im after that, and had been cur-killed.

Hem remembered that when he had first been taken into Sjug'hakar Im, he had been threatened with the Blind House. He had not known then what it meant. His first reaction was to mentally review his behavior over the past days. Was the Slasher character truly convincing? Was he, despite everything, attracting attention to himself? He uneasily remembered how the Hull commander had noticed his combat skills during training. Hem had known immediately it was a mistake, and he was sure that since then the Hulls were taking note of him. Once he had even been drawn out of the block for a demonstration of a particular skill. He had fumbled, not too obviously: he wanted to seem like someone with a natural aptitude for combat but no experience, rather than someone who was hiding what he knew. He still didn't know if his act had worked.

His second thought was to remember the anguished screams from the hut on the other side of the camp that he had heard on his vegetable raiding. He had guessed then the hut was some kind of horrible prison; he felt as sure as he could be that this was the Blind House.

His third thought was that Zelika was probably in there.

After renewing his disguise, Hem spent most of his free time thinking obsessively about how to break into the Blind House and release Zelika. He was caught, as always, between a grinding sense of urgency and anxious caution: if Zelika were in the Blind House, she must be undergoing torments beyond imagining, and yet if he were caught, he would be killed and might as well not have bothered. Every day he dreaded that he might see her taken out for one of the Hull's brutal punishments; if that happened, he did not know what he would do. He certainly could not watch Zelika tortured with even a pretense at equanimity: it was difficult enough with children he did not know. The brutalities of Sjug'hakar Im were furnishing him with an entirely new set of nightmares.

On his nocturnal scoutings, he examined the Blind House from a cautious distance. He tried to sense the minds inside, and thought he caught a faint trace of Zelika's presence, although pained and twisted almost out of recognition. It was enough, however, to confirm his determination to break into it, despite the screams that sometimes came from the hut. Hem never got used to them; every time he heard them, his insides went cold.

The vigilance planted outside the hut was very strong, and this puzzled him. If he was right, the Blind House imprisoned only snouts, and a less powerful vigilance would do just as well. Hem dared not approach it too closely, lest he give himself away; but on the nights when he crept through the camp he spent most of his time gingerly sensing out the vigilance, its shape and mechanism.

Like all vigilances, it was a sorcery woven of shadow and air and tethered to a particular place. This one was particularly unpleasant. If it had been tangible, it would have felt cold, with the chill of a tomb, and at once bristly, as if it were covered in sharp spines of awareness, and slimy too, like a rotting dead thing. Hem was uncontrollably sick the first time he came within ten spans of it.

This vigilance was, Hem realized with a shock a couple of nights later, not merely designed to be an alarm. It was in itself a device of torture. It pulsed with sorcerous energies that entered the minds of the children inside the hut, poisoning them, as if it were a malign spider, with despair and hatred and panic so extreme that they were like constant physical pains. No wonder such terrible cries and shrieks came from the Blind House.

The vigilance, Hem was sure, had been created and set there by the Spider. Perhaps that was how the Hull came by its nickname. Whoever was in the Blind House suffered its sorceries every hour of every day. No one, thought Hem as he probed, could bear it and survive. His mind whirled through the calculations of how long Zelika must have been locked in there. Thirteen days.

Thirteen days!

He willed away his nausea, and immersed himself in the problem of how to disable the vigilance. He could not simply creep past this one: it was impossible. He had helped Saliman disable vigilances on their way through the Nazar Plains, and understood the principles of the task. The Spider's vigilance was especially complex, and would be very difficult to dismantle. It would take considerable magery, and he would need a very powerful shield to hide it; he was not sure that he had the power to make such a shield. And some of the sorceries twisted within it baffled him, sliding away from his understanding and freezing his thoughts. Patiently, he would steel himself and begin again, although soon he was so tired he could barely stand. Whatever he felt, it would be nothing to what Zelika was undergoing.

Despite everything, Hem became absorbed in the fascination of the conundrum, and almost forgot where he was. At last, he looked up and realized with a start that the deep of night had passed and the stars would soon begin to fade. He had lingered for a dangerously long time; and he was so tired he didn't know how he would train that day.

But he thought that he knew how to destroy the vigilance and get into the Blind House.

No matter what urgency he felt, Hem was simply too exhausted the following night to make an attempt on the Blind House. He was especially grateful that he had decided to play Slasher as a simpleton; his stumbling and thick speech that day were quite genuine, and covered his slowness. He got a bad bruise training in unarmed combat with Reaver, and was slapped and spat on by Slitter that evening when he awkwardly fell against her as they entered Blood Block Two after their dinner. He wanted desperately to speak to Irc, but was too tired to attempt mind-touching. Before he fell asleep, he wondered if perhaps he might go to the Elidhu's home, the dreamplace, as he had twice before when tiredness had nearly overcome him; but if he went there that night, he did not remember it.

The following day he was also a little inattentive, because he kept turning over his plan to disable the Spider's vigilance, probing it for flaws. But an announcement to the snouts at the midday break rapidly brought him back to the present. A gong sounded and the Spider emerged from the Prime Hut. An excited murmur ran around the blocks; the Spider only ever came out when a snout was to be punished. The Hull lifted its hand, and a dead silence fell at once.

"Curs of Sjug'hakar Im!" said the Hull. Again Hem could hear what it said perfectly, as if the Spider's voice insinuated itself straight into his mind. "Listen and listen well. We have two announcements. One is something we want all of you to have a care for: there is a traitor and a spy in our midst."

A ripple of enthusiasm ran through the group of snouts: a spy! This would mean some sport later on. Hem's stomach felt as if it had suddenly been removed, leaving only cold air.

"Some filth slips through Sjug'hakar Im at will, under the very noses even of our dogsoldiers," the Spider continued. "This is of great concern to us all, and we ask you loyal curs for your help. Anything strange, anything unusual, is to be reported to your block captain at once. We require your absolute vigilance: this treacherous spy, this lackey of our enemies, cannot be tolerated. If your information leads to this creature's capture, you will be well rewarded. On the other hand . . ." It paused, and Hem felt its empty gaze pass over the ranks of snouts. "On the other hand, anyone found to be hiding information or aiding the spy will be punished with full malice."

Full malice, thought Hem, swallowing. He could guess what that meant. He kept his face carefully blank, his mouth hanging stupidly open.

"We also have some good news, which will be welcomed by you all. Your training is now almost finished. The curs are pleasing us well. Soon we will begin our journey to Dagra,

where you will be welcomed by our Lord himself, the Master of
the Iron Tower. He has great plans for you, great plans! We are
sure you will fulfill his purpose, and please us all."

The Hull turned and walked back into the Prime Hut and
the snouts stirred, as if they woke from a trance, and began to
cheer and yell. The gong sounded again and the snouts
scrambled for the mess hall, talking among themselves.

Hem ran with them, his head whirling. Despite all his precautions, his scouting had been noticed; and the snouts were
moving on, into Dén Raven. Hem most profoundly did not
wish to go anywhere near the Iron Tower; he remembered his
dream of it, long ago in Turbansk, and felt a chill sweat break on
his forehead.

Time was running out. He had to rescue Zelika and escape
the camp tonight. He might never get another chance.

Hem lay with his eyes shut in the stuffy darkness of Blood
Block Two, and waited for the snouts to go to sleep. His nerves
jangled; he was much more afraid than he had been when he
had decided to enter Sjug'hakar Im. Then, he had coldly judged
the odds and decided they were good enough to gamble with.
This time, he felt his chances of success were very small indeed.

I don't want to die, he thought to himself. I don't want to die
alone, in this horrible place. I want to see Maerad again, and
Saliman. I want to eat and drink with my friends in a sunny
garden.

Hem recalled Saliman's house in Turbansk, how the dining
room opened onto the garden, the cool stone flags by the pond,
the perfume of jasmines winding over the walls, the oleanders
and roses that grew under the fruit trees. He tried to remember
the taste of Soron's seedcakes, and realized he no longer knew
what good food tasted like—even its ghost had vanished from
his tongue. His memories seemed leached of all color and very

far away from him. And, he reflected sadly, memory was all that was left of Saliman's house, that lovely, bright place where, for too short a time, he had been happy. That house lay in ruins, razed by earthquake and overrun by the Black Army.

He remembered how he had first met Zelika, how she had collided with him in the marketplace, filthy and half-mad with grief and the desire for revenge. He thought of all the times she had embarrassed or frustrated or angered him: her crazy desire to fight with Har-Ytan when Turbansk fell, her rages against Saliman, her strict Suderain lessons. Images rose into his mind at random: her rage and his merriment when Irc had dunged in her sandal, the serious crease in her forehead when she was concentrating, her gentle expression when she had picked up the little children in Nal-Ak-Burat. He remembered how she had looked when she came out of the bathing room that first day, her black curls shining and wet, with the infected cut under her eye strangely making her seem even prettier than she was.

If ever we grow up, Hem thought, I would like to marry Zelika.

The thought was such a surprise that he smiled. Zelika very likely would not want to marry him, and if they did marry, they would fight all the time. She was wild and unpredictable and maddening, but he loved her, all the same. She was the most beautiful girl he had ever met. One day he would kiss her mouth, even though she would probably slap his face. One day he would tell her that he loved her.

But first he had to rescue her from the Blind House. He could not afford to be afraid.

The breathing around him settled into a regular rhythm and Hem began his preparations. First he wanted to speak to Irc, in case anything went wrong. He made a mageshield and summoned him. Irc's voice came back at once, bristling with anxiety.

I'm sorry I couldn't speak last night, said Hem. *I was so tired.* He told Irc what he had discovered about the Blind House, and what he planned to do.

When he finished, Irc was silent for a time. *I think this is not a good thing*, he said at last.

Maybe not, Hem answered. *But I have no choice. I have to get Zelika out of there.*

Perhaps she is in another place, said Irc. *Are you quite sure they keep her in this cage?*

I'm sure, said Hem; but he could not hide a sudden doubt. Irc was right: she could, possibly, be in another block. What he had sensed was too blurred for him to be absolutely certain. *She might be somewhere else, but I think the Blind House is the most likely.*

I hope you're right, said Irc. *There will not be another chance. They will look for you.*

Hem was thrown by Irc's doubts. *I have to do this*, he said insistently. *I'm sure she's there.*

I hope you're right, Irc repeated. *I want you back.*

It will be soon—tonight, if I can get Zelika. I've seen a place where we can climb the fence, and then we'll meet you and go back to Hared.

Irc was silent again, and Hem felt the vigilance shift. Their time was running out.

I'll see you tonight, the Light willing, he said. *If things go wrong, my friend, my dear friend, go back to Hared.*

You are my friend, said Irc. Hem felt the fear in Irc's mind as if it were his own. *I want you to come back.*

I will be back, said Hem, as they broke the mindtouch, whispering it out loud. *I will be back.*

The preparations for his raid took another hour. He rechecked all his magery: the semblance he left on his pallet, his glimveils and shadowmazes, his shield. They were solid and good. He picked up his pack and stole noiselessly out of the

Blood Block and crept to the Blind House. Thick clouds covered the sky, and it was as black outside the hut as inside. He skirted around the edges of the training yard, watchful: he saw that there were extra guards tonight. Hulls were patrolling the alleys between the huts. He had feared this might happen, and took special care as he flitted from deep shadow to deep shadow. Hulls could cloak themselves as well as Bards, and he didn't want to simply bump into one.

Fortunately, perhaps because of the strong vigilance that guarded it, the Blind House seemed not to be watched at all. When he reached the edges of the vigilance he halted and sat down on the ground. He was already tired; he needed to gather his strength. This was the most difficult part of his task.

He rechecked his shield, hoping nervously that it would be strong enough, and cautiously began to summon his magery. His hands began to glimmer with silver light, which slowly brightened. Every now and then Hem halted and checked his shield again; it was still containing him. Gradually, bit by bit, he summoned his full powers.

When his body was humming with magery, he reached out delicately with his mind and stroked the vigilance. He was invoking the sleep charm he had often used on the mortally wounded to stay their pain. He bit his lip: if this failed, he could do nothing else. The vigilance tensed on the verge of triggering its alarm and he retreated slightly, but then he felt its awareness slow and gradually become numb, until it was quite still.

Hem breathed out with relief, and began the next charm, his lips moving soundlessly as he said the Speech. This would take some time: it was a spell of unweaving, which would pry into the sorceries that bound the vigilance and gently pick them apart. He was on the third stave of the charm when a shriek burst out of the Blind House and shattered his concentration. For a moment he felt the vigilance stir, and he hastily reinforced the sleep charm. Then he started again, admonishing himself: he had to maintain complete concentration for this spell to work, while another part of him kept alert for any sign of approaching Hulls or guards. He had known it would be difficult. As he continued, his hands began to shake with effort. He forced away his weariness and continued.

At last the unweaving was finished. The vigilance was now dismembered, but it was still active. Now began the most difficult part: one by one, he had to annul the sorcery of each of the dozens of energies he had carefully separated. Each required a subtly different magery, and he had to be wary lest he trigger an alarm by mistake. He had planned what he must do in his examination the night before last; he was sure of his memory. Slowly, patiently, he began.

By the time he had annulled them all, Hem had completely lost track of time. He looked up into the sky and let the power drain out of him, leaving him cold and empty. It was still hours before dawn. His shield had held, and he had dismantled the vigilance. Now, at last, he could go into the Blind House and get Zelika.

He swiftly checked to make sure that no Hulls were close by, and tiptoed to the door. As he had hoped, it was locked by only a bolt. Inside he could hear moaning and faint sobbing. Silently he drew back the bolt and opened the door.

The stench hit him in the face like a fist. Briefly he recoiled with disgust: it was foul beyond imagining. It was the smell of human beings locked into an airless room for days on end, a noxious brew of human filth and diseased skin and stale sweat. Hem took a deep breath, steeled himself, and entered.

At first he couldn't see anything at all. Carefully he made a tiny magelight and closed the door behind him. A confused and frightened babble rose around him: the children inside would not be able to see him, and perhaps would think a Hull had entered, or a haunt from the hills. Hem increased his light as much as he dared, and looked around.

The Blind House could not have been more than ten paces square, yet it contained about thirty children. Their faces were gaunt and hollow, their ribs visible through their rags. They sprawled over the earthen floor in a grotesque tangle of limbs. A few lay unnaturally still; others turned listlessly, their eyes drained of any expression; others still, their faces distorted by madness, gibbered and scratched and took no notice of Hem at all. A dozen or so children stared fearfully at Hem's magelight, its glimmer reflecting in their eyes. Hem scowled, suddenly panicked, wrenched by bewilderment and disgust and pity. In their wretchedness, they all looked exactly the same.

He shook himself out of his shock and began to search for Zelika. It wouldn't be long before someone noticed that the vigilance was gone; his time was very limited. He moved methodically around the room, holding the magelight to each child's face. When the child tried to hide, whimpering, he forced its head around so he could see. Fear and haste made him brutal, and he shut his ears to the cries that rose around him.

Zelika was not there.

Hem couldn't believe it. Perhaps he had missed her in his hurry. He forced down his anxiety and checked again, holding the magelight close to each face, pushing them aside as soon as he was sure they were not Zelika. The children began to panic; wild howls and screams began to rise into the night. They scrabbled pathetically against the walls or the floor, as if they could dig a hole to escape this haunt they could not see, which grabbed them with ghostly fingers and flung them aside.

Suddenly, like a shock in his skin, he felt a distant vigilance sounding its alarm, and then another. He was discovered. Still he looked desperately through the children, searching for

Zelika's loved face. Surely she was there, surely. The children yammered and howled and screeched, barely human in their terror. Even through the clamor, Hem could hear footsteps approaching, and the chill presence of Hulls. Hem let the mage-light blaze for a few moments and glared wildly around at the huddled, terrified children. Zelika was not there. And soon he would be trapped in the Blind House himself.

Hem pushed open the door and slid out. Just as he passed the threshold, a Hull reached for him, perceiving his presence even through his glimveil; he dodged its bony hands, twisted violently to avoid another, and ran for his life. There were Hulls and dog-soldiers everywhere, all running toward the Blind House. Hem slipped into the dark between two huts and doubled over: he was now near the gardens, where he could climb the fence. He could escape and meet Irc and flee.

Zelika was not in the Blind House. Where was she? Irc must be correct: she must have been assigned to one of the other blocks. For a terrible moment Hem wavered. Every part of his being screamed to escape from the horror of Sjug'hakar Im. But he could not leave without Zelika.

He had to stay.

Afterward, Hem did not remember his return to Blood Block Two. He slipped past Hulls in the utter blackness, holding his breath, so heavily shielded he could hardly move, wading through thick air, as if in a nightmare. He listened outside the hut for a long time before he dared to enter, unable to believe that the chaos outside had not woken the snouts from their drugged slumber. All he could hear was the whisper of sleep. At last he screwed up his nerve and slid past the vigilance, through the door and into his bed. Beneath his shield he dismantled his semblance and other charms as rapidly as possible, forcing himself to be methodical, not to make a mistake. He was driven by some tough instinct for survival, because he couldn't think. His entire body was racked with spasms of nausea, his muscles cramped with weariness, and his skull rang with pain. But worse than all of these was the knowledge that he had failed to rescue Zelika; the misery sat so thick inside him that he could scarcely breathe.

At last Hem lay on his pallet, his magery deeply hidden, staring up into the dark. Despite his exhaustion, he thought that he would never sleep again; he felt as if his whole body were jangling. Only moments later he felt the vigilance leap to alertness, and the door of Blood Block Two was flung open. A dark, cloaked figure stepped inside.

It was a Hull, but not their usual captain. Hem erased his mind as he felt the Hull's eyes sweep the room, questing for any sign of the spy who had raided the Blind House. Its gaze passed swiftly over him, and alighted nearby, focusing for a second on a girl who groaned in her sleep and turned over. Then it turned on its heel and left, slamming the door behind it.

One of the other snouts cried out and struggled in a nightmare, and then the hut was utterly silent.

XXI

SPIES

THE effect of Hem's raid on the Blind House was immediate and dramatic. Training was suspended the next day as all the blocks were thoroughly searched. Nothing was found: Hem had expected this and guarded against it. After the Hull left Blood Block Two the night before, Hem had mentally run through his possessions, in case something might betray him. The only things that might have caused suspicion were the cloth packets of morralin that he had stolen from the kitchens, but he had been wary enough to hide them in the hut and had buried them under a glimveil near the vegetable gardens. Slowly and painfully, he had cleansed his pallet of any possible sign of magery; there had not been enough to be sensed from a distance, but if a Hull had inspected it closely it might have picked up faint vibrations that would have given him away. Then he had slept briefly, too worn out and afraid even to contemplate trying to speak to Irc.

He was glad he had been cautious, difficult though it had been at the time. The Spider led the searches, and Hem trembled lest the Hull turn its attention directly on him. The Spider's abilities were of a kind that could sense barriers and shields, and it might well pierce his fragile pretense. The consequences of that didn't bear thinking about. He stood outside Blood Block Two with all the other snouts from the Blood Block while the Spider painstakingly searched their hut. The snouts had been pulled from their beds so early that they had not had time to cut their arms and smear their marks on their foreheads, and they stood in the watery winter sunlight, confused and a little frightened.

"They're looking for the spy, that's what they're doing," whispered a small girl. She glanced scornfully across the yard to the other blocks and sniffed. "Well, they won't find it in Blood Block, that's for sure."

Hem was too tired even to be afraid. He just stood and watched vacantly.

"It's probably Slasher," said Reaver, digging Hem in the ribs with his elbow. "Fancy the spike, eh, Slasher? Cur kill would be too good for you, that's for sure." He spat with disgust.

Despite himself, Hem felt his innards clutch with panic. He smiled idiotically, as if he didn't quite understand, but he couldn't hide the unease in his eyes.

"Yes, it's probably Slasher. I'll go and tell the Spider now. Big rewards, he said."

A snout Hem particularly disliked, a weaselly boy with crossed eyes, laughed sadistically. "Come on, Slasher, we'll take you in."

This time Hem really was afraid; he didn't want to be the focus of this attention, with the Spider so close. "No, Tooth, no, I would never spy!" he protested, as Tooth and some of his cohorts gathered around him, grinning. "Don't say that! I'm loyal, aren't I, Reaver? Aren't I?"

He played the butt of the joke, as he often had over the past days, praying that the snouts would soon get bored. Reaver merely sniggered, and the other snouts lost interest; a camp commander had her eyes on them, and even though she was not a Hull, she made them nervous. They scowled and scuffed the dirt with their feet.

It seemed a very long time before the Spider emerged with the other Hulls, nodded to the commander, and moved on to Blood Block Three. Hem felt relief wash through him, leaving him tingling and light-headed. They must not have found anything.

He heard later that a secret package had been found in the camp, which contained powerful spells. Wild rumors swept through Sjug'hakar Im. The spells were reported to be curses that would turn their marrow into hot lead as they slept, or at a word from the spy (who was by now a powerful sorcerer) would become invisible spiders that would enter their ears and eat their brains. Others said that enchanted weapons had been found buried in the vegetable garden. Hem translated the whispered gossip to mean that the Spider had found his packages of morralin. If the news was true, it frightened him: he had put a strong glimveil over them, and had thought they were safe. Hem realized that the only thing that really protected him was his anonymity among the hundreds of snouts: the Spider would be most unlikely to examine them one by one.

He wondered how long it would be before someone connected his arrival at Sjug'hakar Im with the spy. Perhaps he was insignificant enough to fall beneath the view of the master Hulls; the Hull who had interviewed him when he arrived was, he realized now, very low-ranking.

The block searches finished at midday, and the snouts were summoned to assemble in the training yard. There was a head count, which took a very long time. Then the Spider addressed them, but its speech was short and uninformative. It said that the snouts were to march to Dagra the following day.

That night Hem and Irc had their first real argument. Irc was horrified that Hem planned to leave with the snouts for Dagra, and angry when Hem ordered him to go back to Hared and wait for him to return.

We're marching through the Glandugir Hills, Irc, said Hem. *You don't want to follow me there. It's far too dangerous.*

I want never to go back there, answered Irc. In their mindtouch, Hem saw vague images of the things that had frightened Irc when he had followed the snouts, the day that Zelika had been captured: trees that swayed of their own volition, flowers with teeth, beasts with two muzzles or five eyes. *I did not go far. Farther in it would be much worse.*

I don't want anything to happen to you, said Hem. *So go back to Hared.*

You think only of yourself, Irc said. *You don't care about me.*

Stung, Hem said nothing for a while. He realized fully for the first time how difficult Irc was finding his demands, how it must feel as if he were abandoned. At last he said, *I do care about you, Irc. I couldn't do without you. I just can't leave Zelika. I can't. And it's a chance to find out what's really happening with the snouts. If I go to Dagra, I can bring back news that Hared couldn't possibly get otherwise.*

I think Zelika is dead, said Irc. *You chase a haunt, and we will both die for nothing.*

She's not dead, Hem said fiercely.

How do you know?

I can feel her, said Hem.

What do you feel? said Irc angrily. *You have not seen her. You have not spoken to her. Are you all braintwisted? You've spent too long with the warped ones. So what if you find out what the Dark is planning? If you go into the dark land you will not come back.*

I'll come back, said Hem, with a confidence he did not feel. *Of course I will.*

You can't go. Hem felt Irc's alarm running through him.

I must. Underneath, Hem felt a sudden appalling emptiness open up at the thought of going into Dén Raven without Irc, with no chance of even this small contact. Hem tried to focus his mind, to give the clean contours of an order. *Go back to Hared, Irc. Tonight.*

Your head's full of feathers, Irc hissed back. *You're sick like everything here.*

Hem's mind briefly flooded with Irc's anger and fright and desolation, and then he was suddenly pushed out. Hem tried to mindtouch again a few times, but the crow wouldn't respond. Miserable and cold, at last he tried to settle down to sleep. His muscles ached after spending the afternoon preparing for the next day's journey: the Hulls were dismantling the entire camp, packing all that could be carried, and then in the evening there had been another counting. It had been a hard day, and tomorrow would be even harder.

Hem lay still, depressed beyond anything he had ever felt. He saw the justice of some of the things Irc had said. If he were killed, he would never see Irc again, nor Saliman. And Maerad was already alone enough, after Cadvan's death. . . . He would lose everything that mattered to him, including his own life. Was it really worth the terrible risk he was taking?

Perhaps Irc was right, he thought to himself. But, at the same time, he knew that he could not abandon Zelika. He thought of the mind he had touched so briefly when he had searched the camp. She was here, somewhere; he just had to find her. Irc was wrong to say she was dead.

In Dagra, he might have a real chance of finding out what the Nameless One planned for the child army. *Great plans*, the Spider had said; Hem thought that this meant that they must be planning to use the snouts to attack Annar, and probably sooner rather than later. If he could discover exactly what the strategy was, he would be helping Hared and Saliman, and all those of the Light who were fighting so desperately against the Black Army. Even a small advantage could make the difference, could stave off total defeat.

Most importantly of all, he would be helping Maerad.

That final thought decided him. Maerad, too, was in great peril. How could Hem risk any less?

That night, he dreamed of a landscape covered in deep snow. He was a beast running on all fours, his mouth tingling with the fresh, clean scent of the chilly air. He felt muscles ripple under his skin, full of an untapped energy, and his heart lifted: he could run forever, faster and faster, toward the pale sun that hung coldly over the purple mountains hazed in the distance. It was a dream of pure freedom. He ran for the sheer joy of it, toward a horizon far beyond his sight.

The dream shifted to a vivid, brief memory of Maerad, standing in a long, crimson robe in Nelac's sitting room in Norloch. She was lifting a glass of laradhel to her mouth, and laughing at some witticism of Saliman's. Then suddenly Hem's father, Dorn, was standing in the room with them, and Maerad turned to greet him, smiling and unsurprised. In his waking life, Hem couldn't remember what his father looked like: he had been too young when he died. But he knew it was Dorn. He was a big man, taller than Saliman, with a shy, charming smile. He wore a blue robe richly embroidered with gold thread, and his face was dark and handsome, with the same olive skin as Hem's own. Hem was filled with a sudden, radiant joy.

There was a new strength inside him when he woke in the cold, dim light before dawn, and looked around at the squalid hut that had been his home for the past two weeks. He no longer felt that he had spent his whole life in rooms like this one, thick with the stale smell of despair and unwashed human beings. A stubborn hope flowered deep inside him. There was the Elidhu, who was helping him for his own mysterious reasons, and there was Maerad; he was not as alone as he had felt.

That morning the Hulls held yet another counting. They

were anxious about the spy, Hem supposed; and maybe they
feared that a snout might have escaped the Blind House and
was hiding among the others. For the first time since his terrible
incursion into that place, Hem thought about the other children
who had been imprisoned there. He had avoided thinking
about the Blind House: it was too horrific, too pitiful to contemplate. What had happened to those children? Even if Zelika
were not there, should he have rescued them? He had been as
cruel as any Hull: he had ignored their suffering and terror; he
had thrust them aside like objects and then simply abandoned
them to their fate. The thought of what he had done filled him
with guilt. Was this what he was doing to Irc as well? Was he
becoming, without realizing it, something he hated?

Suddenly, he found himself longing with all his soul to
speak with Saliman. Saliman would understand how torn he
felt, would help him see more clearly what it was he was doing.
Even just to see Saliman's smile, the way he would toss his
head back as he laughed, so his braids fell down his back like a
black, shining river, how he would sketch pictures in the air
with his hands as he spoke . . .

But now the counting was finally over. Hem stirred dully,
ready to march back to Blood Block Two to get his pack, but the
Spider was speaking, its voice coiling intimately in Hem's ear
like a soft, deadly snake.

"My little curs," said the Spider caressingly. "My sweet little
bloodmasters. You will be very happy to know that we have
found the louse in our midst, the spy in our belly."

Hem snapped to attention, in his shock forgetting momentarily that he was supposed to be Slasher, and the Hull nearest
to him swung around with a sudden alertness, questing.
Cursing, Hem shored up his shield and emptied his head. He
could not afford a single mistake: every day he stayed here his
situation became more perilous. He cheered boorishly with

the other snouts—although his skin was iced with a sweat of fear—and he saw to his relief that the Hull had turned away.

Furtively Hem traced his path to the fence: perhaps if he covered himself with a glimveil he might make it there, and be able to scramble over it. But he didn't like his chances, with a thousand snouts and the Spider baying after him. He tried to control his panic and to focus on what the Spider was saying.

"Before we leave for Dagra, we will deal with this recreant scum," said the Hull. "Bring the traitor forward!"

Hem tensed for flight, expecting to be grabbed: but then he realized that a shackled figure was already being dragged into the training ground. With an overwhelming astonishment, he saw it was a Hull. The snouts were as dumbstruck as he was: the bloodthirsty growl that had risen when the Spider announced the discovery of the spy died away into blank silence. There would be no cur kill today: Hulls could not be killed by any ordinary means.

It could not be a scapegoat if it was a Hull, Hem thought hurriedly. It must be a real spy. Was it one of Hared's allies? With his mouth open, he watched as the Hull was thrown to its knees in front of the Spider. It stayed perfectly still, its head cowled by its black cloak. With a gesture of contempt, the Spider ripped off the cloak. For the briefest moment, Hem recognized the Hull he had seen on his first night, the glimmer-spelled image of a beautiful woman. Then there was a gasp from the snouts, and Hem knew the glimmerspell had been destroyed. For the first time, the snouts were seeing the true horror of a Hull.

"See what a traitor is, my little curs?" said the Hull, with a bitter edge to its voice. "Dry skin on dry bones, no more. Yea, even as they live, they are dead. This one sneaks to another master and even as our Master stretches out his glorious hand in conquest, plots to ride our power and wrest it from us. She spies for Imank, the Black Captain, who even now proves his disloyalty. And this cannot be borne!"

The final words rose to a thin scream that scorched Hem's ears, making him wince with pain. But now he was bewildered: what did the Spider mean? What did it mean by treachery? It did not seem to be speaking of the Light at all.

"I say again, this cannot be borne! And so this one will be cast into the Abyss that awaits her, where her shriveled soul shall await the judgment of a crueler master than ours. And she will never return!"

For the first time the kneeling Hull moved. It cowered away, covering its eyes. Despite everything, Hem felt a tremor of pity. That small gesture was so human—the futile wish to cover one's eyes against a terrible fate. The Spider lifted its hands, and there was a flash of light, unbearably bright in the dim daylight, and a dreadful shriek that echoed through Hem's very bones. He blinked, half blinded. When the after-shadows cleared from his sight, he saw that before the Spider was no longer anything resembling a human figure: just a pile of dry bones, with the black cloak settling down over them.

"All traitors here, highborn or cur, will suffer so," said the Spider softly. "Remember that, my little insects. We have many enemies, and all our enemies will be flung into the pit of endless torment." The Hull spat viciously on the pile of bones and, gathering its cloak around it, turned and strode swiftly back to the Prime Hut.

Shaking, Hem returned to Blood Block Two with the other snouts, who were very subdued. So, the Hulls hadn't been looking for him at all, but some other spy. He was still baffled by the Spider's words. Did the Light have other allies he didn't know about?

He suddenly remembered a conversation in Nal-Ak-Burat

about the growing rivalry between Imank, the captain who had led the Black Army against Turbansk, and the Nameless One. *Sharma owes Imank much, and I doubt that Imank would be slow to remind him of it,* the Dén Raven Bard Til-Naga had said. *It is possible that Sharma fears Imank more than he fears any captain of Annar.*

Not for the first time, Hem felt frustrated by how little he knew of what was going on in the wider world. Maybe this Hull had been spying for Imank. It made sense that Imank might be plotting to overthrow the Nameless One: Imank was, by all reports, a very powerful sorcerer. And if it were true that the child armies were an important part of the Nameless One's strategy, Imank would be as interested in them as the Light was. It would explain why there had been no snouts at Turbansk, though: the Nameless One would not like them to be under Imank's authority.

Were the curs, then, to be used against Imank? And how was Imank proving disloyal? By declaring an open rebellion against the Nameless One? Or was something else going on? Had Imank simply become too powerful, and had the Nameless One decided to curb the sorcerer while he could?

There was no one Hem could ask. He would have to find out for himself.

He shouldered his pack, which was heavy: all the snouts were expected to carry their own arms and supplies. The food, he had noted sadly, was mostly morralin-dosed pulses, cooked into solid biscuits and wrapped in dirty cloth. How was he to live on nothing? He didn't dare to make any raids on the garden, which had been stripped, in any case, of all its produce. Some meager strings of beans and a few turnips were not going to sustain him.

He pushed the problem away to think about later, and

stepped out with the other snouts. A slight drizzle made the camp look even more desolate than usual. With the dogsoldiers flanking them and Hulls at the front and back of the column, the snouts began to march to Dén Raven.

The trees that covered the Glandugir Hills thickened rapidly, but Hem saw, to his relief, that they were following a road— barely a track, really—which meant they would not have to hack their way through the vegetation as he had at first feared. They all marched in their blocks. The track was wide enough to permit four abreast at most, and the lines thinned out, making the snouts feel vulnerable; they all jostled for a place in the middle of the track, as far away from the trees as possible. Sometimes these arguments came to blows.

It was the first time that Hem had seen the snouts so afraid, and it didn't make him feel any better. Irc was right: he had almost no chance of survival if he went to Dagra. And how would he return, with all of Dén Raven and the Glandugir Hills to cross? For a wild few moments, he almost made a break for it into the trees; but he bit his lip, telling himself not to be a coward. If Zelika was among the snouts, he would have more possibility of finding her on the road; and this was his chance to discover what was really happening with the snouts.

He tried not to think about Irc. He had recklessly attempted to contact the crow again, in the dawn light before the snouts were called from their beds, but he had not answered.

From his position, Hem could not see the beginning or the end of the line, and even the nearest dogsoldier was almost out of sight. He was glad of this; even the snouts found the dogsoldiers uncanny, and the sense of wrongness near them was so strong that Hem could barely avoid retching when one was only a few paces away. It was the same feeling that the deathcrows gave him: a sense of something vital irretrievably blighted. In the camp he had scarcely been aware of them; they guarded the walls, and lived in a hut in the far corner from the Blood Block, a few hundred paces from the Blind House. Now he was painfully aware of their presence.

Earlier that morning, as they marched toward the Glandugir Hills, Hem had seen a dogsoldier close up for the first time. Although, after the past few days, he had thought he was now inured to shock, the sight had left him deeply disturbed.

Dogsoldiers were a weird mixture of metal and flesh: it was hard to tell where their armor ended and their bodies began, and when Hem came close to them he could feel the heat they gave off, like braziers. They were heavily built, half again as tall as a big man, and moved with a deliberate, menacing slowness. In place of hands they had grasping instruments of articulated metal, with retractable claws of blue steel, and in the middle were black holes from which, at will, they could spit the liquid fire that caused such fearsome injuries. They did not carry any weapons: they didn't have to.

But it wasn't their size, or that they so clearly existed only in order to kill and maim, that made him recoil. He had caught a glimpse of the face under a dogsoldier's iron helmet, a face disfigured by the monstrously fanged steel muzzles that projected from its cheekbones, and he saw its eyes. Human eyes, with a human intelligence. In that moment, he realized with a shock that the dogsoldier was, or had once been, a human being.

Had they been ordinary men and women who were, by some sorcery he could not understand, tormented into these figures of nightmare? Did dogsoldiers *breed*? Or did they all have to be formed, like snouts were formed? And if they were fashioned from ordinary people, what did they feel about what they had become?

In that flash of empathy, Hem hoped passionately that the

dogsoldiers felt nothing at all. If they did, then to be a dogsoldier must be ghastly beyond imagining. There was no clue in their distorted faces: their eyes were hard and expressionless, as pitiless as any Hull's. But perhaps, in the depths of those mutilated bodies, there still existed the ghosts of softer memories—even, perhaps, of love . . . The thought filled Hem with a bottomless horror, and he turned away, heaving. They were like the snouts, but worse. And he had not thought that there could be anything worse than the snouts.

He shook himself. He couldn't afford to think like this. Merely surviving was going to be hard enough.

The Hulls set a blistering pace. Despite the track, it was hard going: up and down hills that were sometimes very steep, but climbing more than descending. It wasn't long before they were in a heavy forest, and the canopy above them twined thickly together, so it seemed always to be dusk. The snouts peered anxiously into the trees as they marched and Hem thought about the winged things that had attacked him and Zelika on the edges of the hills, and then tried not to think about it. The path twisted between the trees, churned by their feet to sucking mud, which was slippery and clung heavily to Hem's sandals. The farther they wound their way into the forest, the sicker Hem felt; his legs seemed to be made of stone, and there was a constant foul taste in his mouth. The air was thick and heavy, somehow hard to breathe.

The first day was uneventful. They slept where they stopped, on the track; despite its dampness, none of the snouts dared to venture to the drier ground beneath the trees. The Hulls lit fires by sorcery, slashing wood from the trees nearby to feed them, and the snouts huddled around the heat, staring out fearfully into the night. It was full of strange noises: branches groaning in rhythms that sounded like a kind of language, sinister rustlings, the howls and barks of animals hunting, the shrieks of night birds.

In the moments before sleep overtook him, Hem wished he could speak to Irc. He thought about how angry he had been when they had last spoken, how they had parted with hard words between them. The memory was so painful that he forgot altogether about his inner shield, and realized with a horrified start that, for the first time since he had entered Sjug'hakar Im, he had let it fail. Hastily he restored it, cursing himself. Despite his physical misery, Hem dropped asleep almost at once.

When he opened his eyes, he was staring straight up at a pattern of leaves and sky far above his head, but something was different about it. He sat up and found that he was in a forest, but a very different place from the nightmare woods of the Glandugir Hills. He knew at once, by an echo of music that sounded in his mind, that he was again in Nyanar's home. By some instinct, he knew that this was one of the forested hills that he had seen in the distance from the base of the great tree. The now familiar sense of deep content rose inside him, like sap rising in a tree toward the spring sky.

Again it was dawn, and birds called their morning challenges from every tree. Shafts of light sifted through the canopy high above him, illuminating a clump of toadstools here, green ferns there, and the smell of earth and rotting leaves rose up, rich and heavy. The trees were so old and high, and their canopies so thick, that the ground beneath them was only sparsely covered with vegetation, and he could see ahead for a long way, down a slope into a valley where a small brook gurgled under a lacing of greenery.

Hem could see the damp shadows the sunlight could not pierce, gray with a heavy dew, but he felt no cold; rather, a delicious warmth stole through his body, as if he were sitting in front of a gentle hearth. And the dreadful sense of ill was gone from his body, the tormenting nausea that had been growing with each step he took deeper into the Glandugir Hills. This forest was unhurt.

Unwronged, said Nyanar's voice.

Hem looked around, but could see nothing but the trees.

Where am I? he asked.

Where you have ever been, Nyanar answered. *You are elsewhen.*

With a shock that went through his whole body, Hem finally understood. *It is not where, but when.* He was in the Glandugir Hills, but as they had been, before the Nameless One had poisoned them, before they had been twisted awry by the sickness that afflicted this country.

How . . . ? But Hem couldn't finish the question. An inarticulate grief for the maiming of this beautiful place constricted his throat. He thought of the dread of the trees of Glandugir, the uncreatures that inhabited them, and found his sight blurred with sudden tears.

You know how, said the Elidhu. The details do not matter. The Song was stolen and much was marred.

Hem nodded sadly.

Time is not as you know it, you mortal creatures, said the Elidhu. A new gentleness was in his voice, as if he knew what Hem was feeling. *You think time springs forward, like a river, and you are ripples glinting on its surface, moving ever forward, never back. But to us it is a sea, and all times exist together. Nothing is truly gone . . . Do not be sad.*

Hem nodded, and felt his sorrow dissolve. It would come back, he knew, but now he was utterly content in the strange present he inhabited. But the Elidhu spoke again.

I brought you here, so that you might rest, he said. *But I cannot help you past this point. You are marching out of my ken, out of my*

home, into the dark center. Have a care, Songboy. Remember what is
already spoken on the winds of time. I will await your return.

Then, as suddenly as it had been there, the voice was gone.
Hem set his back to the bole of the nearest tree, and stared down
the slope before him. As always when he entered the realm of
the Elidhu, he accepted what was there without question. He
didn't think about what Nyanar had said. He didn't think anything at all; he just let the deep peace of the forest soak into him.
A huge azure butterfly danced raggedly in a beam of light a few
paces away, its iridescent colors flickering hypnotically in and
out of shadow. Hem gazed at it, fascinated, and was not conscious of the exact moment when he fell back into slumber.

He was woken by a confused hubbub of screams. Automatically
reaching for his sword he started up, bleared with sleep, looking
wildly around him. It was black night. At first the darkness was
so complete he might as well have been blindfolded: the fire
near him had gone out. He could still feel its heat: it was as if it
had been suddenly smothered. Then a Hull farther ahead flared
lividly, as if its whole body were made of lightning, and a bolt of
fire arced into the trees, throwing a confused wrack of light and
thrashing shadow. Almost at the same time two dogsoldiers spat
red flames farther away down the track.

Hem drew a long shuddering breath and kept his ground,
looking around and trying to assess what was happening. The
snouts nearby were panicking, screaming and running in circles,
striking out at each other. Then Hem felt something like a
whiplash across his mind. He reeled, stunned, and watched, his
eyes wide, as the snouts suddenly snapped into focus. Their eyes
went blank, and they turned outward as one to face the darkness. They seemed to be following orders that he could not hear.
Hem had enough presence of mind to copy their movements.

A group of snouts from another block was attacking

something that he couldn't see. A ghastly gobbling sound tore through the darkness, and then a childish scream, and Hem stood rooted to the ground, unable to move for fear. Then there was a crash of branches from another direction, closer to where Hem was standing, and the Blood Block turned to face it. A Hull running down the track toward them cast another bolt of lightning, and in its sharp illumination Hem, carried forward in the rush, had a brief glimpse of a huge, armor-plated creature like a giant scorpion, at least twice as big as a cow. It scuttled with a terrifying rapidity, its tail tipped by a white sting dripping with venom, trembling evilly over its head. Even as Hem stared, the tail struck out like a flail, quicker than the eye could follow, and stung Slitter. She fell back with a high wail, writhing and frothing at the mouth. In the space of three heart-beats the child was still, her sword dropping from her nerveless hand.

None of the other snouts took the slightest notice of Slitter's fate. They swarmed toward the monster, hacking at its eyes and tail with a furious savagery. They had no thought for their own safety. Hem was too close for comfort: his main instinct was to run away, but he feared, even in this chaos, that someone might notice. He made some stabs toward the creature, keeping as far away from its deadly tail and its merciless fangs and claws as possible.

Then someone slashed off the sting, and the creature arced backward in agony, spewing black blood. Some splashed on two snouts, instantly bringing their skin up in welts. The others rushed forward, stabbing its eyes, and it coiled and uncoiled, lashing out with its claws. They slashed off its legs so it could not run, and then, although the creature was still twitching and gobbling, left it where it was.

Hem felt a great band of pressure ease off his forehead. The will that had driven the snouts into such frenzy had let them go; they were no longer in its thrall. The snouts began to wipe their weapons on the grass, chattering excitedly to each other about the battle and complaining about the acrid stench of the blood. They ignored both the dying beast and their wounded or dead comrades. The first lot of snouts had dispatched the other monster already; its mutilated carcass lay twitching not far away. Hem counted six bodies scattered around the dying monsters. A Hull was relighting the fire with sorcery, and it blazed up into the branches above them.

The snouts cheered at the flame, their eyes flashing with triumph. Now they were just normally ensorcelled, Hem thought; the morralin was not the whole of the binding. The Hulls controlled them as well, when it came to battle. He looked at the wounded snouts, resisting the urge to go and help them; nothing would expose him more quickly than any display of compassion. Hulls were moving toward them already; no doubt they had their own methods of healing.

He sat down by the fire and wrapped his cloak around himself. Reaver came up, grinning.

"Goromants!" he shouted. "We bloody showed 'em. We gave it to 'em!"

Hem tried to look as excited as Reaver and punched his fist into the air. But the boy had already passed him by, to whoop at another snout.

Goromants. Hem had heard the name. He had hoped never to see the reality. It was much worse than any rumor.

He closed his eyes, letting the fire's warmth take away the chill of aftershock. He had never thought he would be glad to be around snouts; but maybe only that kind of frenzy could defeat creatures as fearsome as goromants. Even mutilated as they were, they were not dead. The horrible sounds of their dying ran on endlessly beneath the snouts' celebrations of victory, and colored what little sleep he had the rest of that night.

The goromants were still alive the next day, when the snouts marched on. Passing snouts kicked the twitching bodies, or spat on them. Hem averted his eyes.

It took three days to get through the Glandugir Hills. There were several more attacks, always at night, but they saw no more goromants: once, a swarm of the winged things that Hem and Zelika had killed, another time a pack of wild pigs with two heads. These were driven off with less difficulty than the goromants; when one or two were killed, the others retreated back into the trees. Several more snouts were injured. The walking wounded made their own way, more frightened of being left behind than of their own pain; those too badly hurt to march were quickly killed by Hulls.

In the very middle of the hills, in the darkest places, there were trees that cried out at night, strange mouthless calls that sent shivers down their backs and made even the Hulls anxious. Once a snout cut down a branch for firewood, and the tree shrieked and thrashed its limbs like a beast, and the snout was drenched in a downpour of blood. Hem saw another snout caught by a vine that seemed to lie harmlessly across the path; unwisely he had trodden on it, and the plant had lashed itself around his foot. The snout, screeching and writhing, clutching at branches and tufts of grass, was dragged out of sight with appalling swiftness: the snouts halted, aghast and fascinated, as the boy's cries turned into a high, bubbling scream and then abruptly stopped.

Hem witnessed everything with a growing sense of numbness. He no longer even felt afraid. He needed all his energy simply to stay alive. Now, with no prospect of any respite in Nyanar's enchanted home, and without Irc, he was truly alone. In the black depths of the Glandugir Hills hope sank deep within him, where he could barely touch it.

He struggled to stay alert, to keep looking for Zelika among the snouts, but his perceptions narrowed to his immediate surroundings. His hunger was constant and only abated by severe cramps in his belly; a lot of the time he didn't want to eat at all, and forced himself to chew his pitiful rations, reminding himself that he could not afford to become too weak. He eked out his supplies so they would last the journey, but even so there would not be enough to get him to Dagra. He would have to begin thieving again.

When they emerged from the forest, Hem stared incuriously, blinking in the sudden light, over a dun landscape that stretched out from the lower hills. The forest shrank into isolated stunted trees, and then into the low thorny shrubs that studded the sparse grasslands. The track meandered over arid plains toward a smudge on the horizon that might be a small town. Dagra, he knew, was far in the north.

Hem felt only a dull relief. At that moment, he never wanted to see another tree in his life.

XXII

DAGRA

IF it had not been for Irc, Hem might not have survived the next seven days. There had been times in the hills when he had thought that he could not go on, when he fiercely regretted that he had not escaped Sjug'hakar Im when he had had the chance. With the bleak clarity of despair, he examined his plans and justifications—his idea that he would be assisting Hared and the Light against the Nameless One, or that he had any chance of finding and rescuing Zelika—and realized that they were the purest folly. He had been insanely arrogant to think that he could enter Dén Raven and not only survive, but escape and return to his friends. His death, he thought, was only a matter of time.

And now it was too late to turn back.

The first night out of the Glandugir Hills he was trying to sleep, twisting and turning against the hard ground, when something inquiringly stroked his mind. He started, looking wildly around him, thinking that a Hull had discovered his presence; but then he realized that no Hull could feel like that. Only one creature in the whole world had that particular touch: Irc, the White Crow, *Lios Hlaf*, his friend.

Recklessly, for it was very perilous with Hulls nearby, Hem fashioned a mageshield and sent out a summoning to Irc. The crow answered immediately, and Hem felt he was very close, not more than a hundred spans away.

Hello, featherbrain, said Irc. *Are you sorry now?*

Irc! Hem felt as if his insides were melting with relief and gratitude and joy. *By the Light, what are you doing here?*

I thought someone ought to come and make sure you didn't do anything stupid, said Irc. *Someone clever. Like me.*

Hem was so overwhelmed he could not say anything, but in the intimacy of mindtouching his feelings were very clear.

I knew you'd be sorry, said Irc smugly. *Hared wants to kill you, but he said you'd probably be killed before he could get to you, which makes him very regretful.*

The thought of Hared's impotent fury stopped the whirl of Hem's emotions, and he almost snorted with laughter.

Oh, Irc, he said. *You shouldn't have followed me. But I am so glad you did, so glad.*

Hared thought I should. He says I am a very clever and brave bird. Hem could almost see Irc's feathers swelling with pride.

But—but how did you get through the forest? asked Hem, smiling at his friend's vanity.

I didn't. I flew over it. Not going there again. I knew I'd find you this end. And I have a message from Hared that I must tell you. Now the snouts have left, he's going to look at the camp, and he said he is going to meet us at Sjug'hakar Im in three times four days, plus two.

That meant fourteen days, by Irc's counting. It would cut it close, but he might just make it, if he escaped the snouts at Dagra. If he moved swiftly with magery, he could possibly avoid capture, traveling on his own. There was no doubt it would be perilous, but all of a sudden, Hem felt anything was possible. A friendly voice in this terrible place was unimaginable, but here it was.

Can you just follow the snouts, then? said Hem. *You'll be all right?*

Yes, said Irc. *I am a clever bird.*

You are. And brave and wonderful. Hem could feel something waking nearby, and added hurriedly, *I must go, Irc.*

I'll be watching you, featherbrain.

The mindtouch closed. But that night, Hem slept well, undisturbed by bad dreams.

It was seven days' hard march to Dagra. Although the hazards of the Glandugir Hills were now behind them, their journey was not without peril. Dén Raven was, Hem began to realize, a country in the grip of some kind of civil war. As they moved into more populated regions, they began to encounter groups of armed soldiers guarding bridges and crossroads. Most of the time they were waved through without challenge, but once there had been a brief skirmish, during which the Hulls had killed the guards. After that, without explanation, the snouts were marched back the way they had come, and took another road. Hem tried to eavesdrop on the Hulls to discover what was happening, but it was too difficult, and so he was forced, like all the other snouts, to speculate. He assumed that they had almost run into hostile territory—that of those loyal to Imank rather than the Nameless One.

To Hem's surprise, most of the land was not diseased like the Glandugir Hills. He had expected that his sickness would continue all the way to Dagra, but, to his overwhelming relief, his cramps eased to a slight nausea. His physical misery was mostly limited to exhaustion and hunger and cold. The weather stayed clear, but that meant nights of frost, when the snouts would fight viciously for the warmest places, closest to the fires, and they would wake with their blankets stiff with rime.

He was too tired to risk any magery, apart from when he had to renew his disguise. With practice he had become better at the spell, and he blessed his foresight in not changing his appearance radically, but it was still draining, time-consuming, and risky. To satisfy his hunger, he employed some older skills than magery, honed when he had been a famished orphan, and stole food from other snouts while they were sleeping. The thefts were noticed and caused several violent quarrels, but no one suspected the simpleton Slasher.

During their march across Dén Raven, Hem had more of a chance to search among the snouts for Zelika. It was fruitless: he could not find her anywhere. Perhaps, he thought, she had changed out of all recognition, which was always possible; or maybe she had been left behind, or killed in the Glandugir Hills. The latter possibilities frightened him so much that, despite the danger of doing so, he attempted again to feel for her, as he had in Sjug'hakar Im. This time it was much more difficult, but he sensed again the same spark, opaque with sorcery and fear, but still present. She was somewhere among the snouts, but he still couldn't work out where. He dared not try again.

He took as much note as he could of what he saw, storing it in his memory for later. For the most part the snouts journeyed past huge farms, tilled or harvested by long rows of dark-clad laborers. Sometimes Hem saw that they worked with shackles around their ankles, and were guarded by dogsoldiers; others were not chained, but were supervised by men with whips. They passed long, low huts where the laborers lived, which looked exactly like the huts in Sjug'hakar Im. Dén Raven really was, as Saliman had said, a giant prison.

One morning they walked through a small town, marching down the center of its main street. Hem cast furtive glances as they passed through. He had seen poverty in Edinur, but this was on another scale. The houses were mean and poor, little more than hovels holding each other up, patched with scavenged bits of wood or planks or stone. The street stank of middens, and was pitted with deep ruts filled with icy water. Ragged children peered at them from behind tumbledown fences or mossy water butts, their eyes wide with fear; Hem noticed with a pang that he saw none older than about nine years. Someone had placed a flowering geranium in a pot by a doorway, incongruously bright in the squalor around it, and Hem saw that a fence a little farther on had once been painted with a picture of a white horse running free over green grass. The painting had been scrubbed out, but its outline still remained, like a ghostly flag of rebellion. But little else there spoke of cheer or hope.

In the center of the town were two grand buildings, rising several levels behind high stone walls on large grounds. They were in shocking contrast to the miserable poverty of the rest of the town, and Hem stared at them in amazement: even the gateposts were gilded. For all their air of luxury, he thought the buildings ugly, and he didn't like the look of the carvings of weird beasts that crouched on top of the walls. Indeed, they were ensorcelled vigilances, squatting malignantly above the prosperity that breathed out of the houses.

He suddenly remembered what Saliman had told him about Dén Raven, long ago, in Turbansk: *The Eyes control all supplies; they live well enough, but the people fare poorly, and are given only enough to ensure they live. Those who win favor with the Hulls, of course, can do much better; some, the Grin, live in an obscene luxury and are themselves petty tyrants. They are useful to the Nameless One, and so he suffers them to flourish . . . nothing there is grown or made for pleasure or beauty, and even the leisures of the Grin are stamped with foulness and cruelty . . .*

Perhaps these houses belonged to Grins. It seemed unlikely they would be owned by Hulls; Hulls weren't interested in opulence.

After that, Hem was glad that the Hulls seemed to avoid towns and villages. He found them more depressing than the countryside, which was depressing enough.

In a few days the landscape changed. There were trees, for a start, and stands of forest, although to Hem's relief they did not go near them; even from a distance he could feel an illness within them, like the Glandugir Hills. He wondered what had happened to this land, that it could be patched by such wrongness. At night, where the forests were, the sky would glow a dull, eerie red.

Now they were marching steadily upward, and to the north Hem could see a ridge of mountains, jagged in the haze. They changed color under the light: sometimes they were red, sometimes purple. Sometimes, on days of heavy cloud, they vanished altogether. Hem remembered his dream of the Iron Tower: it must stand in the shadow of those very mountains. They were getting close.

The roads became busier, and were lined with dusty trees. The main routes were wide, and sometimes paved with stone, like Bard roads. On occasion the snouts were herded off the road, where they had to wait while ranks of dogsoldiers mounted on irzuk and other soldiers marched past them. If they encountered farmers or townspeople on the road, the snouts always took precedence; then they would march arrogantly, with a swagger, sneering at the unsoldierly folk who scrambled to get out of their way. They passed several temporary camps, dun rows of hide tents pitched over what had previously been farmland, and towns and villages were now very frequent, although the Hulls avoided most of them.

The snouts took a keen interest in the ranks they encountered, and gossiped freely about their supposed destinations. Some said knowledgeably that they went toward the Kulkilhirien in the west—the desert place by the Kulkil Pass where the Nameless One gathered his armies before sending them on campaign. Hem, who thought this was likely, supposed they would be readying to march on Annar or Car Amdridh. But others were marching in the opposite direction, and he wondered what that meant. He had gathered a number of pebbles that he stored in his right pocket, and each time he saw a rank, he transferred a single pebble to his left; in this way he was able to keep track of their numbers. There were many thousands.

Hem wondered often where Saliman and Soron were; perhaps they had even passed each other unknowingly on the road.

On the fifth day they encountered some more snouts, also going north to Dagra, and on the sixth two more ranks, as their routes converged. The groups would greet each other with yells and whoops, and after that they marched together, swelling their number to more than five thousand. Hem cursed this chance: his efforts to track down Zelika were getting nowhere, and he was running out of time. Even though the Sjug'hakar Im snouts kept together, it made his task much more difficult. He had taken to wandering about idly in the evening, under the pretext of gathering firewood or some other task, casting about for the sense of Zelika; but so far he had found nothing.

He couldn't mindtouch with Irc as often as he would have liked; they managed to speak only once after their initial conversation. But once or twice a day he glimpsed out of the corner of his eye a scruffy bird with mottled gray plumage: either standing like a lump on a fencepost, watching the snouts march past, or searching by the roadside for worms and beetles. He knew that Irc was showing himself to reassure Hem he was alive, and when he saw him, Hem's heart always lifted, no matter how despondent he felt. It was comforting to know he had an ally in this hostile land. Sometimes, if he caught his eye, Irc would bob his head in recognition. Mixed with Hem's pleasure at seeing Irc was a terrible fear that a Hull might notice him. On the other hand, Irc was cunning enough to stay out of sight most of the time; and if you didn't look too closely, in his dyed grayish plumage he looked rather like the large meenah, birds that were very common in Dén Raven.

It occurred to Hem also that perhaps the Hulls were preoccupied with something other than watching for unkempt birds that might be spies. Even the snouts detected a growing anxiety among their captains as they neared Dagra. It was whispered that the Spider had been seen arguing with the other Hulls, and two Hulls had requisitioned horses and now scouted ahead of the main party. When they returned, the Hulls would gather in a huddle, seemingly debating their route.

Hem sniffed the air uneasily: it was heavy with a vague menace, which grew stronger the closer they came to Dagra. It was more than the mountains now looming ahead of them, brooding and grim under a cloudy skyline; or that sometimes he could see through swathes of winding vapors the Iron Tower, a dark finger of warning against the blood-colored crags of the Osidh Dagra. The very ground seemed tense and watchful. He was filled with foreboding.

Despite the Hulls' precautions, the snouts walked into serious trouble a day out of Dagra. Fortunately for Hem, the Sjug'hakar Im snouts were marching at the back of the column, and escaped the worst. The first Hem knew of it was confused shouting farther ahead; the snouts around him craned their necks, straining to see what was happening, as the dogsoldiers marching alongside the Blood Block suddenly ran forward.

The snouts began to look panicky; then there was a call to order, which Hem felt like a whiplash inside his head, and their faces went blank. With the suddenness that Hem could never get used to, the snouts instantly calmed and gripped their weapons, awaiting orders from the Hulls. It seemed that they were not yet needed. Hem loosened his shortsword in its scabbard, praying that the Blood Block would not need to fight.

He was too tired, and he lacked the frenzied energy that sorcery gave the other snouts. He wished he knew what was going on in front, but it was impossible to see past the others.

He could tell by the noise that the fighting was drawing nearer; then a snout suddenly burst through the rows in front of Hem, tumbling over and over on the road, clearly dead, followed by a giant man who carried a spiked, bloodied club. His naked torso and shaved head were painted in zigzags of red and white; now smeared with blood, his beard was plaited in many strands twined with small bones, and his teeth were sharpened. He wore a horned helmet, iron gauntlets, and a skirt of iron links.

Hem almost turned and ran: but before he could move even a step, the other snouts attacked the giant, who was swinging his club with lethal effect. The snouts flung themselves at him, snarling, biting, kicking, and hacking, and the giant was dragged down by their weight, sinking to the ground. Once he was down, the snouts made short work of him.

Hem suddenly found that he was slashing wildly at the body with the rest of the snouts. Shocked, he stepped back, wiping away the blood that had spattered his face, spitting the taste of it from his mouth. He suddenly felt deeply soiled. For a moment, in the heat of battle, he had lost control: he had become one of *them*. Even in the Glandugir Hills, in the nastiest battles, he had fought only to survive, and had quietly stepped away from any extra savagery. How long before he was boasting about his collection of severed ears, like Reaver? The thought made him go cold with disgust.

He would have to escape the snouts soon, or he would end up as braintwisted as they were.

The snouts were released from sorcery and milled about in excitement, boasting about their hits and how many they had killed. Hem listened with more than his usual contempt. A score or so of snouts had been killed, and another score injured, including Reaver, who had caught the edge of a blow on his arm. It had ripped the muscle, but Hem saw that the wound was not disabling; after it had been pressed shut by a Hull, Reaver went around the snouts, showing his wound to anyone who would look. To hear him talk, thought Hem, you would think he had killed the giant on his own.

All the same, whatever he felt about it, Hem was glad the snouts had won; if they had lost, he would be dead. As a fighting force the snouts were fearsome. He thought he understood why the Nameless One was so interested in them.

The survivors were ordered to gather the corpses off the road and cast them into a ditch. Hem saw a pile of dry bones that he knew must have been a Hull, and he counted fifty of the giant men. There had been none like them at Turbansk—at least, not where he could see them.

He was helping three others drag one of the giants to a pit when he saw the Spider not far away, talking intently to another Hull. He decided that an attempt at eavesdropping was worth the risk, as there was a lot of noise and confusion to cover him, and cautiously he opened his listening.

To his amazement the Hulls used the Speech, but it was altered in ways he did not understand. Hem did not realize until that moment how deeply the Speech was part of him; to hear it in a Hull's mouth was monstrous, as if his own inner soul was somehow Hullish. He repressed a strong desire to retch.

". . . can't be true," the Spider was saying.

"Imank is here, I tell you," said the other. "Jagfra tells me that his presence hovers over Dagra. And these are part of his Iguk bloodguard: they are unmistakable. You know that."

The Spider paused, as if it were thinking.

"Why set them here?" it said at last. "Why challenge us?"

"Imank does not wish the Master to have anymore strength in his hand at present," said the other Hull. "Sixteen ranks of curs is not a small consideration; you saw how they defeated the Iguk. I think not all is well in Dagra."

Hem could feel the Spider's doubt. "We should have heard, if the Master were truly threatened," it said at last. "Surely Imank is not strong enough to return without being summoned?"

"Of course he was summoned," hissed the other Hull impatiently. "The Master seeks to rein him in. And Imank seizes his chance. The time is *now*."

The Spider suddenly looked up suspiciously, sniffing, and Hem at once stopped listening and turned his face away.

The conversation he had overheard had only whetted his curiosity. Now he thought he understood the sense of threat that filled the air as they neared Dagra: the Nameless One had called Imank, the Black Captain, back to his side, and if the Hull was right, Imank planned to overthrow him.

The snouts were marching straight into the eye of the storm.

That night, he spoke to Irc. The crow had some observations of his own.

They fight everywhere, he said. *I fly here and I fly there, and all I see is people fighting. Dogmen and others. Many like those you fought today. Others too: I have been listening to the Hull-talk. I think that the Light has a hand in this, as much as the other Dark Master.*

Do you? Hem couldn't keep the surprise out of his voice. Irc had changed much in his recent time on his own; he wouldn't have thought like this a few weeks ago.

Yes, yes. There are other things moving, but it is all very messy. I cannot tell what might happen. We should be well out of here.

Hem said nothing.

All these fights make it easier for us, I think. They will not be looking out for a missing boy; you will slip through the cracks. But it is getting worse. It is like the quake, you can feel that something is going to happen.

Hem knew that Irc was right, and his heart sank. *But I haven't found Zelika,* he said.

If you can't find her tomorrow, said Irc, *you will have to leave her behind.*

The next day Hem volunteered for any task going. Some snouts were sent up and down the lines all day, carrying notes from one Hull captain to another, and so were not corralled in their particular blocks. To his chagrin, Hem was considered too stupid to trust with messages. Slasher's simpleness had been a useful cover, but now he cursed his luck. But there were other, dirtier jobs that captains were happy to give him, which allowed him at least a little freedom of movement.

He had decided to risk feeling for Zelika as they marched; this way he might be able to identify at least which block she marched with. It was very difficult: he had to make a very strong shield, and Hulls walked close by, especially watchful now. And every day he was more tired. Doggedly and patiently he made as strong a shield as he was able, and after recovering from the fatigue this induced in him, began to feel delicately about him.

At first there was nothing: no trace at all of the Zelika-glow he had felt twice before. Could she have been killed in the past few days? But he had checked every corpse he could, to make sure it wasn't Zelika. With a clutch of panic, he ran over in his mind the pitiful bodies he had seen. Some had been so badly hurt it was very difficult to tell who they had been. Always some detail—a hand, the shape of a foot—had reassured him it wasn't his friend. Perhaps he had missed something: he hadn't been able to keep track of every death.

He tried again, and this time, with a wash of relief, caught a tiny flicker he recognized. It was, he thought with a stab of excitement, very close: much closer than he had sensed before. He peered cautiously through the identical heads that bobbed in front of him.

That morning there had been some confusion as they began their march, and the Sjug'hakar Im snouts weren't marching in their usual order. The Blood Block was behind the Tusks, snouts who scarred their forearms with a crude cross. The Tusks usually marched six blocks behind, and were one of the blocks that Hem had thought might contain Zelika. In front of the Tusks was the Knife Block, a group he had crossed off his list. Farther ahead were the snouts who had joined them on the road.

Hem contained his agitation, fearful of betraying himself. Then he tried again. This time he was able to focus his searching a little better, and the trace was stronger. He had finally found her. Zelika was one of the Tusks. He narrowed his searching still more, trying to locate exactly where she was, feeling among the other snouts. At last, with triumph, he managed it. She was three rows ahead, four from the left. So close.

Hem was trembling by now, and exhausted. He relaxed his magery, and looked dazedly about him, conscious of his surroundings for the first time in what seemed like hours. The hairs bristled on his neck: they were at last approaching the walls of Dagra.

They had stopped climbing and now marched along a broad road flagged with red stone that drove straight through a vast, rocky plateau. Hardly anything grew there but a few stunted trees and bushes, and the entire plateau was studded with encampments of soldiers. To his left was a wide lake of black water, fed by a sluggish river, and black reeds rattled in the cold winter winds.

The city walls loomed high in the dull sunlight, built of the hard, red stone of the mountains. Hem studied them uneasily as they drew closer: he could see only one gate, and that was well guarded. The walls themselves were impassable, dropping thirty spans sheer to the plains below. Even at this distance he could feel their power: the entire barrier was also a vigilance, each stone of it sensate and aware. As they drew closer, Hem saw Dagra clearly for the first time. He stared, his heart plummeting to his feet, and his courage shriveled.

The city was shrouded in fumes and ragged mists that twisted idly in the icy winds, obscuring its battlements. The vapors briefly tore open to reveal a snaggled roofline or a tower as sharp as a gimlet, before hiding them again in veils that distorted perception so they seemed even more ghastly— impossible pinnacles or bridges arcing over abysses of shadow. The stench of sorcery was thick and bitter, drying out Hem's mouth so that he could barely swallow.

He longed to turn away, to crawl into a hole and hide from the monstrous awareness that stood before him, but he couldn't tear his eyes from it. It drew his gaze as a snake did its prey, and he was helpless to resist. For the first time Hem fully realized the folly of his hopes: such might as he saw before him would suffer no defeat. The city saw everything, and knew everything, and brooked no rebellion. Not even a mouse could escape its thrall.

As he stared, the vapors swirled and revealed the spike of the Iron Tower thrusting arrogantly above the battlements of the citadel. He quailed at the sight of it, of this stronghold within a stronghold: it seemed to him like a cruel, massive blade whose very existence wounded the sky. The tower's lower levels were buttressed with massively ridged shoulders of iron that bled long trails of rust, and its innumerable wards and keeps and parapets and towers drew up above them, one inside the other, black rows of fanged rock.

Unwillingly, drawn by a fascinated loathing, Hem's gaze traveled up its jagged heights to the tower's bitter pinnacle, where a long white blade pierced the clouds. A stray sunbeam caught the steel and it flashed, stabbing Hem's eyes with a malignant brilliance. He blinked, breaking the bewitchment, and almost fell over. He was so stupefied he scarcely noticed the kick and curse his stumble earned him from the snout marching next to him.

Numbly he marched with the snouts toward the vast iron gate. As they reached it, it drew up with a dreadful groaning of metal, slowly opening like a huge maw. Some of the snouts began to cheer, but their voices fell raggedly on the heavy air and were quickly swallowed in silence. Hem shut his eyes as he passed under the keystone, feeling its shadow crush him like a blow. He was so dizzy he could barely see. With a dull, massive clang, the gate fell shut behind him.

XXIII

THE IRON TOWER

HEM stumbled along, trying to keep up with the snouts, his legs shaking. He looked dumbly from side to side, all thought of action quenched in horror. They marched along a broad avenue of somber grandeur. It was one of the major thoroughfares that radiated from the Iron Tower, and down its center and along each side ran rows of unadorned columns of polished stone or metal, so high their tops were lost in the noxious mists that choked the air of the citadel. The buildings on either side were tall and windowless, sheer faces of polished rock that stared blindly over them, with doors of bronze or copper or brass.

Before long they turned aside into much smaller and meaner streets, from which ran narrow, dark, evil-smelling alleyways and lanes. A metallic clamor rose to meet them and soon was so loud that Hem covered his ears, half-deafened. They were in the Street of the Weaponsmiths. Sulphurous blasts of fire seared his face as they passed huge forges, where hundreds of hammers clanged on hundreds of anvils, and huge bellows worked by teams of half-naked men blew the furnaces white-hot, sending spirals of sparks whirling up into the cavernous darkness. Tiny figures, shining with sweat in the heat, beat and tempered to bitter edges the weapons for the Dark's rapacious armories. Hem saw swords and shortswords, spears, halberds, pikes, and javelins, maces and warhammers and axes, hauberks and cuirasses, helms and greaves and vambraces, armors of chain mail and scale and plate, stacked in their hundreds against the walls.

This was the heart of the Nameless One's war machine. His slaves toiled in the mines far to the south, digging out bright ore from its secret places, and dragging it on heavy wagons to the metalsmiths of Dagra. Hem was momentarily staggered by the scale of the industry. He thought of the weapon forges he had seen in Turbansk: they too had been places of flame and iron, a labor bent on creating instruments of death. They had not filled him with horror. Why not? he thought now, staring appalled through the doors of Dagra's forges. Why not?

They left the foundries behind and wound through other districts: streets filled with leather makers and weavers and cobblers, bakeries and potteries, wagoneries and wheelwright shops, knife grinders and laundries, stables that housed oxen and horses and the metal-armored irzuk. For the Nameless One required all these things as well, and their preparation kept busy his thousands of slaves.

These streets were crowded with soldiers of all kinds, and men and women in rich clothes, flanked by slaves or carried in sedans, for whom everyone else had to stand aside. Hem also passed hawkers crying their wares and people haggling, hod carriers and soilmen, drunkards spilling out of mean, foul-smelling hostelries, barefoot slaves scurrying on errands, and ragged beggars. Many of these bore the marks of terrible injuries, and Hem guessed they had once been soldiers.

After an hour, Hem was totally lost: Dagra was as bewildering as Turbansk. But here no one stopped to gossip, no one fingered bright silks or lingered by the jasmine stalls of the flower sellers, or gathered to clap the antics of jugglers and street minstrels. He suddenly saw what Turbansk might become, now that Imank had taken it, and was swept by a terrible sadness.

The Hulls hurried the snouts along, keeping them under the leash of sorcery so they would not be scattered in the chaotic streets. Hem noticed that most people got quickly out of the way when they saw the snouts. He struggled to keep up; each step was a torment. The foul air was hard to breathe, and the sky was throbbing with strange currents and lights, as if a storm were about to burst over their heads. At last they reached a grim barracks, story upon story of windowless stone, where they were to be housed.

They were each given some hard biscuit and dried meat, and directed into low, dark dormitories lit by smoking oil lamps, the floors covered with filthy straw, on which were placed rows of bug-ridden pallets where they were to sleep. The snouts were released from the Hulls' control. Shaking their heads, too tired even to make their usual boasts and jokes or to inspect their new quarters, they sank down on their beds and stretched out their aching legs, grateful at last to stop and to have a place to lie down that was softer than the bare ground.

Hem sat for a long time with his head bowed, sunk in hopelessness. The other snouts ignored him, as they usually did. When he had recovered from the worst of his exhaustion, he pleasurelessly chewed the dried strips of meat, shoving the morralin-laced biscuit under his pallet.

Whatever the risk of escaping, he could not remain in Dagra. To stay here was certain death: in this place, it could only be a matter of time before he was exposed as a spy. He would rather die trying to escape than die a snout. The thought stiffened his resolve, and he began to run over his grim prospects, forcing aside his nausea.

Somehow, tonight, he had to find Zelika and escape Dagra. It was impossible. How could he identify which snout was Zelika, overpower her, and force her to come with him, without any of the other snouts or Hulls noticing what he was doing? And then, most impossible of all, how could he conceal both of them, and escape unseen over the impregnable city walls? He had not known a vigilance could be so powerful; he doubted that he could make a shield that would be strong enough to hide himself, let alone Zelika, from its awareness.

And where was Irc? Miserably, Hem thought that his friend could not have followed him here. The wards on the walls were so strong it was impossible to imagine how even a small and crafty bird could pass them unseen. And even if, by some unimaginable cunning, Irc had gotten over the walls, how could he trace him through the chaos of Dagra? He dared not send out a summoning. He was alone in the middle of this dark city; there was no one to help him. His head hurt, as if an iron band were slowly tightening around his forehead. And he was so tired.

Well, thought Hem, with an attempt at briskness: first things first.

He had found out that Zelika was a Tusk. The initial shock of entering Dagra had driven the thought of Zelika out of his head, and so he had lost track of her whereabouts; but fortunately they had been hurried into their barracks in the order in which they had marched, and the Tusks were in the same room as the Blood Block.

Warily he searched for any sense of Hulls. Even opening this narrow chink in his awareness made him flinch. The tension in Dagra was nigh on unbearable: the very air seemed to tremble. He suddenly remembered the Hulls' conversation the previous day, and Irc's prediction. Imank was here, in Dagra, seeking the overthrow of the Nameless One: and even the Nameless feared his most powerful captain. No wonder the Hulls had been making them run—they were afraid.

Perhaps this was why there were no Hulls close by. He

could be luckier than he thought: there just might be a chance. Slightly heartened, he brought his awareness back into the barracks. All the snouts were very tired and the morralin dose they had been given added to their exhaustion; and all of them were yawning, although it was still early. He glanced furtively up and down the long room: maybe two hundred snouts. It shouldn't be too difficult to track down Zelika. He curled up, his eyes shut, and waited for all the snouts to go to sleep.

Then, with even more care than in Sjug'hakar Im, checking constantly to ensure that he was not detected, Hem made a mageshield and began the slow labor of searching through the sleeping minds around him. He caught the glow of Zelika almost at once, surprisingly nearby. She was sleeping against the same wall as he was, fourteen places up. Why, then, had he not seen her? He had been too tired, he supposed, and the light here was so bad.

He snapped his mind shut and, after a short rest, began to make a glimveil. The Speech slipped in his head, the words fraying or vanishing entirely, and the charm failed; stubbornly, with agonizing slowness, he began again. This time it worked. Now he was hidden. He was far too tired to attempt to make a semblance to avoid anyone noticing the empty pallet where he had been. He would just have to risk it.

He crept up the line of sleeping bodies, counting carefully, and when he reached the fourteenth, brushed her mind lightly to check he was not mistaken. She was sleeping with her face in the crook of her arm, her roughly cropped hair a matted tangle of short curls. Hem's throat constricted; he had loved Zelika's long hair. It would grow back . . . His heart pounding, he bent down and gently turned her over, preparing himself for the tremendous effort of lifting and carrying her. But then he saw.

To stop himself crying out, he bit his lip so hard that it bled. It wasn't Zelika at all.

It was a boy. A nasty, half-healed scar ran down the side of his face, puckering the skin around it and distorting his features. Hem recalled he had seen this boy before on their march through Dén Raven, without taking much notice of him. Now he looked closely, Hem saw he had Zelika's stubborn chin, her long eyelashes, her delicate cheekbones.

All this time, he had been following Nisrah, Zelika's brother.

XXIV

IRC'S STORY

HEM didn't know how long he sat beside Nisrah in that dark room. The full knowledge of his folly burst over him: how he had been misled by his passionate hope, how he had suppressed his own doubts, how he had arrogantly refused to listen to Hared or even Irc. The Hulls could not have scried Zelika, because if they had, they would have known that he was also spying on the camp. They would have been looking for him. But instead, he had been accepted into Sjug'hakar Im without question: no one had entertained the least suspicion that he was not who he claimed to be. He had known that Nisrah was a snout, but it hadn't even occurred to him that the mindglow he felt might be Zelika's brother. He had explained away his own uncertainty, putting it down to his lack of skill, to the shroudings of sorcery. And yet, now, it was so obvious.

He had endured unspeakable suffering, struggling through the perils of the Glandugir Hills and Dén Raven and finally imprisoning himself in Dagra. He had endangered himself, Irc, and Hared. He might never see Maerad or Saliman again. And all for no reason.

If there had been any tears in Hem, he would have wept, but he was too numb for tears. He was consumed by a choking bitterness.

He was roused at last by a huge crack of thunder, so loud that he thought that the floor shook under his feet. Hem leaned forward and carefully bound Nisrah's hands behind his back with the leather thongs he had stolen in Sjug'hakar Im, and fashioned them into a lead. Then, grimacing, he picked him up. He didn't make any conscious decision to take Nisrah with him: it seemed to Hem that there was no choice. He couldn't simply abandon him, like the children in the Blind House, to a terrible fate.

The boy didn't stir. He was unexpectedly light, worn by his hard life, and his body felt unnaturally hot. Hem swung him over his shoulder and walked to the door, listening for a moment to be sure that no guard waited outside. The barracks seemed strangely empty. He softly unlatched the door and left the room.

He was in an empty corridor lit by flickering torches, with a wooden staircase at the far end. When Hem reached the stairs there came another long peal of thunder, and he clutched at the wall, feeling the building rocking beneath his feet. Perhaps there would be an earthquake; and a storm of the Dark itself was about to break over his head. In a sudden panicked rush he stumbled down the stairs, the noise of his footsteps blotted out by the thunder. When he reached the entrance hall, he saw to his amazement that it was also unguarded. Where were the Hulls? He didn't stop to speculate. He staggered to the door, and pulled frantically. It was locked.

Throwing caution to the winds, Hem blasted the lock off the door with magery and ran out into the street as if there were Hulls at his very heels. He zigzagged around several corners until he entered a laneway empty of people, and finally halted, leaning against an empty, crumbling doorway, sobbing for breath.

He put Nisrah down and wiped the sweat off his own face. The boy no longer seemed so light: Hem's back burned with strain and his legs were trembling. He couldn't carry him all the way out of Dagra, even if he knew where to go, and he had no

confidence that the boy would come with him willingly. He
wished uselessly for some medhyl, to give him some extra
strength. What was he doing? He might have escaped the barracks, but he was still inside the biggest prison he had ever
seen. And he was wholly lost.

He looked up into the sky. The sun was setting, and its low
rays shone redly under a ragged hem of cloud, so the thickening
air seemed to be stained with blood. The narrow alley where he
stood was thrown into deep shadow. Myriad forks of lightning
lit the swirling vapors that coursed around the Iron Tower like
feverish veins, and gusts of wind fitfully kicked up the rubbish
that littered the street. Hem's skin prickled with sorcerous energies but, for the first time since he had entered Dagra, he felt
small and insignificant: the sense of watchfulness had vanished,
as if the awarenesses that were woven through the fabric of the
city were intently focused elsewhere. The rolls of thunder were
now almost continuous, and the ground trembled beneath his
feet. What was happening here?

He glanced at Nisrah, who was slumped on the filthy
doorstep, still sunk in a drugged sleep. The ugly wound on his
face had broken open, and a little blood and pus trickled from
under his eye. Hem regarded him with no emotion at all: neither pity nor disgust nor fellow feeling. Nisrah was just a
burden that he must take with him. He had no thought of leaving him behind; perhaps it was simply that he had to salvage
something from the wreck of his hopes.

He looked away, swept suddenly by a terrible loneliness. On
a wild impulse, without any hope that he would be answered,
he sent out a summoning to Irc. To his amazement, it was
answered almost straight away.

Where have you been? Irc hissed into his mind. *I've been looking
and looking* . . .

Hem was thrown by Irc's prompt answer and stammered,

both delighted and suddenly fearful for Irc. *I-I couldn't call before*, he said. *Are you in Dagra?*

Yes, yes, Irc said impatiently. *Of course I am. But where are you?*

I don't know where I am, said Hem forlornly. *I'm lost.*

There was a pause, and Hem momentarily thought that he had lost contact. But then the crow's voice came back, slightly muffled. *Can you see the Big Tower?* he asked.

Yes.

Bear away from it, with the sun at your sword hand. Wherever you are, you will reach one of those big roads, and they all lead to the walls, and the walls lead to the gate. I'll meet you there, at the gate. Listen for my call.

But—Hem said, bewildered.

I'll meet you there. It's hard to keep the mindtouch, there is so much bad magic here. I couldn't find you. I thought you were dead . . .

As Irc spoke, a green lightning split the sky, bringing with it such a stench of sorcery that Hem reeled, his senses stunned. *A big storm comes. Hurry . . .* Irc's voice grew faint, and then vanished altogether.

Frightened, Hem tried to mindtouch Irc again, but the city was howling with sorceries that burned his mind, and he couldn't hear him. The wind was picking up; the storm was almost upon them. He hesitated, then drew his shortsword and shook Nisrah violently, trying to wake him. The boy grumbled, pushing him away, but at last opened his eyes.

"Get up," said Hem. Nisrah opened his mouth to object, but Hem jerked his bonds roughly, and the boy groggily got to his feet, staring at Hem with a bewilderment turning rapidly to anger.

"What are you—"

"Walk." Hem pressed the point of his blade against Nisrah's back. "Do anything dirty, I kill you."

To Hem's relief, Nisrah sullenly did as he was told. He didn't know if he could struggle with Nisrah and still maintain a glimveil over both of them. They began to march down the alley, away from the Iron Tower, into the darkening night.

It wasn't easy to keep his sense of direction. Quite often Hem completely lost sight of the Iron Tower, and sometimes he and Nisrah seemed to be wandering in circles, picking their way along alleys that were little more than black, filthy crevices between high towers, only to come to a dead end or, worse, to find they were closer to the Iron Tower than they had been before. The backstreets of Dagra were unsettlingly empty: they passed occasional figures who glanced up into the flickering sky as they hurried to shelter, but that was all.

Hem was past tiredness, past thought: he was a single intent, a determination to get to the gate, so he could meet Irc. He put out of his mind the question of what he would do once he was there; he had no idea.

Nisrah walked before him, not saying a word. Once he tried to escape, crying out to a man who was passing by and throwing his body to the ground and rolling to break Hem's grip. The thongs tore through Hem's fingers, burning them; he flung himself after Nisrah and covered his mouth, ignoring the pain as the boy bit him. To Hem's relief, the passerby simply fled, thinking perhaps they were haunts, as he could hear voices but could see nothing. Hem was so angry that he wrenched Nisrah to his feet with no thought of how his bonds might be hurting him, holding his sword to his throat so it cut the skin.

"I said, no dirty tricks," he growled in his ear.

After that, Nisrah marched passively in front of him. Hem began to hate the sight of his slumped, stumbling back: it was one with his own hopelessness and degradation.

As night fell over Dagra, a deep blackness relieved only by the increasing lightnings, Hem began to despair that he would find the gate at all. He was looking for the Street of the Weaponsmiths, through which the snouts had passed on their way to the barracks, but he seemed to be nowhere near it. Instead, they were wandering through an endless maze of many-floored brick buildings, smoke-blackened and foul with the smells of rotting food and human waste. The ground was now shaking continuously, like a shivering animal, and the weight of air was becoming unbearable. It seemed unbelievable that the threatening storm had not yet burst, so heavily did it hang above them.

At last they turned into a wider street, and then stumbled out into one of the broad thoroughfares that radiated from the Iron Tower. At one end the cruel spike of the Iron Tower cut a black wound into the mountains behind. Unlike the backstreets, this road boiled with people. Hem cowered, gripping Nisrah tightly. Everywhere were ranks of soldiers holding flaming torches that threw grotesque shadows: Hulls on horseback, dog-soldiers, infantry. They stood on guard, as if ready for battle, but none moved; and their eyes shone redly through the shadows.

Hem squinted, hoping to see the gate, but it was so dark he couldn't see the road's end. Gasping for breath in the dry air, he thought rapidly. The quickest way to the gate would be down this road: dare he risk creeping along in the shadow of the walls, under the very noses of the Nameless One's forces? And yet, if he went back into the tangle of alleyways behind him, he would at once get lost again, and might never find his way. He wavered, irresolute, for a long moment; then, taking firm hold of Nisrah, who stood dully beside him, plunged into the main street, hugging the shadows of the walls.

He went as fast as he could, steering Nisrah in front of him. It felt too slow: he was encumbered by his prisoner, and despite the cover of the glimveil he feared being sensed by a Hull, and kept as far as possible from those he saw. He worried that

Nisrah might try to escape again at any moment; among so many soldiers and Hulls it would be disastrous. He looked up at the sky, desperately hoping that the storm would break; if it rained it would cover them more effectively than any glimveil. But the rain did not fall: the very walls seemed tense as strung wires, humming with unreleased power, and still the storm built up, still the city shook with its coming.

At last, panting, he looked around to see where he was, and to his disbelief saw that the city gate was straight before him, not more than two hundred paces away. There were fewer soldiers there than farther up the road; his task would be easier now. By sheer blind luck, he had run into the road that led to the gate. For a moment he went limp with relief; then he took a deep breath, preparing to shepherd Nisrah to the gate, to find a place where they might both be hidden from Hulls and look out for Irc, who must have been waiting there for ages.

It was then that things began to go wrong. He noticed that Nisrah was no longer slumped in front of him, but before he could think what that might mean the boy turned, and Hem saw, with a sudden chill, that his eyes had gone blank. The snouts must have been woken by the Hulls, and Nisrah was not beyond their sorcerous thrall.

Hem was taken off guard as Nisrah snarled and kicked him in the shins, knocking him down. He was straining to burst his bonds, the muscles cording out on his shoulders with the effort, and he took no notice at all when Hem threatened him with his shortsword. Hem shouldered him forward roughly, but Nisrah stood his ground, still struggling to break the leather thongs. With a sudden snap they burst, and then, his wrists bleeding, Nisrah swung a fist at him. Cursing, Hem ducked the blows and tried to knock Nisrah over, so he couldn't get away: but the boy lashed out with his hands and feet like a maddened beast, and Hem was knocked against the wall and winded.

Screaming for help, Nisrah got up and started running. He
burst out of the glimveil a few paces in front of an astounded
Hull that snapped to attention, grabbed Nisrah by the arm, and
then glared straight at Hem, its red eyes burning through
Hem's concealment. For a moment Hem was trapped by the
Hull's malign gaze and stared stupidly back, like a rabbit at a
fox, utterly unable to think or move.

Before the Hull could move toward him, however, its attention switched away from him, and it turned sharply toward the
Iron Tower. Involuntarily Hem followed its gaze and saw that
the entire tower was sheathed, from its base to its bitter summit,
in a ghastly flame, first shimmering with the decaying green of
a corpselight and rapidly growing brighter, until the whole
tower blazed brightly as an infernal, frozen lightning. The soldiers yelled and stamped and clashed their weapons against
their shields, and at first Hem thought the ground shook with
their noise, until he realized it was shaking by itself.

The flame died as suddenly as it appeared, but the interruption was enough for Hem to free himself from the Hull. His
glimveil was now broken. Nisrah was standing by the Hull, its
bony fingers clamped around his upper arm: he took no notice
at all of the Iron Tower. He was screaming obscenities at Hem,
his face distorted with fury and anger, his face a mask of blood
where the scar had broken as they had struggled. Even in that
flash of time, Hem wondered if he could still rescue him; but the
Hull was turning again with deadly intent, and he panicked.

Hem heaved the breath back into his body and took to his
heels, dodging and weaving through ranks of soldiers, too fast
for those who reached out to clutch him. At first he ran in sheer
panic; but once he had escaped the burning chill of the Hull's
gaze he remade his glimveil with a word and began to work his
way determinedly toward the gate. His only thought now was
of Irc, that he might see him before he died. He had no expecta-

tion left that either of them would survive—even if he made it to the gate, even if he managed to meet Irc. What could they do then? He was long beyond hope now.

Out of nowhere, it seemed to Hem—though they must have burst from the side streets in an ambush—the road was suddenly swirling with the bloodguard, the giants of Imank's personal forces, and he found himself at the edge of a raging battlefield. Driven by sheer instinct, he twisted and ducked around struggling knots of fighters, trying not to trip over bodies that were writhing on the ground. Then, as if they obeyed an order that Hem couldn't hear, the Dagra soldiers began to run away from the giants, toward the Iron Tower, screaming and howling. There was a noise like the screech of stone in terrible anguish, so loud that Hem thought his ears would burst, louder even than the soldiers and the rising howl of the wind and the great crashes of thunder that might not be thunder at all, but the sound of towers falling. For now the ground was shaking so much and buildings were bulging strangely, their walls rippling as if they were curtains of silk: surely that was a turret falling out of the air and smashing into the road, arcing eerily like a slow fountain of stone, crushing the soldiers in front of him before they could even throw up their hands or cry out . . .

And then at last the storm burst over him in bolts of hail and freezing rain, and out of the sky came cold things of winged flame whose livid, undead faces made Hem utterly lose his mind with fear. He ran like a witless insect through a chaos of rain and stone and wind and blood, not knowing where he ran, not knowing anymore even who he was.

When Hem came to his senses, he found he was lying on a mess of rubble, in a silence that seemed as deafening as the noise that had preceded it. I must have tripped, he thought with wonder. He couldn't remember how. He opened his eyes, which had been jammed shut, and at first thought he must be blind: it was so dark that he could see nothing. Water fell on his face from the sky, and he was shivering with cold.

His body ached all over. Slowly he checked his arms and legs. Miraculously nothing seemed to be broken. He sat up and tried to see where he was. He was in some kind of pit. Maybe, he thought, that's why it's so dark.

On his hands and knees he crawled up the rubble, making little landslides of pebbles and rock that made no sound at all. He peered over the edge of the pit.

At first, all he saw were blobs of red flame swimming in darkness. He shook his head, blinking, and tried to look again. Where was he? He could recognize nothing around him. Gradually, as his eyes adjusted, he made out the jagged mass of the Dagra mountains against the lighter clouds, and then the spike of the Iron Tower; but he couldn't recognize anything else. The Iron Tower seemed to be on fire. Other points of flame moved about crazily, in patterns that made no sense: he blinked again and realized they were people carrying torches.

Still nothing made any sound.

I lost Nisrah, he thought emptily. He ran away. It was all for nothing . . .

And then: Why is it all so quiet? Why can't I hear the rain?

He struggled out of the pit and found himself on top of a mound of rubble. His hands were torn and bleeding, and it hurt to touch the stone: but when he began to retch, he realized the stones were scorching him with sorcery. He began to scramble awkwardly off the pile of rubble, down the side farthest from the Iron Tower. At once his head began to clear a little, freed of the fog of sorcery. He looked ahead: the ground before him stretched out level and wide, and moving columns of flame were streaming toward him. Soldiers, he thought. The armies camped on the plateau.

He realized that the pile of rubble must have been the Dagra walls. He was outside Dagra. He had escaped. But where was Irc?

His mouth felt as if it were made of dust. His pack was still on his back, so he fumbled for his water bag, and took a long gulp.

It made him feel slightly, very slightly, better, and he began to wonder what he should do. His ears were no longer stuffed with silence: they were ringing with a high, irritating noise, and underneath that, he could hear a faint patter of rain falling on stone. He was wet through with the rain. He shook his head again, trying to get rid of the ringing in his skull; he must have been deafened by the noise.

His first thought was to find Irc, if he was still alive. If he was still alive. How could anything have survived those creatures he had seen in the sky? Or had he imagined them in his terror? There was no sign of them now. If Irc was dead, Hem was on his own.

Screwing up what little energy he had, he sent out a feeble summoning.

Nothing.

If he didn't move, someone would trip over him and he would be captured and put to death. But where could he go?

Doggedly he began to crawl away from Dagra, out of the path of the marching soldiers. His only thought was of Irc. He must be dead. Irc was dead, and he was alone on a plain of nightmare, already a haunt, some spider thing that was no longer human at all. But still, he didn't want to die. He kept on crawling.

You're going the wrong way, pebblehead.

The voice lilted into his head as clearly as the bar of a song. He looked up in a daze, squinting through the darkness.

Not ten paces away, Irc stood on a spike of rock. Something dangled from his beak.

Hem froze in shock. Then he staggered to his feet and ran toward Irc, who launched himself off his perch and glided toward Hem. He caught him, gathering the big, clumsy bird in his arms, pressing his cheek against Irc's feathers, which were filthy and smelled of scorching. There were no words for what he felt.

Crooning, Irc pressed against him, rubbing his head against Hem's temple. But then the bird flapped his wings, demanding to be let go. Hem opened his arms, and Irc perched on his shoulder and spoke into his ear.

We must move, my friend. Or we will die.

Where? asked Hem despairingly.

Away from here. Then we will think what to do. And take this, I am tired of carrying it.

Irc dropped the thing he had been carrying into Hem's palm. It was a trinket that the crow must have picked up, a small brass object that was strung on a fine steel chain. Hem felt a sudden hysterical desire to laugh: even here, in the midst of utter devastation and ruin, Irc never forgot his thieving ways. He slipped the chain over his head, feeling the trinket strangely hot and heavy against his skin, and stroked Irc's neck.

Oh, my friend, I'm so glad to see you. I thought you were dead, he said.

It was a close thing, said Irc. *I will tell you later. But now we must go. The soldiers come.*

The rain was beginning to peter out, and as the clouds lifted, an uneasy moon let fall a meager light. Hem glanced back at what was left of the city: it looked as if someone had taken a bite out of the center. The Iron Tower was outlined by a dim glow; it stood intact, but everything in front of it seemed to have been flattened. He wondered vaguely what had happened there, but was simply too tired to care. Irc pushed him on, guiding him away from soldiers he might otherwise, in his weariness, have walked straight into. Somehow Hem renewed his glimveil, somehow he kept walking, although his legs no longer felt as if they belonged to him. If Irc had not continually nagged him, he might have slept where he stood.

Irc did not let him rest until a washed-out dawn began to lighten the gray landscape. Hem looked up and realized they had come a surprisingly long way. He had been heading down-hill for at least an hour, stumbling through slopes of scree that bruised his ankles and tripped him. They had left the plateau on which Dagra stood, and were now on lower ground, near the shores of the black lake that lapped gloomily on dark sands. Hem was too weary to scavenge through his backpack for food: he simply crawled under a bush and went to sleep. He was wet through and cold, and the ground was stony, but he was beyond thinking about creature comforts. Merely to stop walking was all he asked. Irc crept in beside him, and snuggled into his neck.

He was woken some hours later by savage pangs of hunger. Irc was nowhere nearby. Hem was so stiff and sore he could barely move, and his arms and legs were covered in grazes and bruises. He looked at his meager supplies—a strip of dried meat and a couple of moldy dates—and considered how to ration them. It was impossible: he would have to steal some food from somewhere. Then he ate the lot, staring glumly over the reeds that rustled in the thin winds by the shoreline, checked his glimveil, and went back to sleep.

Irc returned at nightfall. He had scouted all around their area, and it was deserted. The countryside was in turmoil: all the roads were blocked by soldiers, some allied to Imank, others to the Nameless One, and he had seen several skirmishes. He had eavesdropped on a couple of conversations between Hulls, and it seemed that no one knew what was happening.

But I know, said Irc, looking smug. *I know more than anyone else.*

Hem, feeling stronger after his long sleep, was amused. *You are just talking big,* he said.

Irc ruffled his feathers with irritation. *I am a crow, not a lying human being,* he said huffily. *I don't make things up. I was there. I saw things that others did not.*

But, but what?

I saw things. But I won't tell if you're not nice.

Hem smiled wanly. *I'll be nice,* he said. *I promise.*

Irc was silent long enough to judge that he had punished Hem for his impertinence, and then began to tell him what he had seen.

He had got past the wards and vigilances of Dagra's walls by the simple expedient of flying over them. This was not, he told Hem, as easy as it sounded: he had had to fly around the city and into the mountains, where the walls ran into the solid rock of the Osidh Dagra. Even so, to get over the wards he had to fly so high that it was hard to breathe, and ice crystals formed on his feathers. But at last, late in the afternoon, he had found his way in.

From above, he could see the heightening tension in the citadel: all the major thoroughfares were beginning to fill with armed soldiers; and artisans and slaves out in the streets hurried to shelter. The increasing winds began to buffet him, and besides the dangers of lightning, there were invisible presences gathering in the upper air that made his feathers stand on end. So he flew low over the roofs of Dagra and began to search for Hem.

Their months of intimate mindtouching meant that Irc could always find him, no matter where he was. It was, he explained to Hem, like the way he always knew where north was: Hem was a star in the guiding constellations in his brain. But this

time, muffled by the warring sorceries that twisted around the
city buildings, the star had gone out. He began to worry that
Hem had been killed, and flew from one end of Dagra to
another, becoming increasingly agitated.

Irc had been both repelled and fascinated by the Iron Tower.
It drew him with a dreadful magnetism. Each time he swept the
city roofline he ventured a little nearer, and, at last, driven by an
insatiable curiosity, he flew up its dire height, a gray mote of
dust against its massive blackness. The higher he flew, the more
uneasy he became; he could feel the prickle of massive protec-
tions, vigilances, and wards woven inside the very substance of
the tower; but in the gathering darkness and wind, he went
unnoticed.

In a watchtower near the top he glimpsed a lighted window,
and something moving inside; but at that moment, he felt
Hem's summoning—Hem had now left the barracks of the
snouts and was wandering lost through the streets of Dagra
with Nisrah at swordpoint. Irc glided away from the tower to
speak to him, fearing to trigger a vigilance, and arranged to
meet Hem at the gate, before the sorceries broke their mindtouch.

He had intended at that time to fly straight to the gate to
wait for him, but his curiosity got the better of him: he just
wanted a closer look at the Iron Tower. A quick reconnoiter
could do no harm . . . The power that he sensed in the walls of
the tower was enough to scorch his feathers, and he knew it
would have sensed him at once, if it had not been preoccupied:
but it was not looking outward. It was intently focused on
something inside.

Irc weighed the danger exactly as he would calculate the
risks of stealing a desirable spoon from a crowded kitchen. As
was usually the case, his inquisitiveness won over the threat of
being caught. Slowly and cautiously, he flew back to the lighted

window, perched on a parapet nearby and craned his neck forward, trying to see inside. In the shadows of the gathering storm, he did not see the small figure that fixed its eyes on him and began to stalk him.

The next thing Irc knew, he had been caught by a leather thong weighted at each end with stones, which whipped itself around his legs and made him fall off the parapet onto the inner walk. It happened so quickly he didn't even have time to caw in alarm. Rough hands picked him up, unwound the thong from his legs, and shoved him, protesting furiously, into a sack (which stank, he said indignantly, of dung).

Irc was very unclear about what had happened next. He had been carried somewhere, and he had heard voices talking and coarse laughter. He suspected that he had been caught for some guard's dinner. He lay very still inside the sack, thinking it might be best to pretend that he were dead. He wondered if his legs were broken and expected any moment that someone would wring his neck. Then he heard new footsteps, another voice giving what sounded like orders. He thought then that his captor was somewhere he shouldn't be, because he seemed to panic. When the other footsteps retreated, his assailant moved with great stealth, still holding onto the sack, and then started running. But he was seen: Irc heard the other voice speaking in anger, and suddenly Irc was flung through the air and landed with a bump on a stone floor. He heard raised voices and a scream and something that felt like a blast of sorcery. He heard footsteps retreating, as if they went down a staircase, and then everything went quiet.

Irc seemed to have been forgotten. He lay half-stunned by his fall, until he realized that the end of the sack was now open. Cautiously he began to struggle and poked his head out. He could see very little: he was in a room of polished black stone, lit by flickering iron braziers attached to the walls. Nearby, obscuring his view, he could see a large round table, also of black stone, on which were engraved strange patterns and runes that glowed with a faint greenish light. Then, to his joy, he saw a window—really an embrasure, an unglazed slit—not more than ten paces away. But before he could do anything about escaping, he heard rapid footsteps approaching the room, and the door was flung open.

A single, appalled glance made him withdraw at once into the fragile shelter of his sack, grateful that chance had thrown him into a pool of shadow.

Here Irc's powers of description began to falter; he did not know how to put what he had seen into the Speech. Hem could visualize, through their mindtouch, a shadowy image of what Irc remembered; but Irc found it so distressing that it was immediately twitched away. What Hem managed to glean from Irc's attempts to describe what he saw was pieced together from several conversations over the next few days.

Two presences had entered the room. The closest, with its back to Irc, was definitely a Hull, but it emanated a power that even Irc could tell was many times greater than any he had previously encountered. It was tall and heavily built, dressed in black plate armor that bore no device, and its helm also was plain and unadorned. Across its back was a scabbard that drew Irc's eye: like all else about the Hull, it was unadorned, a sheath of bright steel that threw off an evil gleam. From the scabbard jutted the pommel of a sword that Irc said hurt his eyes; it was inscribed with many intricate runes that seemed to writhe as he looked at them.

The other being was hidden behind the stone table. Irc could only hear its voice, and this terrified him more than anything he had encountered in his short life. It was worse, he said, than any marred beast he had seen in the Hills of Glandugir. This voice was melodious and beautiful, and it always spoke softly, but somehow the beauty made it more frightening, rather than less so. Irc said that what made it most terrifying was that it seemed to be in pain. A sense of immeasurable physical agony ran underneath everything it said and honed each word to a bitter point of impotent malice. It seemed to be utterly without pity, for itself or anything else: it radiated an implacability that Irc thought was like madness. Not the kind of madness that leaves a soul in fragments, but an irrationality tempered by a malignant, intelligent, immensely strong will.

The entirety of that will was focused on the Hull that stood before it, and the Hull was unshaken and unafraid.

The Hull could only be Imank, the Captain of the Black Army. And, as for the other, Irc guessed that he must be in the presence of the Nameless One, an experience that very few living creatures had endured and survived. Irc withdrew slightly, shivering into his sack, wishing he were anywhere else.

The Nameless One and Imank were arguing, and Irc found to his surprise that he could understand some of it, as they used the Speech. Despite himself, he became intrigued and, as he had not been noticed, his terror lessened slightly. He began to eavesdrop.

The conversation went on for a long time. Irc found it confusing—he couldn't understand most of it. But nevertheless, he worked out that Imank wanted the dominion of the Suderain, as reward for loyal captaincy over the centuries; but the Hull was far from begging. And it seemed that the Nameless One was very reluctant to grant such power. Underneath nearly everything that was said was an implied threat; Irc noticed that Imank used no title for the Nameless One, and simply called him by his usename, Sharma.

"If I do not have the suzerainty, Sharma," said Imank, "I cannot lead my forces into Annar. I cannot with a proper authority exert your full will on the rebels in Car Amdridh. And my forces demand a proper recognition of their loyalty to you."

"When the campaign is completed," said Sharma softly, "then you will gain your true reward."

Irc wondered what this "true reward" might be.

The argument continued for some time, becoming more and more heated. Irc could feel their hatred and mutual fear, and as their anger rose, so the winds and lightning around the tower increased, and the earth tremors that had been shaking Dagra for hours grew in intensity. Imank began to shout, threatening open rebellion if the Nameless One did not accede to his demands. Then there fell a dreadful silence.

"I see no loyal captain before me," said the Nameless One coldly. "I see a creature of greed and treachery."

Quicker than the eye could see, Imank swept out the sword and attacked Sharma. There began a titanic, nightmarish struggle. Irc cowered in his sack, unable to move with fear.

Then something golden arced through the air, hit the wall by the window and landed not far from Irc. It startled the crow out of his dazed terror and he stared at it with a sudden fierce desire. It was clearly a precious thing; a very precious thing. He hesitated for a moment and then hopped out of the sack. His neck thrust forward between his shoulders, he scuttled across the floor to the trinket, grabbed the chain in his beak, and leaped with all his strength for the embrasure. He shot out like an arrow, fleeing for his life, and he didn't look back, not even when the tower itself began to scream and a green fire exploded around him, scorching his feathers and tumbling him down toward the collapsing towers of the city of Dagra, where a terrible battle raged in the streets beneath.

Irc wouldn't talk about what had happened between his flight from the Iron Tower and his meeting with Hem, although

Hem asked him if he had seen the terrifying winged beings that had come out of the air at the gate. Part of Hem still wondered if he had dreamed these things. The only thing Irc would say was that he thought he would die. *But I did not,* he added, fluffing out his feathers. *Because I am a clever crow.*

When Irc had finished his tale, Hem drew out the chain from under his tunic and looked at the trinket thoughtfully. It was fashioned out of brass, a strange forked thing that didn't seem to have any obvious use. Did it belong to Sharma? But why would the Nameless One carry such a humble object around his neck? Perhaps it was a memento, something he kept to remind himself of his vanished humanity? It seemed most unlikely.

He looked at the trinket more closely, and realized it was inscribed all over with tiny runes that he couldn't read. A prickle of wariness made him hide it back underneath his clothes. It looked ordinary, but deeper senses told him that he could not treat it lightly. He would think about it later, when they had escaped.

XXV

RETURN

ALONE, Hem and Irc could move much more swiftly than a thousand snouts, but both of them were very weary. And Hem had to steal all his supplies. Mostly he raided any cultivated fields they passed on the way, but once he managed to break into a storehouse, from which he took some hard, round breads and smoked meats. He filled up his pack, and after that was not so hungry.

They traveled through Dén Raven with extreme caution, sleeping by day and journeying by night. The days were very short now, and this suited them; the skies kept clear, but the nights were hard with frost. Hem concealed himself with heavy shadowmazing and glimveils and avoided roads and any villages and towns. He was relieved that he no longer had to remake the disguising spell. It had been one of the most exhausting aspects of being a snout; but now he was himself again and could wear his own face.

Irc made scouting trips and guided Hem through the safest routes. He reported signs of turmoil and confusion all through Dén Raven: but in a couple of days, order seemed to be returning. In one town Irc had seen a mass hanging; in another, many prisoners paraded through the streets in shackles, watched by a sullen populace.

Somebody must have won, said Hem. *Do you think it was Imank?*

Irc didn't know. Hem puzzled over the question for days, frustrated that he could not go and find out for himself. Irc could understand the Speech, which was spoken by Hulls; but

Hem refused to permit him to go near any Hulls. He dared not take anymore untoward risks: they had already chanced too much, and had barely escaped with their lives.

One morning, Irc returned from one of his scouting forays carrying a parchment that had been nailed to the gate of a Grin's house in a village; he had seen a man reading it out loud, and many people standing nearby, listening.

It might be important, he said, as he dropped it into Hem's hands.

Hem examined the parchment closely, but he couldn't read it. At first it looked like Bardic script, and he thought he could make out a couple of words, but there was something odd about the letters. In the end, he shrugged, folded it carefully and put it in his pack.

He did not think about what might have happened to Zelika or to Nisrah. He didn't permit himself to think, either, about Saliman or Soron or Maerad. Aside from the necessities of his journey, he tried not to think at all; he simply trudged on numbly, letting Irc decide their course. He felt as if he had suffered some terrible wound, which would not begin to hurt as long as he did not look at it. He had to get back to Sjug'hakar Im in six days to meet Hared: that was all that mattered.

They reached the Glandugir Hills after five nights of hard travel, watching the moon dwindle. Despite his fear of the trees, Irc said he would accompany Hem through the forest, to make sure, he said, that he didn't get into any trouble. They decided to march straight through; in that way, they might avoid being attacked. It had taken the snouts three days to get through the hills, but they had not been able to move very fast on the narrow track, and had halted at night; perhaps Hem and Irc could do it in a day. Hem also thought of the Elidhu; they were back in Nyanar's place, and perhaps he might protect them from the horrors of the trees. He feared also that Hared would not wait for them if they were late. To miss their tryst would be too much ill fortune.

It was the dark of the moon, and the nights were long and cold. Hem preferred to go through the hills at night, although he wished for more light. He reckoned that although the snouts had always been attacked at night, it had always been when they stopped, and if he and Irc kept moving they might escape notice. He was now functioning on sheer will; he was long past his limits, and yet still he went on. And now the nausea was rising again, the grinding sense of ill that rose through his feet from the diseased land.

Even after a sleep, Hem was too tired to be afraid. He sat down, ate as good a meal as he could put together, checked his glimveils and started into the hills, Irc either clinging to his shoulder or swooping ahead a short distance down the path. It was so dark that, despite his fear that it would attract notice, Hem was forced to make a small magelight, so he would not lose his way and wander off the track into the pathless forest, or unwarily step on one of the trapvines that would drag him helplessly into the trees.

Afterward Hem could barely remember that journey: it seemed that he had entered a dark, endless tunnel. He didn't know how they made it through. As they had planned, they did not halt, and they were not attacked, although they heard many strange and fearsome noises through the darkness. But the day before Midwinter, more dead than alive, Hem stumbled out of the trees and stood at last on the scrubby slopes that led down to the abandoned camp of Sjug'hakar Im.

Now that he was here, Hem wondered how he was to find Hared. He would be charmhidden, just as Hem was, and he did not know where Hared would make his camp. He looked about him dully; a pale sun threw a gentle light over the Nazar Plains, and made dazzling jewels of the frost as it melted on the grass. For a moment, it almost looked like Nyanar's country . . . Irc lifted from his shoulder, swooped down the hillside, and disappeared. Hem resisted the overwhelming urge to stop and plodded stubbornly forward, down toward Sjug'hakar Im.

It had the forlorn look of all abandoned habitations: its gates swung back and forth in the wind, making a melancholy groan, and already grass was growing back on the training ground. Hem walked through the gate and looked around: there was nothing here. Soon this place would be reclaimed by the wild: creepers would climb the fences and pull them down, the huts would sag and rot. There would be no sign of all the suffering that had happened here.

Hem turned and left the camp. He walked along the road a little way, and then began to climb the slopes, toward the place where he had camped with Zelika, when they were watching Sjug'hakar Im. Somehow, despite his exhaustion, he could not stop walking; it was as if his legs had forgotten how to stop. He was almost at his destination when someone called his name.

It took him a moment to realize that it was not said aloud, that he heard it with his inner ear. Someone very close by was summoning him. Before he answered he looked around distractedly, searching for Hared.

Hem. Answer me.

He made the mindtouch, and realized with a shock who it was. The will that had been holding him together for days suddenly shattered completely; his knees buckled, and the ground rose dizzily to meet him.

I'm here, he whispered, as a black tide rose inside him. *Saliman, I'm here.*

✳   ✳   ✳

A cool hand was on his brow, and his breast was a golden flower opening in petal after petal of light. He floated on water that dazzled with slow ripples beneath a blue, flawless sky.

Hem's eyelids fluttered open. Saliman, shining silver with magery, was staring gravely down at him. *Sleep now*, he said into his mind.

Sleep. How long since he had really slept? He couldn't remember. Hem shut his eyes and slid gratefully into soft, healing darkness.

Hem was woken by the smell of cooking. He lay with his eyes shut, as his mouth flooded with water; it seemed years since he had eaten anything that tasted good, that was not chewed joylessly simply to keep him alive. He raised himself onto his elbow. He was inside a bower of living leaves, woven together and bent to the ground to make a shelter, and a few paces away Saliman sat cross-legged, tending a pan of stew over a fire.

Saliman looked up when Hem stirred, and their eyes met in a long glance of greeting. Saliman did not smile, and neither did Hem: their joy seemed too deep for that. A lump rose in Hem's throat, and he swallowed: he had thought he would never see Saliman again, and yet there he was, cooking dinner. His sheer ordinariness seemed wholly miraculous: his braids were tied in a rough knot on the top of his head, his clothes were travel-stained, and he looked very tired. Hem was filled with a somber, inexpressible delight: despite everything, they had both survived.

There was a flutter of wings and a small thump, and they turned to see Irc landing clumsily by the fire.

"Hello, Irc," said Saliman. "Did you smell the food?"

Irc gave an interrogative caw, and Saliman laughed.

"It smells delicious," said Hem, and came over to join Saliman. "It woke me up."

"Well, it's about time you stirred those legs. The sun came up hours ago."

"The sun?" Hem was taken aback; he had thought it was evening.

"You've slept an entire day and night," said Saliman. He gave Hem a sharp look, as if sizing him up. "How do you feel?"

"I've felt better," Hem said. His muscles still groaned with stiffness and he felt as if he had been beaten all over. "But, I admit, lately I've been feeling a lot worse." He looked at the pan, where some meat was simmering in a sauce of herbs. "Will that take long?"

"Not long," said Saliman, giving him a wide smile. "I thought we could risk a hot meal to celebrate your return. You're looking a bit scrawny."

"But mightn't somebody see a fire?" Hem asked, with a clutch of fear. He had become so used to hiding that even sitting in the open seemed reckless.

"It's unlikely, Hem. I've been here three days, looking around, and my judgment is that we're pretty safe today. The Black Army is nowhere to be seen in the Nazar Plains; the Dark, it seems, is preoccupied elsewhere. We can take advantage of a lull in the storm, and pretend we are camping in the Osidh Am. A little cold, I grant you, but it's pleasant enough. After all, it is Midwinter Day."

Hem drew his knees up to his chin and watched Saliman taste the stew and add some salt from his pack. Irc drew near, demanding a scratch, and Hem absently rubbed the crow's neck until he crouched crooning on the ground. Hem was very hungry; but he was in no hurry. He was content merely to sit with his friends, watching the fire and listening to the gentle simmer of the stewing meat. He realized now that he had forgotten the balm of these easy pleasures, how deeply they reached into his soul and nourished him.

After a while they broke their fast, eating straight out of the pan, with Irc bobbing up and down by their knees demanding scraps. Saliman's simple herbed dish seemed to Hem like a feast, restoring much more than his body. When he had finished his meal, Hem sighed contentedly; he was warm and full, and felt much more substantial. Irc flew off on a private errand, and Hem and Saliman sat in silence for some time and stared at the fire's pale daylit flickering.

"I'm glad to see you back, Hem," said Saliman at last. "I was very worried when Hared told me what you'd done."

"Irc told me that he wanted to strangle me," said Hem.

Saliman grinned. "That's more or less what he said to me. But I was angry too, Hem. It was a foolhardy thing to do, and risked not only your own life, but our larger struggle as well. But amazingly, aside from exhaustion and a lot of bruises and scrapes, there's not much wrong with you. You were very lucky. From what Irc tells me, you ought to be dead."

Hem didn't answer at first, and when he did, his voice was hoarse. "I know it was mad, but I couldn't leave Zelika behind," he said. "And I didn't find her. I couldn't even rescue her brother. It was all for nothing, in the end."

A troubled expression crossed Saliman's face, and he looked away. Hem almost asked him whether he had news of Zelika, but something stopped his question.

"Whether it was all for nothing remains to be seen," Saliman said. "Irc has told me much of what you've done, and I'm eager to hear more: it seems to me that you have done as much, and maybe more, than any Bard has in our struggle against the Dark. It seems that Hared's guess about the child armies was correct, and that is valuable information. And not one of us has been into Dagra itself, and come out alive."

Hem shuddered, remembering the terrible city. "I never want to go there again," he said. "Never."

"I hope you never have cause to," said Saliman gravely. "Now, Hem, if you are able, I'd like to hear your story. Tell me everything."

Haltingly, Hem began to tell Saliman everything that had happened to him since he and Zelika had left The Pit. It felt like four years, rather than four weeks, he thought in wonder; Nal-Ak-Burat seemed far away, and his time in Turbansk another life altogether. His voice strengthened as he continued, and Saliman sat with his face downcast, nodding when Hem paused, to indicate that he was listening, and occasionally asking a question.

Hem emptied the stones out of his pockets, adding up how many soldiers he had seen on his journey through Dén Raven, and told Saliman of his speculations about where he thought they had been going, and he pulled out the parchment that Irc had stolen from the village on their way back.

"The thing is, Irc and me couldn't work out who *won*," he said. "Imank or Sharma? We thought this might give us a clue; it's some kind of announcement, but I can't read it."

Saliman took the notice with an inscrutable expression, glancing at Hem. The boy sat cross-legged next to him, very thin and pale after his ordeal; great shadows were scored under his eyes, and his face was marked by a sorrow that now, Saliman thought, would never quite vanish. His eyes were bright and intent, and he spoke seriously—a Bard discussing weighty matters with another Bard. But in his rags, with his bruised knees poking through tears in his trousers, he looked very young and vulnerable.

"It's written in the tongue of Dén Raven," said Saliman, studying the parchment. "They use the Nelsor script, but they have some extra letters—ah, yes. Well, Hem, I think you are right to think that the Nameless One was not killed. It says here that the rebellion against the high authority of Dén Raven has been crushed, and that all rebels will be hunted down and punished. It lists the punishments; I won't translate them."

"So you think that Imank was destroyed?"

"One or the other must have been," said Saliman. "Neither could suffer the other to live. Even so, Imank must have been very sure, to challenge Sharma outright; I expect that sword was Kinharek, a famous sword with an evil reputation, which Imank is known to possess. Imank must have invested it with a new sorcery, to even think that it could destroy Sharma. But it seems from what you say that the Nameless One called up the Shika; and not even Imank's sorcery would be able to withstand them."

"The Shika?" said Hem.

"Those winged creatures which terrified you so, Hem: I'm sure they were Shika. The Nameless One must have been desperate indeed. You did not imagine them, and you were right to be afraid. The Shika are forces from the Abyss: perhaps the most deadly of the uncreatures bound there. I doubt that even Sharma can control them completely."

Hem shuddered as he remembered the unreasoning terror that had consumed him at the sight of them. "I've been afraid many times that I might die," he said at last. "But this was worse than that."

"They feed on souls," said Saliman softly. "Not even death is an escape from the Shika."

Hem stared bleakly at the ground, and then recollected himself. "But Imank must have thought that the Nameless One could be killed," he said, looking up inquiringly at Saliman.

"The Nameless One cannot be killed."

"But Hulls can be."

"Yes, you can kill Hulls: but only with magery or sorcery. Neither age nor sickness nor ordinary hurts will end their lives. But the Nameless One, Hem, is not a Hull. Some other great spell binds him to this world. And it seems to me that spell has something to do with the Elementals. It is not Bardic magery."

"Do you think it's to do with the Treesong? And that's why Maerad has to find it?"

"It seems very likely. I am not sure how. But the Elidhu Nyanar seems to think it is a question that concerns you as closely as it does Maerad. He said the song was chained, which makes me think that the Nameless has used it for his own ends."

Hem thought of Nyanar, of the strange, wild music that had entered and changed him, of the help he had given him. He doubted he could have survived the snouts without it. *At last, out of the foretimes, you come*, Nyanar had said. *To unchain the song . . .*

Oddly, the thought reminded him of the trinket Irc had brought back from the Iron Tower.

"Did Irc tell you he stole something in Dagra?"

Saliman's eyes sparkled. "He did," he said. "He's quite anxious about it. Now that you're both safe, he wants it back. But I am myself anxious to see it, for quite different reasons."

"I don't know what to think about it," said Hem. "It's not even precious; it's just made out of brass." He pulled the chain over his head and handed it to Saliman. "It must have belonged to Imank or Sharma."

Saliman took the chain and weighed it in his hand.

"It's a little tuning fork," he said, examining it with intense interest. "The kind you might use for a harp. And it has runes engraved on it." He was silent for a long time as he looked carefully at each of the markings. "Hem, do you recognize these runes at all?"

"No, I've never seen anything like them."

"You have, you know." He gave the fork a last inspection, and handed it back to Hem. "These are very like the runes on Maerad's lyre."

Hem's mouth dropped open in astonishment. "Are you sure?"

"I'm quite sure. They are very distinctive. I wonder . . ." Saliman gazed into an abstract distance, lost in thought.

"I've wondered, over the past few months, if the Treesong might not have something to do with those runes? And why not? Maerad's lyre is Dhyllic ware, after all, and was made a very long time ago, when the Treesong perhaps was not forgotten as it is now."

"But Maerad's gone all the way north to find it," said Hem blankly.

"Aye, that she has . . . but there is a riddle here, Hem. Nobody knows what these runes are—they could be anything. But it seems more than a coincidence that the same runes would be on this thing, stolen from the Iron Tower, and on the lyre that belongs to the Chosen. Perhaps they might belong together."

Hem thought distractedly. It made sense, but it also made things very confusing. If they knew what the Treesong was, they might be able to begin to work it out, but the whole thing seemed like a baffling puzzle.

"Remember what the Elidhu said to you?" said Saliman thoughtfully. "Two are foretold, brother and sister, not one: *One for the singing and one for the music.* And now you have found a tuning fork. Well, I don't understand: but I have always suspected there was a part you had to play in this, as important as Maerad's. In any case, whatever it means, it seems very clear that we have to find Maerad and her lyre. And the sooner, the better."

Hem's heart leaped at the thought of Maerad; but at the same time he realized, with a wrenching feeling of desolation, that searching for Maerad would mean finally abandoning any hope of finding Zelika. With that thought, he was overwhelmed by a sense of crushing failure.

"But I'll have to leave Zelika," he said, in a low voice. "And I'll never know what happened to her."

Saliman looked up sharply. He paused for a time, and then came over to Hem and put his arm around his shoulder.

"Hem," he said, very gently. "Zelika is dead."

Hem went white, and bit his lip very hard. "No," he said. "How do you know? She might have escaped. I never found her in the camp—"

"She's dead, Hem. I found her body yesterday, when I was searching through the trees around the camp. It was definitely Zelika. I don't think she even made it into Sjug'hakar Im."

Hem was silent. He stared ahead, his jaw set.

"You know what she was like," Saliman continued softly. "She was afraid of nothing. She must have tried to escape when they captured her, and was killed then. She was in a grave covered with branches, on the other side of Sjug'hakar Im, and with her were the bodies of two other children. They had taken her sword, but she still wore her armor. I gave her a proper burial, not far from here."

Hem's jaw began to wobble, and he bent his head to his chest. "Do you—do you think that she suffered?" he whispered.

"No." Hem looked straight into Saliman's eyes to be sure that he was telling the truth. "No, Hem, she didn't suffer. I'm sure she died quickly."

"So I did all that for nothing." Hem swore savagely and smashed his knuckled fist into the ground. "For nothing. For nothing. For *nothing*." Each time he spoke he hit the ground again, his knuckles bleeding, but he did not feel any pain.

"No, not for nothing, Hem, my dear Hem." Saliman took Hem's bleeding hand between his, and then embraced him tightly. "But you could not save Zelika, nor any of those children. You were so brave, even to try."

A pain beyond anything he had ever felt seemed to be

burning Hem from the inside. He couldn't believe that Zelika was dead, although he knew it was true. He had known, underneath, that she must be dead ever since he had found Nisrah in Dagra, but he hadn't been able to face it. And everything he had risked, all that he had suffered, had changed nothing: not for Zelika, not for Nisrah, not for the half-mad children in the Blind House, not for any of the snouts enslaved in Sjug'hakar Im. Their lives were all destroyed forever, and nothing could make it any better. He didn't want to live in a world where things like that happened.

Hem began to cry helplessly against Saliman's chest, and Saliman just held his shuddering body, stroking his wet face, and said nothing.

A long time later, Hem stood up and walked blindly away from the fire. Saliman watched him go without trying to stop him. For a while Hem didn't know where he was walking. He felt completely empty, as if he would never feel anything ever again.

He wandered first to the place where he had buried his things, before he had entered Sjug'hakar Im. He undid the ward, and dug them out. Very little of the food was worth salvaging. With a shudder he threw away the sword he had used as a snout, and strapped the Turbansk scabbard around his waist. He picked up his spare clothes and his leather armor; he would take off the Sjug'hakar Im clothes later and throw them away. He wanted to wear nothing that connected him to the snouts.

He took up the cloth bag that contained his silver medallion, the lily token of Pellinor that was his only link to his heritage, to his lost family. He tipped it out of the bag and fingered it; it was his oldest possession, and was precious to him. Then he put it back in the bag and hung it around his neck, with the brass tuning fork. Lastly he picked up his Turbansk brooch. He sat back on his heels, studying it closely.

It was unstained by its burial, and its gold rays sparkled in the sun. Slowly and deliberately, he pinned it to his cloak. Now he was a Bard again.

Saliman had told him where he had placed Zelika, and after a while Hem started to make his way toward her grave. She was buried at the foot of an almond tree, on a low hill that looked over the Nazar Plains, and Saliman had put a large boulder to mark the place. Hem sat down by the grave and thought about the wild girl he had known and loved for so brief a time. She was too vivid, too alive, to be there under the soil. He thought, too, of Nisrah, whom he had last seen clutched by the bony hand of a Hull in the midst of ruin, screaming at him with his face distorted by hatred.

In many ways, Zelika's death had been merciful. But Hem would never be reconciled to the unjustness of it.

The sun was beginning to go down when Irc came looking for him. He landed on Hem's shoulder, and wiped his beak on his hair, but he didn't make any of his usual clever remarks. Hem scratched Irc's neck, grateful for the crow's silent sympathy. Then he sighed heavily and stood up, taking one last look at the grave.

"Good-bye, Zelika," he said out loud. "I was going to marry you, you know, when we grew up. It won't happen now. Maybe it wouldn't have happened anyway. But I want you to know that." He stood silent for a time with his head bowed, and then whispered, "May the Light keep you."

He turned and walked steadily toward Saliman's camp, without looking back.

Saliman had damped the fire down during the day, and when Hem returned they both busied themselves with giving it fuel and preparing the evening meal. Neither of them spoke much at first, but after dinner they began to discuss their plans. They were to leave the following morning, to meet Hared and Soron, who were awaiting them at The Pit. Saliman and Soron had returned from their mission in Dén Raven a few days earlier, and Saliman had insisted on coming to Sjug'hakar instead of Hared.

"If you did return," he said, with a twisted smile, "I thought that perhaps it would be better that I met you, rather than Hared. He is still furious that you disobeyed him, and I thought that if you had survived, you would be better met with love than anger."

Hem looked up gratefully, remembering belatedly that Saliman had been on a mission of his own. "What were you doing in Dén Raven?" he asked. "We might have passed each other."

Saliman's face suddenly lit up with mischief. "We might, indeed. We could have waved." Then he added, more soberly, "You saw some of the results of what Soron and I were doing with your own eyes. We met some contacts, and we sent some messages. One of our aims was to force Imank to declare open rebellion against the Nameless One."

When Hem thought about it, it was obvious; he remembered Irc speculating that the Light was involved in the turmoils that racked Dén Raven. "But mightn't that have happened anyway?"

"I think so, certainly. But only when Imank's position was secured. We thought it better if it happened now, before Imank's campaign against the Suderain was completed, and while the Nameless One was pondering how to march on Annar. We have bought ourselves a little time: Sharma has suffered his worst blow so far, and it was from his own. But there was another task . . ."

Saliman trailed into silence, staring into the fire, and Hem looked up inquiringly.

"It is strange," said Saliman at last. "Even to speak of this pains me. You remember, Hem, that I suspected that in

Turbansk there was a spy? After that last terrible night, when it seemed that the Black Fleet was prepared for us, I was quite sure there was. You can be sure that we were very careful—no one but Har-Ytan, myself, and Juriken knew of the plan to call the earthquake, and I believe that desperate tactic worked as we wished, but it is impossible to organize a large assault without many people knowing about it. And I had no doubt that word was passed on; and so many died, who might otherwise not."

Saliman's voice hardened as he spoke, and Hem nodded slowly, remembering his suspicions about Alimbar, the consul of Turbansk.

"So, Soron and I desired to find out the truth of that. And, Hem, although I should not say so, I wished for revenge. Alimbar disappeared from Turbansk the night before the last assault; we could not find him anywhere. It made me almost certain that our suspicions were correct. And I had reason to believe that he was heading for Dén Raven, there to gain his reward. I also thought I knew what name he might be using. You saw the houses of the Grin there; you may understand how the prospect of unlimited wealth might tempt him, especially if all he could foresee was the utter defeat of Turbansk, though the Light knows he was wealthy enough. I do not understand how he could want more." Saliman shook his head. "A man cannot eat more than three meals a day, or live in more than one house at a time. If you have what you need, and more than you need, what is the use of adding to it?"

"It's not about use," said Hem. "It's about something else." Saliman, he thought, was like most Bards; he could not comprehend the empty desire for riches. Even Hulls did not understand it, scorning material wealth for the pure desire for power and domination.

"Did you find him?" asked Hem, when Saliman again fell silent.

"Aye," said Saliman. He grimaced with distaste. "Aye, we did. And when pressed, he revealed a few useful facts, which are good to know, about how much the Dark knows of our doings, and we have the names of those who have been betraying our havens to the Dark."

Hem wondered what Saliman and Soron had done to make Alimbar talk. Perhaps, he thought with a shudder, they had scried him. "Did you kill him?" he asked, in a small voice. He wasn't sure if he wanted to know the answer.

Saliman paused before answering. "I did not. I heeded the Balance. . . . These things have their own justice, which it is not for us to judge, and mercy is always the higher wisdom. But he threw his lot in with Imank, and I think that it will go hard for him, now that Sharma is crushing that rebellion, and he dare not tell anyone what he has revealed to us, since that would make him seem doubly treacherous. He now writhes in a vice of his own making. And, the larger mercies aside, I feel no pity for him."

Hem felt relieved. Somehow the thought of Saliman murdering a man in cold blood distressed him, however just that killing might be.

"I think you were right not to kill him," he said soberly. "There is too much death, everywhere."

"Aye, Hem," said Saliman gently. "Far too much. And what is the use of fighting the Dark, if we forget the Balance and sink to its level? What then are we defending?"

Hem smiled, but there was no joy behind it. He met Saliman's eye, but didn't answer. He was thinking of the moment when he had become like a snout, overcome by the frenzy of slaughter, how soiled the memory made him feel. They sat unspeaking for some time, listening to the sounds of the night. In the distance, Hem could hear the strange cries of creatures hunting in the Glandugir Hills, and he shivered and drew nearer to the fire. Its small, comforting light flickered bravely against the great darkness that surrounded them.

That night, Hem dreamed he was walking through a green meadow full of wildflowers, with grass almost as high as his knees. He reached a high hedge, and unlatched a gate and passed into an orchard of apple trees. It was early spring, and all of them held a heavy burden of pink-and-white blossoms. Blossom littered the ground like snow, and among the white-starred grasses nodded daffodils and bluebells and crocuses of many colors.

He wandered through the orchard into a garden just now greening from its winter slumber, and continued over a path of raked white gravel toward a beautiful house. Hem knew it was his home, although he had never seen such a place before. It was a long, double-storied building of yellow stone, with wide windows that shone in the sunshine.

Hem turned, and began to wander among the apple trees. The blossom made soft drifts on the ground, and its scent rose into the crisp air as he crushed the petals under his bare feet. At the far end of the orchard was a wooden shed, and he made his way slowly toward it, ducking the low branches that swept their damp burdens of blossom into his face. He unlatched the door and entered, breathing in with deep pleasure: inside it smelled sweet and earthy. Stacked along the walls on wooden racks were rows of apples, stored from last season. Taking his time to choose the best, Hem picked one up, stroking its silky, golden skin. A single dried leaf clung to its stem. He wandered back out into the orchard, biting into its white, juicy flesh.

And then he heard someone calling out his name. He looked up and saw Maerad coming down the gravel path toward him. He waved and started running, his face radiant with joy.

She was calling him home.

XXVI

THE SONG

BEFORE they left Sjug'hakar Im the following morning, Hem looked somberly around the camp. The unsettlingly clear weather of the past few days still held, and a pale winter light fell on the lion-colored grasslands of Nazar, lending them a delicate hue that reminded him, with a sudden poignance, of the unstained landscape he had seen when Nyanar had taken him to an earlier time. He turned around and contemplated the dark mass of the Glandugir Hills. The sense of illness beat out of them, like heat from a fevered body; he could feel it on his face. And yet in their depths he had watched the fragile dance of a butterfly in a sunbeam, a long time ago.

He didn't visit Zelika's grave again. He had already said his farewells; her death now lived inside him, a weight he would carry until the end of his days. He hoped that she would not be lonely here, buried in this sad land, which, like Zelika, had once been so beautiful. He thought of what Nyanar had told him about time: that all times coexisted. *Nothing is truly gone* . . . It isn't so for me, thought Hem. Nor for any human being. We can only go forward, unless we are guests in some enchantment that is not ours. We are condemned to an endless present, and we can never go back—the source of all our joy, and all our sorrow.

He sighed heavily, and hefted his pack onto his shoulders. Saliman, who had been clearing any traces of their camp, burying the ashes of their fire, and unpicking the glimveils, came up behind him.

"Ready, Hem?" he said.

Hem turned and met his eyes. Saliman's face was full of a discreet compassion; he guessed what Hem was feeling, but clearly didn't wish to intrude. Hem nodded slowly, and summoned Irc. Then they turned northward and began the trek back to The Pit.

It was back to the old rhythm of concealment and caution, shadowmazing and glimveils. Hem realized that these mageries seemed much simpler and less tiring than they had before; they even seemed a relief after the past few weeks, when he had been maintaining a difficult disguising spell as well as everything else.

He realized, too, that he didn't feel as nauseous as he had. Perhaps his body had adjusted; or maybe it was just that it had been so bad in the Glandugir Hills that the sickness he felt now was comparatively easy to bear. Or maybe, he thought idly, Nyanar had given him some kind of strength against it. He wondered if he would encounter the Elidhu again. When they had last spoken, Nyanar had said he would see him when he returned from Dén Raven, but there had been no sign of him.

Hem and Saliman made their way as quickly as caution would allow, eating their midday meal without stopping to rest. Saliman wanted, if possible, to get back to The Pit within two days. They stayed away from the forest edges, but kept the road in sight. It looked as if the clear weather was going to break; darkening clouds were gathering overhead, and a sharp, thin wind nipped Hem's hands and face. It would be at least one miserable night out in the open, under the rain.

Neither Saliman nor Hem spoke much. Hem was very grateful for Saliman's silent fellowship that day; his steady presence was a great comfort, after so long without human company. But the thought gave Hem a stab of guilt; he felt as if he were being disloyal to Irc, who had been the best of friends, and had saved his life and, probably, his sanity. No human friend could have done more.

But all the same, he had missed Saliman so fiercely, and had feared he would never see him again. Just to have Saliman nearby, to hear the faint rhythms of his breathing and his footsteps, seemed a chance beyond hope. Maerad was now, he thought painfully, much more alone than he was. If Maerad was alive.

But even as his fear for Maerad quickened, he thought of his dream of the night before. The feeling of it was still with him: it was similar to what he had felt in the presence of the Elidhu, but warmer, more intimate. More *mine,* Hem thought. That's what *my* home looks like. Maerad was alive; some inner knowing in Hem pulsed with certainty. Maerad was alive, and he would find her, though all the wastelands of the Suderain and Annar lay between them. Perhaps she, too, dreamed of him.

These thoughts ran underneath Hem's consciousness all morning. He kept his listening alert, and constantly scanned the land around them for signs of sorcery or vigilances. There were old traces of sorcery, but nothing serious; the landscape felt abandoned and empty. He wondered what was happening in the wider world.

As the day wore on, he stopped thinking at all. He was still deeply tired after his ordeal in Dén Raven, and he felt it more and more in his legs, which began to feel heavier and heavier, as if he pushed them through thigh-deep water. Despite the exercise, he felt cold to his very bones. A dullness settled on him, though he forced it aside, willing himself to keep alert. It would be too much, after everything he had survived, to be betrayed by some small mistake now.

Even so, he was startled when Saliman grasped his arm and halted him. Hem looked at the Bard in surprise and saw that

Saliman was staring at something ahead of them, and drawing his sword. At first, he couldn't see what Saliman was looking at. Before them, the ground sloped downward to a thicket of low trees that grew in one of the many shallow dips that littered this area. Then, as Hem stared, he saw something big and dark moving in the shadows of the thicket. Irc, standing on Hem's shoulders, tightened his claws and trembled.

It was a huge stag, with a shaggy winter coat ruffing out to a huge yellow mane around its shoulders. Its seven-tined antlers swept high above its brow, so that Hem wondered how he had possibly missed it; but what compelled his gaze, even at this distance, was the stag's yellow eyes, which were staring straight at Hem.

They were Nyanar's eyes. Then Hem heard it: the music, the achingly beautiful, ungraspable phrases that haunted his waking memory.

Saliman's hand tightened on Hem's forearm, and Hem said, "It's all right. It's Nyanar." Somehow it was difficult to speak; he felt as if he were trying to talk underwater. Hem saw in Saliman's face, without being able to do anything about it, that the Bard was afraid.

Slowly and proudly, the stag stepped up toward them. It was a huge animal, taller at the shoulder than Saliman's height, and its pale antlers seemed as high as a tree. Ten paces away from them it stopped and the air shimmered with a strange light. Hem blinked, and when he opened his eyes again the stag was gone, and in its place was the naked, white-skinned Elidhu, orbed in shifting ripples of light.

Saliman let his sword arm fall to his side.

Greetings, Songboy, said Nyanar, stepping toward them. *I said I would see you again.*

"Greetings," said Hem, a deep happiness rising within him. He realized that he had spoken aloud, and sensed, rather than saw, Saliman turn to gaze at him, his eyes wide with alarm. But Saliman seemed a great distance away. Hem was only half-aware of Irc, who stood unmoving and unspeaking on Hem's shoulder. He was still trembling, though Hem thought that he trembled with delight, not with fear. "But how did you know I'd come back?" said Hem boldly. "I might have been killed."

You were not killed. You are here, said Nyanar. *I said to remember what is written on the winds of time . . . Although you are right: time has infinite forkings, and none can truly foretell what is to come. There are many futures and many pasts, and your present is but a tiny fulcrum, changing all of them . . . And do you bring something back from the Poisoned Lands?*

Hem stared in surprise, and stammered. "Yes," he said. "Yes, I did . . . was that foretold as well?" He fumbled with the chain around his neck, brought out the little brass tuning fork that Irc had stolen from the Iron Tower, and held it up. It twirled on its chain, catching the light on its dull surface.

As he did so, a curious expression crossed Nyanar's face: part fear, part disgust, part longing, part anguish. He shut his eyes, as if mastering himself, and then opened them again.

You have the Song, he said at last.

Hem's mouth dropped open. "I have—what?"

The Song that was stolen. My song.

Impulsively Hem held out the brass trinket to Nyanar. "If it's yours," he said, "then you must take it."

The Elidhu flinched back, as if Hem had thrust a burning brand into his face.

Nay, he said fiercely. *I will not touch that thing. It is an abomination.*

Hem looked at the little tuning fork, dangling harmlessly from the steel chain, and then back toward the Elidhu. He opened his mouth to say something, and then couldn't think of anything to say and shut it again.

An abomination, said the Elidhu again. *A broken thing, twisted to bad ends.*

"What do you mean?" asked Hem, completely baffled.

I know what those things are that are cut into the metal. Do you not feel the anguish within them?

Hem stared again at the tuning fork, realizing that Nyanar meant the engraved runes. His heart started to hammer painfully. He thought he did know, in a shadowy, uncertain sense, what Nyanar meant; there was a power in those runes, and now that he looked closely, it tasted of wrongness . . .

Then the music sounded in his mind again, but stronger than before, almost as overwhelming as it had been in Nal-Ak-Burat, when Nyanar, the tree man, had bent over and breathed it into him. Hem shut his eyes, feeling the wave of it sweep him up. But this time there were words in the music; and Hem did not become part of it, but listened outside it, in some still space, with his whole being, and he felt as if the words the Elidhu sang were engraved on his heart:

I am the song of seven branches
I am the gathering sea foam and the waters beneath it
I am the wind and what is borne by the wind

I am the speech of salmon in the icy pool
I am the blood that swells the leafless branch
I am the hunter's voice that roars through the valley
I am the valor of the desperate roe
I am the honey stored in the rotting hive
I am the sad waves breaking endlessly
The seed of woe sleeps in my darkness and the seed of gladness

The music stopped, its last note ebbing in Hem's blood. There was, for a heartbeat or for an eon, Hem couldn't tell, complete silence: he could hear nothing at all, not even the wind, or the tiny sounds of his own body.

The Song was made into marks, said the Elidhu bitterly. *And those marks devoured it and broke its meanings, so that nothing about it is whole. And since then the Elidhu also are broken . . .*

Hem's hand dropped. The tuning fork suddenly felt very heavy, almost too heavy to hold. It took all his strength and both hands to lift it again. And he saw then that the tiny engraved runes were glowing, as if they were molten metal. He blinked and stared, fascinated.

He could read the runes. Suddenly they seemed as clear to him as Bardic script. Clearer, even; he still struggled with Bardic writing.

Do you understand? said the Elidhu softly.

"I can—I can read the runes," Hem answered shakily.

Read them. Speak them to me.

Slowly, but without hesitating, his voice strengthening as he spoke, Hem read the runes on the fork. *"I am the song of seven branches.* Birt, the birch, which is winter. Lran, winter also, of the rowan. Nerim, the ash, who is spring. Summer, which is Coll, the hazel. The autumn briar, Ku. Muin the vine, autumn also, and Gordh, autumn ivy. Phia, the beech, and Ngierab, the reed, both for winter. And last, Midwinter Day, the elder, who is Raunar. *The seed of woe sleeps in my darkness and the seed of gladness."*

As he read each rune, the fire inside it died back to dull metal. After he finished speaking, Hem saw that the runes had become inscrutable squiggles, without the meanings they had held as he had read them, and the tuning fork seemed once again an insignificant brass trinket, hanging lightly from his hand.

"The seed of woe sleeps in my darkness and the seed of gladness," Hem repeated. The Raunar stanza seemed to echo everything

he had been thinking that day. He looked up at the Elidhu, dazed with wonder, but Nyanar's face was averted, and the ripples of light that laved his skin were dim and blue. At last the Elidhu stirred, and gazed at Hem.

Do you remember the marks? he said. His voice was harsh, and Hem saw a terrible pain in his eyes. *Songboy, inscribe this on your soul. The song belongs to the marks; each mark a line. Remember.*

Hem knew he would not forget the meanings, nor the song that the Elidhu had interleaved with his music. He swallowed and nodded, trying to meet the urgency in Nyanar's voice. "Yes, I'll remember. I can't forget . . ."

Remember, said Nyanar.

And then, without any warning, he was gone. Irc flapped up into the air with a cry of loss.

Released from Nyanar's presence, Hem stumbled and would have fallen if Saliman had not caught his arm.

"Are you all right?"

Hem straightened up. "I need to just . . . sit down for a while," he said. His legs were trembling.

They sat down on the grass where they were, and Saliman pulled some medhyl from his pack and handed it to Hem. He seemed oddly shy; he did not look at Hem as he did so. Hem sipped the liquor gratefully, and a little strength began to return to his legs.

Saliman did not ask any questions, but sat patiently, pulling idly at a tuft of grass and twirling it around his fingers. After a long silence, haltingly, Hem tried to explain to him what had just happened.

"You heard what Nyanar said," he began.

"Yes, I heard it," said Saliman gravely. For the first time since the Elidhu had vanished, he met Hem's eye. "But Hem, I did not understand a word. It is a great wonder to me to see an Elidhu with my own eyes. But I am not sure that it is not a greater wonder, to see you speaking to an Elemental in his own language."

Hem stared at Saliman, not understanding.

"Hem, it was not the Speech that you were using then. Nor Annaren, nor Suderain, nor any tongue that I know. It seems the Elemental speech is within you, as the Speech is inborn in Bards, unless you speak it from some enchantment that the Elidhu brings with him." Saliman smiled, but it was a very sad smile. "It should not be so surprising. Maerad too has the Elemental tongue."

Hem cleared his throat, embarrassed. He didn't like the way Saliman looked at him. His glance was gentle, but tinged with something like awe or fear, and it made Hem feel estranged from him. He felt a great loneliness sweep over him. He had gone beyond Bardic knowledge, and Saliman could not follow him there. Hem shook his head, trying to clear it, and cast about for something to break the odd mood.

"Well, I think you were right in what you said yesterday," he said at last. "Nyanar said the Song was on this tuning fork. He must mean the Treesong. And now I know what the runes mean."

Saliman lifted his eyebrows with astonishment, and Hem repeated the stanzas that the Elidhu had sung, and then explained the runes. Saliman listened, his brows drawn with concentration. When Hem finished, he looked at him with wonder; but he was smiling, and Hem saw with relief that the brief feeling of estrangement had passed.

"I said, back in Nal-Ak-Burat, that we were not alone, and that that was a basis for hope," he said. "I did not realize how right I was. This matters, Hem. It is a turning point in this war with the Nameless One. I just wish we knew what to do with it."

"Me too," said Hem, a little forlornly.

"One thing," Saliman said, frowning again with thought.

"Some runes are missing. Four for winter, but only one each for spring and summer. One for Midwinter Day, but none for Midsummer . . ."

"The others must be on Maerad's lyre," said Hem. "Like you said."

"Aye," said Saliman. "I think it must be so. And now we must search all Edil-Amarandh to find her." He stared gloomily down at the ground. "I knew we had to find her," he said, "But I didn't know why. Knowing is like that. And now that I know why, I have no idea where to begin looking. Or what we will do, when we do find her."

A silence fell between the two, but this time it was the comfortable silence of friendship. Hem gazed over the empty lands of the Nazar Plains without really seeing anything. Irc had flown down to the thicket where they had first seen Nyanar, and perched in a tree. He was scarcely visible against the tangled branches. It would be dark soon.

"The Nameless One must have stolen the Treesong from the Elidhu," Hem said. "But when I tried to give it back to Nyanar, he wouldn't take it. He wouldn't even touch it."

"Perhaps he couldn't take it, as it is," said Saliman. "Some great sorcery was needed to harness the Treesong, to make these runes. Somehow they must contain the power of the Elidhu's Song. No doubt that's what Nyanar meant by unchaining the Song."

"He said the Song was broken," said Hem thoughtfully.

Saliman looked searchingly into Hem's face. "Are you a little recovered, Hem? Because we must leave here. It will be twilight soon."

They stood up, brushing themselves down, and Irc swooped back onto Hem's shoulders and pecked his ear.

He is beautiful, said the crow. He sounded elated.

Hem knew Irc was speaking of Nyanar. *Yes,* he said slowly.

He stroked Irc's neck, suddenly conscious that the crow was a wild creature. He had known that, of course, but he had never really thought about what it meant.

But he is sad, said Irc. *So sad. I am happy to have seen him, but he is so sad.*

Irc launched himself off Hem's shoulder and soared high into the air until he was just a dark fleck against the gathering clouds, gliding and diving and tumbling in ecstatic arcs of flight.

Hem watched Irc for a long time, caught up by the sheer joy of his play. In those boundless realms of air, Irc was utterly free; and against the mountains of cloud he was so small, a fragile being of feathers and muscles and light bones, held together by . . . what? What was that spark that was Irc, his wild and crafty friend? Why did he love Hem? Because it seemed miraculous that this living creature should give Hem his loyalty and his friendship, even in the face of death.

Hem's heart constricted with a sudden sweet anguish. It seemed impossible, and yet it was so. And Saliman, too, and Maerad, and Zelika, who had loved him also. Even her death did not change that. They were no less wild and no less free than Irc, and yet they chose to love him. Hem, who scarcely deserved such riches, who stumbled blindly on these paths and yet found himself loving them back, despite all the terrible darknesses in his being.

At last Hem stirred, and turned to Saliman. The Bard stood unspeaking beside him, a smile of unconscious pleasure quirking the edges of his mouth as he watched the crow dancing in the darkening sky. As he met Hem's eyes, Saliman's smile widened and a spark of pure delight flashed between them.

"Well, we'd better leave," Hem said, smiling back. "We have a long way to go."

HERE ENDS
THE THIRD BOOK
OF PELLINOR

Appendices

A S in the previous books, *The Naming* and *The Riddle*, these notes are intended to fill in a little background for those readers curious about the societies and cultures of Edil-Amarandh, and are intended as complementary to the earlier appendices. In the first and second books of Pellinor, I outlined a short history of Edil-Amarandh and the Bardic institutions of Annar, and also looked briefly at the different peoples and societies encountered in the narrative. Those interested in the provenance and powers of the Speech and the Elidhu might also wish to consult my introductions to these fascinating subjects in the previous books.

I am very conscious as I write this of my limited ability to keep up with all the available work in Annaren studies, one of the fastest-growing areas of contemporary scholarship. Translation of the Annaren scrolls and research into their implications in diverse fields of academic disciplines continues apace—most notably under the auspices of the University of Querétaro, which is currently leading the way in scholarship and publications, though many other institutions are contributing to our growing understanding of Edil-Amarandh. My thanks are due to all those whose work and conversation have enriched my understanding.

Once again, as an invaluable introduction to the field for the general reader I recommend Jacqueline Allison's pioneering study of the histories of Edil-Amarandh, *The Annaren Scripts: History Rewritten.*

A BRIEF INTRODUCTION TO
THE SUDERAIN AND AMDRIDH

THE Suderain was the largest of the Seven Kingdoms, and for many eons the most powerful in influence, knowledge, and wealth. It was closely aligned, politically, economically, and culturally, with the coastal realm of Amdridh, and together these two kingdoms dominated the south of Edil-Amarandh. The autonomy of the Seven Kingdoms and their ability to resist the depredations of both the Nameless One and the Kings of Annar after the Restoration was due in great part to the ancient independent power of these two great southern realms.

The Suderain comprehended the major cities of Turbansk, Baladh, and Jerr-Niken, all famous centers of Bardic Lore and Knowing, which themselves had close ties to the Amdridh Schools of Zimek and Car Amdridh.

The almost total lack of archaeological artifacts and sites that is the great frustration of Annaren studies can make some things hard to determine—the great and still largely unexplored trove of Annaren documents discovered in Morocco in 1991 still remains the single source of knowledge of Edil-Amarandh. Consequently, the question of whether Turbansk predates Afinil is currently a focus of some dispute among Annaren authorities. Certainly, some fiercely disputed dating[1] of the extant documents seems to point to the Suderain scrolls being among the oldest of those discovered, which suggests that its claim to be the first School in Edil-Amarandh may be not entirely unfounded. There is reason to believe that Turbansk was built at around the same time as the great Howes of the Pilanel in Zmarkan.[2]

Among the many literary treasures uncovered in the past few years are some tantalizing fragments of what is undoubtedly the most ancient epic poem in human history, *The Epic of Eribu*. The poem is written in Suderain, and claims to be a translation of a much older text dating back to the Inela—or pre-Dawn—Age, about a quest taken by the king of the ancient undergound city Nal-Ak-Burat in order to save his city from approaching destruction. Sadly, so little of the poem remains—and that itself is badly scored with elisions—that it is impossible to descry much more information about Nal-Ak-Burat than is available in the *Naraudh Lar-Chanë*, where its mystery is its chief characteristic, and there is no trace so far of the original text from which the translation is made. However, it is now generally agreed that an ancient civilization existed in the Suderain that predated Turbansk and that appeared to have close links to, or perhaps even to worship, the Elidhu Nyanar.

Although so far no records have been found of the fate of the inhabitants of Nal-Ak-Burat, some linguists argue that it is probable that their descendants were the peoples who lived in the Neera Marshes in Maerad's time. One theory—that remains controversial, though in some quarters it is rapidly gaining credence—is that Savitir, Nazar, and Dén Raven in the eastern Suderain were settled by nomadic tribes from the deserts to the south, who later founded Nal-Ak-Burat. According to this model, the peoples who populated the area around the Lamarsan Sea and the Amdridh peninsula represent a completely different racial and linguistic group.[3] The theory is that the nomadic tribes spoke a language that later diverged into several distinct tongues, including the language spoken in Dén Raven and by the tribes of the Neera Marshes. This ur-language (known as NAB-1) would explain the marked differences between classical Suderain and the languages spoken by the tribes of the Neera Marshes, and the otherwise puzzling relationships between the languages of the Neera Marshes and that of Dén Raven, which suggest a common root language of which, so far, no record can be found.

The discovery of NAB-1—and, one would hope, its subsequent decipherment—would resolve many controversies in Annaren studies, since so far arguments for its existence have depended wholly on secondary evidence. The fragmentary Suderain translations of *The Epic of Eribu* remain so far the most significant pieces of this fascinating puzzle; if a parallel text of the original could be unearthed, it would be as significant to our understanding of Edil-Amarandh as the Rosetta Stone was to deciphering hieroglyphs.

Comprehensive written records in the Suderain and Amdridh seem to have been kept from around A2200, when the Library of Turbansk—along with the Library of Thorold, one of the oldest in Edil-Amarandh—was founded by Bards anxious to keep the Knowing alive after the destruction of Afinil. The Library of Car Amdridh was founded around a century later, while those of the other southern Schools seem to date from after the Restoration. Unfortunately, very few of the southern records have survived; the Annaren Scrolls are generally agreed to have been the contents of the great library of Norloch which, although it held copies of what the Bards considered the most significant documents from all the Bardic Libraries, by no means reproduced the contents of all of them.

The Southern Monarchies

Both the Suderain and Amdridh were ruled by monarchs, respectively the Ernani of Turbansk and the Po of Car Amdridh.[4] The non-Bardic rulers in the other cities of the kingdoms were consuls, answerable to the Ernani or the Po. After the foundation of the School of Turbansk, the dual system of government that held sway through most of Edil-Amarandh meant that the monarchs were equal in authority and power to the First Bards of Turbansk and Car Amdridh. Before the collapse of the Annaren monarchy in the Long Wars, and the subsequent conflation of the triple scepter of the Annaren Kingship into the role of the First Bard of Norloch, this situation made the First Bard of Turbansk the most politically powerful Bard in Edil-Amarandh.

The inheritance of the monarchies of Turbansk and Amdridh was in general determined by primogeniture, regardless of the sex of the oldest child. There were, however, exceptions; succession was ultimately determined by the reigning monarch, and in rare cases he or she bestowed the crown elsewhere among his or her children or, in the event that the monarch was childless, to another branch of the ruling family. Given this, and given also that neither the Ernani nor the Po married but instead chose a consort (sometimes, as in the case of Har-Ytan, a succession of consorts), it is perhaps surprising that there are no records of wars of succession like those that destroyed the Annaren monarchy. Perhaps the authority of the rulers was such that any decision of succession was considered unarguable; or perhaps the wealth of the Suderain and Amdridh, together with the strict application of the social rules of the Balance, gave the kingdom a stability the northern monarchy lacked. Certainly, many extant records claim as a matter of pride that even in times of famine and hardship—at the height of the struggle with the Nameless One during the Great Silence, for example—starvation and privation among the common people of the Suderain was almost unknown.[5] There is only one account of civil unrest against the monarchy: after Aleksil the Tyrant forcibly imposed crippling taxes to fund his luxurious court, he was overthrown in a bloodless coup in A1333 by a popular uprising that was, intriguingly, supported by the Bards of Turbansk. This underlines how crucial the support of the Bard Schools was to the maintenance of political power in Edil-Amarandh.

The Bards of the Suderain

Unlike Afinil, the Bard Schools of the Suderain were never destroyed in the millennium-long Great Silence after the conquest by the Nameless One. This meant that traditions of the Light in the Suderain had continued unbroken for some thousands of years, and that in the south the Reformation under Maninaë had minimal impact—unlike in Annar, where the *Paur Libridha* (Maninaë N23) was the most influential and authoritative text on the constitution of the Schools. The *Paur Libridha* was in many ways a reforming text, written out of an urgency to ensure that the Light was never threatened again as it had been during the Great Silence and, as Alannah Casagrande points out, some of its innovations—for one, the explicit outlawing of dialogue with Elementals—were never quite accepted in Schools in the Seven Kingdoms. In Thorold, for instance, where the people believed that they owed their defeat of the Nameless One's forces to the mountain Elidhu Lamedon, this proscription was quietly ignored.[6] The Suderain also continued to use the Afinil year count, rather then the Norloch count instituted by Maninaë, but for clarity I will use the Annaren convention here.

The southern Schools were therefore run on southern lines, which sometimes led to conflicts between the northern and southern Bards. The most striking cultural difference between Annar and the Suderain was the persistence in the south of forms of worship of the Light (although Bards were seldom strongly associated with this) and, sometimes, of what appear to be Elemental figures. This is to say that a tradition of organized religion existed in the south that was completely unheard of in Annar, and was inflected subtly through Bardic culture. It is no accident that the mysticism of the Way of the Heart originated in Turbansk.[7]

Another key—and perhaps, given the above, paradoxical—difference was in the considerable sophistication of what we would think of as scientific and mathematical discourses in the Schools of the south. Of course, given the constant communication between Bard Schools, the discoveries and theories of the southern Bards became influential in the north, but many documents attest to the fact that any Bard interested in these areas of the Knowing would travel south to study.

Jerr-Niken and Turbansk, in particular, were considered leading centers of theoretical exploration in mathematics and science, and we know that the Suderain Bards had a sure theoretical grasp of many surprisingly modern concepts. Although often practiced for its own sake,

as part of the play of thought that was understood between Bards to be
an expression of the Light, recent evidence also compellingly suggests
that this knowledge was often applied practically: in medical techniques, for example, that show that the Bards had an accurate
understanding of bacterial and viral infections, or in the field of astron-
omy. The science of optics was highly developed in Jerr-Niken and
Turbansk, and researchers have unearthed star maps of considerable
complexity, rivaling those of the astronomers of the Maya. It also
appears that the southern Bards had developed a workable theory
of evolution, and we know Malikil of Jerr-Niken theorized genetic
inheritance in N755,[8] recording her meticulous observations of breed-
ing and cross-pollinating ikil plants. Discoveries such as these allowed
Intathen of Gent to theorize an evolutionary model of competing populations of species, using the game of Gis, a complex board game using
counters, which was very popular among Annaren Bards.[9] Some schol-
ars argue that the prevalence of the spiral or double helix in the
artwork and even the architecture of the south (the floor plan of the
Ernan of Turbansk, the great palace of the Ernani, was, for example,
famously based on a two-dimensional representation of a double helix)
suggests that the southern Bards were aware of the existence of DNA.

Many of the most interesting recent discoveries have been in the
area of mathematics. The Suderain worship of Light led to intense
Bardic studies of its properties, which in turn resulted in an early discovery of refraction. As early as A2500, Mulgar of Jerr-Niken described
Snell's Law (that when light bends as it passes from one medium to
another, the angles are related trigonometrically—the sine of the angle
of incidence equals the sine of the angle of refraction). This meant that
trigonometry and spherical geometry became a focus of mathematical
thinking early on and led, among other things, to the precocious discovery two centuries later of Fourier Analysis by the mathematical
genius Abin-Kan of Jerr-Niken. Abin-Kan's discovery, which he called
Edhi-Delar (in the Speech, "light building") meant that Bards could
represent any arbitrary shape in terms of an aggregation of simpler

sinusoidal waves. Abin-Kan also, almost simultaneously, discovered that light is a wave, by means of a device very like Young's slit apparatus (a glass slide blacked by soot, with two lines scraped very close to each other). Together, these two discoveries permitted later Bardic thinkers to sketch out what appears to be a full mathematical basis for quantum mechanics, despite the fact that they had not made the physical hypotheses.

Their number theory had intriguing parallels with that of the Greeks, leading some to speculate that Turbanskian mathematics may have survived into the classical Greek era. Like the Pythagoreans, Turbanskian Bards linked numbers with harmony: one was the primordial unity from which all else is created, two was the symbol for the female, three for the male, and four symbolized harmony (because two is even, so four—two times two—is "evenly even"). Four also symbolized the four elements out of which everything in the universe was made (earth, air, fire, and water). The Suderain Bards, after Lilora of Turbansk (N230), also theorized prime numbers, and held the prime factor theorem—that every whole number can be expressed as a unique product of prime factors—in great reverence. Lilora's proof of this tenet used a nonlinear logic that has parallels with that of Brouwer and the intuitionists, in which any mathematical object is considered to be a product of a construction of a mind and that, therefore, the existence of an object is equivalent to the possibility of its construction.[10]

Dén Raven and the Rise of the Nameless One

The Nameless One, known most often in the Suderain by his usename Sharma, was the king of Dén Raven before he became one of the most adept mages in Edil-Amarandh. When he studied with the Bards of the Light in the Dhyllic city of Afinil, it was said his innate powers rivaled even those of Nelsor, the legendary Bard who invented the first Bardic writing and who is also credited with creating the Treesong runes. The story of Sharma's journey to Afinil in A1567 is well known; what is more puzzling is why he traveled hundreds of leagues north, rather than to Turbansk, where it might be surmised that he would find such knowledge as he desired closer to home. The answer seems to lie in a mysterious animus against the Bards of the south; the Bard Nindar remarked on Sharma's commonly expressed contempt for the Bards of Turbansk, "It was said that his face would darken at any praise of a Turbanskian Bard, and but for courtesy, he would spit," he wrote. "Some said they had never seen such bitterness in another human being, without seeming reason or foundation; and if anyone asked him the reasons wherefore his black feelings, he would look so threateningly that no more questioning was ventured."[11]

Nindar also records Sharma's fascination with the Elidhu who visited Afinil, most notably the Winterking Arkan, later known throughout Annar as the Ice Witch and reviled by the Bards for his alliance with Sharma. While Nindar appears to believe that Sharma's primary interest was in the Elemental Wars, it seems likely that he was more interested in the Elidhu's possession of endless life. In the *Naraudh Lar-Chanë* it is strongly suggested that it was at this time that Nelsor, who may have been Arkan's lover, captured the power of the Elidhu Treesong in the Treesong Runes, inscribing them on a Dhyllic lyre and a tuning fork (in connection with this event, it is worth remembering that one of the magical qualities of Dhyllic lyres was that they never needed to be tuned). We can conjecture that Sharma, suspecting that the secret of the Elementals' eternal life was held in the power of the runes, stole the tuning fork from Nelsor and immediately left Afinil for Dén Raven. His abrupt disappearance certainly caused speculation in Afinil, enough for it to be recalled later, when the extent of his ambition became evident. However, as the existence of the Treesong Runes was a secret known to very few Bards, perhaps only to Nelsor and Sharma, it was not until much later, when Maerad was called to fulfill her quest for the Treesong, that Sharma's theft became clear. Given that Sharma did not steal the whole Song, it seems fair to speculate—with many Bards who wrote later about these events— that his knowledge of the Runes was dishonestly gained. "There were many who distrusted Sharma, even before he cast aside his Name and revealed his dark design," wrote Callachan of Gent."[12] It was said that he would spy on his own shadow, and that his right hand would cheat his left."

How Sharma used the Treesong Runes to make the Spell of Binding that ensured his deathlessness is unknown; but many Bards speculated that the lack of half the runes meant that the spell was only partially successful. Although the spell gave Sharma eternal life, it was eternal life in torment; it seemed that the magery he exerted in the Spell of Binding was too powerful for his human body to sustain. Certainly, the few extant descriptions of the Nameless One all mention his physical anguish, and it was often claimed that his form was unimaginably monstrous.

After his return to Dén Raven, nothing more was heard from Sharma in Annar or the Suderain for another three centuries. It was during this time that he began the transformation of Dén Raven into the vast prison camp and armory that it became in Maerad's day, and set up strategic alliances with powerful Elidhu, including Arkan in Zmarkan and Karak in Indurain (perhaps the same Elemental known later as the Landrost, although this is by no means certain). In A1810 he began his campaign to defeat the Bards of Annar with an invasion of South Annar, and in A2041, after many grievous wars, succeeded in his aim of conquering Annar and completely destroying the civilization of the Dhyllin.

Few documents exist to record the Great Silence, which lasted for more than a millennium, until Maninaë cast Sharma out of Annar in A3234 and began the Restoration of the Light. Those few that do remain record an absolute militaristic tyranny, in which entire populations were enslaved—the archetype, perhaps, of a totalitarian regime. The Light continued undefeated in the Seven Kingdoms, and even continued to flourish in the Suderain, but was nevertheless under constant attack from Sharma's powerful sorcerers, the corrupt Bards known as Hulls who had given up their Bardic Names for a shadow of

Sharma's immortality. Unlike Sharma, Hulls could be killed, even if only by magery; but they did not die of normal physical wounds or disease or age. Most of the time they used glimmerspells to disguise their horrific appearance. Callachan of Gent describes them thus:

> The bodies of the Hulls do not remain youthful, but as the centuries pass, show the depredations of their extreme age: they appear as withered skeletons clothed with skin as dry and yellow as parchment, and their eyes burn with a red light in the hollow skulls of their faces. And with their comeliness, so any pleasure in living vanishes; and they are filled with a hatred for anything fair or good, or that flourisheth in its innocence and joy in the gentle meadows of the world, and all that they make in their cunning is designed to hurt or to do ill or to cause despair, even when it seemeth that to do so makes little sense. For there is a wantonness in how the Hull makes others suffer that is beyond most human cruelty, that taketh an active joy in the pain inflicted, even in its seeming indifference; and this evil joy and indifference together seemeth to me to be the very essence of the Dark.
>
> A Hull employs the Speech, as doth a Bard; but in its mouth the Speech hath not its true virtue, and it is a hurt to hear it twisted so that it signifies often the very reverse of what it should intend. Thus Bards call it the Black Speech, to differentiate its use from our own; for if the *words* are the same, the *meanings* and *powers* summoned by the Black Speech are as if torn from the grace of the Balance, and an injury to the fabric of magery. This is the Dark Art of Sorcery, which draweth from our powers, only in order to destroy them.[13]

After the Restoration, it was widely believed that Sharma had fled Dén Raven, taking refuge in the southern deserts. For some five hundred years Dén Raven was free of Sharma's tyranny, although his shadow did not pass from the kingdom: there had been much hurt done to the land by his sorceries that even the Suderain Bards were unable to heal, and later it was discovered that some Hulls secretly remained, working for the eventual return of their master. The isolated kingdom opened up relationships with its neighbors, instituted a system of parliament, and founded several Bardic Schools. However, after millennia of absolute rule by Sharma these institutions and reforms were fragile, and the coup by the Hull Imank in N654 under the kingship of Ukbra led to the slaughter or banishment of all Dén Raven Bards, the destruction of the Schools, and the return to petty tyranny and isolation.

By N750, under the apparent leadership of the Hull Imank, a powerful sorcerer in his own right and also Captain of the Black Army, Dén Raven began to make aggressive forays against the eastern reaches of the Suderain. When the great School of Jerr-Niken was sacked and burned to the ground in N939, many in the Suderain began to fear that the Nameless One had indeed returned. In the face of widespread skepticism from Annar, the Ernani Har-Ytan and First Bard of Turbansk, Juriken, began to prepare their defenses for the invasion that eventually occurred in N945.

Unlike most of Annar and the Seven Kingdoms, where the influence of Bards meant that social status was usually a fluid concept, Dén Raven society was strictly hierarchical. At the apex, beneath the authority of Sharma himself, were the Hulls, but even within the Hulls there were strictly observed rankings. During the Great Silence, the Nameless One had instituted a system of Circles, each of different status. There were nine Circles of the Dark, ranging from the Sick (or Sickle) Moon— to which belonged all the most powerful Hulls, including Imank—to the Eyes—Hulls who were in charge of surveillance in Dén Raven and were greatly feared (the Hull known as the Spider in Sjug'hakar Im was most probably an Eye)—to the Circle of Insects—the lowest rank, from which were drawn petty officials such as slave masters. Beneath the Hulls was an intricate caste system, kept in place by fear: the Hulls used their sorceries for both surveillance and punishment, and employed a wide system of spies. Any sign of rebellion among the populace was crushed with terrifying ruthlessness. The most powerful class beneath the Hulls were the Grins, fabled for their greed and cruelty, who ruled the small towns and often ran the huge farms and mines and armories. The Grins were invariably extremely wealthy. Below them were artisans, valued for their skills; these trades were usually hereditary and each had its own status. Below them, at the bottom of society, were the numerous slaves who were required to labor in the industries of Dén Raven and to serve in its huge armies.[14]

THE ELIDHU

P ROBABLY the most fascinating and ambiguous entities of Edil-Amarandh, the Elidhu have been the focus of intense speculation in Annaren studies. Literally hundreds of references are scattered through the available literature, but many are so contradictory that it is difficult to decide definitively who or what the Elidhu were. Sometimes they seem like gods, mythic personifications of natural forces or events, as the Winterking can be seen as the personification of a possible Ice Age; at other times (as in many Thorold stories) they are protagonists of folktales; at still others they are presented matter-of-factly as any other historical figure taking forestage in human events. Yet it is not the variousness of the reports about them, but their remarkable consistency, that gives us pause. However they were regarded—as gods or as actual people, as allies or as unpredictable and dangerous foes—every reference to the Elementals since the beginning of written records in every region of Edil-Amarandh remarks on their slotted, inhuman eyes, their immortal status, and their ability to change their physical form.

One difficulty in understanding these entities is the nature of the Elidhu themselves—they are held to be mysterious beings who generally are little interested in human affairs. Of course, the irony is that the records we are likely to find are only of those Elidhu who *did* associate with human beings. The two Elidhu who feature most in the earlier books—Ardina and Arkan—are often said to be atypical of the Elementals, and certainly appear more humanlike than otherwise, especially as both of them have taken humans as lovers.[15]

Books IV and VI of the *Naraudh Lar-Chanë* (translated as *The Crow*) fill out further our picture of the Elidhu. In *The Crow*, Hem encounters Nyanar, an Elidhu (who appears to be a forest Elemental) associated with the regions of Savitir and Nazar in the eastern Suderain, bordering on Dén Raven. Nyanar's name has been the subject of some philological speculation. *Nyan* in the classical Suderain tongue (circa A1000, some three millennia before the events of the *Naraudh Lar-Chanë*) is the word for "change" or "transformation" (hence *nyanil*— "ritual"—a word with religious connotations not found farther north in Edil-Amarandh), and also is related to *nya*, "blossom" (as in English, a noun as well as a verb). However, others argue that the name Nyanar must be derived from the so far undiscovered language (NAB-1) spoken by the mysterious peoples of Nal-Ak-Burat.

Nyanar brings a somewhat stranger dimension to the Elidhu than we have heretofore seen in the *Naraudh Lar-Chanë*. In Maerad's meeting with Ardina in her various guises as wood Elidhu, moon avatar, and otherworldly Queen of Rachida, there is a current of understanding and a sense of kinship; even her unsettling dialogues with Arkan the Winterking only suggest things beyond what can be humanly understood. Arkan questions human polarizations and morality. "What is the Light without the Dark? It cannot be. And the Dark was first . . ." he says, confusing Maerad's certainties. "Only humans lie, because they think that language can give them another reality," he declares later, claiming that human beings, hampered by language, can understand nothing of what he calls truth.[16] Although he is described in the Annaren as *inikuel* (literally, "double-faced," a word that does not have our connotations of hypocrisy but instead invokes strangeness, beyond the Knowing), Arkan seems in many ways humanly legible: he claims to love, and displays sadness and anger in ways that Maerad can understand, even if she objects to them and ultimately rejects them. Nyanar is not nearly so recognizable, and might therefore be closer to a "typical" Elidhu than either Arkan or Ardina.

As John Carroll points out in his study *The Elidhu of Edil-Amarandh*:

Traces of the Absolute,[17] Hem's initial meeting with Nyanar, in stark
contrast with Maerad's dialogues with Arkan, culminates in word-
lessness, a profound experience of Elemental "music." It is deeply
ambiguous: at once an experience of inexpressible beauty, it also opens
Hem to obliterating terror. Perhaps the most unsettling evocation of
this terror—a fear of the inhuman implacability of the natural world—
is Hem's Elidhu-inspired dream, "He watches as the impossible wave
surges inexorably toward him, swallowing the earth in its path. It will
devour everything, even the clouds. Mercy is a human vice; the wave
knows nothing of it. Soon everything will be silent."[18] As the author of
the *Naraudh Lar-Chanë* comments, "The music of the Elidhu was shot
with darkness, which both deepened its mystery and beauty and drew
it far beyond Hem's grasp. The Elidhu were neither good nor evil; such
words were invented by human beings to explain human actions."[19]

Against this vision of amoral destruction is posited something
more benign, an idea of "at homeness." Nyanar speaks of the landscape as "home," but his environment is, literally, his being. "This is
myself," he tells Hem at one point, speaking of the landscape; and at
another, "I am all that is here. There is no here that is not me." This is
also evident when the Winterking speaks of the anguish of his banishment from Arkan-da. Place is more than a location to inhabit: it is the
ground of an Elidhu's being.

In many ways the Elidhu are anarchic, and deeply antagonistic to
Bardic ideas of the social Balance. As Dr. David Lloyd argues in his
provoking meditation on the place of the Elidhu in the *Naraudh Lar-
Chanë*, one of the defining aspects of the Elementals is their direct
challenge to Bardic ideas of rationalistic causality. This is expressed in
part through a different experience of time, which Lloyd characterizes
as *mythic* time. "Time is not as you know it, you mortal creatures,"
Nyanar tells Hem. "To us it is a sea, and all times exist together.
Nothing is truly gone . . ." The Elidhu concept of time, as a primordial
place of origin, is an idea familiar to us through ritual, which is always
a return to origin and creation. In cultures as diverse as the Australian

Arunta, the New Guinean Kai, or in Hindu or Tibetan or Catholic ritual, appeal is made to a "beginning" as an expression of the "true" and the "sacred," which authorizes human meaning.[20]

The Elidhu's actual experience of primordial or mythic time, and their concomitant understanding that all times coexist, challenges the rational historicism of the Bards in fundamental ways, and at least partly explains the Bardic distrust of the Elidhu as fickle and danger- ous, as "pathological." The Elidhu represented a possibility of renewal and even, perhaps, of revolution, which, after the Restoration, the Annaren Bards sought to repress. David Lloyd in *Elements of the Sublime* writes:

> Myth . . . is not defined by its content, but by its temporal struc- ture. That is, where Adorno and Horkheimer emphasize the anthropomorphic tendency that defines myth for them as against the abstraction of reason, I would stress—against that still historicist division of the mythic (as past and as a relation to the past) from the enlightened—precisely what historicism itself distrusts as myth—its appearance as the rhythmic return of the past in an uneasy haunting of progress by the ghosts of its unfinished business.[21] It is the persistence and insistence of the archaic that reason should have eradicated, exhibiting the tenacity of irrational attachments and the violence of primor- dial drives. The putatively archetypal content of the Elidhu is less significant, however readily invoked, than its unruly capacity to return. In this, of course, the Elidhu share the char- acteristics of the unconscious to which, on a social and an individual level, they are generally assimilated. . . . Insofar as Bardic historicism itself participates in the rationalization that represses the past and reduces its multiple forms to a single, serial narrative, it must perforce envisage the mythic Elemental as pathological. Where myth was, historical time must come, to lay the past to rest and cure its violence with reason and

progress. The therapeutic drive of historicism, which relates the
universal narrative of civility, is thus peculiarly repressive,
seeking less to release the past in the unruliness of its ever-
present possibilities than to discipline it.[22]

Banished from Annaren history after the Restoration, the Elidhu nevertheless haunt Edil-Amarandh as unfinished business; behind their
unacknowledged or demonized presence is the forgotten crime of the
transcription and theft of the Treesong, in which both the Light and
Dark were equally culpable. As Cadvan says at the end of *The Riddle*,
"This is a matter of undoing what Light or Dark should never have
done."

On the other hand, as is shown by Nyanar's persistence even in the
midst of Sharma's wreckage of his "home," the Elidhu are also harbin-
gers of possibility. Lloyd argues elsewhere that the Elementals
demonstrate the reconnection of the past with the present, not as a
process of nostalgia, but as reclamation of a possible future. "The work
of history is not merely to contemplate destruction, but to track
through the ruins of progress the defiles that connect the openings of
the past to those of the present," he says. Through the figure of Nyanar,
present despite the degraded and poisoned environment that Sharma
has made of his place and self, "the form of the imagined future is
sketched in the ruins of the present."[23] One might add that, as symbols
of a natural environment betrayed and exploited by a civilization now
long vanished, the Elidhu resonate uneasily into our own present.

THE TREESONG RUNES

AT the end of *The Riddle*, I include some notes on the Treesong runes, to which I refer interested readers. The Treesong was an alphabet of twenty symbols. Ten—those with the phonetic values A, E, I, O, U, F, S, H, D, and T—were inscribed on Maerad's Dhyllic lyre. The other runes—B, L, N, C, Q, M, G, P, NG, and R—were on the tuning fork stolen by Irc from the Iron Tower.

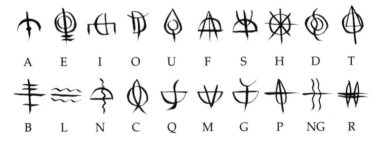

| A | E | I | O | U | F | S | H | D | T |

| B | L | N | C | Q | M | G | P | NG | R |

Each Treesong rune was a complex constellation of meaning, even if considered only in its lexical sense. It was not only a letter with a phonetic value; it encoded a line of the twenty-line poem that made up the Treesong, and also worked as a calendar, with the fifteen consonants symbolizing different seasons or significant days, and the vowels representing phases of the moon. Each rune was also associated with a different tree, each of which had its own network of associations. The density of symbolism associated with each rune is made even more complex by the suggestion of both Nyanar and Arkan that the runes as writing were significantly incomplete: that to be wholly meaningful, they required music. The source of their power is, like the Speech, only imperfectly understood.

The complete Treesong stanzas (with the moon-associated runes running first, and the others in seasonal order) now reads:

I am the dew on every hill
I am the leap in every womb
I am the fruit of every bough
I am the edge of every cliff
I am the hinge of every question

I am the song of seven branches
I am the gathering sea foam and the waters beneath it
I am the wind and what is borne by the wind
I am the falling tears of the sun
I am the eagle rising to a cliff
I am all directions over the face of the waters
I am the flowering oak that transforms the earth
I am the bright arrow of vengeance
I am the speech of salmon in the icy pool
I am the blood that swells the leafless branch
I am the hunter's voice that roars through the valley
I am the valor of the desperate roe
I am the honey stored in the rotting hive
I am the sad waves breaking endlessly
The seed of woe sleeps in my darkness and the seed
    of gladness

In an unpublished monograph, Professor Patrick Insole of the Department of Ancient Languages at the University of Leeds has made a thorough study of the extant sources on the Treesong, and on the symbolism of the runes.[24] I have drawn extensively on his monograph for this book, and Professor Insole, generally regarded as the foremost authority on the scripts of Edil-Amarandh, has kindly permitted me to quote extensively from his monograph for these notes.

The runes on the tuning fork and the stanzas and values pertaining to them

B	I am the song of seven branches
L	I am the gathering sea foam and the waters beneath it
N	I am the wind and what is borne by the wind
C	I am the speech of salmon in the icy pool
Q	I am the blood that swells the leafless branch
M	I am the hunter's voice that roars through the valley
G	I am the valor of the desperate roe
P	I am the honey stored in the rotting hive
NG	I am the sad waves breaking endlessly
R	The seed of woe sleeps in my darkness and the seed of gladness

B	Birt	Winter	Birch
L	Lran	Winter	Rowan
N	Nerim	Spring	Ash
C	Coll	Summer	Hazel
Q	Ku	Autumn	Briar
M	Muin	Autumn	Vine
G	Gordh	Autumn	Ivy
P	Phia	Winter	Beech
NG	Ngierab	Winter	Reed
R	Raunar	Midwinter Day	Elder

Some conjectural interpretations of the rune designs

WINTER is indicated as a flat line, which has been interpreted as representing ice or, more opaquely, as simply the absence of sun/light.

 B is represented by seven branches, referring to the stanza "I am the song of the seven branches." It also appears to represent a tree in winter.

L shows two levels of water, one above and one below the central horizon, referring to the line "I am the gathering sea foam and the waters beneath it."

SPRING is indicated by a rising sun motif, perhaps representing growth or the coming of light.

 N refers to the wind.

SUMMER is indicated by a circle, representing the sun.

 C shows a vertical fish form, representing a leaping salmon.

AUTUMN shows an inverted semicircle, indicating falling.

 Q shows a "leafless branch," or perhaps flowing blood.

 M represents a valley.

 G is obscure but may indicate the horns of the "desperate roe" (cf. the development of the ancient Semitic letter *aleph*).

WINTER

 P shows a leaf form that appears also to represent a hive, with a vertical line marking a center, possibly representing honey.

 NG is two vertical waving lines representing both the reeds and their reflection and also the "sad waves, breaking endlessly."

 R repeats the horizontal line for emphasis and implies Midwinter Day. The two vertical ellipses represent the two seeds of woe and gladness.

NOTES FOR THE APPENDICES

1. I have referred elsewhere to the myriad difficulties of dating the Annaren Scrolls. The negligible presence of C14 in any of the documents suggests that they must be more than 50,000 years old, although their remarkable state of preservation makes them appear to be no older than three or four hundred years. Some progress is being made using isotopic dating methods on the ingredients of the inks, but the methods the Bards used to preserve their documents, which still remain a mystery to scientists, appear to have affected the molecular makeup of these materials—mainly parchment and reed paper—in certain fundamental and profoundly puzzling ways. See "Dating the Annaren Scrolls" by Jean-Paul Carrier, *Libridha: A Journal of Annaren Studies*, Issue III, Vol 1, 2003.

2. See *The Riddle.*

3. See *The Languages of the Suderain*, Jack Collins, (Chicago: Sorensen Academic Publishers, 2004).

4. *Genealogies of Light: Power in Edil-Amarandh* edited by Alannah Casagrande (Chicago: Sorensen Academic Publishers, 2000) and also Jacqueline Allison's *The Annaren Scripts: History Rewritten* (Mexico: University of Querétaro Press, 1998).

5. For examples of this kind of claim, *see Keepers of the Balance,* Markabul of Turbansk, A2578; *Sharers of the Light,* Inior of Jerr-Niken, A3145; *The Gifts of the Gift,* Vacarsa of Turbansk, N56.

6. *Genealogies of Light: Power in Edil-Amarandh,* edited by Alannah Casagrande (Chicago: Sorensen Academic Publishers, 2000).

7. "Idols of Light: Aspects of Religious Worship in the Suderain of Edil-Amarandh," Camilla Johnson, *Libridha: A Journal of Annaren Studies,* Issue V, Vol 2, 2004.

8. *The Loom of Light* by Malikil of Jerr-Niken (N755).

9. *The Breathing Waves of Gis* by Intathen of Gent (N560).

10. For the above information, I am deeply indebted to Dr. Randolph Healy, Margaret Louise Mathematics Fellow at Bray College, Ireland, for his valuable conversation and insights.

11. *Sharma, King of Nothing,* the Bard Nindar, Library of Busk (A2153).

12. *A Chronicle of the Black Kingdom* by Callachan of Gent, translated by Jessica Callaghan (Albany: State University of New York Press, 1996).

13. Ibid.

14. Ibid.

15. For more on these two Elidhu, see "The Elidhu" in the appendices of *The Riddle.*

16. *The Riddle,* Part IV.

17. *The Elidhu of Edil-Amarandh: Traces of the Absolute* by John Carroll (Mexico: University of Querétaro Press, 2005).

18. *The Crow,* III.

19. Ibid.

20. "Toward A Definition of Myth," Mircea Eliade, *Greek and Egyptian Mythologies* (Chicago: University of Chicago Press, 1991).

21. *Dialectic of Enlightenment* by Theodor W. Adorno and Max Horkheimer (Stanford: Stanford University Press, 2002).

22. "Ruins/Runes" by David Lloyd, University of Southern California. Unpublished monograph, 2004.

23. "Elements of the Sublime" by David Lloyd, University of Southern California. Unpublished monograph, 2005.

24. "The Symbolism of the Treesong Runes," by Professor Patrick Insole, Department of Ancient Languages, University of Leeds. Unpublished monograph, 2003.